William Thomas McKinley

All photos and musical examples courtesy of William Thomas McKinley.

William Thomas McKinley

A Bio-Bibliography

JEFFREY S. SPOSATO

Bio-Bibliographies in Music, Number 56

GREENWOOD PRESS
Westport, Connecticut • London

Library of Congress Cataloging-in-Publication Data

Sposato, Jeffrey S.
William Thomas McKinley : a bio-bibliography / Jeffrey S. Sposato.
p. cm.— (Bio-bibliographies in music, ISSN 0742-6968 ; no. 56)
Includes bibliographical references, discography, and index.
ISBN 0-313-28923-9 (alk. paper)
1. McKinley, William Thomas, 1939- —Bibliography—Catalogs.
I. Title. II. Series.
ML134.M485S66 1995
780'.92—dc20
[B] 95-14503

British Library Cataloguing in Publication Data is available.

Library of Congress Catalog Card Number: 95-14503
ISBN: 0-313-28923-9
ISSN: 0742-6968

First published in 1995

Greenwood Press, 88 Post Road West, Westport, CT 06881
An imprint of Greenwood Publishing Group, Inc.

The paper used in this book complies with the Permanent Paper Standard issued by the National Information Standards Organization (Z39.48-1984).

10 9 8 7 6 5 4 3 2 1

To those who first set me on the path to music—

to Robert Gottshalk,...

...Gerhard Steiff,...

...and, of course, my parents.

Contents

Abbreviations

Premiere Performance Notation

†	World Premiere Performance
† (*City or Country*)	City or Country Premiere Performance

Instrumentation

Alt	Alto
Bar	Baritone
BCl	Bass Clarinet
Bs	Bass
Bsn	Bassoon
BTbn	Bass Trombone
Cb	Contrabass (Double Bass)
CbCl	Contrabass Clarinet
CBsn	Contrabassoon
Cel	Celesta
Cim	Cimbalom
Cl	Clarinet
Dr	Drums
EHn	English Horn
Elec	Electric
Ens	Ensemble
Fl	Flute
Gtr	Guitar
Hn	Horn
Hp	Harp
Hpschd	Harpsichord
Improv	Improvisation
Mar	Marimba
MSop	Mezzo Soprano
Narr	Narrator
Ob	Oboe

ObD'am	Oboe d'amore
Org	Organ
Perc	Percussion
Pic	Piccolo
Pno	Piano
Rec	Recorder
SATB	Soprano, Alto, Tenor, Bass Chorus
Sax	Saxophone
Sop	Soprano
Strings	String Orchestra
Tape	Tape Recorder
Tba	Tuba
Tbn	Trombone
Timp	Timpani
Tpt	Trumpet
Vcl	Violoncello
Vib	Vibraphone
Vla	Viola
Vln	Violin

N.B. The key of the instrument may be listed directly before the abbreviation if it is in some way unusual, but otherwise the following associations may be assumed:

All Piccolo Clarinets are in E♭
All Clarinets are in B♭
All Piccolo Trumpets are the combined D/E♭ instrument
All Trumpets are in B♭
All Trombones are tenor.

For an explanation on the instrument doubling notation system, see the PREFACE.

Other Abbreviations

Ed.	Editor
GM	GunMar Music, Inc.
m.	Measure
mm.	Measures
MMC	Master Musicians Collective
MS	Manuscript
MSS	Manuscripts
Mvt.	Movement
No.	Number
Trans.	Translator
Vol.	Volume

PREFACE

Without a doubt, "pioneering" research poses unique challenges—among which are the sheer amount of work and organization required behind the scenes and the responsibilities one is faced with regarding that work. The first of these responsibilities is the one the "pioneer" has to those who may wish to continue his or her research—the fulfillment of which extends far beyond the finished product, into the background work itself. If this responsibility is adequately addressed, the end result will not be a work unto itself, but a guide to this greater project as a whole. In the case of the present enterprise, the first full-length monograph on the life and works of William Thomas McKinley, the background work entailed organizing and in some way preserving over thirty years of the composer's writings and related materials. That accomplished, I hope that this volume, in accordance with the "first responsibility," will serve as a guide to a newly defined area of research which now awaits exploration.

When I first began work on this project in the late summer of 1992, I found McKinley's works and memorabilia in complete disarray—the scores stacked in a closet in tattered envelopes, and sketches, newspaper clippings, and concert programs tossed into unmarked boxes. Thus, before anything so grandiose as a book tabulating all of this material could even be considered, a significant amount of organization was required—a process which in itself took several months. Once that task was completed, however, I attempted to fulfill the "first responsibility" by making the materials publicly available in one form or another. In the case of the music itself, this involved making arrangements for the scores and sketches to be stored someplace where they would be both protected and accessible. By the time this book goes to press, the final stages of such an arrangement with the Boston Public Library will have been completed and the bulk of McKinley's works transferred there. However, since personal memorabilia, such as McKinley's copies of concert programs, commission letters, and the like, were not to be included in the Boston Public Library arrangement, some other solution had to be found to make that material available. I decided, therefore, to include within this volume all of the pertinent data contained in such items: complete performance listings, commission information, award citations, and, most importantly, program notes.

It is no doubt clear that this "first responsibility" of pioneering research is oriented toward future scholarship. The pioneer must not, however, overlook the needs of the present. This is the second responsibility—to realize and account for the fact that the work, as the only one of its kind for the time being, might appeal to a broader audience than researchers alone. Since no complete listing of McKinley's works has ever been available, this work is as much pioneering research to performers as it is to musicologists. In order to adequately serve this greater audience, I chose not to model this book on any single composer's catalog. Instead, I started fresh and critically evaluated the numerous catalogs I have used over the years, taking from them those features I felt were particularly strong—the specifics of which are outlined below. The result, I believe, is a book which should serve as an easy to use guide for performers, musicologists, and anyone else interested in the work of this very prolific master.

The numbering system used in the WORKS, PERFORMANCES, AND BIBLIOGRAPHY chapter of this book represents a significant departure from the other volumes in this series, which place the pieces into categories and then catalog the complete oeuvre with a simple number series. In general, I find the use of a simple number series for works that are not chronologically ordered somewhat misleading—as do listeners, who assume that catalog numbers invariably have some chronological meaning. In choosing a new system, one could make a case for the use of opus numbers, since a few of McKinley's works from the 1970s do have them. However, McKinley's use of the numbers was imprecise—there are, for example, only two works between opus 80 and opus 99, while there are seven works between opus 99 and opus 103—making this an unviable option. Therefore, I have adopted a system of numbering similar to that used in the Hoboken catalog of Haydn's works. This has the advantage of grouping the pieces in a way which makes it easier for performers to find works for their instrument or group of instruments and at the same time keeps them logically ordered. In this system the pieces are first separated into broad categories or groups that are labeled with Roman numerals, such as "Works for Orchestra (I)," "Concerti (II)," "Works for Brass Ensemble (III)," and so forth. Each of these groups is then broken down into sub-groups designated by capital letters, such as "Symphonies (I.A)," and "Overtures (I.B)." Within each of these sub-groups fall the pieces themselves, each complete work receiving an Arabic numeral, such as "Symphony No. 1 in One Movement (I.A.1)," and each unfinished work receiving a lower-case letter and having its title struck through, such as "~~Canons for Orchestra~~ (I.C.a)." The works appear in chronological order within each sub-group, with the exception of the unfinished works, which appear at the end of each sub-group. In some cases, when a work appears in two versions, an additional lower-case letter is appended to the work's number, as is the case with the two versions of *Scarlet* (III.A.2a and III.A.2b).

Much of the information that appears in the entries for the pieces themselves reflects the writing on the manuscripts, with additions from other sources surrounded in brackets and explained in the *Editorial Notes*—this includes the titles of the pieces, the material in the *Date, Dedication, Commission,* and *Movements* sections, and the notations in the *Markings* section of the manuscript description. Unusual changes to these sections which would not be appropriate to place in brackets, such as typographical corrections, are marked with asterisks (*) or double-crosses (‡) and are explained in the *Editorial Notes.* As for the nicknames attached to the various locations of composition, all are outlined and explained the BIOGRAPHY.

In regard to dating, McKinley has generally been careful to write at least the year of composition on his works. In cases where he did not, however, I have usually determined the date of composition either by examining the premiere performance date, or simply by asking the composer. In some cases, I myself was present as a witness during the work's composition. In situations where none of these solutions was possible, I have attempted to determine an approximate date through paleographic analysis. While the question of the reliability of such work for twentieth-century composers has recently been raised with regard to Ives, it is not an issue in the case of McKinley, as his writing style and materials changed quite distinctly over time—particularly during the sixties and seventies (see the BIOGRAPHY and the Photos and Musical Examples for more information). In all cases, the method used to determine the date is listed in the *Editorial Notes.* It should also be noted that since McKinley did not always record more than the year of composition on his works, it was not possible to construct a completely accurate CHRONOLOGICAL LIST OF WORKS. Although I have tried to use supplementary evidence to refine the list somewhat, there are bound to be some lingering errors.

The *Instrumentation* listing for each piece is based on the ABBREVIATIONS found at the front of the book and makes use of a rather unique doubling notation system. Contrary to the growing trend towards brevity, the system used here does not make use of complex numbering schemes which, while compact, are inaccurate in that they make assumptions regarding the playing of multiple instruments by a single performer, or "doublings"—assumptions which, while possible with the nineteenth-century repertory, cannot be made with twentieth-century music. The system used here, therefore, attempts to be more precise. In situations where doublings are required, the instruments to be doubled are separated by a slash (/) and each is preceded by the number of players required on that instrument at any one time. Thus the largest number in any doubling set represents the total number of players required, while the smaller numbers represent how many of that total will be required to double up. For example, the indication "2 Pic/3 Fl" means that a total of three flutists will be required for the piece, two of whom must also double on piccolo. This same idea follows for instrument "triplings" and the like: the notation "Pic Cl/Cl/BCl" indicates that only one clarinetist is needed, but he or she must also be able to play both piccolo clarinet and bass clarinet. Also of note in the *Instrumentation* section is the manner in which strings are listed in orchestral works. When the exact number of each string instrument is listed on the manuscript, those numbers are likewise listed here; otherwise they are simply listed as "strings."

McKinley wrote very few sketches in the traditional sense. For the most part, the items listed in the *Sketches* section of some entries were "drafts"—actual attempts to write the piece which, for some reason, were abandoned—and are therefore marked as such. These drafts generally consist of a single sheet of paper, but there are occasionally "extended" or even "complete" drafts of the work, which are also appropriately labeled. Items listed as "sketches," on the other hand, are what one might expect—sheets of paper with thematic scribblings from one or more locations in the piece. For those sketches and drafts I have been able to identify, I have listed the movement and/or measure number to which they correspond. For example, the notation "I/14–20" indicates that the draft or sketch relates to measures 14–20 of the first movement. For drafts and sketches of pieces without bar lines, which account for many pieces from the 1970s, the page number is given in place of the measure number. In general, I have tried to be as precise as possible in identifying the drafts and sketches. Since there were, however, several thousand of them, this has not always been possible, given the time allotted. Those for which I have only been able to determine the piece are listed as "unidentified" within the piece's entry. For those fifty-nine sketches which did not contain enough information for me to identify at all, I have created the UNIDENTIFIED SKETCHES appendix, where each has been numbered and described. In many ways, I am convinced that sorting the sketches and drafts has been the most important part of the entire cataloging process. Having this kind of information available not only stimulates greater interest in the works to which they belong, but it also opens up another whole range of research possibilities, including studies on McKinley's compositional process.

The manuscript description (*MS Description*) is fairly straightforward, listing whether or not the manuscript is in the author's hand (holograph) and in what form, if any, his name appears (printed or signed). The writing instrument used is also listed (ink, pencil, or stencil engraving), as is the physical material on which the piece is notated (paper or vellum—often referred to in library catalogs as "transparencies").

In the *Performance History*, I have tried to assemble as complete a list as possible of all of the performances to date; but there are, no doubt, omissions. All of the performance information presented here stems from actual concert programs, concert reviews, or recordings—information from any other source is enclosed in brackets and is explained in the *Editorial Notes*. Since some of this material is not specific as to whether or not a particular performance was a world or local premiere, I have, when necessary, added that information based on my best estimation regarding the completion status of the performance history. Such editorial citations are always placed in brackets. Only major cities receive special local premiere citations; some smaller cities, which are considered part of a larger municipality, are listed as the premiere citation for that municipality. Thus premieres in, for example, Cambridge, Massachusetts, are listed as Boston premieres.

In the interest of clarity and easy access, the *Bibliography* for each piece contains actual bibliographic citations, rather than cross-listings to a separate bibliography chapter. More general works on McKinley, on the other hand, are listed in the GENERAL BIBLIOGRAPHY. Readers familiar with the other volumes in this series will note the lack of annotated bibliographic entries. The reason behind this, simply, was limited space. The purpose of this book is, after all, to provide information that one could not otherwise easily find on one's own and to preserve information that might otherwise have been lost. While I regret not having been able to provide the bibliographic annotations, I strongly believe that the preservation of materials such as the program notes and the provision of the sketch information more than compensates for the omission.

In effect, this book contains two discographies: one in the *Recordings* section of the entries, and the other in the DISCOGRAPHY chapter—both of which, for the most part, contain the same information. Again, the reason for this is easy access—the reader can either find out everything about a particular piece at a glance or turn to the DISCOGRAPHY and find a complete listing of recorded works. It should be noted, however, that the DISCOGRAPHY chapter also contains listings of McKinley's jazz recordings for those who are interested in exploring the composer's "other side."

When entering the *Program Notes* into this volume, I made a special effort to reproduce them exactly as McKinley and the other authors wrote them. They have not been edited at all, save for the normalization of italicization and the correction of inadvertent typographical errors. As McKinley's writing style is in many ways unique, it is my hope that this hands-off approach will help convey the experience of reading the composer's own words as he wrote them, sometimes carefully—sometimes in haste, for the performance.

As mentioned earlier, this book is but the final product of an intense organizational project—perhaps the best analogy would be that of the proverbial "tip of the iceberg." Remaining submerged beneath the surface are all of the physical materials to which this volume refers, most of which are waiting to be explored at Boston Public Library, many larger music libraries, or even a local record store. It is my greatest hope that this book will serve as an effective guide for any and all researchers and performers—amateurs and professionals alike—to the work of a man I am certain will be remembered as one of the finest, and certainly one of the most prolific composers of his generation.

Acknowledgments

Many kind individuals gave of their time and skill so that this volume might be completed. While it would be impossible to list them all, I would like to take this opportunity to mention those who truly went out of their way to assist me in my efforts.

First and foremost, I must extend my heartfelt thanks to Tom and Marlene McKinley, for their constant support of this project. During the last two and a half years, they gave me unlimited access to Tom's manuscripts, sketches, notes, and letters and permitted me to work in their home for weeks on end. For their time, for their patience, and for their moral support I will always be grateful.

My thanks also go to those who helped provide me with access to some of the manuscript sources not possessed by McKinley himself. To Pamela Miller at Margun Music, Inc., for allowing me to see the manuscripts and fair copies in their possession. To Richard Stoltzman, for granting me access to the manuscripts Tom has given him over the years, and for providing me with a performer's and friend's insight into both the music and the man. To Ray White at the Library of Congress, for providing the manuscript description of the Third Symphony (I.A.3). To those who provided photocopies of works which no longer survive in the original manuscript: Les Thimmig, Irma Vallecillo, and, once again, Richard Stoltzman. Special thanks are due to my friend Craig Thomas of Spaulding Library at New England Conservatory who, in addition to giving me valuable advice, alerted me to numerous items in the library's collection which contained handwritten changes by McKinley, granted me extended access to copies of scores which no longer exist in the original manuscript, and provided me with biographical information about some of McKinley's conservatory colleagues.

Very special thanks go out to my friend Elliott Miles McKinley, without whose intimate knowledge of his father's work the analysis and cataloging of the sketches would never have been completed. His assistance in providing dates of composition, performance information and biographical clues was also invaluable. I especially appreciate his help in the initial sorting through of thirty years of his father's works and papers and in building the shelving necessary to hold them all.

My thanks also to those who provided missing performance information, newspaper and magazine articles, and program notes, including Richard

Nunemaker, Hans-Jörg Modlmayr, Dale Clevenger, David Samuels, Paul Gunther of the Minnesota Orchestra, Gilda Weissberger of Carnegie Hall, and, yet again, Richard Stoltzman. I should no doubt include among this "missing" information those concert programs which I simply could not read—so my special thanks to Bonnie Michal and Vera Deak for their translations of the Russian, Hungarian, and Slovak programs. And to those who graciously allowed their program notes to be reprinted here, my sincere gratitude.

Many friends stepped in from time to time, helping me with various projects and providing me with large quantities of much needed advice. To Patrick Fairfield, who assisted me throughout the summer of 1994, tracking down the authors of program notes, digging up elusive performance information, computing the durations of nearly a hundred works, and performing at least a dozen other tasks I cannot even begin to list here. To Susan Geoffrion, McKinley's personal assistant, for coordinating my meetings with Tom and for checking on numerous small details, thus saving me scores of trips to Reading. To composer Michael Ellison, for his help in establishing the catalog numbering system used in this volume and for the use of his very patient ear. To Professor Robert Marshall of Brandeis University, for his creative tips on the cataloging process and additional advice on the numbering system. To graphic designer Wayne Curtis, for his advice on layout and type selection. Special thanks to my readers, Wayne Curtis, Michael Ellison, James Hill, Elliott Miles McKinley, Craig Thomas, and Robert Marshall for devoting the time necessary for such a hefty project. To my other dear friends who provided plenty of advice and encouragement: Christopher Mossey, Michael Rogan, Hugh Wilburn, Todd Theriault, Gregory Miller, Peter Watchorn, Herman Weiss, Peter Farmer and Peter Kelly. And, finally, to my parents and family, for a seemingly endless amount of love and support.

Biography

William Thomas McKinley was born on December 9, 1938[1] in New Kensington, Pennsylvania—a town founded on steel, aluminum, and other industrial products. The firstborn son of poor Irish-American parents, Daniel Edward and Ellen Lee McKinley, his upbringing was rather less glamorous than the great masters of the eighteenth and nineteenth centuries, but no less inundated with music. His father, a salesman, managed to find time to sing in amateur vaudeville acts with his wife, who would either tap dance or improvise American hymn-like tunes on the piano. Both parents also found time to encourage their son's uncommonly early interest in music. Just as this interest began to surface, however, Tom's parents separated and were divorced by the time he was three years old. Shortly afterward, Tom's mother married Richard Francis Boucher, a third-shift factory worker. Due to their opposing schedules, Tom never saw much of his new stepfather, but both he and Tom's natural father actively supported the boy's leanings towards music throughout his early life.

Tom's earliest exposure to music came from listening to the radio, the primary form of entertainment in those days. Indeed, his earliest memories revolve around listening to the big bands and providing percussive accompaniment using sticks, spoons or whatever else was available. Seeing this obvious musical interest, his mother decided he should receive drum lessons, which he accordingly began at age three and continued until age five. During this time, Tom began to visualize himself as a successful drummer in a big band, hoping that his famous namesake, the jazz drummer Ray McKinley, would help pave the way.

When Tom reached the age of five, his mother decided it would be more advantageous for him to study the family's main instrument, the piano. The drum lessons were discontinued and he began to work with a local amateur piano teacher, Adelaide Weiss. While his experience with Weiss was valuable in that it exposed him to some of the works of the classical and romantic masters, it was insufficient as she was only able to provide him with the most rudimentary of musical skills and she taught him nothing about the music that truly captivated him—jazz. As a result, Tom was forced to do a great deal of work on his own, including teaching himself how to sight-read and, more importantly, how to improvise. In fact, Tom tended to concentrate more on improvisation than on preparing his lessons. And while his mother was a strong supporter of his playing, insisting that he keep practicing, she would never know until years later about this other side of Tom's musical education.

By the age of nine or ten, Tom's playing had advanced to the point where he was able to play in local dance bands. Four nights a week after school and during the day on Saturdays, he would play at the Audrey Ann Dancing Studio. At age eleven he joined the national musicians' union, the American Federation of Musicians, and thus had the distinction of being their youngest member. By the age of twelve, he was playing with performers four times his age and earning enough money "to make a living."[2] At his mother's request, Tom put much of this money aside for college.

During this period Tom found new ways to augment his musical education. He began by making frequent after school visits to Cooper Brothers Music Store, where he would go into the basement and listen to the old "78" recordings of Horowitz and Toscanini—although their names meant nothing to him at the time, their skill captivated him nonetheless. In addition to the classics, he also listened to the latest popular recordings that arrived in the store, with artists like Art Tatum and Fats Waller. While listening to both jazz and concert music recordings broadened his knowledge of repertoire, they had the side effect of planting seeds of conflict within him. Hearing the concert music, on the one hand, made him want to be a concert pianist, while hearing the popular works, on the other hand, would pull him towards a career in jazz. This conflict, which began with his first piano lessons and was intensified by this daily listening, quickly became a major element of stress in Tom's life and would remain so throughout his college years and beyond.

Tom also supplemented his musical education by tapping the extensive sheet music library at the Audrey Ann Dancing Studio. Each week he would take out thirty or forty pieces to play through during his practice sessions. During his years of association with the studio, he learned hundreds of popular tunes, including the works of Cole Porter, Irving Berlin, and George Gershwin. Many of these works he had already learned by ear, not having had the luxury of printed music from which to read. The sheet music, however, gave him the opportunity to see and learn the works as they were originally written and not just as one performer interpreted them. Once learned in their "pure" form, he could go on to make interpretations of his own. Aside from satisfying his curiosity, the study of this music had real practical value in that it expanded his performance repertoire, which led to even more dance gigs.

Between these new activities and his already hectic schedule, Tom's daily routine became flooded with music: he would get up at 6 a.m., go to school, go to the dancing school, then play a gig, then return home and practice some more, and then, finally, go to sleep—only to wake up a few hours later and begin the whole cycle again. There was no time for school-related activities; no time for sports—music was, quite literally, his life.

When Tom reached the age of thirteen, arrangements were made for him to meet Johnny Costa, New Kensington's premiere jazz pianist. In addition to his local fame,

Costa was already quite well known in Pittsburgh and is perhaps best remembered today for his playing on *Mr. Roger's Neighborhood* on the Public Broadcasting Service television network. A graduate of Carnegie Institute of Technology (now Carnegie–Mellon University), Costa pursued a program of study identical to the one Tom would follow years later: he entered as a piano performance major and then switched to composition, studying under Nikolai Lopatnikoff (students were not permitted to enter the composition program until their third year).

After Tom had played for Costa, Costa decided to take him under his wing and teach him some of his jazz techniques. They met somewhat irregularly, Tom's lessons with Costa supplementing those he continued to receive from Weiss. Despite this multiplicity of instruction, Tom's devotion to Costa was complete. Whatever music Costa played, Tom would play—from Bach inventions to the latest works of Art Tatum. Due to his ability to play just about any piece or to improvise in just about any style he heard, a benefit of growing up without the luxury of written music, his playing improved to the point that Costa began to recommend him for gigs, and even had Tom substitute for him when necessary.

Tom's years in high school were also infused with music during school hours through his participation in the high school choir. The choir's director, Carolyn Bruno (now Carolyn Schankovich), also instructed him in history and improvisation, and helped expand his general music knowledge. Tom enjoyed the experience so much that he went on to sing in state choruses while still in high school and later sang with the chorus of the Pittsburgh Symphony during his college years. It was also while in the high school choir that Tom met his future wife, Marlene Marie Mildner.

During their time in the choir together Tom and Marlene were just acquaintances—it was only when Marlene happened to hear Tom play at a club in Cheswick that she began to take an active interest in him. By the time Tom was fifteen he had begun to spend more time playing outside of New Kensington, in neighboring towns as well as in the city of Pittsburgh, and had even begun to take road trips during the summer to play in the big dance halls of Chicago. One Saturday night Marlene was at one of these club engagements. Her mother, who worked in the club's restaurant, had brought her along to work as a hat-check girl. Marlene, at first, was surprised to hear that Tom would be playing that evening, as she thought that a mere high-school student would be too inexperienced to satisfy the club's sophisticated clientele. But after hearing him play and speaking to him at intermission, she realized that she had underestimated him.[3] Less than two years later, on April 11th, 1956, Tom and Marlene were married.

During his senior year, Tom prepared for college auditions. From the outset Tom based his college plans on those of his mentor, Johnny Costa—this included his first choice of school, his course of study, and even the teacher he would study with, if accepted. Therefore, he applied to Carnegie Tech to study piano during his first two years and then composition with Nikolai Lopatnikoff during the last two. In preparation, Tom left his teacher of twelve years, Adelaide Weiss, and studied with "the Hayes sisters," both of whom were graduates of Carnegie Tech.[4]

Tom's recollection of the actual audition is quite vivid. He began with Chopin's *Fantasie Impromptu* in C♯ minor, followed by Bach's C major Invention, after which the jury told him to stop. Feeling that the audition was not going particularly well, he suddenly decided to change his approach. "I can do something else," he told them, "I can make up anything." He remembers Lopatnikoff or one of the others on the panel replying, "Well, make up a piece, then. Let's hear you do it." For the next fifteen minutes Tom improvised in the style of Ravel, during which "Lopatnikoff's eyes went up." Shortly afterward, Tom was admitted as a piano performance major for the 1956-57 academic year.[5]

Although he was accepted on the basis of his compositional skills, Tom, in accordance with the school's policy, would not be allowed to pursue that course of study until his third year. In the meantime, he studied piano with Leonard Eisner. Since Eisner was able to accept Tom's compositional bent and long term goals from the start, their relationship was always sound. During his sophomore year, Tom remembers Eisner saying:

> You know, you could have been a great concert pianist. You have everything it takes except one thing—your heart. There's an extra spark when you make up your own music. ... You should be a composer.[6]

However, the positive aspect of his relationship with Eisner, not to mention the gradual strengthening of his relationship with Lopatnikoff, were unable to prevent these first two years from being, in Tom's opinion, the most stressful in his life. A great deal of this tension came from the split allegiance he still felt between jazz and concert music, leading to what Tom has called a "Dr. Jekyll/Mr. Hyde" existence.[7] As in high school, Tom continued to play jazz gigs in his spare time. It was a slow start after his arrival in Pittsburgh, but by the time he reached his sophomore year he was playing in clubs like the Midway Lounge—sometimes known as the "jazz oasis" of Pittsburgh—as often as six nights a week.[8] The performers he had the opportunity to play with were also more distinguished by this time and included musicians like saxophonist Sonny Stitt and singer King Pleasure, who often sang with Charlie Parker. He also took on independent accompanying jobs, which included playing for Neil Sedaka and The Four Freshmen. All of these experiences tended to draw him towards a career in jazz. Drawing him away, however, were his concert music gigs. In addition to his jazz work Tom found time to work as a coach and accompanist for the opera workshops at Carnegie Tech and to play in the pit orchestra of the Pittsburgh Playhouse. Also pulling him towards the European classical tradition was the influence of two men for whom he had great respect: Lopatnikoff and musicologist Frederick Dorian.

Beyond the difficulties caused by this internal existential debate were the even more devastating external stresses of his personal life. During his first academic year alone, his mother, who had always been a source of strong moral support, passed away, and his first child, Joseph Thomas, was born. Because of the disastrous timing, this latter event, which normally would have been a joyous one, only served to further darken Tom's already gloomy outlook on the future.

The situation, and Tom's mood, bettered somewhat when he entered his junior year and began to study with Lopatnikoff. This improvement was partially due to the excitement Tom felt about working with someone who "represented...all the things you read about [composers]."[9] Lopatnikoff had been a student of Ernst Toch in Berlin and was a close friend of both Hindemith and Stravinsky. He was also an expatriate of the Russian revolution. After his family had been killed while he was still quite young, he went to Europe, eventually making a name for himself in England and France. When Hitler came to power, he emigrated to the United States and eventually ended up at Carnegie Tech. Thus when Tom met this man, who had lived the quintessential romantic vision of a composer's life, "it was just an incredible kind of encounter with history. It was like meeting Beethoven or meeting Brahms or something."[10] Eventually the two became quite close, with Lopatnikoff becoming a kind of father figure to the young composer—himself having little contact with his own father at this time. The strength of their relationship was such that Lopatnikoff was able, at least temporarily, to resolve Tom's internal conflict between jazz and concert music—all it took was the simple declaration that he should be a composer:

> [W]hen *he* said I should be a composer, my life changed. It was like everything I had been was no good—I didn't want jazz anymore. I didn't want nightclubs anymore. I didn't want that kind of 'decadence' anymore. ...Not the music being decadent, but a lot of the life that goes with it. ...I suddenly saw myself as a composer.... It hit.[11]

But Tom found changing his daily habits to be difficult. The gigs continued to roll in, and he had a wife and child to support; so his work habits were forced to remain, for the most part, unchanged. What he did with the little free time he had, however, changed dramatically. Instead of going out to the local clubs, he would stay home with Marlene and read, concentrating on works he believed would help prepare him for his future composing career: philosophical writings, among which were those of Plato and Aristotle, and the scores of many great musical masterpieces, including the Bartók string quartets.

In the meantime, Lopatnikoff provided Tom with what Marlene has described as a "quintessential foundation in the grand European manner"[12]—teaching him score reading, harmony, and orchestration. Tom also adds that "he instilled within me a sense of historical identity connecting with the big stream of European music ranging from Bach to Bartók."[13] Lopatnikoff also taught Tom about the principles of organic musical development, similar to those used by Beethoven, Brahms, and Hindemith.[14] In short, he believed that music should be improvised from a spontaneously composed original idea—a philosophy which Tom was able to blend with his own jazz influences and reflect in the pieces written during this time. These were the String Quartet No. 1 (IV.C.1), written in 1959 and played during Tom's senior year by the Phillips Quartet, and the Adagio for Violin and Piano (VI.F.1), written in 1960 and also played that year by Tom and violinist Joe Bishkoff. He also began work on a symphony, but never completed it. (The sketches, written in a notebook in piano short-score, have since been lost.) All of these works were in the neo-classic tradition, patterned after Lopatnikoff's own style. Since he was also listening to a great deal of Copland at the time, the works were also infused with a strong, syncopated feeling—no doubt Tom's jazz background played a role in this as well. Of these early works Tom writes:

> My earliest mentors at Carnegie Tech did not believe in 'cerebral' music. They taught that the mystical union of mind with spirit is paramount to the creative psyche, and they helped me to see the line of descent from the great masters to the present. When this heritage was coupled with my purely American jazz spirit, it was clear how my musical instincts would be revealed, and how my "Americanness" would manifest itself from the duality I traversed during these years.[15]

The last of the mentors of whom Tom speaks was Alexi Haieff, who was brought in as Lopatnikoff's replacement when the he took a sabbatical during Tom's senior year. At this point Tom was fairly self-sufficient as a composer, so Haieff's main responsibility was simply to oversee Tom's work. Haieff was a very close friend of Stravinsky, however, and as such gave Tom a further chance to learn a great deal about the master—beyond what he had already learned about him from Lopatnikoff. At this time Tom also began to take on private theory and composition students, among whom were saxophonists Eric Kloss and Steven Grossman. Both went on to lead very successful performing careers.

All in all, these last two years at Carnegie were a significant improvement over the two which preceded them, but obviously problems of the magnitude Tom experienced during those years did not dissipate so quickly. The torn allegiances between jazz and concert music continued, and, if anything, multiplied. As Tom describes it, during the day he was torn between following Dorian's love of Beethoven and Weber and Lopatnikoff's love of Stravinsky and Hindemith, while at night he was torn between the "commercial world" of "pure jazz" and the more modern jazz of Charlie Parker.[16] While he was unable to resolve the greater jazz–concert music conflict during these years, he was at least able to come to terms with this new stylistic struggle:

> I became an idealist. It was either going to be that I was going to play the most modern jazz of the day and suffer, like Charlie Parker had suffered, or write [the most] modern music of the day and suffer like Bartók had suffered.[17]

The idealism to which Tom refers took the form of an attempt to live a romantic vision of an artist's life—a vision which, in his mind, revolved around waiting for discovery and acceptance by the public and, in essence, taking a rather passive approach to one's career.

Due to the economic realities of his situation, however, Tom could not afford his new-found idealism—at least not when it came to his performing career. Since the "commercial world" of "pure jazz" was popular, Tom was forced to continue playing it. He also realized that, when and if he were ever able to become a pure idealist, he would probably have to continue to both perform *and* compose in order to stay afloat. He therefore began to contemplate ways of making the two careers compatible—but the solution was not quickly forthcoming.

In the spring of 1960, Tom graduated from the Carnegie Institute. The time had come for him to get his name as a composer before the public. But the idealism which had sprung up during his senior year prevented that—his mind still filled with those romantic visions of what it meant to be an artist. Rather than going out into the world and creating his own success, he waited for the world to come to him. Naturally his performing continued out of economic necessity. But so drained was he by the amount of performing required to support his family, which now included two more sons (Derrick Scott and Jory Damon), that not a single new work was completed at the end of two years after he had left Carnegie. Finally, in the spring of 1963, he wrote the Trio [No. 1] in One Movement (V.F.1). This work is, according to Tom, an imitation of the styles of Leon Kirchner, Aaron Copland, and William Schuman—the composers he was interested in at the time.[18] Here again, Tom's ability to imitate the style of others is readily apparent. Indeed, this practice of imitating the individual styles of contemporary neo-classic composers and the lack of a distinct compositional voice all his own is indicative of what one could call his first compositional period (1959–1964).

Tom's own disinterest in his career did not discourage his friends and family, however. Eventually, they were able to persuade him to at least present this latest work to the Tanglewood Music Center for possible admission and to enter it in the BMI (Broadcast Music, Inc.) music competition. The effort was well rewarded: Tom received a Fromm fellowship to attend Tanglewood during the upcoming summer, and he won the 1963 BMI prize.

When summer finally arrived, Tom borrowed some money, packed up his family, and went to Tanglewood. Once there, he had the opportunity to work with some of the greatest composers of the day, including Aaron Copland, Gunther Schuller, and Lukas Foss. He also got a taste of different compositional styles, including atonal and serial composition. By far the most important aspect of the experience, however, was the evaluation of his work for the first time by outsiders—an experience which, in a sense, marked the official beginning of his composing career.

After Tanglewood, Tom returned to Pittsburgh re-inspired to compose and filled with the new confidence which came with the premiere of his Trio and the completion of his new *Orchestral Study* (I.C.1). He was also very excited to have had the opportunity to work with Gunther Schuller. Schuller, unlike many of the composers and instructors at Tanglewood that summer who were wrapped up in the new serialist rage, was interested in unusual fusions—a concept of obvious interest to Tom and one which helped strengthen the relationship between the two men over the years. Schuller eventually went on to explore the very fusion Tom was interested in—jazz and concert music—in his "Third Stream" work. Overall, Tom returned from Tanglewood a different man; unfortunately the world around him remained unchanged. As Marlene writes:

> The creative nourishment of the eight weeks at Tanglewood was not lasting.... Soon after his inevitable return to his demanding club schedule, it seemed that Tanglewood had been a mirage. Tom stopped composing, even attempting to compose.[19]

Over the next two years, the situation worsened to the point that,

> By the winter of 1965-66, all creativity seemed lost. Even improvisation was severely limited, virtually non-existent, for patrons of the clubs at which Tom was playing demanded only "popular melodies." Indeed, Tom, in despair, thought himself condemned to a life of "sing-alongs."[20]

No doubt the arrival of yet another child (Gregory Sëan) did little to lighten Tom's burden or help to pull him out of this creative slump.

Tom began several new works during this fallow period, but completed only one, *Directions '65* (VIII.E.1). To Tom, *Directions '65,* a serial work, represented the new direction music was taking—the same direction which was in the air at Tanglewood.[21] It also represented the new direction Tom would take in this, his second compositional period (1965–1980): atonality.

Despite the connotations associated with atonal composition, this stylistic shift was actually prompted by Tom's desire to integrate jazz into his compositions. Tom believed that such a fusion might be more easily obtained through atonality because of the greater rhythmic freedom atonal composition allowed over the compositional styles of the common practice period. But as Tom would discover over the next fifteen years, "rhythmic freedom" in this context was, as he has described it, merely a synonym for "rhythmic chaos." With total rhythmic freedom there is no basic pulse, and it is upon this pulse that the rhythms of both jazz and concert music depend.[22]

Along with Tom's change of style came a change in work habits. During his first compositional period, Tom generally composed in pencil at the piano, but over the next few years he began to spend more and more time composing at a drafting table. The advantages of the latter were greater space and a more stable writing surface, both of which allowed Tom to produce the same kind of exquisitely penned scores as his contemporaries were writing at the time. The disadvantages of this location change were quite clear to Marlene, however:

> I think it imposed a greater rift between Tom's "composition self" and his "jazz self"—a more pronounced split which, looking back, I think began at Carnegie Tech., where jazz was denigrated, and jazz playing was banned even in the practice rooms.[23]

As he and many other composers would discover in the late seventies, this rage for elaborate calligraphy in scores, or for the writing of what might be called *Augenmusik,* was merely a substitute for, as Tom says, "beautiful" music. Calligraphy was the "last vestige of hope for anything resembling real music. It was the final stages of the disease."[24]

> The mania for calligraphy was an extension of the fact that composers were only writing music for the eye. And if it were going to be beautiful, it had better be for the eye because it wasn't going to happen anywhere else.[25]

Even in the early days of this newly born compositional period, Tom struggled with this paradox. But the style of the times seemed to dictate that atonality was the future and so he remitted, in the hope that a successful fusion of jazz and concert music would soon reap its rewards and overcome his misgivings.

His newly acquired style not withstanding, by the late spring of 1966 Tom was at the lowest ebb of his creative slump. One night, while very drunk, he decided to call pianist and composer Mel Powell at Yale University. The two had never spoken or met, but Tom had listened to Powell's playing a great deal and felt a certain camaraderie with him due to their similar backgrounds. Tom told Powell his life story, after which Powell requested that he send him some of his music. A few months later, Tom rather unexpectedly received an invitation to come to Yale for his Masters and DMA. This news was exactly what Tom needed to snap him out of his creative slumber. It was not long before he resumed practicing, improvising, and, most importantly, composing.

Going to Yale was like wiping the slate clean and starting a new life—a three-year protected period during which Tom could finally prepare himself for a career. However, his pre-Yale idealism and romantically passive approach to his career was once again beginning to surface and was proving to be nothing less than a curse. As Tom himself has said, "I wanted to be famous, but I didn't want to have anything to do with it."[26] Luckily, those around him were unwilling to let his talent go unnoticed. They would drop his name to influential people and even enter him in competitions without his knowledge. It was through such channels that Tom received his first Fromm commission for *Premises and Expositions* (VIII.A.1) in 1968—a commission which included another summer at Tanglewood, this time as a guest composer. Despite his initial reluctance to participate in his own career, these initial pushes helped him gain enough confidence to begin to take steps of his own.

Going to Yale did not, of course, lessen his financial burden. He continued, in this new setting, to find jobs playing in jazz clubs at night. But this time the experience was different. Perhaps due to his new desires and attempts to bring jazz into his compositions, he was, "for the first time,...able to keep [his playing] in perspective."

> When I went to play a job, it didn't affect my other being. I knew why I was doing it and it had more meaning and it was even more fun....[27]

In addition to playing nightclub gigs, Tom formed an improvisation ensemble which gave numerous performances at the various Yale colleges. He also resumed coaching, this time with the New Haven Opera, and accompanying, now with the Yale dance troupe. The dance troupe position proved especially fruitful, since it not only gave Tom ample opportunities to improvise but also provided him with a great deal of exposure. While in their employ, he had the privilege to play for classes by Daniel Wagner and perform in several National Educational Television projects with Paul

Taylor. Indeed, unlike his previous educational experiences, the work he did outside of school while at Yale only contributed to his overall experience, making this one of the happiest times of his life.

As expected, during his tenure at Yale Tom studied composition with Mel Powell; Powell quickly replacing Lopatnikoff as Tom's surrogate father. At the time of their encounter, Powell was deeply involved with electronic music and the works of Babbitt and Webern. As a result, Tom's new atonal leanings were nurtured and focused. But Powell did not encourage Tom to become a pure serialist. Rather, he told him to compose "the music that was inside" and "to be intuitive."[28] The result was music that was improvised in a serialist style, using repeated melodic patterns, but not strictly defined tone-rows. This new spin on his recently adopted atonal style allowed Tom to take further advantage of his dual background. While Tom did continue to occasionally experiment with the pure serialism of his pre-Yale years, the majority of works from the second compositional period are in this new style he developed under Powell. Tom soon came to disdain compositional systems as a whole—he believed they robbed the composer of his creativity. This belief eventually evolved from a mere philosophy regarding composition to an almost obsessive spirituality. Music should be tied directly into the spirit of the composer himself, Tom believed, and therefore into the spirit of music itself—an opinion reflected in the dedication of many works from the second compositional period "to the spirit of...."

> When I wrote atonal music, I was still writing intuitively. This was not the way one wrote atonal music.... Which meant that occasionally...in the middle of all this *Angst*, something beautiful would occur. "To the spirit of..." was my way of holding on to the intuition—that I wasn't writing this music at all, it was coming through me in a way that I felt a kinship with the prolific masters of the past....[29]

It was also during his study with Powell that Tom solidified the compositional method he would continue to use until the present day. As this writer's analysis of the sketches suggests and Tom confirms, the pieces are conceived organically, as Lopatnikoff had taught him to do: a great deal of time is spent on the opening of a particular work, usually the first five to ten measures, and this, once settled, catapults the rest. Throughout the remainder of the piece, much of the editing involved is done mentally, before being put down on paper. Occasionally, a change will come after the fact—in flashes of inspiration, sometimes in the middle of the night, as Tom says—which will lead him back to the score to make written changes. In the special case of large-scale works, some additional planning is usually involved—the form and, in some cases, motives being written out in advance on scraps of paper.[30]

In addition to providing Tom with a compositional technique with which he could build a career, Yale also provided him with useful contacts and friendships which would help propel that new career forward. By far the most valuable of these friendships were the ones he formed with performers also studying at Yale, among whom were Les Thimmig, Syoko Aki Erle, Michael Finegold, and Richard Stoltzman—all of whom would go on to become major advocates of Tom's music.

Saxophonist Les Thimmig and Tom were particularly close friends at Yale. A composer himself, Thimmig was a strong advocate of new music and had the benefit of being blessed with the talent necessary to play the exceedingly complex works Tom and others would place before him. While at Yale, he and violinist Syoki Aki Erle played Tom's *Interim Pieces [No. 1]* (VIII.G.2). After Yale, however, Thimmig went on to a position at the University of Wisconsin at Madison and became the primary source of performances of Tom's works for several years. During the early seventies, the number of performances in Wisconsin would equal or outnumber those in either Chicago or Boston—the cities in which Tom would eventually settle.

By far Tom's strongest advocate throughout his career was (and is) clarinetist Richard Stoltzman. Stoltzman first met Tom in 1967 when Tom asked him to play his latest work, *Attitudes* (VIII.F.1), along with flutist Michael Finegold and bassist Eric Jensen. After Yale, the two lost contact until 1975. Once they became re-acquainted, however, Stoltzman's concerts regularly included McKinley works.[31]

Yale also provided Tom with the experience necessary to begin a teaching career. In addition to the teaching assistantships common to most graduate students, Tom was given some rare opportunities. The first came in the spring of 1968, when one of his professors, Larry Moss, recommended him for a one-semester position as an associate professor at the State University of New York at Albany (SUNYA), and even went so far as to arrange for him to have an interview. Not long afterwards, SUNYA offered Tom the position, which he readily accepted. So, during the fall of 1968, his third year at Yale, he took a leave of absence, packed up, and moved to Albany to teach, among other things, opera history. As a guest professor, Tom had a certain level of distinction at Albany, one which opened up an exceptional performance opportunity with the American String Trio, for whom he wrote his *Studies for String Trio* (IV.F.1). Upon his return to Yale in the spring of 1969, he was asked to fill another teaching position, this time at Yale itself, for a graduate harmony course. This, combined with the birth of his fifth and final son, Elliott Miles, made Tom's last months at Yale some of his busiest yet.

Tom's fairly extensive teaching experience, both institutional and private, was no doubt responsible for the fact that after he had graduated from Yale in May of 1969, he was immediately hired by the University of Chicago to begin teaching that fall. Needless to say, it was quite an honor to be chosen for such a position right out of graduate school. By becoming a member of the University of Chicago faculty, he was joining the ranks of some of the best composers and musicologists in the field—Ralph Shapey, Easley Blackwood, Edward Lowinsky, Robert Marshall, and Leonard Meyer, to name a few. Tom would spend the next four years working among these well-respected individuals; but overall, the experience was not a pleasant one. The university was very scholarship-oriented at that time, and this did not readily appeal to the performance-oriented composer. He also felt that the composition faculty had little respect for his jazz leanings, causing him once again to feel alienated.[32]

There were, of course, some positive events that had occurred during Tom's tenure in Chicago. By far the most significant was a commission from the Chicago Symphony Orchestra for the Triple Concerto (II.B.2) in 1970. The commission was sanctioned by the general director of the orchestra, John Edwards, who had known Tom back when he was playing jazz piano in Pittsburgh. The experience was as educational as it was prestigious, in that it provided Tom with an opportunity to experiment with large orchestral forces and hone his orchestration skills. The piece, like most of the works of this period, is firmly rooted in Tom's improvised, atonal style.

Shortly before the Chicago Symphony commission, Tom had another chance to work on his orchestration when, for his second Fromm commission, he wrote *Quadruplum* (II.B.1) for Ralph Shapey and his ensemble in January and February of 1970. In addition to performing this new work, in 1971 Shapey gave Tom his first recording opportunity as the piano soloist in Shapey's *Rituals* with the London Sinfonietta.

Aside from these greater events, the only other pleasant aspects of his time in Chicago involved performing opportunities inside and outside the strict confines of the university. Outside, he was playing at one of the best jazz clubs in Chicago, the Modern Jazz Showcase, where some of the greatest jazz performers would play on a regular basis. Inside, he formed the University of Chicago Contemporary Jazz and Improvisation Ensemble. While under Tom's direction, the group performed about a dozen concerts, many of which contained Tom's music and arrangements. Due to the adversity he was encountering at the university, jazz performance took on a very special role in Tom's life during this time—the warm, friendly feeling of the clubs no doubt counterbalancing the cold animosity of the university. He was also feeling more comfortable with his playing during these years—one might say that the world had finally caught up with him. Since the modern Charlie Parkereque jazz he played during the sixties was now popular, he could play the music he most wanted to play without the fear of upsetting his listeners or his employers.

The events in Chicago did little to change Tom's passivity towards his composing career. Indeed, considering the level of the performances and commissions he received, there would seem to have been little reason for his attitude to change. As he had always believed would happen, people were coming to him, rather than vice-versa, and it appeared he would be able to afford the luxury of continuing to be an idealist. In fact, the events in Chicago only served to encourage that idealism further. Eventually it expanded to the point that Tom felt that all that was necessary to become a successful composer was simply to write large quantities of music. And, since his teaching duties were rather light, about six hours a week, that was exactly what he did.

> I composed, day after day, I wrote piece after piece—many of which have never been played. They sit on my shelves. A lot of which don't deserve to be played and were just pure abstract experiments, but the notes were flowing, the mind was flowing, the ink was flowing.[33]

But as this statement from 1986 indicates, this philosophy of waiting for performances to fall into his lap, as, for all intents and purposes, the Chicago performances had done, would eventually come back to haunt him.

For Tom, a particularly memorable work which came out of all this flowing ink was the *Fantasies and Inventions for Solo Harpsichord* (VII.H.4). What makes this work special in Tom's mind is its unusually strong connection to "the spirit of" Bach:

> [I]f you looked at the manuscript [of the *Fantasies and Inventions*], and you had studied Bach's manuscript, you would say, "That looks like Bach wrote that." Now, I wasn't copying his handwriting. My handwriting would change in every piece, because I was living a re-incarnation through every piece. I was feeling what I felt the masters would have felt from the muses and...that's ageless. That's timeless. And so this one piece stands out, particularly, because it looks like...Bach—it looks like he copied it out—it has the curved beams and everything. And I felt like he was next to me the whole time.[34]

The ability to imitate the styles of others was obviously more than a useful skill to Tom—like the use of his own improvisational style, it too was a spiritual matter.[35]

Despite Tom's dislike of Chicago, there was one compelling reason to remain—it was, after all, a job, and one with a tenure track at that. When, however, offers from other schools began arriving during the spring of 1973, Tom considered them very seriously. The first was an offer from Swarthmore College to become chairman of their composition department. But Swarthmore, Tom felt, would be too much like Chicago with its academic focus. The interviewing process did allow Tom to meet George Crumb, however. The second offer came from Tom's old Tanglewood instructor, Gunther Schuller, from the New England Conservatory of Music (NEC) in Boston, where Schuller was now serving as president. Excited at the prospect of becoming a colleague of Schuller's and feeling that Boston had more to offer in terms of a musical life than Chicago, Tom quickly accepted the position on the composition faculty. In August of that year, he once again packed up his family and moved to Boston.

Upon their arrival in the Boston area the McKinley family settled in the town of Reading in a house that Tom would later nickname "Linnea Lane," after their street address, and write on some of the pieces he would later compose there. The family would live in a total of five different locations between this first home and their current residence. The two homes following "Linnea Lane" were both in Manchester, Massachusetts: the "Carriage House" (from August 1975 to July 1977) and "Hickory Hill" (from August 1977 to July 1978). After Manchester would follow two more homes back in Reading: the "Barn" (from August 1978 to July 1981) and their current residence, a yellow house nicknamed "Lells."

The move to the Boston area was fortuitous for Marlene, as well, who, having just finished her Ph.D. in Medieval Literature at the University of Chicago, was now able to find temporary teaching positions at several of Boston's fifty-plus colleges. Eventually she went on to receive a full-time professorship at Suffolk University.

As he still had a month before school began in September, Tom took the time to seek out the other jazz musicians in town and acquaint himself with the various clubs. On one of these nights out he met one of his future students, Thomas Oboe Lee, a jazz major at the conservatory, who was playing at the Orson Welles Theater in Cambridge. Lee's playing affected Tom greatly as, in Tom's words, "this was the first time I heard the jazz music being played the way I had wanted to play it as early as the late fifties."[36] Instantly, Tom wanted to be back in the jazz scene. When Lee saw Tom's keen interest in his playing, he asked Tom to join him and some of his friends. Together they formed a group called "Departed Feathers." The band, and Tom himself, quickly became known around town and Tom's jazz career was once again flourishing.

In September, Tom began teaching at the conservatory. Despite his extensive jazz background and the formation of a new jazz department at the conservatory by Schuller, Tom was brought in as a member of the composition faculty. But Schuller never discouraged Tom, or anyone else for that matter, from intermingling concert music and jazz—a policy which gave Tom a new sense of freedom. Eventually, Tom did become deeply involved with the new jazz department, taking on some jazz piano students and becoming director of the NEC Contemporary Improvisation Ensemble. In fact, due to a crisis in the jazz department in 1978, Tom was asked to take over the department chairmanship for three years, during which he added several prominent jazz musicians to the faculty.

Throughout these early years at NEC, Tom continued to write a great deal of music, since, as an experienced teacher, class preparation required little of his time. But it took quite some time for the people of Boston to become interested in what he was writing. In fact, as mentioned earlier, the majority of performances during these first couple of years took place with Les Thimmig's ensemble in Wisconsin—Boston itself only saw three performances of Tom's music in 1974 and only two in 1975. The disadvantages of his lingering idealistic philosophy were rapidly becoming apparent.

In the latter part of 1975, however, Tom finally decided to try to turn things around and to take a greater interest in his career. He began by entering himself in competitions and applying for grants. By lucky happenstance, the time of this resurgence of interest coincided with a chance encounter with Richard Stoltzman. The two had not spoken since their days at Yale, but when Stoltzman arrived in Boston with his newly formed chamber group, "Tashi," he decided to contact Tom. Tom brought them out to the house in Reading, and at the end of the evening, "Dick left [the] house with thirty-five pounds of music" for clarinet and various other instruments and left Tom with a commission to write even more.[37]

It took time for the effects of Tom's career efforts to be felt, but when they did eventually come though, they came in abundance—some even within the first year. In 1976 alone he received his first grant from the National Endowment for the Arts—he would go on to receive seven more over the next ten years—and his

Concerto for Grand Orchestra [No. 1] (II.A.1) was nominated for the Pulitzer Prize. In 1977 he received a grant from the Massachusetts Arts and Humanities Foundation, and in 1978 he received a commission from Boston Musica Viva's director Richard Pittman for his Six Impromptus (VIII.D.3). In 1980, the Artists Foundation of Massachusetts also presented him with a monetary award. Tom's efforts also had an effect on the number of performing groups willing to program his works—the number of works performed locally more than doubling between 1976 and 1979. The caliber of the ensembles was also improving steadily and began to include groups such as Collage, the John Oliver Chorale, and the various ensembles under Gunther Schuller. Schuller's publishing company, Margun Music, also began accepting and publishing Tom's works. With success came further teaching opportunities; in this case in the form of two summers at Tanglewood. In 1979 came two other tributes to Tom's success: the Minnesota Orchestra's seventy-fifth anniversary prize for his Symphony No. 1 (I.A.1) and the first recording ever of his music, *Paintings No. 2* (VIII.C.1) on Golden Crest Records.

Indeed, the ball was rolling to such a degree that Tom stopped playing in clubs entirely and devoted himself solely to teaching and composition. As Marlene notes, however, there was a price for such devotion:

> It seemed to me that he wanted to eradicate jazz from his life. The rift I discerned during our Chicago days now seemed irreparable. Even though he was teaching jazz at the conservatory, it played no part in his life as a performer or composer. In disowning jazz, Tom disowned part of himself.[38]

The only opportunity for Tom to play during the late seventies came as result of his duties as chairman of the jazz department at the conservatory. Tom was required to take on some jazz performance students and would, as a result, play along with them during lessons, but never in public. Only after he appointed bassist Miroslav Vitous to the jazz faculty in 1980 and the two began taking professional gigs together did Tom re-emerge in the public eye as a performer.

By 1979, Tom's interest in his career had evolved into a fervent desire for fame. Indeed, the situation was now completely reversed from four years previous: rather than waiting for people to come to him to commission works, he was now actively seeking out performers and groups to write music for. And while he did receive some response, it was by no means in the volume he was hoping for. In trying to figure out why this was so, he contemplated the possibility that it may have been the style of the music he was writing. Albeit, the music was very complex, virtuosic, and often used gargantuan forces—reason enough to earn the public's admiration, but not their love. The music may have reflected the tastes of academia, but not the public, as the tiny audiences at new music concerts made clear.

In evaluating the music he was writing, Tom tried to understand what had made him choose the path towards atonality in the first place.

> I think I moved in step [with]...the official sanctioned languages of...American universities. ...I was a product...of that education, except part of me wasn't in it. And I did it well enough that I thought maybe that what I was doing...was valid.[39]

In addition to a grudging attempt to keep in step with the tastes of academia, Tom still kept the possibility of a fusion of his dual background constantly in mind as he persevered with this fifteen-year experiment. But the experiment was failing—the music reached neither Tom nor his audience. Tom's intuition began telling him to return to his roots—to tonality. His intuition was not alone, however—the public, in its newly found love of minimalism, was telling him that as well. In many respects, minimalism, with its tonal vocabulary and repetitive structure, was an overt rebellion against the complex, atonal music written by the majority of contemporary composers during the preceding thirty years. Atonal music, by its very nature, was forced to change constantly—so much, in fact, that the audience was unable to keep up. As a result, the public enthusiastically embraced minimalism, while the academic community, with equal enthusiasm, scorned it. As Tom describes it:

> [The minimalists were] sort of taking the complete opposite and saying, "you see how far off the mark you've gone, when we can turn it completely opposite and it works. And the people like it."[40]

At first, Tom found himself in agreement with the judgment of his colleagues, but as he re-evaluated his own style, he began to think that the minimalists might have something after all. Minimalism's call to follow one's "stream of consciousness" certainly appealed to Tom's improvisatory nature, and its lack of academic approval helped it earn Tom's respect. But it was the basic elements behind the success of minimalism that affected Tom most greatly: tonality and repetition. As Tom has described it, the great music of the common practice period was based on controlled use of both these elements, while pure, "ritualistic" minimalism simply took the latter to an extreme. Thus, the success of minimalism served to inform Tom that it was these two basic qualities that the public craved—qualities that were completely absent from the music of his second compositional period. It was, therefore, the *influence* of minimalism, rather than a desire to become a minimalist himself, that began to push Tom further toward developing a new style. In the future, Tom would, occasionally, experiment with pure minimalism, as he did in 1985 with *Golden Petals* (II.C.2), but Tom preferred to use what he calls "developing" minimalism—a process that he says is found in the repeated patterns, motives, and harmonic sequences of the common practice period.

> [My minimalism is] a more developing minimalism which leads from stasis to change, and that change represents something much more contrasting to its counterpart than you would find in minimalism.[41]

What gave Tom the final incentive to seek out a new style was a commission to write out some of his jazz arrangements from Richard Stoltzman. When Stoltzman first made this proposal in 1980, Tom resisted. He felt that writing out jazz was a contradiction in terms—if he was going to write, he would write "serious" music. Stoltzman continued to push the idea until Tom finally relented and in 1981 agreed to write a piece based on Gordon Jenkins' *Goodbye*. The result, *Goodbye* (X.B.1), was more than an arrangement—it was a new piece, which simply used the *Goodbye* melody as a *cantus firmus*. In writing this piece, the first of what Tom would later call his "neo-tonal" period, Tom realized that it would be possible to use the same approach to write symphonies, concerti, and numerous other forms—all incorporating his jazz improvisation skills, but formalized in written form.

> [T]he tonality of my background from all this music, bringing back harmony, melody and what I would consider biological pulses or human pulses, all of...which made me want to be a composer in the first instance. And I sort of see it as a sort of return to innocence. ...I'm just going to write what pleases me so much, like a little kid. This beautiful chord, I don't care if its academically correct,...I don't care about common tonality or Princeton dogmatics, or whether the instruments are new or electronically filtered...I don't care about any of it. All I know is that I gotta go back to that period of innocence. ...It's old and new at the same time. ...It embraces everything up through the early twentieth century plus my jazz. ...[A]nd I think that without jazz, you can't call yourself an American composer.[42]

Positive response to Tom's new style as represented in this first piece was immediate:

> Dick [Stoltzman] reported to me what happened in the rehearsal. He said they started reading the piece. [After] about three or four minutes Richard Goode said, "Now, this is my kind of modern music." That's all that I heard. I didn't hear any more. Dick told me the story. And I said, "Oh, isn't that nice." And...I got off the telephone once again and I thought, "that's a deep comment that he just made." Not only said "*my* kind," but "*modern*." He didn't say "my kind of music," he said "my kind of *modern* music." And I knew that I had something that was quite modern, but that was reaching into the traditional sensibility more—no one had ever responded to my music that way. Ah, this is beautiful!...[T]his was a pure, unadulterated emotional response, like a little kid again. He was feeling my innocence and he was responding and he was saying I wish all contemporary music had whatever was going on here. And I knew what he was reacting to and I said to Dick,..."My God, it's so simple! ...Now I'm ready to compose! Now I can really compose, because now I don't have to hide anything. ...Is that all it takes? You mean all I have to do is be my basic self?"[43]

The piece was performed as part of a Benny Goodman tribute tour; a tour which included a performance by Stoltzman and Goode at Carnegie Hall, with both Tom and Benny Goodman in attendance. The experience, for all intents and purposes, was the final nail in the coffin of the second compositional period, as it gave neo-tonality the blessing of both the public and Tom himself.

> When Benny took a bow, I knew for perhaps the very first time what being connected to the great tradition meant. That moment was unforgettable and cathartic, and it confirmed in my spirit my reasons for returning to the tonality of my youth.[44]

The success of Tom's new style inspired him to make numerous changes in the ways and forms in which he wrote music in this, his third, and probably last, compositional period (1981–). He began by leaving his drafting table and returning to the piano to compose.

> [U]sing the piano again affirmed my return. Since this was the instrument that stimulated my earliest improvisations, returning to it gave me a renewed sense of connectedness to the sound.[45]

He also returned to the multi-movement forms of his youth, as well as added others popular in the common practice period, such as multi-movement symphonies, concerti, and so forth. During the second compositional period, most of Tom's large scale works, such as the Concerto for Grand Orchestra [No. 1] (II.A.1) and the Concerto No. 1 for Clarinet (II.E.1) were written as single movement works and often for enormous forces. In the third compositional period, however, single movement works occur fairly infrequently—three to four movements are instead the standard—and the forces required fall more in line with the traditional orchestral complement.

As with any stylistic change of this magnitude, it took time for Tom to become fully comfortable with his new voice. The "epiphany" of change, as Tom calls it, may have occurred in 1981, but it was certainly not the end of the transformation. In fact, only since 1991 has Tom felt confident that he has "a language" all his own and that his writing is completely free and intuitive.[46] It took, however, a lot of confidence building and "on the job training" along the way to reach that point.

Tom's now zealous interest in his career found an effective partner in his new style. Prominent orchestras, chamber groups, and soloists all began to respond to Tom's requests for performances, since they could now program his music and have a reasonable chance of attracting an audience. Groups friendly to new music, which were once reluctant to program Tom's works because of the large forces and/or virtuosity required, were now programming them on a regular basis—groups such as the New York Chamber Symphony, Boston Musica Viva, and the Pittsburgh New Music Ensemble. Even groups not known for their excessive interest in new music, such as the Boston Pops, the Pasadena Symphony, and the Seattle Symphony began to commission works. His circle of soloists, which still prominently included Stoltzman, expanded to include such artists as Walter Trampler, Stan Getz, Glenn Dicterow, and many others.

A few of these soloists, along with some private individuals, also became philanthropists, sponsoring Tom to write new music for themselves or for groups which could not afford to commission them. Richard Stoltzman was by far the most supportive of these, commissioning a total of twenty-three works between 1976 and 1990. Since then, German poet Hans-Jörg Modlmayr has taken an active interest in Tom's works, especially in terms of getting them performed abroad. Modlmayr's texts have appeared in five works since 1991, including one of Tom's most successful compositions, the *Emsdettener Totentanz* (IX.B.5). Three of these five were commissioned by Modlmayr and his wife, Hildegard. Indeed, the credit for Tom's fame in Germany, which may soon rival that in the United States, should go to Modlmayr.

Of the hundreds of performances of his music during the 1980's, two were particularly memorable for Tom, in that both helped re-affirm the wisdom of abandoning his atonal style. The first was a performance of *The Mountain* (I.C.4) by the Pittsburgh Symphony under John Harbison in 1982. To Tom, the piece represented a strong shift away from his atonal style, since it was heavily rooted in the style of Brahms. What made the performance itself special, however, was the presence on the program of one of Harbison's own works—a waltz—also written in a style similar to Tom's own neo-tonality. This excited Tom greatly, as it was the first time he realized that he was not alone in his return to tonality—that "there was a common language coming about." The second confidence-building experience was a 1985 New York performance at Alice Tully Hall of his Concerto No. 1 for Clarinet (II.E.1), an atonal work from 1977, with Richard Stoltzman and the American Composers Orchestra conducted by Gunther Schuller. Hearing this older work in the context of all of the performances of his neo-tonal works which were going on at about that same time only served to further reinforce Tom's conviction that he had made the right decision.[47]

As Tom, through the success of his music, became better known, requests for him to take up residencies at various institutions began to arrive, many of which he accepted. In June of 1985, he was composer-in-attendance at the Thirteenth International Viola Conference in Boston, where he participated in a "Meet the Composer" gathering. During the summer of 1989, he spent time as composer-in-residence at the Tidewater Festival of St. Mary's College in Maryland, where his *When the Moon is Full* (IX.B.3), written for the occasion, was premiered. In the summer of 1990, he was guest composer at the Pennsylvania Composer's Forum at Dusquesne University; this was quickly followed by an attendance of the Logan Seminar at Chautauqua Institution that same summer.

Awards and grants also began to arrive with increasing frequency. In addition to the eight aforementioned National Endowment grants, Tom, in 1983 alone, won the American Academy and Institute of Arts and Letters award for the making of a recording of *For One* (VII.B.3) and *Paintings No. 7* (VIII.B.3) on CRI, a commission by the Koussevitzky Music Foundation at the Library of Congress for his Symphony No. 3 (I.A.3), and an honorable mention in the New England Composers Competition, sponsored by the League of Composers–ISCM, Boston. In 1985, these awards were followed by perhaps the most prestigious of all—a Guggenheim fellowship.

Despite a plethora of performances, commissions, and awards, Tom was still unsatisfied. Performances, he felt, were fleeting, leaving no legacy for the composer. Therefore in 1991, Tom decided to create his own legacy and formed Master Musicians Collective (MMC) Recordings—a company which would record his works and the works of others who felt the need to leave a more permanent mark.

When Tom started MMC Recordings, he had no idea how many other composers shared his ideals. By the spring of 1992, the new business from recordings, when added to the already heavy time commitments of commissions and performances—both of his works and as a jazz pianist—made the prospect of continuing his teaching career at the conservatory almost unthinkable. So he left—and not without a little satisfaction. As he discovered back in Chicago, the academic life did not suit him—he never, for example, believed in practicing a particular style simply because it was in favor in the academy. He also believed music schools did little to prepare composers for survival on the outside—a situation he found difficult to remedy without the school's support. Tom continues to teach privately, however, choosing those students who want to "write beautiful music." For them he tries to be "a wedge" between academia and the "real" world, all the while trying to prepare them for the latter.[48]

> What I've tried to do in my teaching is get the student back in touch with their intuitions. And to realize that that is the one gift that separates them from all other walks of life. That's what creativity in art is, in music. It's sensing the right thing at the right time. There are no rules.[49]

Notes

1. Due to a misprint in an earlier McKinley biography, the year of McKinley's birth has often been incorrectly listed as 1939.
2. Ev Grimes, "Yale University American Music Oral History Series: William Thomas McKinley," Oct 1986, Yale University School of Music, 11.
3. Marlene Marie McKinley, "The Creative Processes of Composer William Thomas McKinley," *Music Theory Explorations and Applications* 1(Fall 1992): 20.
4. William Thomas McKinley, interview by author, Reading, MA, 7-8 Nov 1994.
5. Grimes, 21-22.
6. Grimes, 22.
7. Grimes, 24.
8. Grimes, 23.
9. Grimes, 25.
10. Grimes, 25.
11. Grimes, 26.
12. M.M. McKinley, 21.
13. W.T. McKinley, interview by author, Reading, MA, 7-8 Nov 1994.
14. For more information on organicism in the works of Beethoven and Brahms, see Heinrich Schenker, *Beethoven's Ninth Symphony* (New Haven: Yale University Press, 1992) and Walter Frisch, *Brahms and the Principle of Developing Variation* (Berkeley: University of California Press, 1984).
15. M.M. McKinley, 21.
16. Grimes, 28.
17. Grimes, 28.
18. Grimes, 35
19. M.M. McKinley, 22.
20. M.M. McKinley, 22.
21. W.T. McKinley, interview by author, Reading, MA, 7-8 Nov 1994.
22. W.T. McKinley, interview by author, Reading, MA, 7-8 Nov 1994.
23. M.M. McKinley, 23.
24. W.T. McKinley, interview by author, Reading, MA, 7-8 Nov 1994.
25. W.T. McKinley, interview by author, Reading, MA, 7-8 Nov 1994.

26. Grimes, 49.
27. Grimes, 50.
28. Grimes, 51.
29. W.T. McKinley, interview by author, Reading, MA, 7-8 Nov 1994.
30. W.T. McKinley, interview by author, Reading, MA, 7-8 Nov 1994.
31. The details of Stoltzman's renewed presence in Tom's life will be outlined below.
32. M.M. McKinley, 23.
33. Grimes, 64.
34. Grimes, 64.
35. A sample of the *Fantasies and Inventions* manuscript has been reproduced in the Photos and Musical Examples section of the BIOGRAPHY.
36. Grimes, 68.
37. Grimes, 74.
38. M.M. McKinley, 24.
39. Grimes, 81.
40. Grimes, 83.
41. W.T. McKinley, interview by author, Reading, MA, 7-8 Nov 1994.
42. Grimes, 88, 93.
43. Grimes, 90-91.
44. M.M. McKinley, 25.
45. M.M. McKinley, 26.
46. W.T. McKinley, interview by author, Reading, MA, 7-8 Nov 1994.
47. W.T. McKinley, interview by author, Reading, MA, 7-8 Nov 1994.
48. W.T. McKinley, interview by author, Reading, MA, 7-8 Nov 1994.
49. Grimes, 107.

The composer and clarinetist Richard Stoltzman in front of *Fat Tuesday's* in New York.

McKinley's String Quartet No. 1 (IV.C.1, 1959), I/91–96. Pencil on vellum.

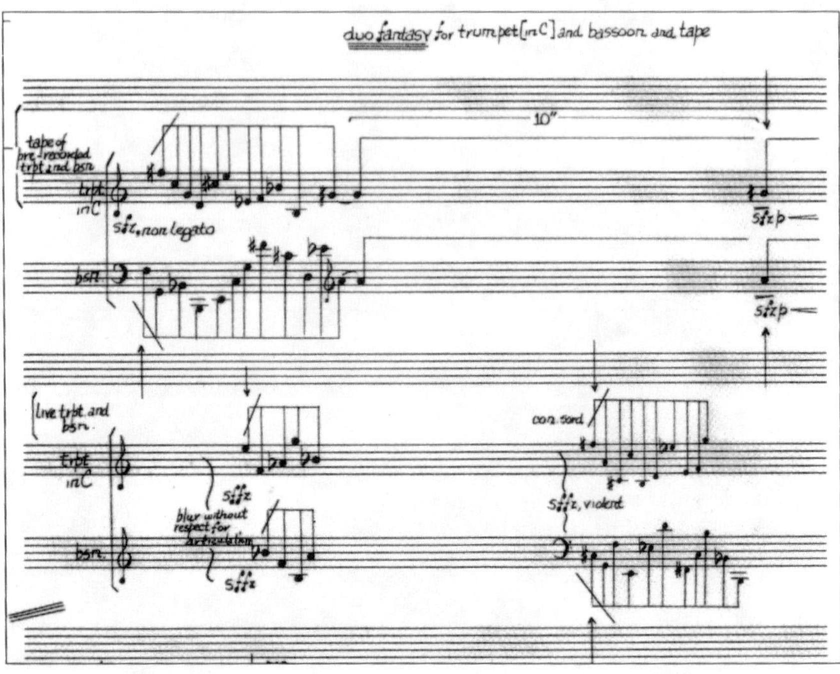

McKinley's *Duo Fantasy* (VIII.G.c, 1969), page 1. Pencil on vellum.

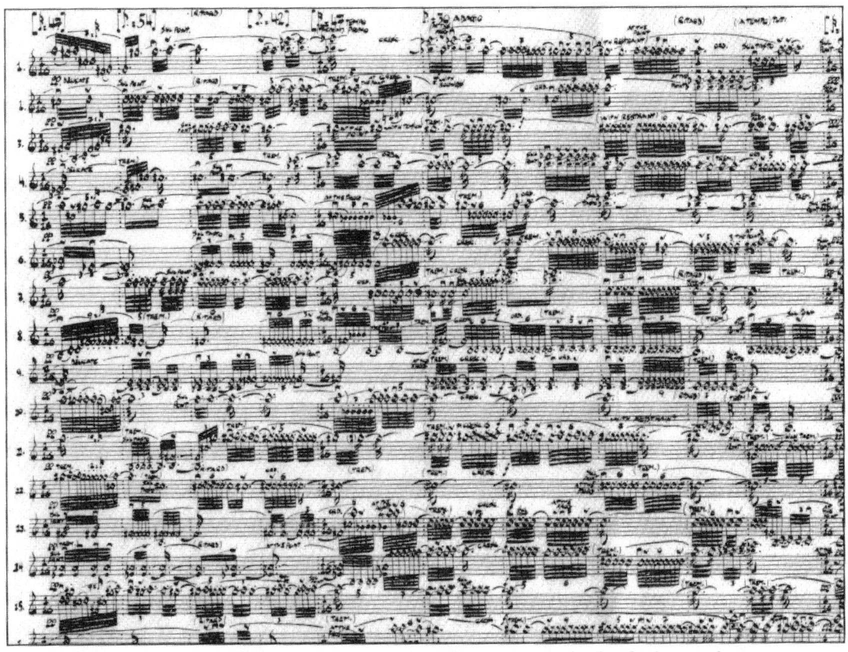

McKinley's Concerto for Grand Orchestra (II.A.1, 1974), draft of Vln I. Ink on paper.

McKinley's *Lightning: An Overture* (I.B.4, 1993), mm. 1–3. Pencil on paper.

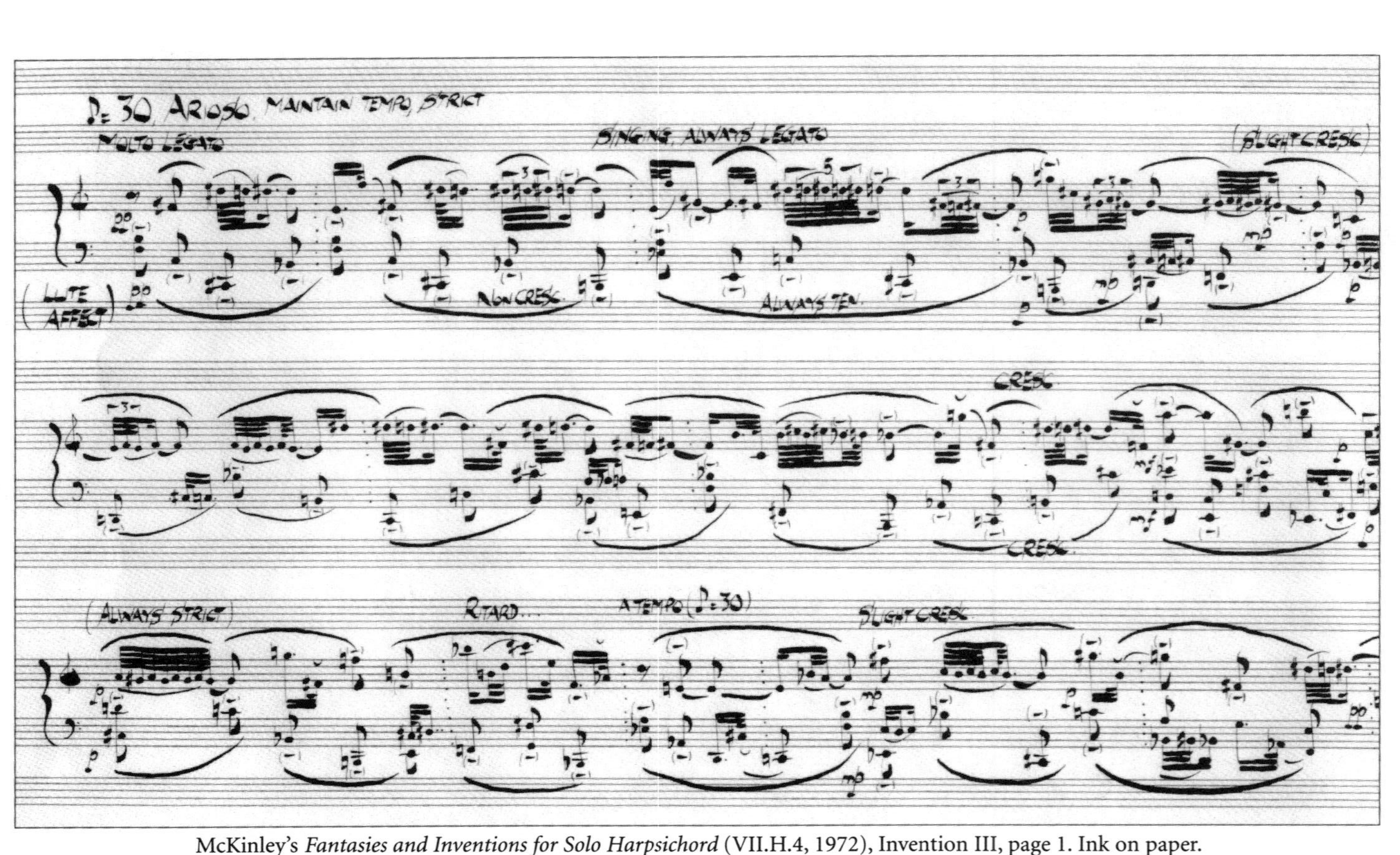

McKinley's *Fantasies and Inventions for Solo Harpsichord* (VII.H.4, 1972), Invention III, page 1. Ink on paper.

Works, Performances, and Bibliography

Group I: Works for Orchestra

Group I.A: Symphonies

I.A.1 Symphony No. 1 in One Movement

Date: 10 Feb 1977 in Manchester, MA ("Carriage House") *Duration:* 10'00"
Dedication: "To the memory of Nikolai Lopatnikoff"
Publisher: Margun Music Inc.

Movement(s):
Adagio, religious, contemplative (♩=52)

Instrumentation:
Orchestra (3 Pic/3 Fl, 3 Ob, EHn, 3 Cl, BCl, 3 Bsn, CBsn, 4 Hn, 2 C Tpt, 2 Tbn, Tba, 4–5 Perc, Pno, Hp, 30 Vln, 12 Vla, 10 Vcl, 8 Cb).

Sketches:
8 drafts of the opening.

MS Description:
Holograph with printed name, ink on vellum. *Location:* Boston Public Library.

Editorial Notes:
Winner of the Minnesota Orchestra 75th Anniversary Composers Competition.

Performance History:
† 3, 5 Jan 1979: Orchestra Hall, Minneapolis, MN
The Minnesota Orchestra, Gunther Schuller, Cond.
6 Jan 1979: O'Shaughnessy Auditorium, Minneapolis, MN
The Minnesota Orchestra, Gunther Schuller, Cond.
[† (Hartford)] 20 Feb 1980: Bushnell Memorial Hall, Hartford, CT
The Hartford Symphony Orchestra, Gunther Schuller, Cond.

Bibliography:
Dyer, Richard. "William Thomas McKinley." *Showcase: The Magazine of the Minnesota Orchestra* 11(29 Nov 1978–6 Jan 1979), no. 3: 13–14.

Feldman, Mary Ann. "Symphony No. 1 in One Movement." *Showcase: The Magazine of the Minnesota Orchestra* 11(29 Nov 1978–6 Jan 1979), no. 3: 24–27.
Israel, Robert. "A Conversation with Gunther Schuller." *Showcase: The Magazine of the Minnesota Orchestra* 11(29 Nov 1978–6 Jan 1979), no. 3: 15.
Anthony, Michael. "Minnesota Orchestra Presents Program of Many Types of Music." *The Minneapolis Tribune* 4 Jan 1979.
Close, Roy. "Schuller Serves Mixed Bag of Music." *The Minneapolis Star* 4 Jan 1979: 16C.
Hawley, David. "Orchestra Offers Rousing Potpourri." *St. Paul Dispatch* 4 Jan 1979.
Barnes, William S. "High Marks for HSO's 'All-American Program.'" *The Bristol Press* 21 Feb 1980.
Sellars, James E. "Symphony Concert Spotlights America." *The Hartford Courant* 21 Feb 1980: 32.
Hansen, Burt. "It Was All-America Night for Schuller and the HSO." *West Hartford News* 28 Feb 1980.
Grimes, Ev. "Yale University American Music Oral History Series: William Thomas McKinley." Oct 1986, Yale University School of Music: 76.
Zagorski, William. "On the Building of Pipelines: William Thomas McKinley and the Master Musicians Collective." *Fanfare* 17(Nov–Dec 1993), no. 2: 126.

Program Notes:

"The Symphony No. 1 in One Movement was begun in 1976 shortly after the premiere of my Concertino for Orchestra during the Festival of Contemporary Music at Tanglewood in August of that year. After the performance, the sound of the orchestra would not leave my imagination. It was an inner necessity that I continue to compose in the orchestral medium. And since the Concertino is a work of relatively brief duration, lasting approximately eight minutes, I wanted to expand the musical thoughts and ideas I discovered upon first hearing it. The earliest inspiration for the First Symphony thus began with an intensely Romantic impulse. In fact, all of my symphonic works and orchestral concerti strive to achieve a dramatic expansion as well as elaborate tonal connections with musical elements found in the marvelously fertile symphonic achievements of the mid–late 19th and very early 20th centuries.

"The reasons are well-known and evident why many contemporary composers do not compose for the orchestra. But I have never been discouraged by these reasons. The marvel of the entire orchestral organism, cosmic in potential, has been the source of my personal commitment and life's work in trying to create the largest body of orchestral compositions that my imaginative spirit will dictate.

"The First Symphony is a continuous and cyclic structure. Many movements, transformations of energy and mood are contained within the single movement. Perhaps one may view it as a novel without chapters. Call to mind the temporal flow that exists in each of our personal, private, and public lives—the overlapping episodes, the dramatic counterplay, the contrapuntal order and even at times disorder—all the continuous and developmental themes, motifs, and human juxtapositions, and, most important, those few precious 'moments' when all rings TRUE in each of our psychic minds and spirits—the epiphanies of self-enlightenment and inner progress. My Symphony hopes to embrace the listener in this way—to transcend a purely technical world and to communicate universal passions and qualities of feeling and mind which we all share, and which I believe we can all hear. The Symphony should manifest as a dream-awakening—a diary of the composer's fantasy and intuition, private, and yet to be shared by all.

"No one will deny that the work has a contemporary 'surface'. We are children of our times and is that not as it should be? I would not argue that most contemporary music lacks universal depth, power, and the intense singing that is manifest in the great works which have remained in the symphonic literature. We must constantly search to find this universal quality and personal voice which, if found, would yield to all of us a psychic power and strength that is not merely 'novel' and 'contemporary'. This power could unite both past and present with a profoundly significant force.

"But perhaps the Symphony in One Movement is fundamentally, but not simplistically, a diary of my relationship—and in the listener's relationship—to its internal dramatic content. And this relationship must be subliminal, spiritual, intuitive and psychical, seeking the Divine. Recall the divinity that Brahms so often spoke of, the moment of blind fury within the creative psyche of Beethoven, the creative labor in the life's work of Bach, the feverish creative fire that would at times possess the musical and creative thoughts of Schoenberg, Berlioz, and Mozart. The common factor which binds them all and the common element to be found in great creative achievement, with rare exception, is fundamentally related to the power of intuition and psychic guidance. These are divine elements—divine patterns and principles. If each of us were able to witness the essence of these elements, we would in our own way and in our own time attain greatness.

"It is my hope that listeners will allow this Symphony to openly embrace their ears and hearts, enabling them to honestly experience the power of a musical communication that humbly attempts to reveal a meditative and psychic experience. And after one has allowed the content of the Symphony into the vibrations of personal experience and consciousness, a perception of new textures and orchestrational combinations, as well as the use of the orchestra as a total organism, will be revealed.

"The connection to an expansion of late 19th and early 20th century tonality, the continual evolution, transformation and dissolution of motivic elements, the unrestricted interplay of improvisatory, fantasia-like rhythmic gestures and arabesques, and the aural conception of the orchestra as a potentially cosmic-sonic force with infinitely variable musical colors and timbral possibilities—all of these elements have been interwoven to cause a totally dramatic and powerful, kaleidoscopic effect. But ultimately, it is my primary desire to communicate an atmosphere of musical joy and innocence which can be perceived by all."

—William Thomas McKinley (© 1979), from 3, 5, 6 Jan 1979 and 20 Feb 1980 programs and Margun Music, inc. MP5004 published score.

I.A.2 Symphony No. 2 ["Of Time and Future Monuments"]

Date: 9 Mar 1978 in Manchester, MA ("Hickory Hill") *Duration:* 38'00"
Dedication: "To my wife Marlene"
Publisher: MMC Publications

Movement(s):
Adagio, with granite structure (♩=40)

Instrumentation:
Orchestra (6 Pic/6 Fl, 2 Ob, EHn, 4 Cl/4 A Cl, BCl, 3 Bsn, CBsn, 4 Hn, 4 C Tpt, 4 Tbn, 2 Tba, Timp, 2 Perc, Pno, Hp, Strings).

Sketches:
20 drafts of the opening. 3 drafts of mm. 64–66. 1 draft of mm. 117–20. 1 draft of mm. 191–96. 1 draft of mm. 291–97. 1 draft of mm. 339–43.

MS Description:
Holograph with signature, ink on paper. *Location:* Boston Public Library.

Editorial Notes:
The symphony was given the title *Of Time and Future Monuments* in 1987. New title first appears on a blueprint copy of the MS in which the original titles have been cut out.

I.A.3 Symphony No. 3 for Chamber Ensemble ["Romantic"]*

Date: Feb 1984 in [Reading, MA ("Lells")] *Duration:* 22'00"
Dedication: "To the memory of Serge and Natalia Koussevitzky"
Commission: Serge Koussevitzky Music Foundation at the Library of Congress
Publisher: MMC Publications

Movement(s):
I. Allegro vivace (♪=120)
II. Largo (♪=42)
III. Valse: Presto (♩.=60)

Instrumentation:
Orchestra (2 Fl, 2 Ob, 2 Cl, 2 Bsn, 2 Hn, 2 Tpt, 2 Tbn, Timp/Perc, Pno, Hp, Strings).

Sketches:
6 drafts of the opening of I. 1 folio of thematic sketches from III. 7 unidentified drafts.

MS Description:
Holograph with signature, pencil on vellum. *Location:* Library of Congress.

Editorial Notes:
*The designation of this work for "chamber ensemble," as printed on the MS, is incorrect. It is, in fact, for full orchestra. The additional title "Romantic" occurs only on the copyist's fair copy. Location of composition from McKinley's notes.

Performance History:
† 18 May 1984: McCarter Hall, New York, NY
Y Chamber Symphony, Gerard Schwarz, Cond.
19–20 May 1984: Theresa L. Kaufmann Concert Hall, The 92nd St. YM-YWCA, New York, NY
Y Chamber Symphony, Gerard Schwarz, Cond.

Recording(s):
MMC Recordings, Ltd.: MMC2003, ©1993 (CD)
Warsaw National Philharmonic, Robert Black, Cond.

Bibliography:
Driver, Paul. "McKinley's New Symphony." *The Boston Globe* 24 May 1984.
Page, Tim. "Concert: Y Chamber Group." *The New York Times* 24 May 1984: C 22.
Grimes, Ev. "Yale University American Music Oral History Series: William Thomas McKinley." Oct 1986, Yale University School of Music: 96.
Zagorski, William. "On the Building of Pipelines: William Thomas McKinley and the Master Musicians Collective." *Fanfare* 17(Nov–Dec 1993), no. 2: 130.
De Jong, Diederik. "Collections: Master Musicians Collective *Recordings.*" *American Record Guide* 57(Mar–Apr 1994), no. 2: 189–90.
Snook, Paul A. "Asia: Symphonies No. 2; No. 3." *Fanfare* 17(May–June 1994), no. 5: 96.

Program Notes:
"In 1983 while I was in New York for the premiere of my *Symphony for Thirteen Instruments* (conducted by Gerard Schwarz on the Music Today Series at Merkin Hall [19 Oct 1983]), Gerard Schwarz and I discussed the Y Chamber Symphony as a possible home for my Koussevitzky Commission. But it was not until I heard this marvelous orchestra rehearse at

Kaufmann Concert Hall that I was able to conceptualize the sound ideal that was to become the inspiring basis for my Third Symphony. Even though of Mozartian proportions, the Y orchestra displayed an incredible richness of tone and personality which helped to guide me in important details of composition and orchestration. I could hear strong lines, long melodic connections, dark timbres, and violet-like hues; and since I envisioned a large harmonic canvas, one of my most challenging musical tasks was to mold, balance, and integrate the exact orchestral proportions of my ideas, thus giving a rich perspective as well as bringing to the foreground the transparent and delicately fragile nature of an orchestra this size. For further preparation, I listened carefully to many Mozart symphonies as well as to the Schubert symphonies, the Prokofiev *Classical* Symphony, and, oddly enough, to the Shostakovich Eighth Symphony, which is, of course, a work for considerably larger forces. But I never used any of these works as models to be stylistically imitated. Instead, some of them provided an evocative guide to the general texture and physiognomy of the classical orchestra. My Third Symphony, then, is in three movements, all of which are traditional in their dramatic character, formal structure, and development.

"The first movement is a rondo (Allegro Vivace) which supports brilliant lines of great velocity and pulse, sweeping movement, punctuated harmonies, and a sustained and dramatically lyrical violin solo. The first movement also introduces a source harmony (C, E flat, G, B flat, D, F, A flat) that serves as a transition (without pause) into the second movement, becomes the principal harmonic pillar of that second movement and moreover, is the final harmony of the last movement.

"The second movement is a broadly suspended Largo, with dark harmonies, a significantly dramatic French horn solo, and a consistently lamenting dramatic orchestral fabric. It is tragic in character.

"The third and final movement is a carefree, optimistic, lyrically soaring and dancing waltz (Presto) which derives from several historical streams. Although it is a blend of the Viennese, the French, the Russian, the Polish, and other sources, all wrapped in a crepe of contemporary jazz 3/4 feeling, I nonetheless felt very close to a singular spirit manifest in this movement, finding that it often transcended its components to enter its *own* dancing-waltz sphere.

"All of the movements are thematic and are bonded together with recurring harmonies (in addition to the source harmony) and rhythmic motifs. The overall dramatic discourse is developmental, and many of the principal musical themes are treated in a Romantically rhetorical fashion similar to the elaborations found in many of the symphonies of Schubert or Mahler—although the Mozartian orchestral forces for which I composed could not permit a grander conception and therefore an even greater rhetorical palette. In short, my Third Symphony tries to honor traditionally expected elements of harmony, melody, pulse, thematic character, color, development, and the like; and it strives to endow these elements with personal character, continuity, and comprehensibility throughout."

—William Thomas McKinley (© 1984), from 18 May 1984 and 19–20 May 1984 programs.

I.A.4 Symphony No. 4

Date: 1985 *Duration:* 27'00"
Dedication: "to Robert Black and Prism"
Commission: [Prism]
Publisher: MMC Publications

Movement(s):
I. Dawn Blues: Allegro (♩.=58)
II. Sunrays: Presto giubilante (♩=112)
III. Night Fancies: Largo misterioso (♩=48)

Instrumentation:
Orchestra (2 Pic/2 Fl/2 Alt Fl, 2 Ob/EHn, 2 Cl/2 BCl, 2 Bsn/CBsn, 2 Hn, 2 C Tpt, Timp, 2 Perc, Pno, Hp, Strings).

Sketches:
1 folio of thematic sketches from I.

MS Description:
Holograph with signature, pencil on vellum. *Location:* Boston Public Library.

Editorial Notes:
Commission taken from McKinley's notes.

Performance History:
† 25 Mar 1986: Symphony Space, New York, NY
Prism, Robert Black, Cond.
[† (Boston)] 5 Apr 1988: Jordan Hall, New England Conservatory of Music, Boston, MA
Members of the New England Conservatory Symphony Orchestra, Susan Clarke, Cond.

Recording(s):
MMC Recordings Ltd.: to be released in 1995
Slovak Radio Symphony, Robert Stankovsky, Cond.

Bibliography:
Lifchitz, Max. "Composer of Note: William Thomas McKinley." *Living Music* 4(Fall 1986), no. 1: 2.
Grimes, Ev. "Yale University American Music Oral History Series: William Thomas McKinley." Oct 1986, Yale University School of Music: 96.

Program Notes:
"My Fourth Symphony was begun after a conversation I had with Robert Black during the winter of 1985. He had heard my Third Symphony (performed by the Y Chamber Symphony and Gerard Schwarz) and we discussed the new language possibilities inherent in tonality. I was (and am) convinced that there are great harmonic and rhythmic tonal plateaus that still can be attained. Although confident of the dramatic results of the Third Symphony, I knew I had much more to express. And since the PRISM Orchestra is about the same size as the Y Orchestra, I was excited to continue the path of the Third Symphony into the proposed Fourth. Very shortly after Bob agreed to premiere the new work I set out with great eagerness and expectation. I cast the new Symphony into three movements. If I may coin a term, I feel this Symphony encompasses a new 'maximalism'—that is, it takes into account *all* of the recent tendencies and mocks *none* of them. To this composer, the vision of our musical future will be an 'embracive' one—not a selective or partisan vision—and it has always struck me that as a given condition of creative existence, the artist attempts to synthesize all that is of spiritual, technical, and historical importance, and in this synthesis lies the seeds of personal style and personal testimony."
—William Thomas McKinley (©1986), from 25 Mar 1986 program.

I

through the late veils of snow
the first green begins to gleam,
from the native soil the springs
are urging forth, in the mountain lake
the cottonwood clouds are floating
to the ground, the songbirds
chase away the ice flakes,
mosquitoes inaugurate the dance

against your brow the sun
burns, in the evening
our shadows darken,
thunderstorms approach, the light
is refracted in the rock,
into the valley shoots the flash

II

the death hour has come.
my fear dissolves, from the walls of rock
the echo returns, we
recall the flower chains,
the water veins begin to swell,
in the twilight grow the
phosphorescing lichens

from the new darkness
the dead free themselves, it is
grief, I am alone, over the
moor wanders the will–o'–the–wisp,
the sheets of fog slumbers,
the dream song becomes mute

III

in the deadly calm, you recognize
the soundless flaring tongues,
you feel grief and pain,
slowly yet over and over again
the corn-poppy rocks about
the blood-saturated battlefield,
the graveyard yews grow
over the mossy stones

in this brown blue night
the cloud mountains sink down
on you, you forged fear,
the dawn again threatens
you, the peregrine falcons
a Hacking you awaken

—William Thomas McKinley (© 1994), from his notes.

I.A.5 Symphony No. 5 (The "Irish")

Date: 1989 *Duration:* 19'00"
Dedication: "to Jorge Mester and the Pasadena Symphony Orchestra"
Commission: [Pasadena Symphony Orchestra]
Publisher: MMC Publications

Movement(s):
I. Ben Bulben: Adagio maestoso (♩=69)
II. Tinkers: Allegro e tempestoso (♩=132)
III. The Streets of Dublin: Largo (♩=50)

Instrumentation:
Orchestra (Pic/3 Fl, 2 Ob, EHn, 2 Cl, BCl, 3 Bsn, CBsn, 4 Hn, 3 Tpt, 2 Tbn, BTbn, Tba, Timp, 2 Perc, Pno, Hp, 30 Vln, 12 Vla, 10–12 Vcl, 8 Cb).

Sketches:
2 folios of notes on themes and orchestration.

MS Description:
Holograph, pencil on paper. *Location:* Boston Public Library.

Editorial Notes:
Commission taken from McKinley's notes.

Performance History:
† 18 Mar 1989: Pasadena Civic Auditorium, Pasadena, CA
Pasadena Symphony, Jorge Mester, Cond.

Recording(s):
Vienna Modern Masters: VMM 3005, ©1991 (CD)
Warsaw Philharmonic Orchestra, Robert Black, Cond.
MMC Recordings Ltd.: to be recorded in 1995.

Bibliography:
Thomas, Robert D. "In Concert: Pasadena Symphony." *Pasadena Star-News* 17 Mar 1989: Extra–4.
Farrell, John. "PSO's 4th Concert Is Pure Ambition Fulfilled." *Pasadena Star-News* 19 Mar 1989.
McQuilkin, Terry. "Violinist Elmar Oliveira in Tchaikovsky Program." *Los Angeles Times* 20 Mar 1989: 6.2.
Rich, Alan. "McKinley Paints an Irish Landscape in Pasadena." *Los Angeles Herald Examiner* 20 Mar 1989: B4.
Heindl, Christian. "Eine Symphonie aus den USA." *Wiener Zeitung* 17 Nov 1992: 4.
Zagorski, William. "On the Building of Pipelines: William Thomas McKinley and the Master Musicians Collective." *Fanfare* 17(Nov–Dec 1993), no. 2: 122.

Program Notes:

"I made two trips to Ireland. It was really the second excursion that inspired the symphony. I took time to examine the central part of the country and absorb it, and I heard music as I traveled through this region. I knew from that point that I would write an 'Irish' symphony as a sort of tribute to my heritage. The entire process of conceiving the work has taken about two years.

"There were so many inspiring places that I initially considered writing an elaborate musical travelogue with fourteen movements, but it would have been totally impractical for this occasion. I eventually elected to write a quasi-traditional three movement work.

"The first movement is titled *Ben Bulben*, an imposing mountain that I photographed at various times of day and night from the town of Sligo. It was a mountain that inspired many artists and writers, particularly Yeats. It has a certain omnipresence since it can be seen from many areas, so the music has a mammoth quality. The orchestra uses triple woodwinds and a large battery of percussion.

"After the grandeur of the opening, the second movement, *Tinkers*, comes as a great contrast like letting in the sun. The tinkers are the Irish gypsies who populate the cities, the roadsides, and everywhere else. In my work, they symbolize the earth, people at their most basic level. The movement has the feeling of a scherzo. It is fast-moving and more light-hearted in imitation of the tinkers' bustling lifestyles. At the same time, there is a sort of mischievous dark side to the tinkers that I have tried to evoke.

"The first two movements each have a single focus but the third movement, called *The Streets of Dublin*, will juxtapose music of various types. Although it was built primarily from impressions of the city at night, the music will contain a number of surprises."

—William Thomas McKinley (© 1989), from an interview with Doug Ordunio in 18 Mar 1989 program.

I.A.6 [Symphony No. 6]

Date: 25 Jul 1990 *Duration:* 30'00"
Dedication: ["to John Curro and the Queensland Youth Orchestra"]
Commission: [Queensland Youth Orchestra]
Publisher: MMC Publications

Movement(s):
I. Tragico e tenebre (♩=52)
II. Prestissimo e vivace (𝅗𝅥.=72)*
III. Adagietto e seriamente (𝅗𝅥=72)

Instrumentation:
Orchestra (Pic/3 Fl, 2 Ob, EHn, 2 Cl, BCl, 4 Bsn/CBsn, 4 Hn, 3 C Tpt, 3 Tbn, Tba, Timp, 4 Perc, Cel, Pno, Hp, Strings).

Sketches:
1 draft of the opening of I (earlier title: "Europe"). See also *New York Overture.*

MS Description:
Holograph with signature, pencil on vellum. *Location:* Boston Public Library.

Editorial Notes:
*The second movement of this symphony was written earlier as the *New York Overture* (I.B.2, 1989) and appears as a fair copy (in copyist's hand) in this manuscript. See *New York Overture* for additional information. Title and dedication taken from printed cover page of the MS. Commission taken from McKinley's notes. The original conception of this work, according to Elliott Miles McKinley, was for seven movements, each being based on one of the seven continents. That assessment is supported by the sketches.

Performance History:
† 8 Sep 1990: Mayne Hall, University of Queensland, Australia
Queensland Youth Orchestra, John Curro, Cond.

Recording(s):
MMC Recordings Ltd.: to be recorded in 1995.

Bibliography:
Turner, Megan. "Popular Composer Puts Jazz, Classics Together." *The Courier Mail (Brisbane, Australia)* 7 Sep 1990: 16.
Hebden, Barbara. "Young Players Equal to Best." *The Courier Mail (Brisbane, Australia)* 10 Sep 1990.

Program Notes:
"When I visited Brisbane in 1989, I was struck by the wonderful performances which John Curro played for me of the Queensland Youth Orchestra. I heard works of Debussy, Rossini, Brahms, and others—works of great difficulty which the major symphonies throughout the world still polish and struggle to master. Thus, it was natural for me to undertake the challenge of creating a new symphony which did not look down on the 'youth' in the orchestra, but rather treated them as equals to any of the major world-class orchestras who have performed my other symphonies.... Put simply, I did not spare the difficulties and wrote what for me is a highly intense orchestral work of large proportions and a large-framed, narrative structure, moving widely between diversely dramatic musical moods. Inspired by Mahler, I used the full organ-like resources of the orchestral palette, particularly so in the first and last movements. The second movement acts as a contrast between the pillars of sound in the first and third movements and, in fact, uses a lighter orchestration to obtain the proper effect and contrast of a fast-moving, but highly developed Scherzando.

The last movement uses the fullest orchestration, making use of a third trombone and third trumpet along with an additional percussionist.

"I view my Symphony No. 6 as a panorama, embracing the melting pot idea which signifies the true meaning of American music—a music which is generally opposed to nationalism (although we do have nationalistic American music) and which in its place puts forth a global attitude embracing the best that world culture offers. Therefore, it would not surprise me if the listener observed in my symphony emblems of Mahler or Ravel, American jazz, American theater, eastern ideas, and so forth. I humbly submit that in this last decade of the twentieth century and its turn into the twenty-first century, 'classical' music will more and more encompass the melting pot perspective, and the more gifted creators of modern music will have absorbed the many streams that have developed throughout our history and by virtue of their inner ear and highly developed intuitions (this latter being most significant) will be expressing this marvelous global synthesis filtering into one main stream of common vestiges and emblems, augmented by the singularly most important elements in a composer's arsenal—personal energy, fire, and an individual creative will towards a higher and higher order of spiritual truth and vitality.

"As a final note, I do not want to leave an impression against the great history of nationalistic styles and schools of thought; but our global consciousness has in the past decade been ignited, and the great amalgam lies just around the *fin de siecle* corner. My new symphony only touches the surface, for it will only be in the composer's total output that we will be able to discern the whole palette. No one score can embrace the totality. But I have tried in this new score to give as large as possible panoramic view of human emotions, rhythms, melodies, contrapuntal interaction, and timbral-orchestrational brilliance—all owing greatly to the great traditions of the past and all pointing to the future with personal individuality and style, for one must be modern in the language of one's day, but not at the avant-garde expense of the values of what tradition has most nobly established in the realm of the beautiful."
—William Thomas McKinley (© 1990), from 8 Sep 1990 program and his notes.

Group I.B: Overtures

I.B.1 Boston Overture

Date: 1986 *Duration:* 8'30"
Dedication: "to John Williams"
Commission: Boston Symphony [Pops] Orchestra [for the opening of their 101st season, 1986/Chiles Foundation of Portland, OR]
Publisher: MMC Publications

Movement(s):
Allegro molto (♩=132)

Instrumentation:
Orchestra (Pic/3 Fl, 2 Ob, EHn, 3 Cl/2 BCl, 2 Bsn, CBsn, 5 Hn, 4 Tpt, 3 Tbn, Tba, Timp, 5 Perc, Pno/Org, 2 Hp, Strings).

MS Description:
Holograph with signature, pencil on vellum. *Location:* Boston Public Library.

Editorial Notes:
The Chiles Foundation awarded the Boston Pops $75,000 to commission new works, among which was *Boston Overture* (*AMC Newsletter* 29(Jan–Feb 1987), no. 1: 24). Additional commission information from 31 May 1986 program.

Performance History:
† 6 May 1986: Symphony Hall, Boston, MA
Boston Symphony Pops Orchestra, John Williams, Cond.
[† (Pittsburgh)] 31 May 1986: Heinz Hall for the Performing Arts, Pittsburgh, PA
Pittsburgh Symphony Orchestra, Michael Lancaster, Cond.

Recording(s):
MMC Recordings, Ltd.: MMC2008, ©1993 (CD)
Silesian Philharmonic, Robert Black, Cond.

Bibliography:
Bouchard, Fred. "An Unlikely Duo Jazz Up Pops' Debut for 1986." *The Patriot Ledger* 7 May 1986: 24.
Katz, Larry. "Williams Hits High Note." *The Boston Herald* 7 May 1986.
Buell, Richard. "Pops Opens 2d Century in Own Style." *The Boston Globe* 8 May 1986: 86.
Croan, Robert. "Composers' Presence Enhances Symphony's American Concert." *Pittsburgh Post-Gazette* 2 Jun 1986: 10.
Spousta, Holly. "A Man of 'Eminently Worthwhile Music': Profiling Reading's William T. McKinley." *Reading Daily Times Chronicle* 21 Aug 1986: 1, 14A.
Lifchitz, Max. "Composer of Note: William Thomas McKinley." *Living Music* 4(Fall 1986), no. 1: 2.
Grimes, Ev. "Yale University American Music Oral History Series: William Thomas McKinley." Oct 1986, Yale University School of Music: 96–97.
Rosenberg, Donald. "New Kensington Composer in Demand." *The Pittsburgh Press* 28 Apr 1991: F1, F4.

Program Notes:
"When John Williams and I discussed the possibility of a new orchestral overture, he emphasized that he wanted a work in keeping with the highest standards of the classical tradition, a work which could serve a BSO [Boston Symphony Orchestra] subscription audience as well as a sophisticated Pops audience. Thus, when I received the formal commission from the BSO, I was deeply honored to be chosen and doubly honored by John's confidence in my abilities to augment this very rich genre and tradition.

"I set out, therefore, to create a musical panorama, opening with a powerful and gripping orchestral gesture, punctuated by a repetitive rhythmic motive (the 'Boston' motive!) which is thoroughly developed from start to finish, interrupted only by a slow middle section which provides contrast. Dominant throughout, orchestrational brilliance intensifies an aural experience encompassing vivid colors of celebration and jubilance and, at the same time, sustaining the dramatic form and virtuoso character of a symphonic overture.

"I have tried to provide a musical palette which is evocative and which allows the audience to discover some important references to their own musical background, experience, and taste—references ranging from Strauss to Gershwin, from Barber to Williams, from early blues to modern jazz, from minimalism to maximalism—organically blended in the McKinley style which is at once euphonious, contemporary, and filled with musical surprise."
—William Thomas McKinley (© 1986), from 31 May 1986 program and his notes.

I.B.2 New York Overture

Date: 1989 *Duration:* 11'30"
Dedication: "to the 92nd Street Y and the New York Chamber Symphony"
Commission: [New York Chamber Symphony]
Publisher: MMC Publications

Movement(s):
Prestissimo e vivace (♩.=72)

Instrumentation:
Orchestra (Pic/2 Fl, 2 Ob, 2 Cl, 2 Bsn, 2 Hn, 2 C Tpt, Timp/Perc, Pno, Hp, Strings).

Sketches:
Formal plan for the work, including some themes.

MS Description:
Holograph with signature, pencil on paper. *Location:* Boston Public Library.
Markings: Final page: "Thanks Georg!"

Editorial Notes:
This work later became the second movement of the Sixth Symphony (I.A.6). Commission taken from McKinley's program notes.

Performance History:
† 12–13 May 1990: Theresa L. Kaufmann Concert Hall, 92nd St. YM-YWCA, New York, NY
The New York Chamber Symphony of the 92nd St. Y, Gerard Schwarz, Cond.

Recording(s):
Vienna Modern Masters: VMM 3005, ©1991 (CD)
Warsaw National Philharmonic Orchestra, Robert Black, Cond.
MMC Recordings Ltd.: to be recorded in 1995.

Bibliography:
Ellis, Stephen. "McKinley: New York Overture, Symphony No. 5 ('Irish'). P. Kelly: Symphony No. 1." *Fanfare* 15(Jul–Aug 1992), no. 6: 215–16.
Heindl, Christian. "Eine Symphonie aus den USA." *Wiener Zeitung* 17 Nov 1992: 4.
Zagorski, William. "On the Building of Pipelines: William Thomas McKinley and the Master Musicians Collective." Fanfare 17(Nov–Dec 1993), no. 2: 122, 126.

Program Notes:
"*New York Overture* was commissioned by the New York Chamber Symphony and composed for the rich and bright sound that this orchestra reveals under Gerard Schwarz's wonderfully buoyant and energetic leadership. Having worked with these intense artists many times before, I found it easy to imagine, in a single vision, a dramatic overture cast in a traditional and serious manner. My impressions and memories of New York provided a direct catalyst. Woven into the overture are a number of 'hints' derived from well-known melodies which have endured as popular romanticizations of New York's manifold personality. Coupled with these 'hints' are my own Tin-Pan Alley and jazz experiences, presented and transformed throughout the melodic and harmonic fabric. Rhythmically, the New York Overture seeks to create perpetual motion and movement as a metaphor for what we see and encounter in the New York streets, with their intricate rhythmic patterns of pulsing energy. Listeners will, I hope, discover in it their own feelings and memories, aroused by the aura of this dazzling, varied, and yet monolithic city."
—William Thomas McKinley (© 1990), from 12–13 May 1990 program and his notes.

I.B.3 Patriotic Variations ["Reading Festival Overture"]

Date: Sep 1993 in Reading, MA ("Lells") *Duration:* 8'00"
Dedication: "Dedicated to the Town of Reading on its 350th Birthday"
Commission: [The Reading Symphony Orchestra, the Reading 350th Anniversary Steering Committee, and the Reading Arts Council]
Publisher: MMC Publications

Movement(s):
Tempo di marcia (♩=126)

Instrumentation:
Orchestra (2 Pic/2 Fl, 2 Ob, 2 Cl, 2 Bsn, 4 Hn, 2 Tpt, 2 Tbn, Tba, Timp, 4 Perc, Strings).

MS Description:
Holograph with signature, pencil on paper. *Location:* Boston Public Library.

Editorial Notes:
Commission taken from 7 May 1994 program.

Performance History:
† 7 May 1994: Reading Memorial High School Auditorium, Reading, MA
Reading Symphony Orchestra, Daniel Abbott, Cond.

Recording(s):
MMC Recordings Ltd.: to be released in 1995
Slovak Radio Symphony, Robert Stankovsky, Cond.

Bibliography:
Iovanni, Sharon. "'Reading Festival Overture' Presented to RSO." *The Reading Suburban News* 20 Nov 1993: 1.

I.B.4 Lightning (An Overture)

Date: 17 Nov 1993 in Reading, MA ("Lells") *Duration:* 15'00"
Commission: "Commissioned by Absolut Concerto (for Avery Fisher Hall Premiere, March 1994)"
Publisher: MMC Publications

Movement(s):
Presto e brillante (♩=116)

Instrumentation:
Orchestra (3 Pic/3 Fl, 2 Ob, EHn, 2 Pic Cl/2 Cl, BCl, 2 Bsn, CBsn, 4 Hn, 3 Tpt, 2 Tbn, BTbn, Tba, Timp, 4 Perc, Hp, Pno, Strings).

MS Description:
Holograph with signature, pencil on paper. *Location:* Boston Public Library.

Performance History:
† 30 Mar 1994: Avery Fisher Hall, New York, NY
New Jersey Symphony Orchestra, Lawrence Leighton Smith, Cond.

Recording(s):
MMC Recordings Ltd.: to be released in 1995
Prague Radio Symphony, Vladimir Valek, Cond.

Bibliography:
Fruchter, Rena. "Symphony to Offer 3 World Premieres." *The New York Times* 27 Mar 1994: 13NJ–9.

Program Notes:
"The *Lightning Overture* is a large-scale, virtuoso orchestral work with a twofold musical purpose, both formal and programmatic. Formally it is cast as a rondo with multiple musical sections and a continually expanding and imbricated architecture. Programmatically, its purpose is to metaphorically simulate the power and multileveled nature of perhaps one of Earth's most frightening and primordial forces. From the crackling electric edges of near lightning to the cool-hot silence of distant lightning, the overture commands the listener's attention to focus on the blend of contrasting passions and formal unity—one could say a synthesis of heart and mind."
—William Thomas McKinley (© 1994), from 30 Mar 1994 program.

Group I.C: Other Orchestral Works

I.C.1 Orchestral Study

Date: [Summer] 1963 in Lenox, MA (Tanglewood) *Duration:* 5'38"
Dedication: "to E.P. Mellon II"
Publisher: MMC Publications

Movement(s):
♩=60

Instrumentation:
Orchestra (Pic, Fl, Ob, Cl, BCl, Bsn, CBsn, 2 Hn, Tpt, 2 Tbn, Tba, Timp, 4 Perc, Pno, Hp, Strings).

Sketches:
1 complete draft. 10 drafts of the opening.

MS Description:
Holograph with printed name, ink on paper, with additions and corrections in pencil.
Location: Boston Public Library.
Markings: Cover page: Original title, *Improvisation for Orchestra*, and later title, *Study*, both crossed out. Page [1]: Original title and date crossed out.

Editorial Notes:
Season of composition from biographical study (see BIOGRAPHY). Performance information from McKinley's notes.

Performance History:
[† 1970: Yale University, New Haven, CT
Yale University Symphony, Gustav Meir, Cond.]

I.C.2 Circular Forms for Grand Orchestra

Date: 3–10 Mar 1970 in Chicago, IL (Univ. of Chicago) *Duration:* 30'
Dedication: "to my wife, Marlene"
Commission: [University of Chicago for the University Symphony Orchestra]
Publisher: MMC Publications

Movement(s):
[One untitled movement.]

Instrumentation:
Orchestra (3 Pic/3 Fl, 2 Ob, 3 Cl/BCl, 3 Bsn, 3 Hn, 3 Tpt, 3 Tbn/BTbn, Tba, 6 Perc, 18 Vln, 8 Vla, 8 Vcl, 4 Cb); Tape Recorder.

Sketches:
70 folios and 5 bifolios of unidentified notes and sketches.

MS Description:
Holograph with signature, ink on vellum. *Location:* Boston Public Library.

Editorial Notes:
Commission taken from 23 May 1970 program.

Performance History:
† 23 May 1970: Mandel Hall, University of Chicago, Chicago, IL
University Symphony Orchestra, Eugene Narmor, Cond.

Program Notes:
"*Circular Forms* is divided into three principal sections and a coda: the first section Allegro; the second section Adagio; the third section, Allegro. Pitches, rhythms and melodic lines are strictly composed and the architectural structure embraces both teleological and non-teleological compositional processes. An interesting aspect of the work is that the conductor is free to shape the non-teleological sections, e.g., those events which are chosen in a circular pattern as opposed to those events which move forward in time. These events are called fields. Each player has a special number of composed fields for which he is responsible. The conductor then chooses these fields from a pre-compositional set-up.

"The piece exploits mobile and immobile sound combinations: some pitches are frozen in certain registers for varying periods of time. The aural effect of the dichotomy between immobility and mobility is intended to produce a highly intense Guernica-like canvas of violence juxtaposed against areas of introspection."
—William Thomas McKinley (© 1970), from 23 May 1970 program.

I.C.3 October Night for Orchestra

Date: Oct 1976 in Manchester, MA ("Carriage House") *Duration:* 6'08"
Dedication: "To the 'Spirit' of *All Humanity*—"
Publisher: MMC Publications

Movement(s):
♩=52+

Instrumentation:
Orchestra (2 Fl, 2 Ob, EHn, 2 Cl, BCl, 2 Bsn, CBsn, 4 Hn, 2 Tpt, 2 Tbn, Tba, 3 Perc, 30 Vln, 12 Vla, 10 Vcl, 8 Cb).

Sketches:
42 drafts of the opening. 4 drafts of mm. 7–9. 1 draft of mm. 14–17. 1 draft of mm. 34–39. 1 draft of mm. 54–56. 9 drafts of mm. 65–69.

MS Description:
Holograph with printed name, ink on paper. *Location:* Boston Public Library.

I.C.4 The Mountain for Large Chamber or Full Symphony Orchestra

Date: 31 Aug 1982 in [Reading, MA ("Lells")] *Duration:* 19'00"
Dedication: "to John Harbison"
Commission: [Pittsburgh Symphony Orchestra]
Publisher: MMC Publications

Movement(s):
Adagio, brooding (♩=52)

Instrumentation:
Orchestra (2 Fl, 2 Ob, 2 Cl, 2 Bsn, 2 Hn, Tpt, Timp/3 Perc, Pno, Hp, Strings).

MS Description:
Holograph with signature, pencil on paper. *Location:* Boston Public Library.

Editorial Notes:
Location of composition and commission taken from McKinley's notes. Premiere performance information from *AMC Newsletter* 28(Mar–Apr 1986), no. 1: 16 and McKinley's notes.

Performance History:
[† 17 Oct 1982: Heinz Hall for the Performing Arts, Pittsburgh, PA.
Pittsburgh Symphony Orchestra, John Harbison, Cond.]

Recording(s):
MMC Recordings Ltd.: to be released in 1995
St. Petersburg Philharmonic, Alexander Titov, Cond.

Bibliography:
Rosenberg, Donald. "New Kensington Composer in Demand." *The Pittsburgh Press* 28 Apr 1991: F1, F4.

I.C.5 SinfoNova (A Sinfonietta for String Orchestra in Two Movements)

Date: Sep 1985 *Duration:* 19'10"
Dedication: "to Aram Gharabekian"
Commission: [SinfoNova]
Publisher: MMC Publications

Movement(s):
I. Prelude: Andante arioso (♩=54)
II. Overture: Allegro magico (♩=104)

Instrumentation:
String Orchestra (11 Vln, 4 Vla, 3 Vcl, 2 Cb).

MS Description:
Holograph with signature, pencil on vellum. *Location:* Boston Public Library.

Editorial Notes:
Commission taken from McKinley's program notes. Los Angeles premiere implied by 13 Nov 1986 article.

Performance History:
† 14 Mar 1986: Jordan Hall, New England Conservatory of Music, Boston, MA
SinfoNova, Aram Gharabekian, Cond.
11 Nov 1986: Jordan Hall, New England Conservatory of Music, Boston, MA
SinfoNova, Aram Gharabekian, Cond.

[† (Los Angeles)] 16 Nov 1986: Dorothy Chandler Pavilion, Los Angeles, CA
SinfoNova, Aram Gharabekian, Cond.

Recording(s):

MMC Recordings, Ltd.: MMC2001, ©1993 (CD)
Slovak Radio Symphony Orchestra, Robert Black, Cond.

Bibliography:

Pfeifer, Ellen. "SinfoNova Fits Together Very Nicely." *The Boston Herald* 15 Mar 1986: 23.
Miller, Nancy. "A Memorable 'Four Seasons' by Chase." *The Boston Globe* 17 Mar 1986.
Dyer, Richard. "SinfoNova Tunes Up for West Coast Visit." *The Boston Globe* 13 Nov 1986.
Pasles, Chris. "SinfoNova Plays Armenian Works." *Los Angeles Times* 19 Nov 1986: 4.
Benoit, Frank. "A Tale of Two Orchestras and an Opera Premiere." *South End News (Boston)* 20 Nov 1986: 10.
De Jong, Diederik. "Collections: Master Musicians Collective *Recordings*." *American Record Guide* 57(Mar–Apr 1994), no. 2: 188–89.
Zagorski, William. "On the Building of Pipelines: William Thomas McKinley and the Master Musicians Collective." *Fanfare* 17(Nov–Dec 1993), no. 2: 126, 129, 130.

Program Notes:

"A commission with stipulated guidelines—such as the idiosyncrasies of a given performer or a conductor's style—always inspires me. When I was given a commission by SinfoNova to consider working within the guidelines of a unifying theme or character, my musical thoughts were thus set in motion at once. As this theme was to have Baroque connotations and overtones, my first explorations went directly to the world of Bach and Vivaldi. I then planned a string symphony cast in two-movement form (slow–fast) which was to evoke what I consider to be two of the most important characteristics of the Baroque: monolithic structure and homogeneous texture. Interestingly enough, these two characteristics have much in common with our modern musical mainstream and it was therefore not difficult to invent analogies that seemed compositionally appropriate. Having always been interested in the *Affektenlehre* or Baroque doctrine of affections or emotions, I chose a 'sighing' motive for the first movement and a 'running' motive for the second. The 'sighing' motive is derived (in terms of rhythmic shape and tempo) from the F Minor Prelude in Book II of Bach's *Well-Tempered Clavier*. The 'running' motive, although original in plan, has much in common with the kind of perpetual motion so often heard in Vivaldi. Each motive is ubiquitous, and both are supported by the kind of harmonic evolutions and repetitive characteristics inherent in the high Baroque style. Imagine Bach working in 1986: what might he do? What might his interests be? I am certain that he would be fascinated by the wide range of tonal possibilities available to explore and expand upon. Indeed, Bach helped to foster the beginnings of expanded tonalities. The influence of his works was to be far-reaching, particularly in the 19th century, when Romantic harmony developed its own path of tonal riches, a path that nonetheless owed each step of its way to Bach. Perhaps this is the main reason why I too have returned to the tonal path, not in an anachronistic manner, but in a manner which both preserves and adds to this great harmonic heritage. I hope that this new symphony, *SinfoNova*, brings this heritage to new light while at the same time satisfying the natural tonal laws which have been ignored by so many of the avant-garde."
—William Thomas McKinley (© 1986), from 14 Mar 1986 program.

I.C.6 Adagio for Strings

Date: [1987] *Duration:* 21'00"
Dedication: "to Aram Gharabekian [and the SinfoNova Chamber Orchestra]"
Commission: [SinfoNova and the Massachusetts Council for the Arts]
Publisher: MMC Publications

Movement(s):
Adagio molto (♩=40)

Instrumentation:
Strings.

MS Description:
Holograph with signature, pencil on vellum. *Location:* Boston Public Library.

Editorial Notes:
Date taken from 11 Apr 1989 program. Additional dedication information from McKinley's program notes. Commission taken from McKinley's notes.

Performance History:
† 20 Nov 1987: Sanders Theater, Cambridge, MA
SinfoNova Chamber Orchestra, Aram Gharabekian, Cond.
† (New York) 11 Apr 1989: Merkin Concert Hall, New York, NY
Prism Orchestra, Robert Stankovsky, Cond.

Program Notes:
"The tonal nature of the string orchestra is a perfect coupling with the formal dynamic and dramatic purpose of the *Adagio.* Together they offer a rich palate for the composer's imagination and a greater stimulus for darker and more tragic lyricism than can often be wrought from certain other instrumental-dramatic couplings. It was this uniqueness which attracted me to this form.

"I initially gave much consideration to finding the kind of theme which could be developed into an extensive musical canvas. The theme serves as cantus firmus throughout the entire *Adagio*, and the musical architecture that ensues is Mahlerian and Gothic in construction, thereby communicating throughout an intuitive and romantically expansive musical atmosphere.

"But despite these complexities, the *Adagio*'s main dramatic purpose, for the audience, is to communicate the tragic and dark lyricism which I felt so very often during its creation, so reinforced by the amiability of this wonderfully flexible and fertile genre.

"My *Adagio* is warmly dedicated to Aram Gharabekian and his string orchestra and owes, as did my earlier *SinfoNova*, to the 'sound' personality of Aram's splendidly disciplined ensemble."

—William Thomas McKinley (© 1987), from 20 Nov 1987 and 11 Apr 1989 programs and his notes.

I.C.a ~~Canons for Orchestra~~

Date: [1965]
Dedication: ["To my Wife"]
Publisher: Unpublished

Movement(s):
I. ♩=52–60
II. ♩=60

Instrumentation:
Orchestra (2 Fl, 2 Ob, 2 Bsn, 2 Hn, 2 Tpt, Tbn, Strings).

Sketches:
1 draft of the opening of I. 8 folios of tone row sketches. 101 folios and 16 bifolios of unidentified notes, sketches and drafts (earlier titles: *Time Pauses for Orchestra; Orchestra Composition; Composition for Orchestra; Synthesis and Changes for Orchestra; Synthesis for Orchestra; Two Movements for Orchestra; Music for Orchestra; Music for Alto Saxophone, Piano, Percussion and Orchestra; Events for Piano and Chamber Orchestra; Events for Chamber Orchestra*).

MS Description:
Holograph, pencil on paper. *Location:* Boston Public Library.

Editorial Notes:
MS ends on the first page of the second movement. First movement has incomplete sections. Date and dedication taken from the sketches.

I.C.b ~~Proportionalisms~~

Date: [ca. 1968]
Publisher: Unpublished

Movement(s):
♪=72

Instrumentation:
Orchestra (Pic, Fl, Ob, Cl, BCl, Bsn, Hn, Tpt, Tbn, Tba, 30 Vln, 12 Vla, Vcl).*

Sketches:
7 folios of rhythmic outlines. 3 unidentified sketches.

MS Description:
Holograph, pencil on paper. *Location:* Boston Public Library.

Editorial Notes:
*Instrumentation list reflects known complement. Sketches do not reveal complete instrumentation. There is no MS for this work.

I.C.c ~~Set No. 1 for Orchestra~~

Date: [ca. 1975]
Publisher: Unpublished

Movement(s):
Hazy (♪=120)

Instrumentation:
Orchestra (3 Fl, 3 Ob, 3 Cl, 2 Bsn, 4 Hn, 2 Tpt, 2 Tbn, Tba, Perc, Strings).

MS Description:
Holograph with printed name, ink on vellum. *Location:* Boston Public Library.

Editorial Notes:
MS ends after 9 measures (2 pages). Date determined through paleographic analysis (style almost identical to Quartet No. 1).

Group II: Concerti

Group II.A: Concerti for Orchestra

II.A.1 Concerto for Grand Orchestra [No. 1] (op. 53)

Date: 2–22 Mar 1974 in Reading, MA ("Linnea Lane") *Duration:* 13'00"
Dedication: "To the spirit of..."
Publisher: MMC Publications

Movement(s):
Grave, with introspection and quiet tension, as if anticipating a violent outburst! (♩=40)

Instrumentation:
Orchestra (8 Pic/8 Fl, 4 Ob, 4 Cl/4 BCl, 3 Bsn/3 CBsn, 4 Hn, 3 C Tpt, 3 Tbn/BTbn, Tba, 6 Perc, Amplified Gtr, 2 Hp, 2 Pno, 30 Vln, 12 Vla, 10 Vcl, 8 Cb).

Sketches:
53 drafts (one extended) and 5 sketches of the opening. 16 unidentified drafts. 1 folio of unidentified sketches.

MS Description:
Holograph with signature, ink on paper. *Location:* Boston Public Library.
Markings: Cover page: Title changed from Concerto for Orchestra to Concerto for Grand Orchestra, opus number changed from 52 to 53.

Editorial Notes:
Photocopy of the fair copy used by Christopher Morris is stored at New England Conservatory of Music in Boston, MA. It contains numerous performance markings and clarifications. Front page markings: "To Tom—| W. Thomas McKinley.""

Performance History:
† 19 Nov 1980: Jordan Hall, New England Conservatory of Music, Boston, MA
Conservatory Symphony Orchestra, Christopher Morris, Cond.

Bibliography:
Buell, Richard. "NEC Symphony in World Premiere." *The Boston Globe* 22 Nov 1980: 10.

Program Notes:
"This Concerto in one movement for Grand Orchestra represents a very personal and significant milestone in my compositional development. After I had written many orchestral works of standard size, I wanted to create a virtuosic tone poem for grand orchestra. The winds, percussion, and keyboards were considerably expanded to create a rich musical fabric which supports other orchestral families and augments and enriches the overall dimension and aural impression.

"The instruments are treated with great virtuosic interplay and dialogue, amplified with sudden and brilliant waves of color, texture, attack, and changes of movement. Debussy envisioned an orchestra 'without feet,' liberated from periodic tonal-rhythmic movement;

and to this end I was deeply dedicated, trying to evoke this concept by sustaining a constantly shifting and multiple metric structure. Added to this, I wanted to have the entire orchestra breathe as if it were one organism, a technique witnessed too infrequently in contemporary orchestral literature. For this point of view I am indebted to the late Romantic orchestral statements of Mahler and Strauss in addition to important orchestral works of the early 20th century, such as Schoenberg's Opus 16, Stravinsky's *Sacre du Printemps*, Debussy's *Jeux*, and Ravel's *Daphnis and Chloe*. The Concerto is approximately thirteen minutes in length, during which time one will not only be drawn to these influences, but will also experience a vast canvas of shifting arabesques and multiple levels of color and dramatic punctuations which create a cinematic transformation of motives, all in perpetual variation, renewal, and fantasy."
—William Thomas McKinley, from 19 Nov 1980 program.

II.A.2 Concertino for Grand Orchestra (op. 71)

Date: 30 Apr 1976 in [Manchester, MA ("Carriage House")] *Duration:* 7'00"
Commission: [National Endowment for the Arts]
Publisher: Margun Music Inc.

Movement(s):
As silver wind (♩=48+)

Instrumentation:
Orchestra (4 Fl, 5 Ob, EHn, 4 Cl, BCl, 3 Bsn, CBsn, 4 Hn, 2 Tpt, 2 Tbn, Tba, 4 Perc, Strings.)

Sketches:
13 drafts of the opening. 7 drafts of m. 46. 2 unidentified drafts.

MS Description:
Holograph with signature, ink on paper. *Location:* Boston Public Library.

Editorial Notes:
Location of composition and commission taken from McKinley's notes.

Performance History:
† 16 Aug 1977: Tanglewood Theater-Concert Hall, Lenox, MA
Berkshire Music Center Orchestra, Gunther Schuller, Cond.

Bibliography:
Pincus, Andrew L. "Five Contemporary Successes." *The Berkshire Eagle* 17 Aug 1977: 10.
Dyer, Richard. "A Stylish 'Jazz Symphony." *The Boston Globe* 18 Aug 1977, evening ed.: 17.
Henahan, Donal. "Tanglewood." *The New York Times* 18 Aug 1977: 3.21.
Kerner, Leighton. "Fromm–BMC Week: Looser and Livelier." *The Village Voice* 29 Aug 1977: 78.

Program Notes:
"In writing the Concertino for Orchestra, I wanted to create a scenario in which concentration of form and clarity of detail are immediately perceivable. Having previously written a Concerto for Orchestra, a work of considerably larger proportions and technical difficulties, I felt it necessary to compose a work that would be more accessible, easier to prepare, and which would require far less rehearsal time than was demanded by the larger Concerto. However, the Concertino never compromises. Within the frame of this 'small concerto' form I endeavored to bring forth many levels of musical energy and patterns which are continually transforming and woven within a strongly linear-polyphonic environment, clothed in a kaleidoscopic garb of color and temporal interplay. The architectural plan of the Concertino is ternary, and the largest sections subdivide into many smaller areas that are

improvisatory in nature—in much the same fashion as Schoenberg's String Trio, Opus 45. Of additional importance is the characteristic of collective virtuosity. I wanted to maintain some semblance of the dramatic principles of the Concerto for Orchestra. Within the dimensions of a Concertino, there was not time to develop elaborately lengthy soloistic passages of 'concertino' groups—hence the notion of collective virtuosity—to display the orchestra as a brilliant organism and progenitor of dynamic color and movement as in a Pollock painting or a Strauss tone poem."
—William Thomas McKinley (© 1977), from 16 Aug 1977 program.

II.A.3 Concerto for Orchestra No. 2

Date: Summer 1993 in Reading, MA ("Lells"), mvts. 1–3 and 5, and in Bratislava, Slovakia, mvt. 4* *Duration:* 22'16"
Dedication: "For the Seattle Symphony's 90th Anniversary Season"
Commission: [Seattle Symphony]
Publisher: MMC Publications

Movement(s):
I. March: Marcia e con fuoco (𝅗𝅥=120)
II. Ballad: Largo e lamento (♪=52)
III. Burlesco e agitato (♩.=152)
IV. Valse triste (𝅗𝅥.=40)
V. Danse Macabre: Feroce, Danse macabre (𝅗𝅥=138+)

Instrumentation:
Orchestra (Pic/3 Fl, 2 Ob, EHn, 2 Cl, BCl, 2 Bsn, CBsn, 4 Hn, 3 Tpt, 3 Tbn/BTbn, Tba, Timp, 3 Perc, Pno, Hp, Strings).

MS Description:
Holograph with signature, pencil on paper. *Location:* Boston Public Library.
Markings: Final page of IV: "Mvt IV, Bratislava | June, '93."

Editorial Notes:
Commission taken from McKinley's notes. *Author received movements as they were completed in the following order: 1, 2, 4, 3, 5. Actual completion date 26 Jul 1993.

Performance History:
† 27–28 Sep 1993: Seattle Opera House, Seattle, WA
The Seattle Symphony, Gerard Schwarz, Cond.

Recording(s):
MMC Recordings Ltd.: to be recorded in 1995.

Bibliography:
Zagorski, William. "On the Building of Pipelines: William Thomas McKinley and the Master Musicians Collective." *Fanfare* 17(Nov–Dec 1993), no. 2: 126.
Bargreen, Melinda. "Olivera Dazzles Audience with Energetic Performance." *The Seattle Times* 28 Sep 1993: E3.
Campbell, R.M. "Olivera and SSO Put on Their Best." *Seattle Post–Intelligencer* 29 Sep 1993: C4.

Program Notes:
"A work in five movements, this concerto owes its dramatic basis to the grand symphonic tradition; each movement portraying a central dramatic idea, (i.e. the first movement march) and casts the different orchestral families into varying degrees of prominence, featuring both solo and group combinations, as well as the virtuosity of the full orchestra in brilliant display.

"The concerto is spiritually dedicated to Gerard Schwarz, the composer's close friend and interpreter for nearly two decades."
—William Thomas McKinley (© 1993), from 27–28 Sep 1993 program and his notes.

Group II.B: Concerti Grossi

II.B.1 Quadruplum for Four Soloists and Chamber Ensemble

Date: 30 Jan—25 Feb 1970 in [Chicago, IL (Univ. of Chicago)] *Duration:* 20'12"
Dedication: "to Paul Fromm"
Commission: [Fromm Music Foundation]
Publisher: MMC Publications

Movement(s):
[One untitled movement.]

Instrumentation:
Sop, Pic/Fl, Pno, Vln soli; Ob, Cl/Sop Sax/BCl, Bsn/CBsn, 2 C Tpt, Tbn, 2 Perc, Vln, Vla, Vcl; Tape (some sections must be prerecorded).

Sketches:
4 incomplete drafts of earlier versions of the work with sketches (earlier versions included two for voice and piano, a symphony, and a concerto for two violins). 1 incomplete draft of the final version in short score. 8 drafts of the opening. 1 draft of page 6. 28 folios and 14 bifolios of unidentified drafts and sketches. 8 folios and 1 bifolio of notes, including formal plans and a chorale melody.

MS Description:
Holograph with printed name, pencil on paper. *Location:* Boston Public Library.

Editorial Notes:
Commission information from the Fromm Music Foundation and McKinley's notes. Location of composition from McKinley's notes.

Performance History:
† 10 Apr 1970: Mandel Hall, University of Chicago, Chicago, IL
Elsa Charlston, Sop; [Untitled ensemble], Ralph Shapey, Cond.
23 Apr 1971: Mandel Hall, University of Chicago, Chicago, IL
Elsa Charlston, Sop; Jan Herlinger, Fl; John Cobb, Pno; Everett Zlatoff-Mirsky, Vln; The Contemporary Chamber Players of the University of Chicago, Ralph Shapey, Cond.
17 Nov 1971: Krannert Center for the Performing Arts, University of Illinois, Urbana, IL
The Contemporary Chamber Players/The Ineluctable Modality, Paul Zonn, Cond.

Bibliography:
Grimes, Ev. "Yale University American Music Oral History Series: William Thomas McKinley." Oct 1986, Yale University School of Music: 59, 61–62.

Program Notes:
"The word *Quadruplum* originates in the second generation of the Notre Dame School, a period associated with Perotin, when a third (*Triplum*) or even a fourth voice part (*Quadruplum*) was added to a pre-existing *cantus firmus*. In the process of becoming acquainted and understanding this music I was stimulated by the idea of having a *cantus firmus*, namely, the solo soprano part (for which I composed the text in a stream of

consciousness[—a] daily recording of my reflecting attitudes toward world affairs and tensions) against which were added in melismatic fashion the fabric of sound created by three other soloists. I further augmented the idea by pitting these four soloists against a large chamber ensemble in the manner of a Baroque Concerto—i.e., ripieno vs. concertante [*sic*].

"The use of speaking voices, pre-recorded and live, using Latin phrases also germinated out of the idea of setting one sound body against another—in this case the mixture of Latin and English causing a kind of murmur and blur of meaning and context as well as the mixture of speaking against singing; and furthermore the mixture of speaking and singing against the instrumental sound body itself divided into various timbral combinations. I conceived the work as an explosive dramatic statement which evokes at times ambiguous but multi-layered meanings which can be perceived either as a totality or as individual events in a dense contrapuntal maze of musical information."

—William Thomas McKinley (© 1971), from 23 Apr 1971 program.

II.B.2 Triple Concerto for Piano, Contrabass, Drums, and Grand Orchestra

Date: 4–12 May 1970 in Chicago, IL (Univ. of Chicago) *Duration:* 27'36"
Dedication: "to the Chicago Symphony"
Commission: [Chicago Symphony]
Publisher: MMC Publications

Movement(s):
Tempo rubato (♩=60)

Instrumentation:
Pno, Cb, Dr soli; Orchestra (2 Pic/2 Fl, 2 Ob, 2 Cl/Sop Sax/BCl, 2 Bsn/CBsn, 2 Hn, 2 C Tpt, 2 Tbn, Tba, 5 Perc, 38 Vln, 12 Vla, 11 Vcl, 8 Cb).

Sketches:
1 complete draft.

MS Description:
Holograph with printed name, pencil on paper. *Location:* Boston Public Library.

Editorial Notes:
Commission taken from McKinley's notes.

Performance History:
† 12 Jun 1970: Orchestra Hall, Chicago, IL
William Thomas McKinley, Pno; Roger Cooke, Cb; Richard Olderman, Perc; The Chicago Symphony Orchestra, Irwin Hoffman, Cond.

Bibliography:
Grimes, Ev. "Yale University American Music Oral History Series: William Thomas McKinley." Oct 1986, Yale University School of Music: 59–62, 78.

Program Notes:
"In the Triple Concerto for Piano, Bass, Drums and Orchestra, the choice of solo instruments reflects the jazz-oriented character of the work, with the 'trio' acting in concert with a fairly standard orchestra (with the addition of soprano saxophone and an enlarged battery of percussion).

"Many varieties of improvisation are employed by the trio; at times their parts consist of chord symbols, a series of pitches, or merely rhythmic patterns. Near the end of the work each member of the trio is featured in a cadenza with a select group from the orchestra: the bass plays antiphonally with the orchestral basses; the piano is combined with a quartet of strings; and the drummer is joined with the percussion section. During these cadenzas, the soloist improvises freely, and, as the composer explains, derives his inspiration from the orchestral group with which he is playing.

"The orchestra (whose parts are entirely written out) is used at times in massive *tutti* climaxes, or broken up into smaller solo groups which contrast with the primary trio of piano, bass, and drums. This treatment of the orchestral forces provides for a variety of textures and colors ranging over the entire spectrum of dynamic possibilities. The piece ends 'quietly and lyrically.'"

—John Buccheri for the Chicago Symphony Orchestra (© 1970 by The Orchestral Association), from 12 Jun 1970 program.

II.B.3 Interruptions for Improvisation Ensemble and Wind Orchestra

Date: 29 Jan 1975 in Reading, MA ("Linnea Lane") *Duration:* 21'03"
Dedication: "to the University of Wisconsin"
Commission: [University of Wisconsin, with funds provided by the Vilas Estate]
Publisher: MMC Publications

Movement(s):
[One untitled movement.]

Instrumentation:
Improv Qt (Sop Sax, Dr, Pno, Cb); Wind Orchestra (3 Pic/3 Fl, 3 Ob, 3 Cl, 2 Bsn, 4 Hn, 2 Tbn, BTbn, 2 Tba, 4 Perc).

Sketches:
1 draft of page 5. 1 draft of page 9. 2 unidentified drafts.

MS Description:
Holograph with signature, ink on paper. *Location:* Boston Public Library.

Editorial Notes:
Commission taken from 19 Mar 1975 program.

Performance History:
† 19 Mar 1975: Mills Concert Hall, University of Wisconsin, Madison, WI
Les Thimmig, Woodwinds; William Thomas McKinley, Pno; Dick Olderman, Perc; Steve La Spina, Cb; University of Wisconsin Wind Ensemble, H. Robert Reynolds, Cond.
[† (Boston)] 17 Feb 1977: Jordan Hall, New England Conservatory of Music, Boston, MA
Les Thimmig, Woodwinds; William Thomas McKinley, Pno; Rodger Ryan, Perc; The Conservatory Wind Ensemble, Frank L. Battisti, Cond.

Program Notes:
"Interruptions—structures forming in space—massive sound blocks interjecting, affirming. High levels of energy, Fires abated—Explosions—volcanic eruption—at times quiet but at the core seething—organically self-contained. Big band tuttis—the rhythm section embarking on journeys which never end. A solitary horn mediating—layering blocks of poly-energies—at once saturated, never diluted—interrupting time—and space—black holes through which our senses must travel—enriched—violence and quiet justified—again

interrupted, but continuing forward—naked teleology—no systems—all systems—world culture—universal symbols—and cymbals!—still again interrupted—eighth quarter eighth—I got rhythm—the Eroica—Ivesian insurance—assurance—and yet again interrupted."
—William Thomas McKinley (© 1975), from 19 Mar 1975 program.

"The difficulties in attempting to synthesize improvised and fully composed musical structures are mainly ones of syntax. In my opinion, most attempts at bridging the gulf between these two styles through 'Third Stream' composition fail. One is always aware of the separate stylistic languages being amalgamated. In *Interruptions* I have attempted to cement this gulf. All of the woodwind ensemble music is written out and all of the *trio concertanti* (piano; percussion; contrabass, bass clarinet; sopranino, soprano, tenor saxophone) music is improvised. The trio does not play an independent set of guidelines, such as jazz chord changes or modes, but instead draws its material from the written sections of the woodwind ensemble. In other words, the members of the trio are required to be score readers and to derive their musical ideas from this written material. Therefore the overall form and syntax become homogeneous and the structural balance is maintained by way of antiphonal and responsorial contrasts."
—William Thomas McKinley (© 1977), from 17 Feb 1977 program.

II.B.4 Sinfonie Concertante for Piano, Harp, Viola, Cello, Percussion, and Orchestra

Date: 1985 in Reading, MA ("Lells") *Duration:* 18'00"
Dedication: "to Collage"
Commission: [Collage and The Massachusetts Council for the Arts and Humanities]
Publisher: MMC Publications

Movement(s):
Frenetico, con appass[ionato] e bravura sempre (♩=160)

Instrumentation:
Perc, Pno, Hp, Vln, Vcl soli; Orchestra (Pic/3 Fl, 2 Ob, EHn, 2 Cl, BCl, 2 Bsn, CBsn, 4 Hn, 2 C Tpt, 2 Tbn, 2 Tba, Timp, Perc, Strings).

MS Description:
Holograph with signature, pencil on vellum. *Location:* Boston Public Library.

Editorial Notes:
Commission taken from McKinley's program notes.

Performance History:
† 1 May 1986: Symphony Hall, Boston, MA
Collage; Boston Composers Orchestra, Gunther Schuller, Cond.

Recording(s):
MMC Recordings Ltd.: to be recorded in 1995.

Bibliography:
Noble, David. "Composers Orchestra Plays a Promising Debut Concert." *The Patriot Ledger* 5 May 1986.
Kimmelman, Michael. "Redefining the Role of Orchestras." *Philadelphia Inquirer* 8 May 1986: 9C.

Program Notes:

"*Sinfonia Concertante* [*sic*] was commissioned by COLLAGE on behalf of the Massachusetts Council for the Arts and Humanities. It was designed to be a large single-movement quintuple concerto with violin, cello, piano, harp, and percussion set against a grand orchestra.

"Having already composed three chamber works for COLLAGE (the last of which, *Paintings VII*, was recently released on CRI), I have become very familiar with their individual capabilities as well as their overall sound and musical persona. Therefore, when I received the new commission, I was particularly inspired by the possibilities of exploring COLLAGE's talents together with orchestra. And at first it was natural that the 'sound' of the Boston Symphony would be in my imagination, no doubt reinforced by the fact that the core members of COLLAGE are members of the Boston Symphony Orchestra. Thus, although I eliminated the most problematic notational difficulties, thereby making the Concerto quite accessible to most orchestras, I still envisioned a rather complex virtuoso-orchestral result and set out to cast my musical ideas within a brilliant orchestral palette—a palette for which I have a strong attraction and in which I believe myself to be suited, having learned considerably from hearing a large number of my recent orchestral works performed.

"Although it was my choice to adopt a single movement structure in this new work, one could possibly argue that it would be historically more accurate (and therefore 'pure') to have created several movements. I weighted this consideration carefully, but since there are five soloists, it seemed that a multi-movement structure could have extended to such great length that practical exigencies would completely prohibit this indulgence. I therefore decided to create an intensely concentrated, distilled, and yet monolithic movement of approximately 20 minutes duration during which all of the soloists are amply featured and in which extended developments, great contrasts, solo cadenzas and orchestral *tutti*s all have adequate presentation.

"The general overall language of the *Sinfonia Concertante* is a continuation of the direction I have taken during the past four years and is, I believe, a composite of extended tonalities which have their strongest roots in 1) Rachmaninoff, 2) Ravel, 3) Scriabin, 4) Berg, and American jazz. The development and evolution of these tonalities in the manner in which they are presented here is indebted most to the period of the 'Great Romantics,' and the twists, turns, juxtapositions, and extensions of these tonalities as well as their tonal-rhythmic manifestations owe considerably to Stravinsky, Copland, Shostakovich, Britten, and again jazz harmonic structures, often framed in a manner which might suggest traits of minimalism to some ears. However, none of these influences are ever presented in an ironic or mocking manner and beyond them I strive to make a very original statement which hopes to foster a personal and recognizable expressive style. The *Sinfonia Concertante* thus attempts a palatable fusion—a *tour d'horizon* or summing up of these influences."

—William Thomas McKinley (© 1986), from 1 May 1986 program.

II.B.5 Can You Sing Me a Song[?] (A Lyric Concerto for Tenor Saxophone, Eight Soprano Voices, Jazz Rhythm Section, Bass and Drums, and Grand Orchestra in One Movement)

Date: 20 Nov 1988 *Duration:* 33'00"
Dedication: "to Stan Getz"
Commission: [Stan Getz]
Publisher: MMC Publications

Movement(s):
Ballad tempo, very slowly (♩=52)

Instrumentation:
Ten Sax, 8 Sop, Pno, Cb, Dr soli; Orchestra (Pic/3 Fl, 2 Ob/EHn, 3 Cl/BCl, 3 Bsn, CBsn, 4 Hn, 3 Tpt, 3 Tbn, Tba, Timp, 3 Perc, Hp, Strings); Optional: Female Chorus, Sop soloist.

MS Description:
Holograph with signature, pencil on paper. *Location:* Boston Public Library.

Editorial Notes:
MS written in short score format. Commission taken from McKinley's notes. Flyer and review confirm 2 Mar 1989 as premiere performance.

Performance History:
[†] 2 Mar 1989: Jordan Hall, New England Conservatory of Music, Boston, MA
Stan Getz, Tenor Sax; Kenny Barron, Pno; Dave Holland, Cb; Lewis Nash, Dr; The New England Conservatory Philharmonia, Robert Black, Cond.

Bibliography:
Elman, Steve. "Stan Getz's Natural Lyricism." *The Boston Globe* 1 Mar 1989: 63.
Gonzalez, Fernando. "Getz in Fine Form for Premiere of McKinley Work." *The Boston Globe* 3 Mar 1989: 45.
Gewertz, Daniel. "Jazz-Classical Fest a Grand Finale." *The Boston Herald* 4 Mar 1989: 26.
Creasey, Beverly. "Brighton Flutist Celebrates Modern Works." *The Allston-Brighton Journal* 9 Mar 1989: 9.
Blumenthal, Robert. "Consider Getz and Taylor and Mourn Roy Eldridge." *The Boston Phoenix* 10 Mar 1989: 10, 18.
Bouchard, Fred. "Jazz and Third Stream Festival: New England Conservatory/Boston." *Downbeat* June 1989: 50–51.

Program Notes:
"*Can You Sing Me a Song* is the second work I have composed for Stan Getz. The first, *Tenor Rhapsody*, was premiered by Stan Getz in San Francisco [*sic*] at Stanford in June, 1988, and follows strictly classical lines. The recent work follows the lines of a classical-jazz synthesis, and although the overriding dramatic effect and design is symphonic, augmented by eight soprano voices singing mostly syllabically with occasional references to a main theme or *idée fixe* (which emerges towards the early middle section of the score and which is derived from the title *Can You Sing Me a Song*), the jazz quartet functions independently (as do the sopranos) within this symphonic design as a kind of Saturnic ring around the whole orchestra. The work is Mahlerian in scope, composed as a single movement and yet divided into multi-faceted inner movements or sections which feature the various 'grooves' or profiles of style for Stan Getz to stretch out upon and to express the various facets of his personality. The tenor part is harmonically governed and melodies are abundantly given throughout with ultimate emphasis on the *Can You Sing Me a Song* melody which the listener should clearly hear as the work develops and progresses. I suppose one cannot help hearing the Ravelian legacy which from harmonic-melodic standpoint has had the greatest influence on the language of jazz and which (although extended in my work) creates a fabric for the great lyricism, purity, and honest singing quality so characteristic of Stan's great legacy and hence the inspiration for the title, *Can You Sing Me a Song*, which suggests the importance of

heartfelt and emotionally direct tunefulness and singing so vital to all forms and styles of musical expression."
—William Thomas McKinley (© 1989), from 2 Mar 1989 program.

II.B.6 Jubilee Concerto for Brass Quintet and Symphony Orchestra

Date: 1 Jan 1990 in Reading, MA ("Lells") *Duration:* 20'00"
Dedication: "to the Town of Bad Kreuznach, Germany (a spiritual musical gift and message to a great culture)"
Commission: [Rheinische Philharmonie]
Publisher: MMC Publications

Movement(s):
Giubilante (♩= 120)

Instrumentation:
2 Tpt, Hn, Tbn, BTbn soli; Orchestra (4 Pic/4 Fl, 4 Ob/EHn, 4 Cl/BCl, 4 Bsn/CBsn, 4 Hn, 2 Tpt, Tbn, BTbn, Tba, Timp/2 Perc, Hp, 25 Vln, 8 Vla, 7 Vcl, 6 Cb). Optional: Pno, Org.

Sketches:
2 folios of notes on orchestration.

MS Description:
Holograph with signature, pencil on paper. *Location:* Boston Public Library.
Markings: Final page: Date followed by "Happy new year!"

Editorial Notes:
Commission taken from McKinley's notes. 7 Jul 1991 performance information from BMI records.

Performance History:
† 9 Feb 1990: Ev. Pauluskirche, Bad Kreuznach, FRG
Blechbläserquintett der Rheinischen Philharmonie, James Lockhart, Cond.
6 Nov 1990: Burghalle, Mayen, FRG
Blechbläserquintett der Rheinischen Philharmonie, James Lockhart, Cond.
1 Jan 1991: Atrium, Wittlich, FRG
Blechbläserquintett der Rheinischen Philharmonie, James Lockhart, Cond.
[† (United States) 7 Jul 1991: Symphony Space, New York, NY
New Amsterdam Symphony Orchestra.]

Recording(s):
Staatsorchester Rheinische Philharmonie: SRP-D 92, ©1992. (CD)
Staatsorchester Rheinische Philharmonie, James Lockhart, Cond.

Bibliography:
Reitershan, Jürgen. "Herz mit Kopf: McKinley über Uraufführung in Bad Kreuznach." *Rhein-Zeitung* 10/11 Feb 1990.
Märzhäuser, Gernot. "Weltaufführung mit etwas Magie." *Allgemeinen Zeitung (Bad Kreuznach)* 2 Dec 1990.

Program Notes:
"Die Freundschaft mit David Tasa, dem Leiter des Frankfurter Blechbläserensembles, führte zur Ausführung des Festlichen Konzertes für Blechbläserquintett und Großes Orchester. Dieses Werk wird durch das Blechbläser ensemble und das Staatsorchester Rheinische

Philharmonie unter der Leitung von James Lockhart eigens für das Stadtjubiläum Bad Kreuznach in diesem Konzert uraufgeführt; der Komponist wird bei der Weltpremiere persönlich anwesend sein. Zum Zeitpunkt der Niederschrift dieses Textes hat das neue Werk noch niemand gehört, wir müssen es also dem Publikum von Bad Kreuznach überlassen, sich selbst sein Urteil zu bilden."
—Author Unknown, from 9 Feb 1990 program.

II.B.7 Concerto for the New World for Wind Quintet, String Orchestra, and Percussion

Date: Oct 29 1991 in Reading, MA ("Lells") *Duration:* 24'00"
Dedication: "to the Quintet of the Americas"
Commission: [Quintet of the Americas]
Publisher: MMC Publications

Movement(s):
Introduction and Thema: Andantino (♩=84)
Variation I: Allegro (♩=152)
Variation II: Larghetto (♩=66)
Variation III: Presto (♩=176)
Variation IV: Moderato (♩=126)
Variation V: Adagio (♩=76)
Variation VI: Scherzo, rag (♩=208)
Variation VII: Nobile (♩=80)
Variation VIII e Finale: Allegro molto e baccanàle (𝅗𝅥=132+)

Instrumentation:
Fl, Ob, Cl, Hn, Bsn soli; 2 Perc, Strings.

Sketches:
Formal plan for the work, including some themes and key designations.

MS Description:
Holograph with signature, pencil on paper. *Location:* Boston Public Library.

Editorial Notes:
Commission information from 13 Jan 1992 review and 9 Jan 1992 program notes.

Performance History:
† 9 Jan 1992: Carnegie Hall, New York, NY
Quintet of the Americas (Marco Granados, Fl; Matthew Sullivan, Ob; Christopher Jepperson, Cl; Barbara Oldham, Hn; Thomas Novak, Bsn); The Manhattan School Chamber Orchestra, Glen Cortese, Cond.

Recording(s):
MMC Recordings, Ltd.: MMC2002, ©1993 (CD)—variation 5 only
Slovak Radio Symphony Orchestra, Robert Black, Cond.
MMC Recordings Ltd.: to be released in 1995
Quintet of the Americas; The Manhattan School Chamber Orchestra, Glen Cortese, Cond.

Bibliography:
Kozinn, Allan. "Quintet of the Americas: Carnegie Hall." *The New York Times* 11 Jan 1992: 13.
Groves, Robert. "Covering Nome to Tierra del Fuego." *The Record* 13 Jan 1992: B–7.

Zagorski, William. "On the Building of Pipelines: William Thomas McKinley and the Master Musicians Collective." *Fanfare* 17(Nov–Dec 1993), no. 2: 129.
De Jong, Diederik. "Collections: Master Musicians Collective *Recordings.*" *American Record Guide* 57(Mar–Apr 1994), no. 2: 189.

Program Notes:

"In spirit, I humbly dedicate my new *Concerto for the New World* as a gift to America—in all of her many hats and guises and with all of her foibles and strengths. And with eternal fervor I hope to be continually inspired by her lofty ideals and aspirations in support of an America which grows steadily towards the fulfillment of her most positive dreams and challenging struggles—an America which when fully awakened can allow her voice to 'ring forth.' Loudly, bravely—embracing all men—all humanity while preserving the most precious gift of individual liberty and the power of conscience within each of us. And by the way of this medium of a quintet-concerto (cast as a *concerto variasioni* with an *idée fixe* or blues theme and eight variations and finale) I was easily facilitated in being able to symbolically portray those musical conflicts (and resolutions) which exist between the soloist(s). The quintet and the whole (*tutti*) orchestral body as parallel metaphorical equivalents to those very same relationships which Socratically exist within our own contemporary American culture and which range from the individual (encompassing his personal conflicts and resolutions) to the largest body of the most powerful macro-cosmic forces which hold the magnetism and power to historically change and engender virtual new discovery as well as the potential to bring forth an even better America to our collective futures."
—William Thomas McKinley (© 1994), from his notes.

"The wind section of an eighteenth century orchestra was essentially a wind quintet, whose function was to boost the sound of the far more fundamental strings. As if to show just how far these instruments have come, William Thomas McKinley has placed the quintet in front of the strings and showcased them in a concerto. The piece, commissioned especially for this event [the 9 Jan 1992 performance at Carnegie Hall by the Quintet of the Americas], reflects not only the group's origins, but also the Quintet of the Americas' fascination with the American musical kaleidoscope. It is a Baroque concerto grosso in the form of a Classical theme and variations, with stylistic splashes of Brahms, blues, and ragtime—a quintessentially (post)modern work. Like much of the music that flows from Mr. McKinley's easy pen, *Concerto for the New World* is jazzy, fun, and eclectic, building from an elegant introduction to the concluding thunderous bacchanale. The composer writes: 'The musical conflicts and resolutions between the wind quintet and the orchestral body are intended as metaphorical equivalents to the conflicts and relationships that exist within our contemporary American society. I dedicate this concerto to the New World and to an America which, when fully awakened, can bravely embrace all men and women, while preserving the most precious gift of individual liberty and the power of conscience within each of us.'"
—Author Unknown, from 9 Jan 1992 program.

II.B.a ~~Music for Improvisation Ensemble and Orchestra in Three Movements~~

Date: [ca. 1965]
Publisher: Unpublished

Movement(s):
I. ♩=120
II.
III.

Instrumentation:
Perc, Pno, Cb soli; Orchestra (Pic, 2 Fl, 2 Ob, EHn, 2 Cl, BCl, 2 Bsn, CBsn, 4 Hn, 2 Tpt, 2 Tbn, BTbn, Tba, 3? Perc, Hp, Strings).

Sketches:
1 folio and 1 bifolio of unidentified sketches and notes.

MS Description:
Holograph, pencil on paper. *Location:* Boston Public Library.

Editorial Notes:
There is no MS for this work.

Group II.C: Double Concerti

II.C.1 Double Concerto ("Lucy" Variations on a Theme of Richard Stoltzman for Violin, Clarinet in B♭ and Chamber Orchestra)

Date: [1984]
Duration: 23'48"
Commission: [Richard Stoltzman]
Publisher: MMC Publications

Movement(s):
Theme: Tranquillo (♩=90)
Variation I: Scherzando (♩=120)
Variation II: Contemplative, fantasia (♩=48)
Variation III: With sweeping motion (♩.=60)
Variation IV: Prestissimo (♩=120+)

Instrumentation:
Cl, Vln soli; Orchestra (2 Fl, 2 Ob, 2 Cl, 2 Bsn, 2 Hn, 2 Tpt, Timp/Perc, Hp, 10 Vln, 4 Vla, 4 Vcl, 2 Cb).

MS Description:
Holograph with signature, pencil on paper. *Location:* Boston Public Library.

Editorial Notes:
Date taken from cover page of fair copy. Commission from orchestral music advertisement/ catalog and McKinley's notes. Flyer for 7 Jun 1986 indicates premiere performance.

Performance History:
[†] 7 Jun 1986: Sanders Theater, Cambridge, MA
Richard Stoltzman, Cl; Lucy Stoltzman, Vln; Pro Arte Chamber Orchestra, Kent Nagano, Cond.

Bibliography:
Miller, Nancy. "For Pro Arte, It Just Wasn't Their Night." *The Boston Globe* 9 Jun 1986.
Noble, David. "Rewarding Performance by Pro Arte." The Patriot Ledger 10 Jun 1986.

Program Notes:
"William Thomas McKinley completed his 'Lucy Variations', a double concerto for violin, clarinet and orchestra, in 1982 [*sic*]. It is written in the form of three variations on a long, lyrical, almost romantic theme originally written by Richard Stoltzman for his wife, Lucy, several years before. The theme is in a 32-bar framework (AABA). McKinley later reharmonized the theme in a style that related it to the modern jazz harmonic world, a style to which the tune is suited, for it suggests a jazz ballad tune. The variations contrast with

each other but are related in overall mood and are organically connected. The 'Lucy Variations' should not be considered a jazz piece; it is a work with jazz influence that nevertheless lies within the classical tradition."
—Mary Alyce Groman (© 1986), from 7 Jun 1986 program.

II.C.2 Golden Petals (A Duo Concertante for Solo Contrabass, Soprano Sax and Chamber Ensemble)

Date: Jan 1985 in [Reading, MA ("Lells")] *Duration:* 22'50"
Dedication: "to Les Thimmig, Miroslav Vitous, Richard Pittman and Boston Musica Viva"
Commission: [National Endowment of the Arts]
Publisher: MMC Publications

Movement(s):
Vivace (♩=120)

Instrumentation:
Sop Sax/BCl, Cb soli; Pic/Fl, Pic Cl/Cl/Alt Sax, Bsn, Hn, C Tpt, Tbn, 2 Perc, Pno, Gtr, Cb.

Sketches:
Orchestral seating plan. 38 drafts of the opening. 4 drafts of mm. 6–10.* 4 drafts of mm. 11–15.* 3 drafts of mm. 21–25.* 8 drafts of mm. 26–30.* 5 drafts of mm. 41–45.* 17 drafts of mm. 61–65.* 1 draft of mm. 77–82.

MS Description:
Holograph with signature, pencil on vellum. *Location:* Boston Public Library.
Markings: Cover page: "—a treatise on minimalism—'maximus minimalas'—."

Editorial Notes:
*Due to the minimalistic nature of this work, it is impossible to determine the exact sources for these sketches with any certainty. Finalist: Kennedy Center Friedheim Awards. Commission and location of composition taken from McKinley's program notes.

Performance History:
† 26 Apr 1985: Jordan Hall, New England Conservatory of Music, Boston, MA
Les Thimmig, Sop Sax/BCl; Miroslav Vitous, Cb; Boston Musica Viva, Richard Pittman, Cond.
[† (Washington, DC)] 4 May 1985: Festival of American Chamber Music, The Library of Congress, Coolidge Auditorium, Washington, DC
Les Thimmig, Sop Sax/BCl; Miroslav Vitous, Cb; Boston Musica Viva, Richard Pittman, Cond.
[† (Houston)] 2 Feb 1989: Hammen Hall, Rice University, Houston, TX
Richard Nunemaker, Sop Sax/BCl; Kenneth Harper, Cb; Pierrot Plus Ensemble, David Colson, Cond.
1 May 1990: Hammen Hall, Rice University, Houston, TX
Richard Nunemaker, Sop Sax/BCl; Peter Herbert, Cb; Pierrot Plus Ensemble, David Colson, Cond.
† (Austria) 20 Mar 1994: Theater, Innsbruck, Austria
Richard Nunemaker, Sop Sax/BCl; Peter Herbert, Cb; Camerata Bregenz, Christoph Eberle, Cond.
21 Mar 1994: Kulturhaus, Dornbirn, Austria
Richard Nunemaker, Sop Sax/BCl; Peter Herbert, Cb; Camerata Bregenz, Christoph Eberle, Cond.

[† (Vienna)] 22 Mar 1994: Großer Saal, Musikverein, Vienna, Austria.
Richard Nunemaker, Sop Sax/BCl; Peter Herbert, Cb; Camerata Bregenz, Christoph Eberle, Cond.
[† (Salzburg)] 24 Mar 1994: ORF-Studio, Salzburg, Austria.
Richard Nunemaker, Sop Sax/BCl; Peter Herbert, Cb; Camerata Bregenz, Christoph Eberle, Cond.

Recording(s):
MMC Recordings, Ltd.: MMC2005, ©1993 (CD)
Richard Nunemaker, Sop Sax/BCl; Peter Herbert, Cb; Pierrot Plus Ensemble, David Colson, Cond.

Bibliography:
Gonzalez, Fernando. "Third Stream and All That Jazz." *The Boston Globe* 29 Apr 1985.
Bouchard, Fred. "Boston Musica Viva: Jordan Hall." *Downbeat* Aug 1985: 53.
Zagorski, William. "On the Building of Pipelines: William Thomas McKinley and the Master Musicians Collective." *Fanfare* 17(Nov–Dec 1993), no. 2: 124.
Bradshaw, Tangela. "Right Note: Musician to Make Solo Debut at Carnegie Hall." *Houston Chronicle* 9 Mar 1994: 1, 4.
Strohal, Ursula. "Viel Lebensgefühl und ein Andachsjodler." *Tiroler Tageszeitung* 22 Mar 1994.
Kräutler, Walter. "Fesselnde 'Grenzüberschreitung': Mitreißende Demonstration der Camerata Bregenz unter Christoph Eberle." *Vorarlberger Nachrichten* 23 Mar 1994.
Heindl, Christian. "Grenzgänge im Goldenen Saal." *Wiener Zeitung* 24 Mar 1994.
Howard, Aaron. "Richard Nunemaker, Saxophonist and Clarinetist, Performs in Houston and San Francisco." *Jewish Herald-Voice (Houston)* 2 May 1994: 36.
Gingras, Michèle. "Record Reviews—Richard Nunemaker: Golden Petals." *The Clarinet* 21(May–June 1994), no. 3: 42–43.
Max, Stephen R. "Richard Nunemaker." *American Record Guide* 57(July–Aug 1994), no. 4: 207.

Program Notes:
"*Golden Petals*, commissioned by a grant from the National Endowment of the Arts, is a large-framed dramatic work originally conceived for the great Czech jazz bassist Miroslav Vitous and for the formidable saxophone-clarinetist Les Thimmig. It was premiered at Boston's Jordan Hall, conducted by Richard Pittman with the Boston Musica Viva, and subsequently performed by the same musicians at the Library of Congress during their 1985 American Festival.

"In an extensive write-up and review of this work in *Downbeat*, Fred Bouchard points to the minimalist-improvisatory qualities in *Golden Petals* and the way in which the gestures unfold in a long-lined dramatically lyric manner. In fact, all of the gestures are precisely notated and only the illusion of improvisation is created directly from the notes themselves. The dramatic persona of the work owes much to the brilliant talents of its original performers, their sounds and technical abilities; for example, the particular sound Miroslav Vitous achieves with his bass—the high harmonics and extensive bowing and lightning-fast pizzicatos. Throughout *Golden Petals* there are grand cadenzas and orchestral *tutti*s all blended into what the composer conceives as a lyrical singing-*cantabile* thread from beginning to end."
—William Thomas McKinley (© 1989), from 2 Feb 1989 and 1 May 1990 programs.

II.C.3 American Blues

Date: 31 Dec 1986 *Duration:* 25'00"
Dedication: "to Gary Burton and Richard Stoltzman"
Commission: [Simon Guggenheim Foundation]
Publisher: MMC Publications

Movement(s):
I. Felicemente (𝅗𝅥=72)
II. Larghetto (♩=58)
III. Valse (𝅗𝅥.=69)

Instrumentation:
Cl, Vib soli; Orchestra (2 Pic/2 Fl, 2 Ob/EHn, 2 Cl, BCl, 2 Bsn/CBsn, 4 Hn, 2 Tpt, 2 Tbn, Tba, Timp, 2 Perc, Pno, Hp, Strings).

MS Description:
Holograph with signature, pencil on vellum. *Location:* Boston Public Library.

Editorial Notes:
Commission taken from McKinley's notes.

Performance History:
† 6 Feb 1987: Symphony Hall, Boston, MA
Gary Burton, Vib; Richard Stoltzman, Cl; The Cross Currents Orchestra, David Hoose, Cond.
† (New York) 7 Jan 1988: Carnegie Hall, New York, NY
Gary Burton, Vib; Richard Stoltzman, Cl; The American Symphony Orchestra, Robert Black, Cond.

Bibliography:
Grimes, Ev. "Yale University American Music Oral History Series: William Thomas McKinley." Oct 1986, Yale University School of Music: 97.
Gewertz, Daniel. "Jazz and Classical Sounds Mix in 'Cross Currents.'" *The Boston Herald* 6 Feb 1987.
Dyer, Richard. "Burton, Stoltzman Unite Jazz, Classical Music." *The Boston Globe* 7 Feb 1987: 17.
Gewertz, Daniel. "Concert Honors Classical, Jazz." *The Boston Herald* 7 Feb 1987.
Tassel, Janet. "From Fat Tuesday's to Carnegie Hall." *Musical America* 107(Jan 1988), no. 6: 21–22.
Kimmelman, Michael. "Concert: McKinley Pieces by American Symphony." *The New York Times* 9 Jan 1988: 12.
Rubinstein, Leslie. "Creative Spirit: Richard Stoltzman." *Carnegie Hall Stagebill* 10(Feb 1988), no. 6: 22, 27–28.
Stevens, Denis. "New York." *Musical Times* April, 1988.

Program Notes:
"With the *American Blues* many wonderful possibilities became realities for me: composing a double concerto for Richard Stoltzman and Gary Burton, two 'giants' in their respective musical worlds; and thereby creating a natural synthesis of America's most indigenous music, jazz, with classical principles.

"In the broadest sense, *American Blues* fuses inventive music elements of modern jazz with euphonious and contemporary classical elements. These jazz and classical elements—color, melody, harmony, and rhythmic design—are mixed and blended into common textures throughout all three movements. The movements are classical in design and through-composed, with ample room for solo, duo and ensemble passages. The theme *American Blues* is presented in both the first and last movements, and it owes considerably to the 'blues' spirit and vision of George Gershwin who believed, as I do, in the fusion of these two currents. This theme is introduced in the jazzy 4/4 time of the first movement and transformed into the jazz-like waltz of the third. The theme should be the main guidepost for the listener as it functions very much in the manner of a fixed idea throughout.

"*American Blues* owes much to our tradition, and I have tried to endow the music with the kind of energy and spirit I have learned in jazz, to express the intangible webbing and intricate melodic weaving of the jazz line. Always my central goal was to transport the performers beyond the confinements of the written note while at the same time preserving total control over the structural development and details. Having such performers as Stoltzman and Burton allowed me to explore the mellifluous properties of both instruments in a way that is unique—both performers have inimitable sound and presence and both have the background, virtuosity, and artistic empathy in concordance with my own goals and ideals."

—William Thomas McKinley (© 1987), from 6 Feb 1987 program.

II.C.4 Nostradamus (A One Movement Melodrama for Narrator, Trombone Soloist and Chamber Ensemble)

Date: 26 Jan 1987 *Duration:* 14'00"
Dedication: "to Ron Borror"
Commission: [Ronald Borror]
Publisher: MMC Publications

Movement(s):
Tempo di marcia (♩=184)

Instrumentation:
Narr, Tbn soli; Pic/Fl/Alt Fl, 3 Perc, Pno, Vcl.

MS Description:
Holograph with signature, pencil on vellum. *Location:* Boston Public Library.

Editorial Notes:
Text prepared and adapted by Marlene Marie McKinley. Commission taken from McKinley's notes. Premiere performance date confirmed by *AMC Newsletter* 30(May–June 1988), no. 1:27.

Performance History:
[†] 4 Mar 1987: Millard Auditorium, Hartt School of Music, W. Hartford, CT
Marlene M. McKinley, Narr; Ronald Borror, Tbn; Hartt Contemporary Players, Douglas Jackson, Cond.
[† (New York)] 31 Mar 1987: Weill Recital Hall, New York, NY
Marlene M. McKinley, Narr; Ronald Borror, Tbn; The New Music Consort, Claire Heldrich, Cond.
[† (Boston)] 19 Oct 1987: Jordan Hall, New England Conservatory of Music, Boston, MA
Marlene M. McKinley, Narr; Ronald Borror, Tbn; The New Music Consort, Claire Heldrich, Cond.
9 Dec 1987: Merkin Concert Hall, New York, NY
Marlene M. McKinley, Narr; Ronald Borror, Tbn; The New Music Consort, Claire Heldrich, Cond.

Bibliography:
Page, Tim. "Music: Consort Group." *The New York Times* 5 Apr 1987: II–61.
Dyer, Richard. "Heiss-McKinley 'Doubles' at NEC." *The Boston Globe* 20 Oct 1987: 73.

Program Notes:

"Although the narrator verbalizes the prophecies, Nostradamus is represented in the instrument of the trombone. It sometimes announces the prophecies, sometimes states the prophecies along with the narrator and sometimes reacts to and comments on the prophecies. He is, in short, the personal voice of Nostradamus, speaking in a range of tones, from menace and foreboding to awe and ecstasy. Needless to say, then, to convey dramatically such diverse emotions and states of mind and spirit is a virtuosic workout for the trombone in the manner of a concerto grosso, displaying the prodigious brass techniques of Ron Borror. The instrumental setting is based on the make-up of the New Music Consort.

"Though I began writing the text about Nostradamus (1503–1566) by selecting some prophecies which I thought would be familiar to the audience, I could not just want to list them; I wanted to provide a more dramatic context. In other words, a listing seemed to elicit too much of the 'austere voice crying out in the wilderness prophesying doom.' Therefore, I decided to approach the material from the point of view of the wife of Nostradamus. And since Nostradamus did write down his prophecies to be a legacy to his son, I tried to convey the love of the parents for their child and of the wife for her husband. From the vantage point of the wife, then, not only was I able to envision more fully another side of Nostradamus, but I was also able to comment on the prophecies and provide the necessary information for the audience. The narrator's main role is therefore the wife of Nostradamus telling their son about the prophecies, but throughout the course of the text the narrator also shifts into the voice of Nostradamus, stating the prophecies. Because my completed text more than doubled the time specifications for the New Music Consort work, both Tom and I made drastic cuts throughout the text (one cut I especially regret is about the great new nation that would emerge in Nostradamus' future, America). And though Tom plans to use the complete text in a projected work within a larger setting, we have tried to retain our complete vision in tonight's version of the work. Apart from the introductory lines in which Nostradamus tells about his preparations for his visions, the prophecies in tonight's performance progress as follows; Abraham Lincoln, Louis Pasteur, Adolf Hitler's rise to power and his horrible deeds (the Holocaust specified), man's landing on the moon, man's destruction of the Earth and events of the future during such specified years as '1999 and 7 months' to the end of his prophecies, from cataclysms that will annihilate almost all to the renewal of all."

—Marlene Marie and William Thomas McKinley (© 1987), from 31 Mar 1987, 19 Oct 1987, and 9 Dec 1987 programs.

II.C.5 Miniature Portraits for Trumpet, Bassoon and String Orchestra

Date: [Early 1991] *Duration:* 16'00"
Dedication: "to Debbie Greitzer and Jeff Silberschlag"
Commission: [Deborah Greitzer and Jeff Silberschlag]
Publisher: MMC Publications

Movement(s):
I. Burlesco: ♩=144
II. Humoresque: Presto (♩.=152)
III. Satirico: ♩=54
IV. Sarcasmo: Presto (♩=180)
V. Ironico: Moderato (♩=120)
VI. Fantastico: Allegro molto (♩=144)
VII. Triste: Jazzy, andante (♩=76)
VIII. Enigmatico: Prestissimo (♩=184)

Instrumentation:
B♭ Pic Tpt/Tpt/Optional: F Tpt/D Tpt/C Tpt, Bsn soli; Strings.

Sketches:
See *Miniature Portraits for Trumpet and Bassoon* (VIII.G.12).

MS Description:
Holograph with signature, pencil on paper. *Location:* Boston Public Library.

Editorial Notes:
Date interpreted from date of premiere performance. Commission information from the composer. Premiere information taken from 14 Apr 1990 article.

Performance History:
[† May 1991: Bolshoi Theater, Moscow, Russia
Jeffrey Silberschlag, Tpt; Deborah Greitzer Silberschlag, Bsn; Bolshoi Theater Orchestra.]
† (Hungary) 6 Jun 1991: Belvárosi Kultúrpalotája, Budapest, Hungary
Jeffrey Silberschlag, Tpt; Deborah Greitzer Silberschlag, Bsn; Magyar Virtuózok, György Gyorivany-Rath, Cond.
† (United States) 3 Apr 1993: Robert E. Lee High School, Staunton, VA
Jeffrey Silberschlag, Tpt; Deborah Greitzer Silberschlag, Bsn; The Mid-Atlantic Chamber Orchestra, Yuval Waldman, Cond.
18 Apr 1993: Virginia Intermont College, Bristol, VA
Jeffrey Silberschlag, Tpt; Deborah Greitzer Silberschlag, Bsn; The Mid-Atlantic Chamber Orchestra, Yuval Waldman, Cond.

Recording(s):
Delos International Inc.: to be recorded in 1995.
Jeffrey Silberschlag, Tpt; Deborah Greitzer Silberschlag, Bsn; The Seattle Symphony, Gerard Schwarz, Cond.

Bibliography:
Dyer, Richard. "NEC, BU, Harvard Cook Up Hot Week of Student Opera." *The Boston Globe* 14 Apr 1990: 12.
Peric-Kempf. "Poput Janusa." *Vjesnik* 7 Jun 1991: 8.
Pofuk, Branmir. "Raspjevani guaci." *Zapad* 8 Jun 1991: 23.
Cic, Emil. "Glazbeni Virtouzitet." *Glasnik Hrvatski Politicki Tjednik* 14 Jun 1991: 46.

Program Notes:
See *Miniature Portraits for Trumpet and Bassoon* (VIII.G.12).

II.C.6 Concerto Domestica for Trumpet, Bassoon, and Orchestra

Date: [1991] *Duration:* 33'01"
Dedication: "to Deborah Greitzer and Jeff Silberschlag"
Commission: [The Richmond Symphony]
Publisher: MMC Publications

Movement(s):
I. Early Morning Blues: Larghetto (𝅗𝅥=54)
II. Morning Rush: Prestissimo (♩.=160)
III. A Lull: Adagio (♩=72)
IV. Transiting the Meridian: Vivace (♩=176)
V. Siesta: Tango (♩=63)
VI. To Home We Go: Allegro tempestoso (𝅗𝅥=132)

Instrumentation:
G Tpt/B♭ Tpt/C Tpt/B♭ Pic Tpt, Bsn soli; Orchestra (2 Pic/2 Fl, 2 Ob/EHn, 2 Cl/BCl, 2 Bsn/CBsn, 2 Hn, 2 Tpt, 2 Tbn, Tba, Timp, Perc, Strings).

VII. Evening Tranquillity: Larghetto (♩=72)
VIII. Thoughts of Night: Vivace (♩=200)
IX. Burning the Midnight Oil: Presto agitato (♩.=96)
X. Together and Sleep: Larghetto e notturno (𝅗𝅥=44)

MS Description:
Holograph with signature, pencil on paper. *Location:* Boston Public Library.

Editorial Notes:
Date and commission taken from McKinley's notes.

Performance History:
† 6,8 Mar 1992: VCU Performing Arts Center, Richmond, VA
Deborah Greitzer, Bsn; Jeff Silberschlag, Tpt; The Richmond Symphony, George Manahan.

Recording(s):
MMC Recordings, Ltd.: MMC2002, ©1993 (CD)—movement 3 only
Slovak Radio Symphony Orchestra, Robert Black, Cond.

Bibliography:
Taylor, Charles. "'Bilingual' Composer Speaks Classical, Jazz." *The Richmond News Leader* 29 Feb 1992: A–40.
Bell, Molly. "Bassoonist, Trumpeter Star in New Music." *The Richmond News Leader* 7 Mar 1992: A–32.
Bustard, Clarke. "Trumpeter and Bassoonist Cover a Wide Range in New Concerto." *Richmond Times-Dispatch* 7 Mar 1992: B–7.
Zagorski, William. "On the Building of Pipelines: William Thomas McKinley and the Master Musicians Collective." *Fanfare* 17(Nov–Dec 1993), no. 2: 129.
De Jong, Diederik. "Collections: Master Musicians Collective *Recordings*." *American Record Guide* 57(Mar–Apr 1994), no. 2: 189.

Program Notes:
"Mr. McKinley's *Concerto Domestica* for bassoon and trumpet is receiving its premiere performance at this concert, with the composer in attendance. He wrote it for the bassoon and trumpet virtuosi, Deborah Greitzer and Jeff Silberschlag, who are soloists in this lively ten movement concerto. Even as Richard Strauss depicted the everyday life of a family in his *Domestic Symphony*, this concerto, according to Mr. McKinley, represents a day in the life of Ms. Greitzer and Mr. Silberschlag, who are married to each other."
—David Manning White (© 1992), from 6,8 Mar 1992 program.

II.C.7a Concert Variations for Violin, Viola and Orchestra [Version I]

Date: 2 Sep 1993 in Reading, MA ("Lells") *Duration:* 17'00"
Dedication: "to Karen Dreyfus and Glenn Dicterow"
Commission: [Karen Dreyfus and Glenn Dicterow]
Publisher: MMC Publications

Movement(s):
Theme: Lamento (♩=80)
Variation I: Prestissimo (𝅗𝅥=200)
Variation II: Larghetto (♩=66)
Variation III: Con forza (𝅗𝅥.=84)

Instrumentation:
Vln, Vla soli; Orchestra (Pic/2 Fl, 2 Ob/EHn, 2 Cl, BCl, 2 Bsn, CBsn, 4 Hn, 2 Tpt, 2 Tbn, Tba, Timp/4 Perc, Pno, Hp, Strings).

Variation IV: Larghetto (♩=66)
[Variation V]: Presto possible e molto bravura (𝅝=88)
Variation VI: Molto maestoso e largamente (♩=58)
Variation VII: Moderato e molto energico (♩=116)
Variation and Finale: Con brio e fantastico (𝅗𝅥.=104)

MS Description:
Holograph with signature, pencil on paper. *Location:* Boston Public Library.

Editorial Notes:
Commission information from the composer.

Performance History:
† 31 Jan 1994: Town Hall, New York, NY
Glenn Dicterow, Vln; Karen Dreyfus, Vla; Manhattan Chamber Sinfonia, Glen Cortese, Cond.

Recording(s):
MMC Recordings Ltd.: to be recorded in 1995.
Glenn Dicterow, Vln; Karen Dreyfus, Vla; The Seattle Symphony, Gerard Schwarz, Cond.

Bibliography:
Smith, Ken. "Concerts: New York Review." *The Strad* May 1994.
Kandell, Leslie. "Manhattan Chamber Sinfonia: Nelson and McKinley." *American Record Guide* 57(May–Jun 1994), no. 3: 49.

Program Notes:
"*Concert Variations* unfolds a virtuosic concerto setting in a strict variation form with an original theme as the basis, casting the solo violin and viola into a duo-concertante relationship. Both instruments are wedded together throughout the concerto's development into a single voice.

"The theme is divided into three parts: A, B, and Coda. The variations strictly follow this form and the harmonic relationships until the Finale, which is in itself expanded, thus acting as a final dramatic apotheosis.

"Mr. McKinley composed *Concert Variations* with the rich instrumental styles of Karen Dreyfus and Glenn Dicterow in mind. Ms. Dreyfus premiered Mr. McKinley's Third Viola Concerto at Alice Tully Hall last year at Lincoln Center and subsequently recorded this work for MMC with Glen Cortese conducting the MSM [Manhattan School of Music] Chamber Sinfonia."
—William Thomas McKinley (© 1994), from 31 Jan 1994 program.

II.C.7b Concert Variations for Violin, Viola and Orchestra [Version II]

Date: [23 Dec 1993] in Reading, MA ("Lells") *Duration:* 17'00"
Dedication: "to Karen Dreyfus and Glenn Dicterow"
Commission: [Karen Dreyfus and Glenn Dicterow]
Publisher: MMC Publications

Movement(s):
Theme: Lamento (♩=80)
Variation I: Prestissimo (𝅗𝅥=200)
Variation II: Larghetto (♩=66)

Instrumentation:
Vln, Vla soli; Orchestra (Pic/2 Fl, 2 Ob/EHn, 2 Cl, BCl, 2 Bsn, CBsn, 4 Hn, 2 Tpt, 2 Tbn, Tba, Timp/4 Perc, Pno, Hp, Strings).

Variation III: Con forza (𝅗𝅥.=84)
Variation IV: Larghetto (♩=66)
[Variation V]: Presto possible e molto bravura (𝅝=88)
Variation VI: Molto maestoso e largamente (♩=58)
Variation VII: Moderato e molto energico (♩=116)
Variation and Finale: Con brio e fantastico (𝅗𝅥.=104)

MS Description:
Holograph with signature, pencil on paper. *Location:* Boston Public Library.

Editorial Notes:
The MS of this version consists of photocopies of the version I MS, with changes by McKinley made in pencil. Author was witness to date of completion. Commission information from the composer.

II.C.a ~~Double Concerto~~

Date: [ca. 1970]
Dedication: "[Aldo] Parisot, Carr Commission"
Commission: Carr Commission
Publisher: Unpublished

Movement(s):
♩=140

Instrumentation:
2 Orchestras (specific instrumentation unspecified).

MS Description:
Holograph, pencil on paper. *Location:* Boston Public Library.
Markings: Page 1: "Chords, Cadenzas at Beginning | Free to Strict."

Editorial Notes:
MS ends after one measure of short score. Date determined through paleographic analysis and location of discovery (with other 1970 sketches).

Group II.D: Flute Concerti

II.D.1 Concerto for Flute and String Orchestra

Date: [1986]
Duration: 26'30"
Dedication: "to Robert Stallman"
Commission: [Robert Stallman]
Publisher: MMC Publications

Movement(s):
I. [Poem]: Poco adagio (♩=76)
II. Prestissimo (𝅗𝅥=208)
III. Allegretto (♩.=54)

Instrumentation:
Fl solo; Strings.

MS Description:
Holograph with signature, pencil on vellum. *Location:* Boston Public Library.

Editorial Notes:

Date taken from printed cover sheet of the MS. Commission taken from McKinley's notes. The title *Poem* has been used for the first movement when it is performed alone. An arrangement of the first movement for flute and piano also exists (see VI.A.4)

Performance History:

† 9 Dec 1986: Merkin Concert Hall, New York, NY
Robert Stallman, Fl; The PRISM Orchestra, Robert Black, Cond.

† (Boston) 20 Nov 1987: Sanders Theater, Cambridge, MA
Robert Stallman, Fl; SinfoNova Chamber Orchestra, Aram Gharabekian, Cond.

7 Jan 1988: Carnegie Hall, New York, NY (First movement only)
Robert Stallman, Fl; American Symphony Orchestra, Robert Black, Cond.

† (Europe) 3 Nov 1991: St. Barbara, Barkenberg, FRG
Beate Gabriela Schmitt, Fl; Harzer Koncert Orchester, Albert Göken, Cond.

Recording(s):

Owl Recording, Inc: Owl-34, ©1989 (CD)
Robert Stallman, Fl; The Prism Orchestra, Robert Black, Cond.

Bibliography:

Grimes, Ev. "Yale University American Music Oral History Series: William Thomas McKinley." Oct 1986, Yale University School of Music: 94–95.

Rockwell, John. "Concert: The Prism Orchestra." *The New York Times* 11 Dec 1986: C 16.

Tassel, Janet. "From Fat Tuesday's to Carnegie Hall." *Musical America* 107(Jan 1988), no. 6: 21–22.

Kimmelman, Michael. "Concert: McKinley Pieces by American Symphony." *The New York Times* 9 Jan 1988: 12.

Stevens, Denis. "New York." *Musical Times* April, 1988.

Bouchard, Fred. "Jazz and Third Stream Festival: New England Conservatory/Boston." *Downbeat* June 1989: 50–51.

Rothweiler, Kyle. "Flute Concerto & Songs." *American Record Guide* 53(Jul–Aug 1990), no. 4.

Croan, Robert. "Record Reviews: Classical." *Pittsburgh Post-Gazette* 26 Oct 1990.

Talman, Jeff. "The Prism Orchestra." *Ear* May 1991.

Bailosky, Marshall. "A New Recording Project." *Composer/USA* Spring 1991: 10, 13.

Kopanski, H. "'Zeit fürs Überleben': Schülerreaktionen auf McKinleys Orchester-Komposition." *WAZ Dorsten* 29 Oct 1991.

"Komponist aus den USA mag Dorstener Herbst." *WAZ Dorsten* 1 Nov 1991.

"Lebhafter Dialog zwischen Dirigent und Musikern." *Ruhrnachrichten Dorsten* 5 Nov 1991.

"Flöte in heftigem Dialog." *WAZ Dorsten* 8 Nov 1991.

Silverton, Mike. "MacBride: *Nocturnes de la Ventana*; Shore: *July Remembrances*; McKinley: *Concerto for Flute and Strings*." *Fanfare* 16(Jul–Aug 1993), no. 6: 171.

Program Notes:

"My Concerto for Flute and String Orchestra was written for and premiered by soloist Robert Stallman and the PRISM Orchestra conducted by Robert Black. Its second [New York] performance was part of an all-McKinley Evening of Concertos with the American Symphony Orchestra in Carnegie Hall on January 7, 1988. Composed in three movements, the Concerto's overall character develops virtuosic gestures in the solo part and a Vivaldi-Bach-like dialogue and rapprochement between the soloist and string orchestra. The first movement is an introspective tone poem with expansive lyricism coupled with quick changing rhythmic contrasts. The second movement is a brilliantly textured perpetual motion with

incessant drive and motoric energy. The third movement begins with a brooding solo flute cadenza, which builds towards an intense climax recollecting elements from earlier movements and presenting long cantabile lines juxtaposed against lush harmonic backgrounds highlighted with syncopated 'jazzy' patterns and sharp pulsating accents. Ultimately, it is my love of the Baroque which influenced the aural basis and inspiration for this concerto, and it is my intense desire that the listener allow himself or herself to be drawn into the direct and personal emotional experience which this concerto offers, and which, to my mind at least, is the quintessential basis for a genuinely creative appreciation and understanding in all music."
—William Thomas McKinley (© 1987), from Owl Recording Owl-34 liner notes and 20 Nov 1987 program.

"Robert Stallman has lived and worked in France, and McKinley's writing for him is always informed by that connection. *Poem* is the first movement of a flute concerto and stands on its own as an 11-minute tone poem. The composer calls it 'a lament, with a brilliant, active middle section.' It is passionate, with a taxing and strenuous solo part redolent of French impressionism. It begins with a long slow flute melody, the strings providing a harmonic, then rhythmic and broadly lyrical background for the solo."
—Leslie Kandell (©1988), from 7 Jan 1988 program.

II.D.2 Two Movements for Flute and String Orchestra

Date: Mar 1994 in Reading, MA ("Lells") *Duration:* 15'00"
Dedication: "To Bob Stallman" and "In memory of Robert Black"*
Commission: [Bernard Goldberg]
Publisher: MMC Publications

Movement(s):
Largo (♩=48)
Presto e satirico (𝅗𝅥=69)

Instrumentation:
Fl solo; Strings.

MS Description:
Holograph with signature, pencil on paper. *Location:* Boston Public Library.
Markings: *Dedication to Robert Stallman appears on cover page; dedication to Robert Black appears on the first page of music.

Editorial Notes:
Commission information from the composer. Movements are to be performed *attacca*.

Performance History:
[† See *Recording(s)*.]

Recording(s):
MMC Recordings Ltd.: to be recorded in 1995.

Group II.E: Clarinet Concerti

II.E.1 Concerto No. 1 for Clarinet in B♭ and Orchestra ["A Symphony"]

Date: 25 Dec 1977 *Duration:* 23'00"
Dedication: "for Richard Stoltzman"
Commission: National Endowment for the Arts [and Richard Stoltzman]
Publisher: Margun Music Inc.

Movement(s):
With great movement, whirling, nebulous, as golden waves, textured and silvery penetration (♪=110+)

Instrumentation:
Cl solo; Orchestra (2 Pic/2 Fl, 2 Ob/2 EHn, 2 Cl, BCl, 2 Bsn, CBsn, 4 Hn, 2 Tpt, 2 Tbn, Tba, Timp, 2 Perc, 36 Vln, 12 Vla, 10 Vcl, 8 Cb).

Sketches:
71 drafts and 6 sketches of the opening. 10 unidentified drafts and 2 unidentified sketches.

MS Description:
Holograph with printed name, ink on vellum. *Location:* Lost.*

Editorial Notes:
*A photocopy of the MS has survived and been placed in the Boston Public Library collection. Additional commission information from McKinley's notes. Photocopy of MS on file at New England Conservatory of Music in Boston, MA contains a transposition of the closing solo as an appendix. Work's subtitle from McKinley's program notes of 5 Jul 1980.

Performance History:
† 5 Jul 1980: Chautauqua Park, Boulder, CO
Richard Stoltzman, Cl; Colorado Music Festival Orchestra, Giora Bernstein, Cond.
† (New York) 21 Feb 1985: Alice Tully Hall, New York, NY
Richard Stoltzman, Cl; American Composers Orchestra, Gunther Schuller, Cond.

Bibliography:
Rich, Alan. "Colorado Piques." *New West* 11 Aug 1980: 53.
Kandell, Leslie. "Classical Composer With a Passion For Jazz." *The New York Times* 17 Feb 1985: 23, 26.
Page, Tim. "Music: Schuller Leads U.S. Composers Group." *The New York Times* 23 Feb 1985: 12.
Grimes, Ev. "Yale University American Music Oral History Series: William Thomas McKinley." Oct 1986, Yale University School of Music: 78–79.

Program Notes:
"The Concerto was composed in 1979 [*sic*] and was written with the virtuosity of Richard Stoltzman clearly in mind. Since 1976 I have been composing a considerable amount of music for the orchestra and other very large ensemble settings. My first two symphonies were completed around the time of the inception of the Clarinet Concerto. The powerful image of the symphony held its grip on my imagination, and thus the Clarinet Concerto came to be subtitled 'A Symphony.' In the Concerto I wanted to explore a synthesis between these two forms within a single movement structure. The 'normal' size of a single movement structure was therefore inevitably expanded, and within it smaller sections formed into secondary pillars.

"Another reason, more pragmatic in nature, determined the necessity of a one movement structure. The economic factor of rehearsing and performing a multi-movement work is overwhelming. And since I have been having success in getting my single movement works performed by major orchestras, I felt I should continue the pattern out of the obvious practical necessities. However, I have not let this seeming limitation upset the nature of my musical ideas—quite the contrary—in fact, I have felt very comfortable in being able to express an ongoing melodic idea growing from a seedling into the most varied and phantasmagoric transformations, never ending and yet always changing and fostering new ideas one after the other in a drama of perpetual invention and dialogue. In the Concerto the contrast between the symphonic nature of the orchestral writing and the solo virtuosic, cadenza-like passages of the solo B♭ clarinet, which are at times in conflict with the orchestra, and at other times in harmony and conversation with the orchestra, was my greatest challenge. There are times when the solo B♭ clarinet is 'absorbed' into the overall orchestra texture—becoming, as it were, an additional member of the orchestral clarinet family; and there are times when the solo clarinet takes the role of antagonist, breaking away as if unleashed and independent from the orchestral fabric. But finally the clarinet and orchestra resolve into a symphonic union wherein the independent and separate natures of the concerto and symphonic idea are ultimately blended. Perhaps one might more easily perceive the work as a gigantic fantasy: whirling, resolving, changing, whirling, resolving, etc., as if a giant kaleidoscopic mirror were continually reflecting a panorama of exploding and evolving musical atoms throughout an endless galaxy of color, rhythm, and time—a glimpse perhaps at the very universe in which we will all hopefully share a future harmony and creative wealth beyond the confines of our present imaginings."
—William Thomas McKinley (© 1980), from 5 Jul 1980 program.

"The Concerto is in one movement and to a very real extent could be perceived and interpreted as a concerto-rhapsody or grand rhapsody which develops a through-composed and rapidly modulating linear-melodic profile, set against exquisitely rich harmonies and presented in a virtuosic manner. This 'rhapsodic' nature is further enhanced by the fact that the clarinet carries the essential musical line most of the time, culminating in the cadenza which echoes and develops the principal material, adumbrates the future material, and demonstrates in traditional fashion a musical display of the soloist's technical abilities. The Concerto was written very definitely with Richard Stoltzman's talents in mind—his uncanny breath control, his strength to carry forth the long melodic lines, and, above all, his understanding of the melodic tessitura which in this particular work must continually 'soar' above the mighty support of the orchestral tapestry in order to sustain the enormous dialogue and dramatic antiphony which this score demands."
—William Thomas McKinley (© 1985), from 21 Feb 1985 program and Margun Music, inc. MP5003 SC published score.

II.E.2 Rhapsody Fantasia for Solo A Clarinet and Orchestra

Date: Jan 1978 *Duration:* 10'00"
Dedication: "to Richard Stoltzman" and "for my wife"
Commission: [Richard Stoltzman]
Publisher: MMC Publications

Movement(s):
Molto legato, with great richness and expansion, voluminous, penetrating (♪=72)

Instrumentation:
A Cl solo, Orchestra (4 Pic/4 Fl, 2 Ob, EHn, 2 Cl, BCl, 3 Bsn, CBsn, 4 Hn, 2 C Tpt, 4 Tbn/2 BTbn, 2 Tba, Timp, 2 Perc, Strings).

Sketches:
43 drafts of the opening.

MS Description:
Holograph with signature, ink on paper. *Location:* Boston Public Library.
Markings: Page 1: Earlier title, "Symphony #2," crossed out.

Editorial Notes:
Commission information from the composer.

Bibliography:
Grimes, Ev. "Yale University American Music Oral History Series: William Thomas McKinley." Oct 1986, Yale University School of Music: 78–79.

II.E.3 Blues Lament for Dick

Date: [1981] in [Reading, MA] *Duration:* 1'25"
Dedication: "For Dick [Stoltzman]"
Commission: [Richard Stoltzman]
Publisher: MMC Publications

Movement(s):
Blues with gentle movement, sotto voce (♩=48)

Instrumentation:
Cl solo; Orchestra (2 Fl, 2 Ob, 2 Cl, 2 Bsn, 4 Hn, 2 C Tpt, 2 Tbn, Tba, Perc, Strings) or Pno solo.*

MS Description:
Holograph with signature, pencil on paper. *Location:* Boston Public Library.
Markings: Cover: "to be played as encore"

Editorial Notes:
*MS originally for clarinet and piano, then shortly afterward converted to short score format. Date taken from fair copy and McKinley's notes. Location of composition, commission and 6 Nov 1984 performance information taken from McKinley's notes. Premiere performance information from *AMC Newsletter* 25(Summer 1983), no. 3: 14.

Performance History:
[† 11 Jan 1983: Calvin Simmons Theater, Oakland, CA
Richard Stoltzman, Cl; Oakland Symphony Orchestra.]
[† (Dayton) 6 Nov 1984: Montgomery County Memorial Hall, Dayton, OH
Richard Stoltzman, Cl; Dayton Philharmonic Orchestra.]
[†? (Boston)] 6 May 1986: Symphony Hall, Boston, MA
Richard Stoltzman, Cl; Boston Symphony Pops Orchestra, John Williams, Cond.

Bibliography:
Buell, Richard. "Pops Opens 2d Century in Own Style." *The Boston Globe* 8 May 1986: 86.
Bouchard, Fred. "Richard Stoltzman: Clarinet Crossover." *Downbeat* 53(Oct 1986), no. 10: 20–22, 61.

II.E.4 Jean's Dream (Five Musical Visions for B♭ Clarinet and Chamber Ensemble)

Date: 11 Jan 1987 *Duration:* 12'45"
Dedication: "to Jean Kopperud (and the New York New Music Ensemble)"
Commission: [New York New Music Ensemble]
Publisher: MMC Publications

Movement(s):
I. Jack in the Box: Presto (♩=184)
II. Jazz Days: Moderato (♩=116)
III. Climbing Down the Ladder: Larghetto (♩=56)
IV. All Mime: Andante con moto (♩=84)
V. Razzle Dazzle: Presto vivace (♩=104)

Instrumentation:
Cl solo; Fl, Perc, Pno, Vln, Vcl.

MS Description:
Holograph with signature, pencil on vellum. *Location:* Boston Public Library.

Editorial Notes:
Commission taken from McKinley's notes. Premiere performance information from *AMC Newsletter* 30(May–June 1988), no. 1: 27. Information on 4 Oct 1989 performance from BMI records.

Performance History:
[† 25 Feb 1987: Rutgers University, New Brunswick, NJ
Jean Kopperud, Cl; New York New Music Ensemble, Robert Black, Cond.]
† (New York) 1 Mar 1987: Merkin Concert Hall, New York, NY
Jean Kopperud, Cl; New York New Music Ensemble, Robert Black, Cond.
9 Dec 1987: Merkin Concert Hall, New York, NY
Jean Kopperud, Cl; The New Music Consort, Claire Heldrich, Cond.
[† (Boston)] 12 Mar 1989: Jordan Hall, New England Conservatory of Music, Boston, MA
Jean Kopperud, Cl; Collage New Music, Robert Black, Cond.
[4 Oct 1989: Iowa State University, Ames, IA
Performers unknown.]
[† (Russia)] 1 Apr 1991: Rachmaninov Conservatory Hall, Rachmaninov Conservatory, Moscow, Russia
Stephanie Key, Cl; S. Jackson, Fl; J. Shoal, Perc; N. Novichenok, Vln; E. Kolpakova, Vcl; I. Krasovetskii, Pno.

Bibliography:
Webster, Daniel. "With Focus on Clarinetist, a 'Jean's Dream' Premiere." *The Philadelphia Inquirer* 3 Mar 1987: 5D.
Creasey, Beverly. "Brighton Flutist Celebrates Modern Works." *The Allston-Brighton Journal* 9 Mar 1989: 9.
Tommasini, Anthony. "McKinley's Popularity a Mystery." *The Boston Globe* 14 Mar 1989: 29.

Program Notes:
"Staging and movement were the main inspirations for *Jean's Dream* and provided a basis for Jean Kopperud's outstanding talent in combining virtuosic clarinet playing with varieties of mime and dance.

"The work is twofold in purpose and design: first, as a springboard or catalyst for Jean's interpretations, allowing (as a work in progress) for future variations and elaborations *vis-*

à-vis the staging and choreographic movement; and second, as a small chamber concerto, featuring the traditionally virtuosic and technical attributes of the B-flat clarinet.

"The titles of the five visions are of my own invention and provided a helpful stimulus to creating the character and flow of the musical-dramatic events and action. In this sense then, the work is also programmatic and provides the clarinetist with an interpretive basis for staging—although it has to be said that Jean is in a class by herself when one considers the challenge and possibilities of a dual scenario. (However, other soloists, if they so choose, can perform the work in the 'straight' manner of a small chamber concerto.) The treatment of the chamber ensemble is essentially secondary to the activity of the clarinet but from time to time is called upon to compete with equivalent musical action and force. And in this latter sense *Jean's Dream* might be seen to have primarily classical roots and classical characteristics in addition to its theatrical flair and programmatic overtones."
—William Thomas McKinley (© 1987), from 9 Dec 1987 and 12 Mar 1989 programs.

II.E.5 To My Friend Dick

Date: [1988] *Duration:* 16'51"
Dedication: [Richard Stoltzman]
Commission: [Richard Stoltzman]
Publisher: MMC Publications

Movement(s):
♩=100+

Instrumentation:
Cl solo; Fl, Ob, BCl, Bsn, Tpt, Tbn, Pno, Cb, Dr.

MS Description:
Holograph with signature, pencil on paper. *Location:* Boston Public Library.
Markings: Piece contains a great amount of improvisation. In sections where improvisation occurs, only chord symbols and some simple melodies are provided.

Editorial Notes:
Date taken from cover of photocopy of manuscript. Dedication is inferred from the title of the piece. Commission information from the composer. 19 Sep 1988 is first performance present in BMI records.

Performance History:
[†] 19 Sep 1988: J. Leonard Levy Hall, Rodef Shalom Temple, Pittsburgh, PA
Richard Stoltzman, Cl; William Thomas McKinley, Pno; Rodger Ryan, Dr; Jeff Mangone, Cb; The Pittsburgh New Music Ensemble, David Stock, Cond.
[† (New York)] 11 Jun 1989: Merkin Concert Hall, New York, NY
Richard Stoltzman, Cl; William Thomas McKinley, Pno; The Pittsburgh New Music Ensemble, David Stock, Cond.
[† (Boston)] 15 Dec 1990: Tsai Performance Center, Boston University, Boston, MA
Richard Stoltzman, Cl; The Jazz Composers Alliance Orchestra, Ken Schaphorst, Cond.

Bibliography:
Kozinn, Allan. "New Work From Pittsburgh Ensemble." *The New York Times* 13 Jun 1989: C19.
Gonzalez, Fernando. "New Jazz Pieces Show Skill But Lack Soul." *The Boston Globe* 17 Dec 1990: 40.
Garelick, Jon. "Local Jazz Hits Stride." *The Boston Phoenix* 21 Dec 1990: III–15.

II.E.6 From Stadler to Stoltzman for Solo B♭ Clarinet and Orchestra [McKinley Segment]

Date: 1989 in Reading, MA ("Lells") *Duration:* 2'00"
Commission: [Richard Stoltzman]
Publisher: MMC Publications

Movement(s):
Allegro appassionato (♩=132)

Instrumentation:
Cl solo; Orchestra (Pic/2 Fl, 2 Ob, 2 Cl, 2 Bsn, 4 Hn, 3 Tpt, 3 Tbn, Tba, 2 Perc, Pno, Hp, Strings).

MS Description:
Holograph with signature, pencil on paper. *Location:* Boston Public Library.
Markings: Final page: "finale after Sing Sing Sing."

Editorial Notes:
Commission information from the composer and Richard Stoltzman. Premiere performance information from Richard Stoltzman and Frank Solomon Associates.

Performance History:
[† 1989: Constitution Hall, Washington, DC
Richard Stoltzman, Cl; United States Air Force Symphony Orchestra]

II.E.7 [Concerto No. 2 for B♭ Clarinet and Orchestra]

Date: 16 Mar 1990 *Duration:* 25'00"
Dedication: [Richard Stoltzman, Larry Combs, Michele Zukovsky]
Commission: ["A consortium commission from the National Endowment for the Arts for the clarinetists Richard Stoltzman, Larry Combs, and Michele Zukovsky"]
Publisher: MMC Publications

Movement(s):
I. Allegro con dramatico e tempestoso (♩=120)
II. Andantino (♩=69)
III. Prestissimo e vivace (♩.=80)

Instrumentation:
Cl solo; Orchestra (2 Pic/2 Fl, 2 Ob/EHn, 2 Cl, BCl, 2 Bsn/CBsn, 2 Hn, 2 Tpt, 2 Tbn, Tba, Timp, 2 Perc, Pno, Hp, Strings).

Sketches:
2 drafts, in short score, of the opening.

MS Description:
Holograph with signature, pencil on paper. *Location:* Boston Public Library.
Markings: Final page: Date followed by "Happy spring!"

Editorial Notes:
Title, dedication, and commission information from the cover page of the fair copy.

Performance History:
† 2 Jun 1990: Norwalk Concert Hall, Norwalk, CT
Richard Stoltzman, Cl; Fairfield Chamber Orchestra, Thomas Crawford, Cond.

Recording(s):
RCA Victor Red Seal: to be released in 1995.
Richard Stoltzman, Cl; Berlin Radio Symphony, Lukas Foss, Cond.

Bibliography:

Mott, Gilbert H. "Change of Tune: Composer William Thomas McKinley Rejects Atonality to Make Contemporary Classical Music That's Accessible." *Fairfield Fairpress* 1 Jun 1990: F3.
Sweeney, John S. "Clarinetist Shows Technical Quality." *Greenwich Time* 8 Jun 1990: B4.

II.E.8 Concerto for Clarinet and Jazz Orchestra

Date: 2 Dec 1990 in Reading, MA ("Lells") *Duration:* 22'30"
Dedication: "to Richard Stoltzman and the Jazz Composers Alliance"
Commission: [Richard Stoltzman]
Publisher: MMC Publications

Movement(s):
I. Larghetto e magico (♩=66)
II. Scherzando (𝅗𝅥=100)

Instrumentation:
Cl solo; Orchestra (Fl, Sop Sax/2 Alt Sax, Ten Sax, Bar Sax/Ob, 2 Hn, 2 Tpt, 2 Tbn, BTbn, Vib, Gtr, Dr, Perc, Pno, Cb). Optional: Mar.

MS Description:
Holograph with signature, pencil on paper. *Location:* Boston Public Library.

Editorial Notes:
Commission information from the composer.

Performance History:
† 15 Dec 1990: Tsai Performance Center, Boston University, Boston, MA
Richard Stoltzman, Cl; The Jazz Composers Alliance Orchestra, Ken Schaphorst, Cond.

Bibliography:

Gonzalez, Fernando. "Jazz Composer's Alliance Stays Fresh." *The Boston Globe* 14 Dec 1990: 68.
Young, Robert. "Pianist Scores With Fusion." *The Boston Herald* 15 Dec 1990: 23.
Gonzalez, Fernando. "New Jazz Pieces Show Skill But Lack Soul." *The Boston Globe* 17 Dec 1990: 40.
Garelick, Jon. "Local Jazz Hits Stride." *The Boston Phoenix* 21 Dec 1990: III–15.

Program Notes:

"Richard Stoltzman stands in the lineage of our great American clarinetists: Benny Goodman, Artie Shaw, Buddy DeFranco, Jimmy Giuffre, Woody Herman, Eddie Daniels; and since I have had the great fortune to have performed in various settings—both jazz and classical music—with Benny Goodman, Jimmy Giuffre, Eddie Daniels and Richard Stoltzman, I feel particularly close to and proud of this great tradition. It is from this tradition that I draw my inspiration, in synthesis with the great classical tradition that lies as a giant backdrop behind our American-jazz heritage and from which such master composers as Gershwin, Milhaud, Stravinsky, Ellington, and so forth drew their inspiration. I humbly dedicate this, my third clarinet concerto, to the spirit of these great performers and composers both past and present; and I have striven for an amalgamation of classical and jazz style framing the soloist in the traditional concerto-orchestral setting, combined with a language that preserves jazz rhythms ('grooves'), jazz harmonic structures (which owe a great debt to Ravel) and jazz and popular derived melodies, all woven together polyphonically in the manner of a symphonic concerto.

"Contrary to common practice, the third concerto is in two movements: the first, a traditional three-part structure—Adagio–Allegro–Adagio (slow–fast–slow); and the second, a Scherzando ('African boogie'), Cadenza Duo, Latin Samba, Waltz (Andantino), Ballad

(Lento), Cadenza Solo, Scherzando, and Shout (Molto Allegro Vivace) Finale. Essentially, the form of the second movement mixes, combines and weds temporal and mood elements intrinsic to and inherent in more traditional-classical models, with their commonly separated second and third movements, while also attempting to compress, divide and transform these elements (along with other significant musical and dramatic features) into a multi-sectional, rondo-like structure wherein the compositional ideas presented are continuously expanded within the total musical architecture and ultimately strive to distill and synthesize prototypical classical antecedents into a hybrid of a jazz-classical concerto model.

"However, heard as a whole, the musical architecture is formed and divided into two equivalent halves—a bipartite division, the first section lasting 10 minutes, the second 14 minutes—each treated with equal dramatic weight, providing ample areas of interaction replete with several cadenzas (one with Elvin Jones-like drumming) for the clarinetist. There is also a prominent duo obligato-concertante between oboe and solo clarinet in the opening of the second movement scherzo ('African boogie'), as well as a duo concertante section between flute and solo clarinet later in the same movement. In both movements, the listener will hear many contrasting changes of groove and tempo, ranging from popular ballad to Latin samba, all filtered through a 'burnin' groove (of African origin) and up tempo lines. And from time to time these jazz ostinato elements are contrasted against a fabric which is more contemporary and modernistic in its harmonic content (less suggestive of the jazz surface) and classical symphonic temperament. Seen in the most general sense, I wanted to create a scenario that allowed Stoltzman to be a part of a jazz-classical interpretive role which he might have somehow dreamed as one large musical fantasy—eyes closed and with no music, save only his improvisatory ears with which to create an ad hoc, totally through-composed experience!

"I also dedicate this concerto to the JCA [Jazz Composers Alliance]. Many of the composer-founder members were devoted students of mine at NEC [New England Conservatory], and I am proud of their creative achievements, energies, and organizational fortitude to keep this alliance growing in the remarkable way they have, year after year."
—William Thomas McKinley (© 1990), from 15 Dec 1990 program and his notes.

II.E.9 Clarinet Concerto No. 3 ("The Alchemical")

Date: [Jan 1994] in [Reading, MA ("Lells")] *Duration:* 16'10"
Dedication: "To Walter Benzanson on the occasion of his 80th birthday"
Commission: Gail Coffler
Publisher: MMC Publications

Movement(s):
I. Nigredo: Dirge (𝅗𝅥=42)
II. Albedo: Allegro (♩=152)
III. Citrinitas: Molto brillante e luminoso (♩=88)
IV. Rubedo: Scherzo diabolico (♩.=72)

Instrumentation:
Cl solo; Orchestra (Pic/2 Fl, 2 Ob/EHn, 2 Cl, BCl, 2 Bsn, CBsn, 4 Hn, 2 Tpt, 2 Tbn, Tba, Timp, 4 Perc, Pno, Hp, Strings).

MS Description:
Holograph with signature, pencil on paper. *Location:* Boston Public Library.
Markings: Final Page: "'into the red light.'"

Editorial Notes:
Author was witness to date of composition.

Performance History:
[† See *Recording(s).*]

Recording(s):
MMC Recordings Ltd.: to be released in 1995
Richard Stoltzman, Cl; Warsaw Philharmonic Orchestra, George Manahan, Cond.

See also: Scarlet [Version II] (III.A.2b)

Group II.F: Saxophone Concerti

II.F.1 Tenor Rhapsody for Solo Tenor Sax and Orchestra

Date: 22 Apr 1988 *Duration:* 13'00"
Dedication: "to Stan Getz"
Commission: [Stanford Symphony Orchestra]
Publisher: Unpublished

Movement(s):
Largo (♩=48)

Instrumentation:
Ten Sax solo; Orchestra (2 Fl, 2 Ob/EHn, 2 Cl/BCl, 2 Bsn/CBsn, 4 Hn, 2 Tpt, 2 Tbn, Tba, Timp/3 Perc, Pno, Hp, Strings).

MS Description:
Holograph with printed name, pencil on vellum. *Location:* McKinley Residence.

Editorial Notes:
Commission taken from 10 Jun 1988 program. Flyer for 9 Jun 1989 indicates New York premiere performance.

Performance History:
† 10 Jun 1988: Memorial Auditorium, Stanford University, Palo Alto, CA
Stan Getz, Ten Sax; Stanford Symphony Orchestra, Andor Toth, Cond.
[† (New York)] 9 Jun 1989: Symphony Space, New York, NY
Paul Cohen, Ten Sax; New Amsterdam Symphony Orchestra, Robert Black, Cond.

Bibliography:
Johnson, William. "'Karmic' Friendship Leads to Jazz Rhapsody." *San Francisco Times Tribune* 9 Jun 1988: 13.
Elman, Steve. "Stan Getz's Natural Lyricism." *The Boston Globe* 1 Mar 1989: 63.
Gonzalez, Fernando. "Getz in Fine Form for Premiere of McKinley Work." *The Boston Globe* 3 Mar 1989: 45.
Bouchard, Fred. "Jazz and Third Stream Festival: New England Conservatory/Boston." *Downbeat* 56(June 1989), no. 6: 50–51.

Program Notes:
"I had for many years envisioned an orchestral work embellished by the gorgeous tenor sax sound of Stan Getz. But seldom during the earlier years of my career did such liaisons exist between classical music and jazz except for those few circumstances now familiarly etched in the history of American music. Certainly, Ellington, Gershwin, Goodman, and Sauter Finnegan set precedents which foretold of events to come; but only in the past decade

have we witnessed the fruits of these early masters exemplified in our own time by a genuine synthesis and collaboration between the worlds of jazz and classical music and their honored interpreters and improvisers. Not just a third stream, a deep fusion is now occurring in our culture, and the future of American music seems to be assured by its potential riches—all the more significant because of its diversity and intricate eclecticism.

"It was fortuitous that Stan Getz first heard some of my most recent music. During the past five or six years I have become increasingly aware of my own dual heritage and roots and have tried to imbue my music with the most vital characteristics embodied in this contemporary current of fusion without sacrificing or downplaying those elements which I believe most important in our modernist tradition. Stan seems to have heard these characteristics in my work when he called to invite me to compose a new work for tenor saxophone and orchestra. I told him I had been envisioning such a work in my inner thoughts for a very long time and at that very moment (having just then felt a strong sense of deja-vu) I enthusiastically expressed my delight and honor to accept unequivocally his proposal. I then set forth to realize the work I had for so long imagined, and it soon became clear that it would be cast as a tenor rhapsody, with large, slowly evolving and dramatically expansive proportions, fully notated (Stan and I had agreed that this would be a classical work in the sense that I would through-compose his improvisational line but at the same time evoke an atmosphere that would seem as if he were inventing the musical line anew) and unfolding in a grand-rhapsodic manner in much the same temporal format as a set of thirty-two bar choruses on a ballad form. The length of the *Tenor Rhapsody* corresponds to approximately six thirty-two bar choruses of ballad-time with subdivisions and rhythmic pulses deriving and transforming from the original tempo. The melodic line is passionate and lyrical (with some audible but transformed allusions to certain jazz tunes that we have all heard Stan play) and ultimately develops into a full blown tenor-saxophone cadenza followed by a large orchestral *tutti* and a gradual reprise and return to the lyricism and singing of song that characterizes the work's overall musical temperament and communicative purpose."

"It is my hope that the listener will hear this work as neither jazz or classical, pop, new age, new wave, or anything of the kind—but rather as the deep fusion I spoke of above—a fusion that does not force the marriage of opposites but rather sees the potential of an American music which strives towards a higher and more ennobled meeting together of its most creative antecedents."
—William Thomas McKinley (© 1994), from his notes.

See also: Can You Sing Me a Song? (II.B.5)

Group II.G: Horn Concerti

II.G.1 Huntington Horn Concerto

Date: 1989 *Duration:* 18'30"
Dedication: "To Jay Wadenpfuhl"
Commission: [Boston Symphony Orchestra]
Publisher: MMC Publications

Movement(s):
I. Saturday Matinee: Presto e vivace (𝅗𝅥.=84)
II. Broadway Blues: Moderato e sensuale (♩=72)
III. Curtain Calls: Allegro con spirito (𝅝=58)

Instrumentation:
Hn solo; Orchestra (Pic/3 Fl, 2 Ob, EHn, 3 Cl/BCl, 4 Bsn/CBsn, 4 Hn, 2 Tpt, 3 Tbn/BTbn, Tba, Timp, 2 Perc, Pno, Hp, Strings).

MS Description:
Holograph with signature, pencil on paper. *Location:* Boston Public Library.

Editorial Notes:
Commission taken from McKinley's notes. Original MS written in short score format.

Performance History:
† 25–26 May 1989: Symphony Hall, Boston, MA
Jay Wadenpfuhl, Hn; Boston Pops Orchestra, John Williams, Cond.

Program Notes:
"McKinley completed his *Huntington Horn Concerto* early this year. The title puns on the solo instrument for which it is composed (the 'hunting horn') and the street that contains both the building where McKinley works and the building in which the concerto receives its premiere. It was written for and is dedicated to BSO [Boston Symphony Orchestra] horn player Jay Wadenpfuhl. The concerto is both an abstract composition in the traditional three movements and an homage to the world of the theater, in that it depicts a Saturday on Broadway from the early matinee to the end of the evening performance. The names of the movements ('Saturday Matinee,' 'Broadway Blues,' 'Curtain Calls') give a clear indication of the spirit and mood of each, the rhythms and melodies will remind listeners of the great tradition of the American musical theater."
—Steven Ledbetter (© 1989), from 25–26 May 1989 program.

Group II.H: Percussion Concerti

II.H.1 Again the Distant Bells

Date: 20 Dec 1981 in Reading, MA ("Lells") *Duration:* 12'00"
Dedication: "to David Samuels"
Commission: [David Samuels]
Publisher: MMC Publications

Movement(s):
Distant Bells. Memories awake from time's expanse: Largo (♩=42)

Instrumentation:
Vib/Mar solo; 7 Perc.

Sketches:
1 nearly complete draft (pages 1–9, 11–15 missing). 2 folios of notes on the structure of the work.

MS Description:
Holograph with signature, pencil on paper. *Location:* Lost.*
Markings: Throughout the score are descriptions of the various bells and their sonic effects.

Editorial Notes:
*A photocopy of the MS survives and is stored at Boston Public Library. Commission taken from McKinley's notes. Premiere performance information from *AMC Newsletter* 28(Mar–Apr 1986), no. 1: 16 with additional information from David Samuels and McKinley's notes.

Performance History:
[† 5 May 1982: Brooklyn College of Music, Brooklyn, NY
David Samuels, Vib/Mar; Brooklyn College Percussion Ensemble, Morris Lang, Cond.]

See also: Concerto for Oboe and Percussion (VIII.G.5)
Symphony for Thirteen Players [Chamber Symphony No. 1] (VIII.A.3)
A Different Drummer ["An Instrumental Omnibus"] (VIII.D.8)
Paintings No. 4 ("Magical Visions") (VIII.D.4)

Group II.I: Cimbalom Concerti

II.I.1 Concerto for Cimbalom and Chamber Ensemble

Date: 1986 *Duration:* 14'30"
Dedication: "to Theodore Antoniou and Alea III"*
Commission: [Theodore Antoniou and Alea III]
Publisher: MMC Publications

Movement(s):
I. Winter Mists: Allegro moderato (♩=116)
II. Winter Night: Larghetto (♩=54)
III. Winter Rain: Presto (♩.=120)

Instrumentation:
Cim solo; 2 Pic/2 Fl/2 Alt Fl, Ob/EHn, Cl, Timp/2 Perc, Pno, Vln, Vla, Vcl.

MS Description:
Holograph with signature, pencil on vellum. *Location:* Boston Public Library.

Editorial Notes:
*Program notes of 21 Oct 1986 add James Barnes to the list of dedicatees. Commission of the work by Theodore Antoniou and Alea III is also implied in these notes.

Performance History:
† 12 Apr 1986: Longy School of Music, Cambridge, MA
James Earl Barnes, Cimbalom; Alea III, Theodore Antoniou, Cond.
21 Oct 1986: Jordan Hall, New England Conservatory of Music, Boston, MA
James Earl Barnes, Cimbalom; [Untitled ensemble], Theodore Antoniou, Cond.
4 Mar 1988: First and Second Church, Boston, MA
James Earl Barnes, Cimbalom; The Boston Musica Viva, Richard Pittman, Cond.

Bibliography:
Tommasini, Anthony. "McKinley's Recent Works Lack Discernment and Taste." *The Boston Globe* 5 Mar 1988: 14.

Program Notes:
"When Theodore Antoniou asked me to compose this new work, I will admit that a sense of trepidation came over me—I had never used the cimbalom and knew its nature only incidentally *vis-à-vis* Kodály and Stravinsky. Yet, with the help of some technical information concerning the instrument's idiomatic properties provided by James Barnes, the soloist in tonight's performance, I found that after the first moments of the Concerto I began to feel very comfortable with these properties, and the sound of the Cimbalom held clearly in my musical imagination. At first I was not entirely sure that the new work would be a Concerto.

I envisioned shorter pieces, epigrammatic pieces, ragtimes, etc. But as the work took early shape I felt confident in tackling the bigger form, and, coupled with the help of a wide color palette from the ensemble, was able to envision several movements, including virtuosic cadenzas as well as a variety of musical interpolations and dialogues within the *tutti*. Hence, all the natural components of a Concerto took seed.

"The movements are: I. Winter Mists, II. Winter Night, III. Winter Rain, and the programmatic quality of the work owes itself to the varieties of winter moods which are ageless and universal in feeling. And since color and harmony are of great import—the programmatic character of the Concerto is enhanced. Although thoroughly modern in its outcome, the Concerto is most definitely a tonal work with discernible melodies and rhythmic pulses in support of its tonality. If I had to characterize my present language in a phrase, I would call it 'evolving' or 'developmental' *minimalism.*

"On a purely musical level, my Concerto attempts to recombine the apparent differences between an evolving minimalism and a dramatic, continually developing expressionism and to hopefully go beyond them—to ultimately aim at the purpose of communicating: first to the performers, our primary critics; and in the end to the very heart of the listening audience."
—William Thomas McKinley (© 1986), from 12 Apr 1986 program.

"[The] Concerto for Cimbalom and Chamber Ensemble was composed on a commission from Alea III, and premiered by that group last season at the Longy School of Music with Theodore Antoniou conducting and James Barnes playing cimbalom. This is a large-framed work showing off the wide coloristic gamut of the cimbalom's character, and its technical possibilities. Due to the virtuosity and commitment of James Barnes, I think we will see a rebirth of this instrument, its importance (having been used by a number of 20th Century masters), and its longevity. The work is in three movements, broad in scale, brightly colored, multi-rhythmic, continually evolving, and is dedicated to James Barnes."
—William Thomas McKinley (© 1986), from 21 Oct 1986 program.

Group II.J: Harp Concerti

II.J.1 Rhapsody for Solo Harp and Concert Band

Date: 27 Dec 1976 in Manchester, MA ("Carriage House") *Duration:* 11'00"
Dedication: "To Susan Allen with gratitude and respect"
Commission: American Harp Society (29 Nov 1976)
Publisher: MMC Publications

Movement(s):
Brilliant, sustained and broad gesture (♩=50)

Instrumentation:
Hp solo, Concert Band (2 Pic/8 Fl, 4 Cl, 2 Alt Sax, 2 Ten Sax, Bar Sax, 2 Hn, 4 Tpt, 2 Tbn, BTbn, 2 Tba, 6 Perc).

Sketches:
28 drafts of the opening.

MS Description:
Holograph with printed name, ink on vellum. *Location:* Boston Public Library.

Editorial Notes:
Premiere information from National Endowment grant application of 14 Nov 1978 and McKinley's notes.

Performance History:
[† Jun 1977: South Newton High School, Newton, MA
Susan Allen, Harp; South Newton High School Band, Donald Dregalla, Cond.]
25 Jun 1977: [Hall unknown] New London, NH
Susan Allen, Harp; South Newton High School Band, Donald Dregalla, Cond.

Group II.K: Keyboard Concerti

II.K.1 Concerto for Piano No. 1 (op. 60)

Date: 29 Dec 1974 in Reading, MA ("Linnea Lane") *Duration:* 13'12"
Dedication: "to all great concert pianists"
Commission: [Peter Serkin]
Publisher: MMC Publications

Movement(s):
Richly, with intense singing and crying. Blues feeling (♪=52)

Instrumentation:
Pno solo; Orchestra (2 Pic, 4 Fl/Alt Fl, 3 Ob, Heckelphone or EHn, 4 Cl/4 BCl/CbCl, 2 Bsn/4 CBsn, 4 Hn, 3 Tpt, 2 Tbn, BTbn, 2 Tba, 9 Perc, Hp, 30 Vln, 12 Vla, 10 Vcl, 8 Cb).

Sketches:
8 drafts of the opening. 1 draft of m. 9. 8 drafts of mm. 22–23. 4 folios of unidentified sketches.

MS Description:
Holograph with signature, pencil on paper. *Location:* Boston Public Library.

Editorial Notes:
Commission information from the composer.

II.K.2 Poem of Light (A Little Concerto for Piano and Chamber Ensemble)

Date: [Jun 1983] in [Reading, MA ("Lells")] *Duration:* 17'30"
Dedication: ["Written for the Boston Musica Viva's 15th Anniversary season, especially for Randall Hodgkinson. The piece was dedicated to Mrs. Gardner Cox for her valued support over the years."]
Commission: [National Endowment for the Arts]
Publisher: MMC Publications

Movement(s):
Magical (♩=72)

Instrumentation:
Pno solo; Fl, Cl, Perc, Vln, Vla, Vcl.

MS Description:
Holograph with signature, pencil on paper. *Location:* Boston Public Library.

Editorial Notes:
Dedication, taken from 31 Dec 1983 program. Date, location of composition, and commission taken from McKinley's notes.

Performance History:
† 7 Oct 1983: Longy School of Music, Cambridge, MA
Randall Hodgkinson, Pno; Boston Musica Viva, Richard Pittman, Cond.
31 Dec 1983 ("First Night '84"): First and Second Church, Boston, MA
Randall Hodgkinson, Pno; Boston Musica Viva, Richard Pittman, Cond.
15 Oct 1984: Jordan Hall, New England Conservatory of Music, Boston, MA
Randall Hodgkinson, Pno; [Untitled ensemble], Stephen Drury, Cond.
† (New York) 12 Jan 1986: Christ and St. Stephen's Church, New York, NY
Howard Lew, Pno; The North/South Consonance Ensemble, Max Lifchitz, Cond.
5 Jun 1986: Merkin Concert Hall, New York, NY
Cameron Grant, Pno; The New York New Music Ensemble, Robert Black, Cond.
[† (Providence)] 8 Feb 1987: Rhode Island School of Design, Providence, RI
New Music Ensemble, George Goneconto, Cond.
4 Mar 1988: First and Second Church, Boston, MA
The Boston Musica Viva, Richard Pittman, Cond.

Bibliography:
Driver, Paul. "Composer McKinley 'Hears the Muses.'" *The Boston Globe* 9 Dec 1983: 48, 52.
MacPherson, William A. "An Excellent Ensemble." *Providence Journal* 10 Feb 1987.
Tommasini, Anthony. "McKinley's Recent Works Lack Discernment and Taste." *The Boston Globe* 5 Mar 1988: 14.

Program Notes:
"Originally, I set out to compose an ambitious and 'grand' piano concerto for Randall Hodgkinson and the Boston Musica Viva. But as musical ideas unfolded, it soon became apparent that my conception was taking a different course. What finally originated was a music of a much more intimate character: shimmering, lambent, and sparked by occasional touches of 'extroverted' brilliance.

"There is a cadenza for the piano soloist which is essentially introspective and in keeping with the intimate character of the whole form. However, the solo part is not entirely unvirtuosic. There are some concerto like passages which are difficult and demand a mastery of legato, rubato, 'bringing out' of singing melody, control of pedaling—particularly the *una corda*, and smooth execution in trills, tremolandi and arpeggio figurations. Perhaps most important is the tone richness and tone projection required of the soloist—the manner in which the soloist is able to dominate and carry the flow of the entire ensemble, creating the forward energy and projecting the 'illusion' of musical light and the poetic shades of musical color which transform from beginning to end."
—William Thomas McKinley (© 1983), from 7 Oct 1983 program and his notes.

"*Poem of Light* was composed for Randall Hodgkinson and the Boston Musica Viva. Its world premiere, conducted by Richard Pittman, took place last October in Boston. Essentially, the *Poem of Light* is a broadly lyrical tone poem, encased in ornate colors and decorated by motifs which are developed in a chaconne-like manner, undergoing many shifting shades of harmony. The piano is given greatest prominence, culminating in an introspective cadenza."
—William Thomas McKinley (© 1984), from 15 Oct 1984 program.

II.K.3 Concerto for Piano No. 2 ("O'Leary")

Date: 13 Aug 1987 in Reading, MA ("Lells") *Duration:* 16'30"
Dedication: "to David Buechner" and "...to the spirit of..."*
Commission: [Steven and Barbara O'Leary]
Publisher: MMC Publications

Movement(s):
I. Tumultuosamente (♩.=69)
II. Prestissimo (♩=184)
III. Largo e triste (♩=40)

Instrumentation:
Pno solo; Orchestra (Pic/2 Fl, 2 Ob, 2 Cl, 2 Bsn/CBsn, 4 Hn, 2 Tpt, 2 Tbn, Hp, 3 Perc, Strings).

MS Description:
Holograph with printed name, pencil on vellum. *Location:* Boston Public Library. *Markings:* *Dedication to David Buechner on the cover page; dedication "...to the spirit of..." on the instrumentation page. However, 11 Apr 1988 program dedicates the work to "Steven and Barbara O'Leary."

Editorial Notes:
Commission information from the composer.

Performance History:
† 7 Jan 1988: Carnegie Hall, New York, NY
David Buechner, Pno; The American Symphony Orchestra, Robert Black, Cond.
† (Boston) 11 Apr 1988: Symphony Hall, Boston, MA
David Buechner, Pno; SinfoNova Chamber Orchestra, Aram Gharabekian, Cond.

Recording(s):
MMC Recordings Ltd.: to be released in 1995
Jeffrey Jacobs, Pno; Silesian Philharmonic, J. Swoboda, Cond.

Bibliography:
Kimmelman, Michael. "Concert: McKinley Pieces by American Symphony." *The New York Times* 9 Jan 1988: 12.
Stevens, Denis. "New York." *Musical Times* April, 1988.
Tommasini, Anthony. "SinfoNova Makes a Daring and Risky Move." *The Boston Globe* 13 Apr 1988: 34.

Program Notes:
"It is all-out virtuoso writing in the grand style. The neo-tonality embraces the richest kind of harmony without giving up stability. At the same time, the surface is contemporary. I have always dreamt of what Rachmaninoff would be like today. Popular music of thirty years ago had a Rachmaninoff character. I took the quality of passion rather than a direct quote."
—William Thomas McKinley (©1988), from an interview with Leslie Kandell in 7 Jan 1988 and 11 Apr 1988 programs.

II.K.4 Silent Whispers for Solo Piano and Orchestra

Date: [Dec 1992] in [Reading, MA ("Lells")] *Duration:* 10'20"
Dedication: "to Victoria Griswold"
Commission: [Victoria Griswold]
Publisher: MMC Publications

Movement(s):
Prestissimo e lamento bisbigliando (♩=138)

Instrumentation:
Pno solo; Orchestra (Pic/2 Fl, 2 Ob, EHn, 2 Cl, BCl, 2 Bsn, CBsn, 4 Hn, 2 Tpt, 2 Tbn, Tba, Timp, 3 Perc, Hp, Strings).

MS Description:
Holograph with signature, pencil on paper. *Location:* Boston Public Library.
Markings: Sketch for the opening of String Quartet No. 9 occurs on the back of p. 12 of the MS.

Editorial Notes:
Author was witness to date and location of composition. Commission information from the composer.

Performance History:
[† See *Recording(s).*]

Recording(s):
MMC Recordings, Ltd.: MMC2004, ©1994 (CD)
Victoria Griswold, Pno; Warsaw National Philharmonic, Robert Black, Cond.

Bibliography:
Zagorski, William. "Master Musicians Collective Warsaw Series, Volume II." *Fanfare* 18(Sep–Oct 1994), no. 1: 432.

II.K.5 Andante and Scherzo for Piano and Orchestra

Date: 21 Jan 1993 in Reading, MA ("Lells") *Duration:* 10'00"
Commission: [Frances Burnett]
Publisher: MMC Publications

Movement(s):
Andante e dolce e languido (𝅗𝅥=50)

Instrumentation:
Pno solo; Orchestra (3 Pic/3 Fl, 2 Ob/EHn, 2 Cl, BCl, 2 Bsn, CBsn, 4 Hn, 2 Tpt, 3 Tbn, Tba, Timp, 3 Perc, Hp, Strings).

MS Description:
Holograph with signature, pencil on paper. *Location:* Boston Public Library.

Editorial Notes:
Commission information from the composer.

Performance History:
[† See *Recording(s).*]

Recording(s):
MMC Recordings, Ltd.: MMC2009, ©1994 (CD)
Frances Burnett, Pno; Slovak Radio Symphony Orchestra, Robert Stankovsky, Cond.

II.K.6 Fantasia Variazioni (Fantasy Variations) for Harpsichord and Orchestra

Date: 2 Apr 1993 in Reading, MA ("Lells") *Duration:* 15'45"
Dedication: "To Elaine Comparone"
Commission: [Elaine Comparone]
Publisher: MMC Publications

Movement(s):
I. Allegro e sarcasmo (♩=126)
II. Prestissimo e magico (♩=200)
III. Più agitato e diabolico (♩=160)
IV. Moderato e energico (𝅗𝅥=112)
V. Andante e elegante (♩=92)
VI. Allegro e giubilante (♩.=132)
VII. Presto e delicato (o‿♩=63)
VIII. Larghetto e tragico (♩=69)
IX. Vivace (♩=168)
X. Allegretto satirico (♩=160)
XI. Adagio (♩=56)
XII. Allegro finale (𝅗𝅥=152)

Instrumentation:
Hpschd solo; Orchestra (2 Pic, 2 Fl, 2 Ob, 2 Cl, BCl, 2 Bsn, CBsn, 4 Hn, 2 Tpt, 2 Tbn, Tba, Timp, 3 Perc, Hp, Strings).

MS Description:
Holograph with signature, pencil on paper. *Location:* Boston Public Library.

Editorial Notes:
Commission information from the composer.

Performance History:
[† See *Recording(s).*]

Recording(s):
MMC Recordings, Ltd.: MMC2016, ©1994 (CD)
Elaine Comparone, Hpschd; Slovak Radio Symphony Orchestra, Robert Stankovsky, Cond.

II.K.7 [Concerto for Piano No. 3]

Date: [20 May 1994] in [Reading, MA ("Lells")] *Duration:* 19'31"
Commission: [Marjorie Mitchell]
Publisher: MMC Publications

Movement(s):
I. Blues: Andantino (♩=63)
II. Ragtime: Più allegro (♩=160)
III. Slow blues march: Tempo di marchia e bluesy (♩=56)
IV. Struttin': Prestissimo (♩=208)

Instrumentation:
Pno solo; Orchestra (Pic/2 Fl, 2 Ob, 2 Cl, BCl, 2 Bsn, CBsn, 4 Hn, 2 Tpt, 2 Tbn, Tba, Timp, 4 Perc, Pno, Hp, Strings).

MS Description:
Holograph, pencil on paper. *Location:* Boston Public Library.

Editorial Notes:
Author was witness to date and location of composition. Title taken from cover of fair copy. Commission information from the composer.

Performance History:
[† See *Recording(s).*]

Recording(s):
MMC Recordings Ltd.: to be recorded in 1995.

Group II.L: Violin Concerti

II.L.1 Summer Dances

Date: [Sep 1984]
Duration: 28'30"
Dedication: [Syoko Aki Erle]
Commission: [Syoko Aki Erle]
Publisher: MMC Publications

Movement(s):
I. Bolero: Larghetto (♩=63)
II. Valse: Tempo di valse (𝅗𝅥.=50)
III. Ballad: Largo (♩=44)
IV. Jig: Allegro vivace (♩.=126)

Instrumentation:
Vln solo; Orchestra (Pic/Fl, Ob, Pic Cl/Cl, Bsn, Hn, Tpt, Tbn, Timp/Perc, Pno, Hp, Strings).

MS Description:
Holograph, pencil on vellum. *Location:* Boston Public Library.

Editorial Notes:
Date and commission taken from McKinley's notes Dedication is indicated in the parts.

Performance History:
† 28 Sep 1985: Sprague Memorial Hall, Yale University School of Music, New Haven, CT
Syoko Aki Erle, Vln; Yale University Orchestra, Jesse Levine, Cond.
[† (Boston)] 1 Apr 1986: Jordan Hall, New England Conservatory of Music, Boston, MA
Syoko Aki Erle, Vln; [Untitled ensemble], Robert Black, Cond.

Bibliography:
Grimes, Ev. "Yale University American Music Oral History Series: William Thomas McKinley." Oct 1986, Yale University School of Music: 97.

II.L.a ~~Violin Concerto~~

Date: [1970]
Dedication: "for Paul Zukofsky"
Publisher: Unpublished

Movement(s):
♩=52–60

Instrumentation:
Vln solo; Orchestra (Pic, 2 Fl, 2 Ob, 2 Cl, BCl, 2 Bsn, CBsn, 4 Hn, 4 Tpt, 2 Tbn, BTbn, Tba, 2 Perc, Strings).

Sketches:
1 incomplete draft. 1 folio of notes on the formal plan of the work.

MS Description:
Holograph, pencil on paper. *Location:* Boston Public Library.

Editorial Notes:
MS ends after 1 page, draft ends after 3 pages. Dating established through paleographic analysis and location of discovery (formal plan found with the formal plan of *Quadruplum* and on the same orange paper).

Group II.M: Viola Concerti

II.M.1 Concerto Fantasy for Viola and Orchestra [Concerto for Viola No. 1]

Date: 5 Jul 1978 in Boston, MA *Duration:* 17'00"
Dedication: "for Sol Greitzer"
Commission: [National Endowment for the Arts]
Publisher: MMC Publications

Movement(s):
Scherzo, brilliant (♩=60)

Instrumentation:
Vla solo; Orchestra (4 Fl/4 Alt Fl, 2 Ob, EHn, 4 Cl, BCl, 3 Bsn/CBsn, 4 Hn, 2 Tpt, 2 Tbn, Tba, Timp, 2–3 Perc, 30 Vln, 10 Vla, 8 Vcl, 6 Cb).

Sketches:
26 drafts and 5 sketches of the opening.

MS Description:
Holograph with printed name, ink on vellum. *Location:* Boston Public Library.

Editorial Notes:
Commission taken from McKinley's notes.

II.M.2 Viola Concerto [No. 2]

Date: [Aug 1984] in [Reading, MA ("Lells")] *Duration:* 30'30"
Dedication: "to Sol Greitzer"
Commission: [Massachusetts Council for the Arts]
Publisher: MMC Publications

Movement(s):
I. Andante ma non troppo (♩=52)
II. Vivo (♩=120+)
III. Molto maestoso (𝅝=48)

Instrumentation:
Vla solo; Orchestra (Pic/2 Fl, 2 Ob/EHn, 2 Cl, 2 Bsn/CBsn, 2 Hn, 2 Tpt, Timp/Perc, Pno, Hp, Strings).

Sketches:
4 unidentified drafts.

MS Description:
Holograph with signature, pencil on vellum. *Location:* Boston Public Library.

Editorial Notes:
Date, location of composition, and commission taken from McKinley's notes.

Performance History:
† 13 Mar 1987: Embassy Theater, Los Angeles, CA
Sol Greitzer, Vla; Los Angeles Chamber Orchestra, Jorge Mester, Cond.
[† (Pasadena)] 14 Mar 1987: Ambassador Auditorium, Pasadena, CA
Sol Greitzer, Vla; Los Angeles Chamber Orchestra, Jorge Mester, Cond.
[† (Denver)] 15 Mar 1987: Paramount Theater, Denver, CO
Sol Greitzer, Vla; Los Angeles Chamber Orchestra, Jorge Mester, Cond.
† (New York) 7 Jan 1988: Carnegie Hall, New York, NY
Sol Greitzer, Vla; The American Symphony Orchestra, Robert Black, Cond.

Recording(s):
MMC Recordings Ltd.: to be recorded in 1995.

Bibliography:
Kandell, Leslie. "Classical Composer With a Passion For Jazz." *The New York Times* 17 Feb 1985: 23, 26.
Spousta, Holly. "A Man of 'Eminently Worthwhile Music': Profiling Reading's William T. McKinley." *Reading Daily Times Chronicle* 21 Aug 1986: 1, 14A.
Grimes, Ev. "Yale University American Music Oral History Series: William Thomas McKinley." Oct 1986, Yale University School of Music: 97.
Cariaga, Daniel. "McKinley Premiere." *Los Angeles Times* 16 Mar 1987.
Giffin, Glenn. "L.A. Orchestra Brings Strings to Paramount." *The Denver Post* 16 Mar 1987: 1D–2D.
Schilliaci, Daniel. "Chamber Orchestra in Fine Form." *Los Angeles Herald* 16 Mar 1987.
Thomas, Robert. "Mester, at Helm of LACO, Displays Masterful Control." *Pasadena Star-News* 16 Mar 1987.
Tassel, Janet. "From Fat Tuesday's to Carnegie Hall." *Musical America* 107(Jan 1988), no. 6: 21–22.
Kimmelman, Michael. "Concert: McKinley Pieces by American Symphony." *The New York Times* 9 Jan 1988: 12.
Stevens, Denis. "New York." *Musical Times* April, 1988.

Program Notes:
"Composing in a neo-tonal, euphonious, contemporary language, I owe much to the achievements of the American romantic composers such as George Gershwin and William Schuman filtered and synthesized through my own personal experiences in American jazz. Although this new concerto is not meant to be an overtly jazzy work, the listener who is familiar with certain modern tonalities of jazz and popular music will hear the expansion of these tonalities along with modernist rhythmic elements, cast within a wide palette of orchestral color.

"I envisioned Sol Greitzer's role in the manner of *Harold in Italy*. (We have occasionally teased with the idea of 'Sol in Los Angeles' or 'Sol in New York'). The viola part is quite continuous, seldom resting, and moves in and out of phase with the orchestra. Its presence is usually dominant, but sometimes the viola is meant to be heard only as part of the total fabric. This allows me to indulge occasionally in the large sound of the orchestra and, due to intrinsic problems of balance when the viola is used as a concerto solo instrument, I was faced with the traditional task of balancing the viola against the orchestra while at the same time justifying and enhancing the orchestral presence and involvement in the musical dialogue. Thus, as in *Harold in Italy*, my concerto may be viewed as a symphony with the *cantus firmus* or main thread of continuity throughout the work's entirety centered in the solo part.

"There are three movements, the first cast *a la* Haydn in a monothematic or distilled sonata form, the second a veritable presto vivo scherzo type, and the finale a chaconne cast in a very large, developing variation form not entirely unlike the form of the passacaglia in Brahms' Fourth Symphony. There are cadenzas in the first and last movements interspersed with smaller quasi-cadenza-like passages. The cadenza in the third movement begins accompanied and gradually evolves into solo. Although I have used principally classical structures for the concerto's architecture, the overall drama does indeed unfold in a long-lined, romantically lyrical manner. Melody is extremely important. Only in the domain of harmony and color have I consciously sought a modern surface.

"It has up to now been my experience that, with the presence of bona-fide themes and traditional developments, coupled with intense lyricism and emotionally powerful rhythms which retain the vitality of discernible pulse and heartbeat, I could be freed to find freshness and lushness in the harmonies and colors without ever losing communication with the performers and audience alike. Therefore, the listener may here and there perceive elements reminiscent (albeit momentarily) of minimalism as well as other modernistic tendencies. It has never been my desire to develop a language which ignores the best which our present can offer. But at the same time, it has gradually become very important for me also to try to preserve the very best which tradition has to offer. During my private moments of creation, I am never conscious of trying to construct or amalgamate any idea or setting which is prestructured or merely external. All of what I am trying to say comes from an intense internal singing and desire to express my thoughts in a single musical stroke. I have humbly learned this manner from the great masters and at the expense of being criticized or chastised for daring to mention this, I feel duty-bound at this stage of my compositional life and career to say what is for me the most essential and truthful creative impetus. My noted prolificness and fecundity is often the subject of great controversy and occasional misunderstanding. Indeed, I would love one day to tell you the rest of this story."
—William Thomas McKinley (© 1987), from 13 Mar 1987 program.

II.M.3 Ancient Memories (a chamber concerto for viola and chamber ensemble)

Date: 1989 *Duration:* 18'00"
Dedication: "to Walter Trampler, James Dunham and Marcus Thompson"
Commission: National Endowment for the Arts
Publisher: MMC Publications

Movement(s):
I. Ancient Dreams: Andante e sensuale (♩=80)
II. Ancient Passions: Prestissimo (♩=160)
III. Ancient Longings: Larghetto dramatico ma semplice (♩=63)
IV. Ancient Joys: Tempo di valse e giubilante (♩.=69)

Instrumentation:
Vla solo; Pic/Fl, Cl/BCl, Perc, Pno, Vln, Vla, Vcl.

MS Description:
Holograph with signature, pencil on paper. *Location:* Boston Public Library.

Performance History:

† 12 Mar 1989: Jordan Hall, New England Conservatory of Music, Boston, MA
Walter Trampler, Vla; Collage New Music, David Hoose, Cond.

† (Rochester) 21 Sep 1990: Kilbourn Hall, Eastman School of Music, Rochester, NY
James Dunham, Vla; Eastman Musica Nova, Sydney Hodkinson, Cond.

† (New York) 29 Apr 1992: Merkin Concert Hall, New York, NY
Walter Trampler, Vla; New York New Music Ensemble, Christopher Finckel, Cond.

29 Apr 1993: Tsai Performance Center, Boston University, Boston, MA
Marcus Thompson, Vla; Boston University New Music Ensemble, Theodore Antoniou, Cond.

[† (Pittsburgh)] 17 Jan 1994: Levy Hall, Rodef Shalom, Pittsburgh, PA
Marcus Thompson, Vla; Pittsburgh New Music Ensemble, David Stock, Cond.

Bibliography:

Creasey, Beverly. "Brighton Flutist Celebrates Modern Works." *The Allston-Brighton Journal* 9 Mar 1989: 9.

Tommasini, Anthony. "McKinley's Popularity a Mystery." *The Boston Globe* 14 Mar 1989: 29.

Holland, Bernard. "New York New Music Ensemble: Merkin Concert Hall." *The New York Times* 2 May 1992: 16.

Kanny, Mark. "Music Ensemble Opens Year on High Note." *Pittsburgh Post-Gazette* 18 Jan 1994.

Program Notes:

"*Ancient Memories* was commissioned by the National Endowment for the Arts for a consortium of three violists: James Dunham, Marcus Thompson and Walter Trampler. All three have performed and continue to perform Ancient Memories on their recitals as fulfillment of the consortium requirements.

"The principal idea in the concerto is to cast the violist as *dramatis persona* within the broader outlines of a traditional chamber concerto format. There are four movements, each meant to evoke a particular memory or *Sehnsucht* the composer often experiences in thoughts and private moments of contemplation. Those chosen represent a small number from a large category of memories and feelings that seemed most translatable into musical imagery: Ancient Dreams, Ancient Passions, Ancient Longings and Ancient Joys. The viola symbolizes the dreamer and each movement concentrates on one central emotive element, often transforming through instrumental development and virtuoso-like embellishments into a wider palette of dramatic expression, suggestive and powerful in re-awakening the unlocked mysteries of our most distant remembrances."

—William Thomas McKinley (© 1989), from 12 Mar 1989 and 29 Apr 1992 programs.

II.M.4 Concerto No. 3 for Viola and Orchestra

Date: [Aug 1992] in [Reading, MA ("Lells")] *Duration:* 21'55"
Dedication: "to Karen Dreyfus and the Manhattan Sinfonia"
Commission: [Karen Dreyfus]
Publisher: MMC Publications

Movement(s):
I. Lamento (♩=56)
II. Largo (♩=44)
III. Prestissimo e diabolico (𝅗𝅥=120)

Instrumentation:
Vla solo; Orchestra (2 Pic/2 Fl, 2 Ob, 2 Cl, 2 Bsn, 4 Hn, 2 Tpt, 2 Tbn, Tba, Timp, 2 Perc, Hp, Strings).

MS Description:
Holograph with signature, pencil on paper. *Location:* Boston Public Library.

Editorial Notes:
Author was witness to date of composition. Commission information from the composer.

Performance History:
† 22 Feb 1993: Alice Tully Hall, New York, NY
Karen Dreyfus, Vla; Manhattan School of Music Chamber Ensemble, Glen Cortese, Cond.
23 Feb 1993: Borden Auditorium, Manhattan School of Music, New York, NY
Karen Dreyfus, Vla; Manhattan School of Music Chamber Ensemble, Glen Cortese, Cond.

Recording(s):
MMC Recordings Ltd.: to be released in 1995
Karen Dreyfus, Vla; The Manhattan School Chamber Orchestra, Glen Cortese, Cond.

Program Notes:
"I have had the good fortune to have worked with and composed for some of America's finest violists, among whom several stand out: James Dunham of the Cleveland Quartet, Marcus Thompson, Walter Trampler, Sol Greitzer, and, most recently, Karen Dreyfus, who will give the world premiere of my Viola Concerto No. 3.

"It is to the many lessons and experiences taught me by these wonderful violists that my new concerto owes its creative and spiritual stimulus. My third concerto seeks to compress the most resonant tonal areas inherent in the viola, and at the same time, expand these areas into a romantic weave of dialogue and argument.

"Cast in three movements, there are strong Baroque and Classical reminiscences which nourish the musical narrative in traditional fashion.

"Throughout the Concerto's extended development, the intrinsic difficulties of balance and compatibility between the solo viola and the orchestra are compensated for in several ways. There are many interspersed cadenzas of varying length, as well as antiphonal passages between solo and tutti and strong orchestral developments which allow the viola to remain silent from time to time.

"I was not content with 'baby-fied' accompaniments behind the soloist. Rather, I sought a rich and texturally interesting orchestral backdrop, giving the orchestra players an interactive role in the narrative. At the same time, I hoped to preserve and showcase the richness of the viola's most sonorous properties, or *dramatis personae* if you will.

"Beyond all explanation, the Concerto strives for direct and visceral communication, so as to draw the listener into its action and emotional drama."
—William Thomas McKinley (© 1993), from 22 Feb 1993 and 23 Feb 1993 programs.

Group II.N: Violoncello Concerti

II.N.1 Concerto No. 1 for Cello and Orchestra (op. 80)

Date: 18 Jan 1977 in Manchester, MA ("Carriage House") *Duration:* 55'00"
Dedication: "to Aldo Parisot"
Commission: [Aldo Parisot]
Publisher: MMC Publications

Movement(s):
With wild abandon, unleashed energies, always brilliant (♪=as fast as possible)

Instrumentation:
Vcl solo; Orchestra (3 Pic/3 Fl, 3 Ob, EHn, 3 Cl, BCl, 3 Bsn, CBsn, 4 Hn, 2 Tpt, 2 Tbn, Tba, Timp/4 Perc, Pno, Hp, 30 Vln, 12 Vla, 10 Vcl, 8 Cb).

Sketches:
1 draft of mm. 4–5. 3 drafts of mm. 42–44. 1 draft of mm. 96–99. 1 draft of mm. 306–308.

MS Description:
Holograph with printed name, ink on paper. *Location:* Boston Public Library.
Markings: Cover page: "The cellist may feel at liberty to use a high quality pick-up microphone. No distortion of the natural sound should be present. The basic nature of the piece is to allow the solo cello to at times recede into the background activity...at other times to completely dominate the prevailing texture...never does the soloist cease to play. In this respect the work might be considered a fantasy concerto. This score is the original manuscript...it represents 3 stages of completion and interruption...hence the enormity of its duration."

Editorial Notes:
Commission taken from McKinley's notes.

Group II.O: Contrabass Concerti

II.O.a ~~Concerto for Solo Double Bass~~

Date: [ca. 1982]
Publisher: Unpublished

Movement(s):
I. Allegro moderato (♩=60)

Instrumentation:
Cb solo; Orchestra (3 Fl, 2 Ob, 2 Bsn, 4 Hn, 3 Tpt, 2 Tbn, 2 Tba, Perc, Strings).

MS Description:
Holograph, pencil on paper. *Location:* Boston Public Library.

Editorial Notes:
MS ends after 4 measures.

Group III: Works for Brass Ensemble

Group III.A: Works for Concert Band

III.A.1 A Short Symphony for Brass and Percussion (Op. 103)

Date: 20 Jul 1979 in Reading, MA ("Barn") *Duration:* 11'00"
Dedication: "To my wife Marlene Marie"
Commission: [National Endowment for the Arts]
Publisher: MMC Publications

Movement(s):
♩=42

Instrumentation:
4 Hn, 4 C Tpt, 4 Tbn, 2 Tba, 4 Timp, 3 Perc.

Sketches:
24 drafts of the opening. 2 drafts of mm. 9–10. 1 draft of mm. 19–20. 1 draft of mm. 32–33.

MS Description:
Holograph with printed name, ink on vellum. *Location:* Lost.*

Editorial Notes:
*A photocopy of the MS survives and is stored at Boston Public Library. Commission taken from McKinley's notes.

Performance History:
† 14 Nov 1979: Jordan Hall, New England Conservatory of Music, Boston, MA
The Conservatory Wind Ensemble, Frank L. Battisti, Cond.

Program Notes:
"Completed within the last year, *A Short Symphony for Brass and Percussion* offers the listener an unusual sound experience. On top of a subdued presence of sound, one hears constantly shifting tonal colors and activity centers, as the musical 'action' moves back and forth between families of instruments, as well as individual players, each part displaying its own character before dissolving back into the thick audio mist.

"The piece may be heard as one large crescendo, beginning quite calmly, reaching several points of lesser arrival along the way, but moving overall towards the final concentrated explosion of energy."
—William Thomas McKinley (© 1979), from 14 Nov 1979 program.

III.A.2a Scarlet [Version I]

Date: [Mar 1984] *Duration:* 10'30"
Dedication: "to Bob Brookmeyer and Mel Lewis"
Commission: [Mel Lewis]
Publisher: MMC Publications

Movement(s):
Lyrical 3/4, rich and floating, lazy (♩=76)

Instrumentation:
Big Band (Fl/2 Sop Sax/2 Alt Sax, 2 Fl/2 Ten Sax/2 Cl, Bar Sax/BCl, Hn, 4 Tpt, 2 Tbn, 2 BTbn, Dr, Pno, Cb).

MS Description:
Holograph, pencil on paper. *Location:* Boston Public Library.

Editorial Notes:
Date taken from McKinley's notes. Commission information from the composer.

Performance History:
† 24 Apr 1984: Jordan Hall, New England Conservatory of Music, Boston, MA
The Conservatory Big Band, Miroslav Vitous, Cond.
30 Oct 1984: Jordan Hall, New England Conservatory of Music, Boston, MA
The Medium Rare Big Band, Pat Hollenbeck, Cond.

Bibliography:
Driver, Paul. "Cornucopia Sampled at New England Conservatory." *The Boston Globe* 26 Apr 1984: 71.

III.A.2b Scarlet [Version II]

Date: [ca. 1985] *Duration:* 10'30"
Dedication: "to Bob Brookmeyer and Mel Lewis"
Commission: [Mel Lewis]
Publisher: MMC Publications

Movement(s):
Lyrical 3/4, rich and floating, lazy (♩=76)

Instrumentation:
Cl solo; Big Band (Fl/Sop Sax/Alt Sax, 2 Fl/2 Ten Sax/2 Cl, Bar Sax/BCl, Hn, 4 Tpt, 2 Tbn, BTbn, Dr, Pno, Gtr, Cb).

MS Description:
Holograph, pencil on paper. *Location:* Owned by Richard Stoltzman.
Markings: Cover page: "N.B. This score has been adapted for performance with Richard Stoltzman and the Woody Herman Band. Clarinet replaces Alto/Sop Sax I and is given most solos, with the exception of piano solo at [rehearsal] G. Guitar replaces Trombone III (hence Tbn IV becomes the sole bs. tbn part) and at times covers Alto I lines as well. All changes are indicated in this score."

Editorial Notes:
MS is a photocopy of the copyist's fair copy with changes made by the composer in pencil. Dating based on date of last original version performance. Commission and premiere performance information from the composer.

Performance History:
[† ca. 1985: Location unknown
Richard Stoltzman, Cl; Woody Herman Band.]

See also: Rhapsody for Solo Harp and Concert Band (II.J.1)

Group III.B: Works for Brass Quintet

III.B.1 Canzona for Brass Quintet

Date: 19–24 Dec 1975 in Manchester, MA ("Carriage House") *Duration:* 4'12"
Dedication: "To the spirit of..."
Publisher: MMC Publications

Movement(s):
Dots: Delicate and introspective (♪= 147)
Squares: As fast as possible
[Canzona:] As fast as possible, as silver winds

Instrumentation:
Hn, 2 C Tpt, Tbn, BTbn soli.

Sketches:
24 drafts of the opening of III. 76 unidentified drafts.

MS Description:
Holograph with printed name, ink on vellum. *Location:* Boston Public Library.

Editorial Notes:
In the 8 Nov 1982 performance, the *Canzona for Brass Quintet* was performed with the *Brass Quintet* (III.B.2) under the title *Brass Music.*

Performance History:
† 8 Nov 1982: Jordan Hall, New England Conservatory of Music, Boston, MA
Krista Smith, Hn; Paul Perfetti, Jonah Rabinowitz, Tpt; Robert Blossom, Tbn; James Messbauer, BTbn; Theodore Antoniou, Cond.

Bibliography:
Dyer, Richard. "Opposites in Harmony." *The Boston Globe* 10 Nov 1982: 67.

Program Notes:
For 8 Nov 1982 notes see *Brass Quintet* (III.B.2).

III.B.2 Brass Quintet

Date: [ca. 25–31 Dec 1975] in Manchester, MA ("Carriage House") *Dur.:* 3'26"
Publisher: MMC Publications

Movement(s):
I. Overture: ♪=52
II. Sinfonia: 𝅗𝅥=52

Instrumentation:
Hn, 2 Tpt, Tbn, BTbn soli.

Sketches:
1 draft of I/16. 5 drafts of the opening of II. 1 draft of II/13.

MS Description:
Holograph with printed name, ink on vellum. *Location:* Boston Public Library.

Editorial Notes:
Program of 8 Nov 1982 and McKinley's notes indicate composition in 1975. Sketches for this work and *Canzona* were intermingled, but those for *Canzona* were decidedly earlier. Therefore, this work was most likely composed immediately after *Canzona*, but before the

end of 1975. In the 8 Nov 1982 performance, the *Canzona for Brass Quintet* was performed with the *Brass Quintet* under the title *Brass Music.*

Performance History:

† 8 Nov 1982: Jordan Hall, New England Conservatory of Music, Boston, MA
Krista Smith, Hn; Paul Perfetti, Jonah Rabinowitz, Tpt; Robert Blossom, Tbn; James Messbauer, BTbn; Theodore Antoniou, Cond.

Bibliography:

Dyer, Richard. "Opposites in Harmony." *The Boston Globe* 10 Nov 1982: 67.

Program Notes:

"Traditionally, the brass quintet consists of two trumpets, French horn, trombone, and tuba. During the time of composing my *Brass Music,* I recall choosing an additional trombone as substitute for the tuba because of what I then perceived to be its contemporary capabilities—those of a more extended dynamic and soloistic range, a greater accuracy of attack and ensemble response, and an overall agility and homogeneity throughout the entire range and sound spectrum. The additional trombone thus stands in much the same relationship to the entire group as the English horn does as Stockhausen's wind quintet *Zeitmasse,* wherein the English horn substitutes for the French horn to effect, ostensibly, the execution of gestures which, due to extreme speeds and disjunct leaps, demand maximum agility and split second instrumental interplay and response. (I might add that since then my judgment and perception in this matter has tempered somewhat, and I have composed a large number of brass works including a Brass Symphony in which the tuba parts display great virtuosity and figure prominently in the overall dramatic intensity.)

"Nevertheless, the intense musical energy in the *Brass Music,* the polyphonic complexity and the complete equality among the instrumental parts, owe their fundamental inspiration to these notions; and perhaps there is a slight gain in the overall balance and homogeneous fluency brought about by the presence of the second trombone.

"*Brass Music* consists of five principal sections: Overture, Sinfonia, two pieces 'Dots' and 'Squares' (and coda), and Canzona. They were originally designed to be played in any order or as separate movements. For this performance I have chosen the order which to me creates the best dramatic balance and continuity. In one sense what I have constructed perhaps suggests a kind of eclectic Suite or Divertimento, but nonetheless there are clear connections among the movements which are often characterized in extroverted, festive, and brilliantly 'brassy' idiomatic figuration and gesture. And within individual movements, particular emphasis is often given to specialized coloristic detail, for example, the arpeggiated overtones or harmonics at the beginning of 'Dots.' Most important, the Overture, Sinfonia, and Canzona have 'spiritual' connections to their historical antecedents. The voluminous and extroverted expressive world which I perceive as an indigenous quality in early brass music was a constant stimulus to my musical invention, and I paid particular attention to the sonorous world of Gabrieli and the extent to which he explored the 'pure' sound in relation to the contemporary world of the late Renaissance. This perspective was far more significant to me than adopting formal analogs from a neo-classic perspective which could only hope to echo or mimic an archaic icon from ages already past. Quite to the contrary, the formal ideas in *Brass Music* are intricate and their understanding demands great attention to the score. The movements are not of great length, however, and this helps to balance the density and gestural intricacy elaborated in the polyphonic webbing and formal development. The listener should find this balance satisfying and be able to discern the true 'spirit' of the music on first hearing. In some way, all of my music, from simple jazz to the complex realms of esoterica, has a common

bond—that of improvisation. And despite the challenge in listening to polyphonic music—of any kind and of any epoch—I would wish my music to retain, after all the details are mastered, a genuine 'spirit' of improvisation in which all the musical ideas are revealed anew in an unending rebirth and stream of invention. It is this last point towards which the musical expression contained within *Brass Music* seeks its prime fulfillment."
—William Thomas McKinley (© 1994), from his notes.

III.B.3 Dedication Overture for Brass Quintet

Date: 1 May 1985 *Duration:* 3'30"
Dedication: "To the College of Liberal Arts and Sciences and the Department of English of Suffolk University on the occasion of the retirement of Dr. Stanley Vogel, Dr. Edward Clark, and Dr. Mary Mahoney."
Commission: [Suffolk University]
Publisher: MMC Publications

Movement(s):
Maestoso (♩=152)

Instrumentation:
Hn, 2 Tpt, Tbn, Tba.

MS Description:
Holograph with signature, pencil on vellum. *Location:* Boston Public Library.

Editorial Notes:
Commission information from *AMC Newsletter* 27(Summer 1985), no. 3: 10

Performance History:
† 10 May 1985: Suffolk University, Boston, MA
Huntington Brass Quintet.

III.B.4 [Concert Music for Brass Quintet]

Date: Oct 1985 *Duration:* 12'00"
Commission: [Eroica Brass]
Publisher: MMC Publications

Movement(s):
Moderato (♩=104)

Instrumentation:
2 Tpt, Hn, Tbn, BTbn soli.

MS Description:
Holograph with signature, pencil on vellum. *Location:* Boston Public Library.

Editorial Notes:
Title and commission taken from the parts.

Performance History:
† 5 Jun 1986: Merkin Concert Hall, New York, NY
The Eroica Brass Quintet (Charles Olsen, Donald Barchelder, Tpt; Susan Panny, Hn; James Becker, Richard Ford, Tbn).
8 Feb 1987: St. Ignatius Episcopal Church, New York, NY
The Eroica Brass Quintet.
8 Feb 1987: Merkin Concert Hall, New York, NY
The Eroica Brass Quintet.

Bibliography:
Holland, Bernard. "Music: Works by McKinley." *The New York Times* 7 Jun 1986.
Lifchitz, Max. "Composer of Note: William Thomas McKinley." *Living Music* 4(Fall 1986), no. 1: 2.

III.B.5 Overture for Brass Quintet

Date: 20 Nov 1987 in Reading, MA ("Lells") *Duration:* 10'00"
Dedication: "to the Eroica Brass Quintet"
Commission: [Eroica Brass Quintet]
Publisher: MMC Publications

Movement(s):
Giubilante (♩=120)

Instrumentation:
Hn, 2 C Tpt, Tbn, BTbn soli.

Sketches:
1 incomplete draft (earlier title: *Herbst*). 4 drafts of the opening (one in short score). 1 draft of mm. 293–96.

MS Description:
Holograph with signature, pencil on paper. *Location:* Boston Public Library.

Editorial Notes:
Commission information from the composer.

Performance History:
† 9 Dec 1987: Merkin Concert Hall, New York, NY
Eroica Brass Quintet (Charles Olsen, Donald Barchelder, Tpt; Susan Panny, Hn; James Becker, Richard Ford, Tbn).

III.B.6 New Year's Carol

Date: 29 Dec 1987 *Duration:* 3'15"
Dedication: "to the Eroica Brass Quintet"
Commission: [Eroica Brass Quintet]
Publisher: MMC Publications

Movement(s):
Allegro, gioiosamente (♩.=104)

Instrumentation:
Hn, 2 C Tpt, Tbn, BTbn soli.

MS Description:
Holograph with printed name, pencil on vellum. *Location:* Boston Public Library.

Editorial Notes:
Commission taken from McKinley's notes.

Performance History:
† 7 Jan 1988: Carnegie Hall, New York, NY
Eroica Brass Quintet (Charles Olsen, Donald Barchelder, Tpt; Susan Panny, Hn; James Becker, Richard Ford, Tbn).

Bibliography:
Kimmelman, Michael. "Concert: McKinley Pieces by American Symphony." *The New York Times* 9 Jan 1988: 12.
Stevens, Denis. "New York." *Musical Times* April, 1988.

Group IV: String Quintets, Quartets, and Trios

Group IV.A: Flute Quintets

IV.A.1 Quintet Romantico

Date: 13 May 1987 *Duration:* 29'00"
Dedication: "to Bob Stallman and the Marblehead Chamber Players"
Commission: [Robert Stallman]
Publisher: MMC Publications

Movement(s):
I. Andante con moto (♩=88)
II. Prestissimo e vivace (♩=138)
III. Largo (♩=44)

Instrumentation:
Fl, 2 Vln, Vla, Vcl soli.

MS Description:
Holograph with signature, pencil on vellum. *Location:* Boston Public Library.

Editorial Notes:
Commission taken from McKinley's notes.

Performance History:
† 2 Aug 1987: Marblehead Chamber Music Festival, Marblehead, MA
Robert Stallman, Fl; The Muir Quartet (Bayla Keyes, Lynn Chang, Vln; Steven Ansell, Vla; Michael Reynolds, Vcl).
[† (Boston] 19 Oct 1987: Jordan Hall, New England Conservatory of Music, Boston, MA
Robert Stallman, Fl; The Muir Quartet.
† (New York) 9 Dec 1987: Merkin Concert Hall, New York, NY
Robert Stallman, Fl; Alexander String Quartet (Eric Pritchard, Frederick Lifsitz, Vln; Paul Yarbrough, Vla; Sandy Wilson, Vcl).

Bibliography:
Dyer, Richard. "Heiss-McKinley 'Doubles' at NEC." *The Boston Globe* 20 Oct 1987: 73.
Lifsitz, Frederick. "Artists on Repertoire." *Chamber Music* 6(Fall 1989), no. 3: 11.

Program Notes:
"My *Quintet Romantico* was written specifically for Robert Stallman and the Muir Quartet. It was premiered on the Marblehead Chamber Music Festival this past August.... It is a large framed romantic work in which extended developments and probing themes are continually woven together. Autobiographical in nature, the 'Quintet' firmly asserts extended tonalities, supporting a varied range of surfaces from the static to the highly active with varied rhythmic modulations."
—William Thomas McKinley (© 1987), from 19 Oct 1987 and 9 Dec 1987 programs.

Group IV.B: Clarinet Quintets

IV.B.1 From Opera No. 2 for B♭ Clarinet and String Quartet

Date: 20 Feb 1976 in Manchester, MA ("Carriage House") *Duration:* 30'00"
Dedication: "Written for Richard Stoltzman" and "to the spirit of..."*
Commission: [National Endowment for the Arts]
Publisher: MMC Publications

Movement(s):
With great expanse, noble and with penetrating command (♩=40)

Instrumentation:
Cl, 2 Vln, Vla, Vcl soli.

MS Description:
Holograph with printed name, pencil on vellum. *Location:* Boston Public Library.

Editorial Notes:
*McKinley's program notes add an additional dedication to "the members of Tashi." Commission taken from McKinley's notes. Notes also state that "*Paintings No. 3* and *From Opera No. 2* are considered as a pair." Premiere performance date from *AMC Newsletter* 20(Fall, 1978), no. 4: 18, advertisement, and 5 Mar 1978 article.

Performance History:
[† 13 May 1978: The 92nd Street YM-YWCA, New York, NY
Tashi (Richard Stoltzman, Cl; Ida Kavafian and Theodore Arm, Vln; Il-Hwan Bae, Vla; Fred Sherry, Vcl).]
16 Mar 1979: Crouse College Auditorium, Syracuse, NY
Tashi.
[† (Boston)] 25 Apr 1981: Jordan Hall, New England Conservatory of Music, Boston, MA
Tashi.

Bibliography:
Kozinn, Allan. "How to Win Prominence Playing the Clarinet." *The New York Times* 5 Mar 1978: D 15, D 20.
Yeiser, Patricia. "Tashi Offers First Hearing." *Syracuse Post Standard* 17 Mar 1980: B 7.
Buell, Richard. "Tashi at BU Is Harrowing." *The Boston Globe* 27 Apr 1981: 24.
Grimes, Ev. "Yale University American Music Oral History Series: William Thomas McKinley." Oct 1986, Yale University School of Music: 75.

Program Notes:
"*From Opera No. 2* for B-flat Clarinet and String Quartet was composed in 1976 and dedicated to Richard Stoltzman and the members of Tashi. In March of 1979, it was given its world premiere by Tashi in Syracuse, New York, and has subsequently become part of the Tashi repertoire in addition to several other of my chamber works: *For One* for solo clarinet, Quartet for piano, violin, cello and clarinet, and a second clarinet quintet, [and] *Paintings No. 3*....

"The listener will probably wonder about the meaning of the title *From Opera*. It is the second work in a series, and, therefore, I suggest that the listener regard this score as an instrumental mono-drama. It is composed in one movement, but its structural outlines encompass a much larger dimension or formal shape. The duration of the movement is about thirty minutes, and throughout that time frame unfolds a wide panoply of dramatic confrontations and resolutions. In the early going, the clarinet acts principally as antagonist, elaborated by numerous interpolations, cadenzas, and recitative-like sections. The recitatives particularly, as in traditional opera, thrust the dramatic tensions forward, and the other sections help to reinforce the forward motion with a continual web of virtuosic and *bel canto*-like linear weaving.

"As the work evolves there is a subtle metamorphosis that takes place and the clarinet's dramatic role is changed from antagonist to protagonist, signaled by the appearance of instrumental arias and arietta-like passages. The Arioso, arietta qualities are particularly evident during the last third of the work's progress when one becomes aware of a gradual *poco a poco* retard and a general calming of tensions. The dramatic confrontations which are developed early on through the middle-later stages are ultimately resolved at that point, and the work ends quietly and with tranquillity.

"Throughout the entirety of the work, the strings function in several ways: to react against the antagonist in the manner of dialogue; to provide a support in the manner of texture, harmony, and density; and to put forth their own manner of virtuosic independence which strengthens the overall tonal 'effect' resulting from the timbral integration of wind against string sound.

"In a simpler sense, the clarinet represents vocal attributes (both cantabile and melismatic), and the strings represent the orchestra. And I have tried to transfer into instrumental form by analogy, the dramatic powers intrinsic to opera. This was a demanding task, but one which has intrigued me for many years. The great operas of Mozart, Verdi, Wagner, and Berg are my spiritual precedents—but I do not invite comparison on that level. My personal vision is continually nourished by the study of the great works which abound both past and present, and, in my humble judgment, the contemporary composer must strive to discover the analogies, metaphors, and other forms of relationships which do in fact exist in the tradition."

—William Thomas McKinley (© 1981), from 25 Apr 1981 program.

See also notes for *Paintings No. 3* (IV.B.2).

IV.B.2 Paintings No. 3 for B♭ Clarinet and String Quartet (op. 70)

Date: Mar 1976 in Manchester, MA ("Carriage House") *Duration:* 9'39"
Dedication: "Written for Richard Stoltzman" and "...and to the spirit of | in all humanity | stirring, | yielding, | melting, | violins rendering | to | all clarinets | and | love...charity | above all | men...."
Commission: [Richard Stoltzman]
Publisher: MMC Publications

Movement(s):	*Instrumentation:*
I. Worlds: With wildness and violent passion (as fast as possible)	Cl, 2 Vln, Vla, Vcl soli.
II. Dusk: With some flow (♩=40)	
III. Coins: Lilting, with air and purity (♩.=52)	
IV. Dust: With complete flow, molto legato (♩=40+)	
V. Light: Frozen, motion suspended (𝅗𝅥=30)	
VI. March Day: ♩=60+	
VII. Coda: As fast as possible	

Sketches:
25 drafts of the opening of I. 15 drafts of the opening of II. 1 draft of the opening of IV. 2 drafts of the opening of VI. 1 draft of the opening of VII. 1 draft of VII/9–11. 2 unidentified drafts.

MS Description:
Holograph with printed name, pencil on vellum. *Location:* Boston Public Library.

Editorial Notes:
Commission taken from McKinley's program notes. Confirmation of 4 Mar 1982 as premiere performance from McKinley's notes. Notes also state that "*Paintings No. 3* and *From Opera No. 2* are considered as a pair."

Performance History:
[†] 4 Mar 1982: Jordan Hall, New England Conservatory of Music, Boston, MA
Conservatory Contemporary Ensemble, John Heiss, Cond.
7 Mar 1982: Symphony Hall, Springfield, MA
Conservatory Contemporary Ensemble, John Heiss, Cond.

Program Notes:
"*Paintings No. 3* was commissioned by Richard Stoltzman as one work in a series of compositions for clarinet combined with various instrumental combinations, including two concertos for clarinet and orchestra, two clarinet quintets, a Tashi Quartet, and numerous other chamber works and solo pieces. *Paintings No. 3* is scored for B♭ clarinet and string quartet and is the second of the two clarinet quintets. The first clarinet quintet is entitled *From Opera No. 2* and was given its world premiere in Syracuse, New York, in April of 1979 by members of Tashi with Mr. Stoltzman as soloist. Subsequently, *From Opera No. 2* has been performed by that ensemble throughout the United States and Canada and most recently at Jordan Hall, Boston, in May [*sic*] of 1981.

"*Paintings No. 3* was begun immediately following the completion of *From Opera No. 2,* and it displays considerable formal-dramatic contrasts when compared with its predecessor. Although both works undoubtedly possess some characteristics in common—a carry over from the energy of one into the other, and even perhaps some gestural flashbacks—the differences far outweigh the similarities. *From Opera No. 2* is a work in one movement, lasting nearly forty minutes. It makes extreme demands on performers and listeners, challenging their aural skills, memory perceptions, and powers of attention and concentration. It extends the thresholds of listening and performing to maximum levels of skill and endurance. Antithetically, *Paintings No. 3* is less formidable in its demands. It is a set of five movements and a coda, and each movement is composed in epigrammatic fashion, revealing a separate ethos or spirit. However, the epigrammatic style of *Paintings No. 3* should not invite comparison with the aphoristic principles and compositional elements at work in the music of Anton Webern. Rather, *Paintings No. 3* portrays musical ideas and musical developments of a nature far more rhetorical in kind, and it suggests conceptual characteristics which are peculiar to or indigenous in the Romantic tone poems (or 'paintings') composed throughout the early-middle years of the nineteenth century.

"The movements of *Paintings No. 3* are titled 'Worlds,' 'Dusk,' 'Coins,' 'Dust,' 'March Day,' and 'Coda.' Each is clearly designed of simple formal construction, although an improvisational character prevails which is in perfect keeping with the overall manner of Romantic gesturing and rhythmic movement throughout the work's entirety. The 'affect' of each movement is created with conscious effort to portray an individualized tone portrait or 'painting.' These 'affects' are not conceived incidentally and are genuine motivators of the musical invention, continually nourishing the compositional process and the composer's creative habitus.

"The concept of the tone portrait has its roots in the Baroque and derives from the *Doctrine of the Affections*. This doctrine, although open to subjective interpretation and speculation, implies that within a single musical movement (or entire composition), one 'affect' or character will dominate and undergo little or no significant transformation or contrast. The listener should find it easy to understand this particular parallel, and the 'affects' in *Paintings No. 3* should be readily sensed, if not at first entirely understood. The *real* difficulties for the listener lie in the abstract realm of rhetoric and syntax. *Paintings No. 3* reflects many characteristics of contemporary musical language. Its rhetoric is contrapuntal and virtuosically complex, and its syntax is, for the want of a better term, pantonal, although some ears might hear it as 'free' atonality. Rhetorical complexity and in particular syntactical complexity will not be difficult to fathom for those whose musical instincts and apprehensions are more learned and refined. But to those listeners who do find difficulty comprehending (and apprehending) contemporary musical rhetoric and syntax, it must be emphatically stated that the specific kinds of contemporary musical problems which have to do with aural perception, understanding, etc., are not indigenous to *Paintings No. 3* alone—rather, they are indigenous to our present 'state of the art' irrespective of one's compositional 'personality' or style. A key to understanding contemporary musical language lies in repeated hearings and sincere effort on the part of the interested listener. 'Lend me your ears' is a most apt proposition and one too infrequently adopted among musical listeners. *Paintings No. 3* attempts to mediate these numerous problems and presents its various 'affects' (or paintings) in the form of separate and relatively brief movements, thereby eliminating the aspect of extended duration and the ensuing difficulties that this aspect imposes upon powers of concentration. The separation and individualization of movements thus helps the listener (and performer) to gather concentration, to absorb mentally the events transpired, and to prepare expectations for the aural experience of the next musical painting. But it should be stressed once again that each movement is a self-contained organism and that *all* of the movements in *Paintings No. 3* are extremely rich, providing a nearly constant web of contrapuntal complexity and an intricate maze of temporal transformations and coloristic details—brilliantly engaging the individual performer as well as the entire ensemble. In addition, it should be kept in mind that *Paintings No. 3* is above all a clarinet quintet. The role of the clarinet is one which acts both as a catalyst for the ensemble and as an antagonist pitted against the ensemble. The differentiation of color—string against wind sound—is yet another important characteristic, and it adds to the already brilliant coloristic details which are musically embroidered within the string parts. And finally as in all of my works which include the B♭ clarinet, the dark, brooding, richly contemplative and transcendental sound of Richard Stoltzman's clarinet reigns supreme in my musical imagination."
—William Thomas McKinley (© 1994), from his notes.

See also: All the Things You Are (X.B.3)

Group IV.C: String Quartets

IV.C.1 String Quartet No. 1

Date: [1959] in [Pittsburgh, PA (Carnegie-Mellon Univ.)] *Duration:* 16'31"
Publisher: MMC Publications

Movement(s):
I. ♩=120–126
II. Andante [(♪=60)]

Instrumentation:
2 Vln, Vla, Vcl soli

MS Description:
Holograph with printed name, pencil on paper. *Location:* Boston Public Library.

Editorial Notes:
Fair copy is a McKinley holograph (ink on vellum, printed name). In the MS, mm. 60–66 of the second movement are unwritten. Metronome mark for the second movement obtained from the composer. Date taken from binding of fair copy. Location of composition and performance history from McKinley's notes.

Performance History:
[† May 1960: Carnegie-Mellon University, Pittsburgh, PA
Phillips String Quartet.]
[Jun 1960: Young Man's Hebrew Association, Pittsburgh, PA
Phillips String Quartet.]

Bibliography:
Grimes, Ev. "Yale University American Music Oral History Series: William Thomas McKinley." Oct 1986, Yale University School of Music: 29–30

IV.C.2 Galaxy (A Short Sonata for String Quartet) [String Quartet No. 2]

Date: Dec 1973 in Reading, MA ("Linnea Lane") *Duration:* 12'31"
Dedication: "to my wife"
Publisher: MMC Publications

Movement(s):
[One untitled movement.]

Instrumentation:
2 Vln, Vla, Vcl soli.

MS Description:
Holograph with printed name, ink on vellum. *Location:* Boston Public Library.
Markings: Dedication page: "Energy through | self...with | empty shells... | ...awaken... | on fire... | ...yes again...."

Performance History:
† 27 Apr 1990: Jordan Hall, New England Conservatory of Music, Boston, MA
New England String Quartet (Ellen Jewett, Heidi Yenney, Vln; Holly Barnes, Vla; Kris Yenney, Vcl).

Program Notes:
"It has long been my desire to have *Galaxy* premiered. And frankly, after seventeen years, I wasn't counting on it. *Galaxy* represents one of my most substantial statements from that period just preceding my better known *Painting* series. *Galaxy* represents in a single

concentrated movement the major concerns of its day. The piece offers complex richness and multiplicity of detail, explosive contrasts, a high level of dissonance set against extended and transformed modern age sonorities, as well as clearly audible vestiges of tonality."
—William Thomas McKinley (© 1990), from 27 Apr 1990 program.

IV.C.3 Quiet

Date: [1973] *Duration:* 12'14"
Publisher: Unpublished

Movement(s):
Quasi ad libitum, religioso (♩=52)

Instrumentation:
2 Vln, Vla, Vcl soli.

Sketches:
23 drafts of the opening (earlier titles: *Quiet Memories; Stasis*).

MS Description:
Holograph, pencil on paper. *Location:* Boston Public Library.

Editorial Notes:
MS is a first draft, written partially in short score. Contains many corrections and additions (some in red pencil). Labeling of *Stasis* drafts with a roman numeral "I" may indicate that McKinley's original conception was for a multi-movement work. Date appears on one of the drafts of the opening of the work.

IV.C.4 Fantasia Concertante for String Quartet [String Quartet No. 4]

Date: 21 Aug 1976 *Duration:* 16'30"
Dedication: "To the Sequoia Quartet" and "to the spirit of..."*
Commission: The Sequoia Quartet and the Naumberg Foundation
Publisher: Margun Music Inc.

Movement(s):
Delicate, then suddenly brilliant (♪=48+)

Instrumentation:
2 Vln, Vla, Vcl soli.

MS Description:
Holograph with printed name, ink on vellum. *Location:* Boston Public Library.
Markings: *Page ii: Additional dedication: "a particular note of affection for Yoko Matsuda. Her confidence in my work is a constant source of deep inspiration and her dedication in the performance of Contemporary Music is beyond praise.... It is to the spirit of all musicians of her stature that my work is ultimately dedicated.... To the adventurers, the open-minded artists whose work provides the nucleus of our culture—a world of culture of which Yoko is a devoted member...."

Editorial Notes:
4 and 6 Apr 1977 performance information from a 1 May 1977 letter from James Dunham to McKinley regarding the Sequoia Quartet's concert tour. See also *Sinfonia for String Quartet* [String Quartet No. 3] (IV.C.5).

Performance History:
† 8 Mar 1977: Alice Tully Hall, New York, NY
The Sequoia String Quartet (Yoko Matsuda, Miwako Wantanabe, Vln; James Dunham, Vla; Robert Martin, Vcl).

[† (Los Angeles) 4 Apr 1977: Hall unknown, Los Angeles, CA
The Sequoia String Quartet.]
[6 Apr 1977: California Institute of the Arts, Valencia, CA
The Sequoia String Quartet.]

Recording(s):
GM Recordings: GM 2014, ©1985 (LP)
Sequoia String Quartet

Bibliography:
Kimball, Robert. "Sequoia Quartet Lean and Strong." *The New York Post* 9 Mar 1977: 42.
Zakariasen, Bill. "Sequoia Strings Aren't Wooden." *The New York Daily News* 10 Mar 1977: 75.
Rockwell, John. "Sequoia String Quartet." *The New York Times* 13 Mar 1977: 59.
Oja, Carol J. "Salute to GunMar." *Newsletter of the Institute for Studies in American Music* 16(May 1987), no. 2: 13.

Program Notes:
"My earliest acquaintance with music of the twentieth century was the Bartók six string quartets. As a young student in the composition classes of Nikolai Lopatnikoff, to whose memory this work is dedicated on the spiritual level, I was immediately attracted to the sensuous surface of Bartók's quartets, and ever since they have remained as a constant source of inspiration. The *Fantasia Concertante* attempts to continue forward the discoveries of sound and color in which Bartók had a deep interest. In no way do I consciously quote from Bartók. I have tried to use the coloristic resources of the string quartet in a transcendental manner—to carry them one step further—to expand the implications inherent in them.

"And yet there is another aspect of composition which I did not learn from Bartók. It concerns jazz, improvisation of all orders and genres and it too remains a vital part of my earliest musical training and recollection. It is fortunate to be able to experience both worlds of expression. Somehow this seems to be a large part of the American experience. In the *Fantasia Concertante* I have tried to explore the high levels of energy and intensity characteristic of contemporary Black music and weld them together within a very controlled structural framework.

"The gestures, rapid transformation of time and movement are combined within a pitch world of pantonality and the 'pure' color content about which I spoke before. All of this in search for my own personal language and style. I do not seek eclecticism nor collage.

"There are fixed structural elements. The overall form of the *Fantasia Concertante* is Rondo. Much the same as *Jeux* of Claude Debussy. The opening material returns four times, and throughout the entire quartet there are motivic shapes which likewise return. The minor second and minor seventh predominate, particularly in the solo cello and first violin sections.

"On the global level, the title of the work applies—Fantasy, the continual transformation, mutation, and evolving moment to moment continuity of events, and Concertante, emphasis on the virtuosic, concerto-like gestures of the individual instruments. Within this gamut I have tried to awaken moments of 'violence,' 'wildness,' 'explosion' and moments of 'introspection,' 'prayer,' and 'spiritual' meditation. Ultimately, the listener should attempt to partake in a dramatic experience allowing the content to be heard intuitively and without preconceived expectation. And if not that, to enjoy the sensuous surface of pure color. I am sure all are in agreement that total aural perception is perhaps an activity which reaches fruition after *many* hearings of a new and difficult work. But if the physical and psychical impressions are immediately powerful, then the microcosmic structural elements remain but a small distance behind."

—William Thomas McKinley (© 1977), from 8 Mar 1977 program.

"McKinley's *Fantasia Concertante for String Quartet* was composed in 1976 and is the second of six works for this medium. It was commissioned by the Naumberg Foundation for the Sequoia Quartet.

"The work is, in the composer's words, 'a kind of "Rondo Concerto"—a symphonic form distilled into a one-movement quartet.' The frequent return of the opening upward wave-like gesture... signals the recurring rondo refrain, while cadenzas for cello and first violin act as form-articulating 'concertante' elements. As in most of McKinley's music of the '70s, the tempo is continually fluctuating, unstable—constantly contrasting extremely slow, almost timeless, static interpolation with fast passages of great virtuosic brilliance.

"Despite the generally atonal, fully chromatic language of the work, its tonal harmonic basis derives from the earliest piano styles and voicings of Fats Waller and Art Tatum to those of Richie Bierach and Chick Corea. In a real sense McKinley is here composing with all 'twelve tones by ear, using the natural qualities of the chromatic scale,' and thus linking up with both Bach and jazz.

"The work is also a virtuoso tribute to the Sequoia Quartet in the grand bravura manner of Liszt and Paganini, hence its title and its main aesthetic determinant. In this sense—and in its extended proportions and 'raw expression' (so the composer)—McKinley's *Fantasia Concertante* is a work that belongs well in the big romantic tradition."
—Gunther Schuller (© 1985), from GM Recordings GM 2014 liner notes.

IV.C.5 Sinfonia for String Quartet [String Quartet No. 3]

Date: 8 Sep 1976 in Manchester, MA ("Carriage House") *Duration:* 4'19"
Dedication: " To my wife Marlene ...and to the spirit of the baroque sinfonia"
Publisher: MMC Publications

Movement(s):
With great power and motion, exploding(♩=52)

Instrumentation:
2 Vln, Vla, Vcl soli.

Sketches:
101 drafts of the opening (earlier titles: String Quartet No. 3; *Hurricane*). 1 draft of mm. 12–13.

MS Description:
Holograph with printed name, ink on vellum. *Location:* Boston Public Library.
Markings: Page [1]: Roman numeral "I" at the top of page indicates that McKinley's original conception may have been for a multi-movement work.

Editorial Notes:
The earlier title of "String Quartet No. 3" suggests this work was begun before the *Fantasia for String Quartet* [String Quartet No. 4], temporarily put aside, and finished after the *Fantasia* was complete. Based on McKinley's program note for the *Six Movements for String Quartet* (IV.C.6), however, this later work is still considered to have come before the *Fantasia Concertante*, despite its later completion date.

IV.C.6 Six Movements for String Quartet [String Quartet No. 5]

Date: 26 May 1977 in [Manchester, MA ("Carriage House")] *Duration:* 27'40"
Dedication: "to the Sequoia Quartet"
Commission: [Massachusetts Council for the Arts]
Publisher: MMC Publications

Movement(s):
I. With power (♩=60+)
II. 𝅘𝅥𝅯=as fast as possible
III. Contemplative and yet rich (𝅗𝅥=40)
IV. Presto molto, with volcanic thrust (♩.=90+)
V. ♩=60
VI. ♪=120+

Instrumentation:
2 Vln, Vla, Vcl soli.

Sketches:
8 drafts of the opening of I. 5 drafts of the opening of II.

MS Description:
Holograph with printed name, ink on paper. *Location:* Boston Public Library.

Editorial Notes:
Location of composition and commission taken from McKinley's notes.

Performance History:
† 8 Nov 1982: Jordan Hall, New England Conservatory of Music, Boston, MA
Joel Smirnoff, Gerard Elias, Vln; Katherine Murdock, Vla; Jonathan Miller, Vcl.

Bibliography:
Dyer, Richard. "Opposites in Harmony." *The Boston Globe* 10 Nov 1982: 67.

Program Notes:
"Many of my works were written in sets or in companion fashion; for example, when I composed my Clarinet Concerto for Richard Stoltzman, I followed it immediately with a Clarinet Rhapsody; and when I composed for TASHI my quintet *From Opera*, I followed it with *Paintings No. 3*, also for the same combination. I composed in 1976 a *Fantasia Concertante* for String Quartet (which was commissioned by the Naumberg Foundation for the Sequoia Quartet) which was then followed by the work you hear this evening, *Six Movements for String Quartet*. Each of the 'companion' works (and sometimes there are three or four companions) seems to represent a lighter side of my composing style. The first works (often in one movement) are long, intense, experimental, and tend to take greater risks. In contrast, the companions (often dividing into several movements) tend to be shorter, less intense or not as sustained in their intensity; and they do not take as many musical risks in such areas as form, density, and complexity in the event-making and counterpointing. Often, the companion work refines one or two musical ideas or musical moments and hones them into one clearly defined statement. But the deepest exploration and discovery inevitably takes place in the 'mother' composition. For me, this has always been a vivid learning experience, and I have been fortunate to hear these 'sets' of works which have helped me to more fully understand the compositional process—that human activity in which perception, musical creation, and hearing are united into a single experience demanding the greatest acumen and unceasing creative labor.

"In the *Six Movements* I was able to stand back as it were (after the enormous outpouring in the *Fantasia Concertante*) and objectify and polish some of the string quartet ideas I had discovered and was attracted to in the *Fantasia*. In addition, I had in the back of my mind the wonderful Stravinsky *Three Pieces for String Quartet*. I had always admired their singularity, personal character, intense profiling, and brevity; and I wanted to explore the very same qualities coupled, of course, with my own musical visions and understanding of how it might be possible to transform and transcend those qualities to create my personal expressive world and ambiance.

"Each of the movements explores one of several specific technical and musical problems. There is a pizzicato movement, an extended chordal movement, a virtuosic gestural movement, and a more lengthy narrative movement in which elements in each movement are combined. The listener will have no difficulty in grasping the essential character or 'affect' of each; therefore, lengthy analysis of these aspects is not needed. Each movement is architecturally straight-forward, amplified by strong opening gestures and strong dramatic closures. The subsections are also clearly articulated, marked by definite cadences and points of structural rest. Perhaps most important is the accumulative effect—all of my multi-movement works tend to be more easily understood when perceived as single entities. Perhaps there is a subconscious thread—a never ending flow of temporal existence—which manifests in the artist's stream of ideas and statements. Might not the composer connect with this sub-conscious flow in order to reveal a portion or frame of this existence? Do not in fact the painter, the choreographer, the sculptor, the architect frame their expressive content in a manner which objectifies this sub-conscious temporality and stream of events? Unquestionably, the composer frames his expressive content in a temporally abstract manner. When I divide my work into sets of movements, I posit or invent a series of time frames which are indeed 'formally' separated, but never disruptive to the larger flow and the way in which that flow is able to stimulate and bring to fruition the deepest subconscious levels of musical-dramatic time. The view of the creative process generates a continuous unfolding and 'mysterious aural illumination' which strives for wholeness, uniqueness, and compositional understanding.

"My experiences in listening to Webern, for instance, have borne this out. I love the micro-moments and atomistic event making, but yet the totality seems far more significant, and Webern's jewel-like thoughts take on a grander perspective as one is more and more able to distance oneself from the 'real time' experience inherent in each musical moment. I would hope that my *Six Movements for String Quartet* might be heard in the same way—from the 'affective' experience held in each individual musical moment to the development of that experience into concrete ideas and larger formal periods which eventually evolve through the intricate webbing of the entire work and gather their full impetus, invention, and communicative power at the point of final crystallization into a single organism or a complete and monolithic musical statement—as a pyramid or large mountain viewed from great distance."

—William Thomas McKinley (© 1994), from his notes.

IV.C.7 String Quartet [No. 6]

Date: [1986] *Duration:* 21'00"
Dedication: "to the Muir Quartet"
Commission: [Massachusetts Council for the Arts]
Publisher: MMC Publications

Movement(s):
I. Seducente, tempo di valse (♩.=40)
II. Adagio molto (♩=40)
III. Presto vivace (♩=144)

Instrumentation:
2 Vln, Vla, Vcl soli.

MS Description:
Holograph with signature, pencil on vellum. *Location:* Boston Public Library.

Editorial Notes:

Date taken from McKinley's program notes. Commission taken from McKinley's notes. Premiere performance confirmed in AMC Newsletter 30(May–June 1988), no. 1: 27. Additionally, recording of 12 Oct 1986 (in McKinley's collection) is marked "second performance."

Performance History:

[†] 10 Oct 1986: Symphony Space, New York, NY
Muir String Quartet (Bayla Keyes, Lynn Chang, Vln; Steven Ansell, Vla; Michael Reynolds, Vcl).

[† (Boston)] 12 Oct 1986: Jordan Hall, New England Conservatory of Music, Boston, MA
Muir String Quartet.

24 Jan 1988: Jordan Hall, New England Conservatory of Music, Boston, MA
Boston Composers String Quartet (Clayton Hoener, James Cooke, Vln; Scott Woolweaver, Vla; Andrew Mark, Vcl).

7 Feb 1988: Weill Recital Hall, New York, NY
Boston Composers String Quartet.

28 Jan 1991: Jordan Hall, New England Conservatory of Music, Boston, MA
Boston Composers String Quartet.

7 Jun 1992: Weill Recital Hall, New York, NY
Boston Composers String Quartet.

Bibliography:

Spousta, Holly. "A Man of 'Eminently Worthwhile Music': Profiling Reading's William T. McKinley." *Reading Daily Times Chronicle* 21 Aug 1986: 1, 14A.

Grimes, Ev. "Yale University American Music Oral History Series: William Thomas McKinley." Oct 1986, Yale University School of Music: 97.

Miller, Nancy. "A Perfect Doubles Match at Jordan Hall." *The Boston Globe* 14 Oct 1986.

Page, Tim. "Concert: Red Sneakers." *The New York Times* 16 Oct 1986: C20.

Miller, Nancy. "Brilliant Quartet and New Music." *The Boston Globe* 26 Jan 1988: 68.

Holland, Bernard. "Music: Boston Quartet in 4 Composers' Works." *The New York Times* 8 Feb 1988: C15.

Gann, Kyle. "Boston Composers and Kronos Quartets: Fear of Symmetry." *The Village Voice* 23 Feb 1988: 76.

Porter, Andrew. "Musical Events: Quartets." *The New Yorker* 11 Apr 1988: 113–14.

Dyer, Richard. "Heiss and McKinley: A Study in Contrasts." *The Boston Globe* 29 Jan 1991: 60.

Program Notes:

"My String Quartet (1986) was composed for and dedicated to the Muir Quartet, who are in residence at Boston University. The work is in three movements and of large proportions. The general structure and language is Romantic and neo-tonal. I like to think of its overall character as a blend of classically constructed melodic contours, formally developed into a large narrative in which undeniably minimalistic elements are interwoven. To the listener then, this might aurally suggest a kind of developing minimalism—kaleidoscopically cast."

—William Thomas McKinley (© 1986), from 10 Oct 1986, 12 Oct 1986, 24 Jan/7 Feb 1988, and 28 Jan 1991 programs.

IV.C.8 String Quartet No. 7

Date: 1 Oct 1988 in Reading, MA ("Lells") *Duration:* 20'00"
Dedication: "to the Alexander String Quartet"
Commission: [Alexander String Quartet]
Publisher: MMC Publications

Movement(s):
I. Andante e misterioso (𝅗𝅥=52)
II. Presto e ritmico (𝅗𝅥=168)
III. Lento e tragico (♩=44)
IV. Tempo di valse (𝅗𝅥.=84)
V. Moderato e luminoso (𝅗𝅥=69)
VI. Prestissimo con fuoco e agitato (♩=240)
VII. Allegro con fuoco e brillante (♩=132)
VIII. Adagietto e misterioso (♩=92)

Instrumentation:
2 Vln, Vla, Vcl soli.

Sketches:
1 draft of the opening of I.

MS Description:
Holograph with printed name, pencil on vellum. *Location:* Boston Public Library.

Editorial Notes:
Commission information from the composer. 13 Aug 1989 performance information from BMI records.

Performance History:
† 6 Dec 1988: Theresa L. Kaufmann Concert Hall, The 92nd St. YM-YWCA, New York, NY
Alexander String Quartet (Eric Pritchard, Frederick Lifsitz, Vln; Paul Yarbrough, Vla; Sandy Wilson, Vcl).
† (Boston) 11 Dec 1988: Jordan Hall, New England Conservatory of Music, Boston, MA
Alexander String Quartet.
[13 Aug 1989: Location unknown
Alexander String Quartet.]

Bibliography:
Kozinn, Allan. "Quartet Opts for the Gritty Over the Pretty." *The New York Times* 8 Dec 1988: C16.
Miller, Margo. "Writer-Critic Smith to Edit *Opera News*." *The Boston Globe* 11 Dec 1988: B11.
Pfeifer, Ellen. "Boston Composers Spotlighted." *The Boston Herald* 13 Dec 1988: 37.
Tommasini, Anthony. "Birthday Concert for McKinley." *The Boston Globe* 13 Dec 1988: 73.
Townsend, Douglas. "New York: Alexander String Quartet: McKinley String Quartet No. 7 (Premiere)." *Musical America* 109(May 1989), no. 3: 45–46.
Lifsitz, Frederick. "Artists on Repertoire." *Chamber Music* Fall 1989: 11.

Program Notes:
"In String Quartet No. 7, each movement depicts a specific character or dramatic persona. The full technical resources of the quartet medium are explored throughout the work's entirety, and the accumulative effect is designed with a single thread of dramatic connectedness and developmental continuity. Thus, none of the eight movements can be deleted or shuffled as is often done in many smaller multi-movement works of a programmatic nature. The composer wishes the listener to concentrate principally on elements of

spontaneity, emotional expressiveness, and dramatic appeal, even though abstract elements of structure, organization and the like are indeed important. The work is dedicated to the Alexander String Quartet whose aural-personality is uniquely rich and dark and whose dedication and care in preparing my *Quintet Romantico* (premiered last year in New York City with Robert Stallman at Merkin Hall) greatly inspired the compositional devotion which I put forth in creating the eight movements of the new String Quartet No. 7."
—William Thomas McKinley (© 1988), from 6 Dec 1988 and 11 Dec 1988 programs.

IV.C.9 Greene and Blues

Date: 8 Nov 1991 in Reading, MA ("Lells") *Duration:* 5'15"
Dedication: "to the Greene Quartet"
Publisher: MMC Publications

Movement(s):
Swinging, waltz groove (𝅗𝅥.=50)

Instrumentation:
2 Vln, Vla, Vcl soli.

Sketches:
1 draft of the opening.

MS Description:
Holograph with signature, pencil on paper. *Location:* Boston Public Library.

IV.C.10 [String Quartet No. 8]

Date: 2 Mar 1992 in Reading, MA ("Lells") *Duration:* 25'20"
Commission: [Silesian String Quartet]
Publisher: MMC Publications

Movement(s):
I. Maestoso e tempestoso (♩=112)
II. Lento e appass[ionato] (♩=42)
III. Scherzando e tumultuoso (𝅗𝅥.=120)

Instrumentation:
2 Vln, Vla, Vcl soli.

MS Description:
Holograph with printed name, pencil on vellum. *Location:* Boston Public Library.

Editorial Notes:
Title taken from parts and cover page of fair copy. Commission information from the composer.

Performance History:
[†] 25 Apr 1993: Jordan Hall, New England Conservatory of Music, Boston, MA
Silesian String Quartet (Marek Mos, Poitr Janosik, Vln; Arkadiusz Kubica, Vla; Lukasz Syrnicki, Vcl).
†(New York) 26 Apr 1993: Merkin Concert Hall, New York, NY
Silesian String Quartet.

Bibliography:
Hampton, Aubrey. "Master Musicians Collective." *Organica Quarterly* 12(Autumn 1993), no. 45: 10–11, 24–25.

Program Notes:
"String Quartet No. 8 integrates the polarities of technique and psyche into a holistic musical utterance communicating my personal vision and testimony to the listener's mind and feelings."
—William Thomas McKinley (© 1993), from 26 Apr 1993 program.

IV.C.11 String Quartet No. 9 (Moments Musicals)

Date: 2 May 1992 in Reading, MA ("Lells") *Duration:* 15'00"
Dedication: "to my friend James Dunham and the Cleveland Quartet"
Commission: [The Cleveland Quartet]
Publisher: MMC Publications

Movement(s):
I. Grandioso (♩=80)
II. Presto (𝅗𝅥=132)
III. Largo (𝅗𝅥=58)
IV. Tempo di valse (𝅗𝅥.=72)
V. Adagio e dramatico (♩=66)
VI. Scherzando e sardonico (♩=152)
VII. Prestissimo e volante (♩.=84)
VIII. Lamento e triste (♩=44)
IX. Tempestoso e sardonico (𝅗𝅥=72)
X. Tempo di marcia (♩=120)
XI. Scherzando e giubilante (𝅗𝅥.=112)

Instrumentation:
2 Vln, Vla, Vcl soli.

Sketches:
2 drafts of the opening of I, one of which is found on the back of page 12 of the *Silent Whispers* MS. 1 draft of the opening of VIII.

MS Description:
Holograph with signature, pencil on paper. *Location:* Boston Public Library.

Editorial Notes:
Commission information from the composer.

IV.C.12 Der Baum des Lebens (The Tree of Life)*

Date: [26 Aug 1993] in [Reading, MA ("Lells")] *Duration:* 15'00"
Dedication: "an Hildegard Modlmayr"
Commission: [Hildegard Modlmayr]
Publisher: MMC Publications

Movement(s):
I. Rilke–Sonnette an Orpheus:
Grandioso (♩=80)
II. Bobrowski–Der Muschelbläser: Tempo di valse (𝅗𝅥.=72)
III. Celan–Du liegst hinaus: Scherzando e sardonico (♩=152)
IV. Modlmayr–Europa: Lamento e triste (♩=44)

Instrumentation:
2 Vln, Vla, Vcl soli.

Sketches:
See String Quartet No. 9 (IV.C.11).

MS Description:
Holograph with signature, pencil on paper. *Location:* Boston Public Library.

Editorial Notes:
*An arrangement of String Quartet No. 9 (IV.C.11). See also *Der Lebensbaum* (IX.B.10). Based on poems by Rainer Maria Rilke (1922), Johannes Bobrowski (1958), Paul Celan (1976), and Hans-Jörg Modlmayr (1989) and graphics by Fritz Möser. Author was witness to date and location of composition. Commission information from the composer.

Performance History:
† 13 Nov 1993: St. Barbara Kirche, Dorsten-Wulfen-Barkenberg, FRG
Silesian String Quartet (Marek Mos, Poitr Janosik, Vln; Arkadiusz Kubica, Vla; Lukasz Syrnicki, Vcl).

Bibliography:
Vonhoff. "Jahrhundert-Querschnitt mit Uraufführung." *Ruhrnachrichten* 15 Nov 1993.
Göken, Albert. "Streichquartett führt ins 'flutende Leben.'" *Dorsten WAZ* 16 Nov 1993.

Group IV.D: Oboe Quartets

IV.D.1 Blues Pieces

Date: [Feb 1994] in [Reading, MA ("Lells")] *Duration:* 14'16"
Dedication: "to Helios"
Commission: [Helios]
Publisher: MMC Publications

Movement(s):
Entrata: Adagio (♩=56)
Coal Train: Prestissimo (𝅝.=60)
Blue Song: Allegretto (𝅗𝅥.=52)
In the Minors: Sarcasmo (𝅗𝅥=132)
Lullaby Blue: Larghetto (♩.=58)
Tango Blue: Moderato e sensuale (𝅗𝅥=56)
Rags in Blue: Allegretto con giubilante (𝅗𝅥=80)

Instrumentation:
Ob, Vln, Vla, Vcl soli.

MS Description:
Holograph with signature, pencil on paper. *Location:* Boston Public Library.

Editorial Notes:
Author was witness to date of composition. Commission information from the composer.

Performance History:
† 24 May 1994: Weill Recital Hall, New York, NY
Helios (Matt Sullivan, Ob; Marshall Coid, Vln; Sam Kephart, Vla; Ted Mook, Vcl).

Bibliography:
Kozinn, Allan. "Helios: Weill Recital Hall." *The New York Times* 28 May 1994: 13.

Group IV.E: Piano Quartets

IV.E.1 Piano Quartet No. 1

Date: 26 Sep 1988 in Reading, MA ("Lells") *Duration:* 19'00"
Dedication: "to the Los Angeles Piano Quartet"
Commission: [Los Angeles Piano Quartet]
Publisher: MMC Publications

Movement(s):
I. Lento dramatico (♩=40)
II. Tempo di valse e elegante (♩.=63)
III. Allegro e giubilante (♩=138)

Instrumentation:
Pno, Vln, Vla, Vcl soli.

MS Description:
Holograph with signature, pencil on paper. *Location:* Boston Public Library.

Editorial Notes:
Pages 59–72 of the MS are lost, but photocopies have survived. An autographed photocopy of the fair copy, with corrections by the composer, is on file at New England Conservatory of Music, Boston, MA. Commission information from the composer.

Performance History:
† 15 Dec 1988: Alice Tully Hall, New York, NY
Los Angeles Piano Quartet (James Bonn, Pno; Joseph Genualdi, Vln; Ronald Copes, Vla; Peter Rejto, Vcl).

Program Notes:
"The piano quartet offers one of the richest genres to the composer's expression. It nearly parallels in dramatic purpose and importance the medium of the string quartet. Dedicated to the eminent Los Angeles Piano Quartet, Piano Quartet No. 1 offered me an opportunity to imbue a large canvas with bold musical designs, rich and varied harmonies, wide-ranging moods, and expressive contrasts—all amplified and expanded by a largely framed, narratively developed musical discourse.

"The first movement evolves from a passacaglia opening into large skyscraper-like sonorities, continuing with and elaborating upon the original passacaglia theme and structure. The second movement, in contrast, spins lyrically from a waltz theme, elegant and magical in mood, but all the while maintaining a serious attitude in its developmental working-out of the lighter and more lyrical waltz character. The third movement erupts into a jubilant pulsating rhythmic statement, cumulatively building from beginning to end, nearly relentless in its driving force but at the same time exalted in dramatic mood and foot-tapping pulse and developing its narrative in a quite ambitious architectonic layout and design of some 800 plus measures.

"The listener will easily recognize the traditional chamber-music aspects of this quartet and it is to the great Brahmsian tradition that this work specifically owes its spiritual homage and dedication."
—William Thomas McKinley (© 1988), from 15 Dec 1988 program.

Group IV.F: String Trios

IV.F.1 Studies for String Trio

Date: Oct 1968 in Albany, NY (SUNY Albany) *Duration:* 7'42"
Dedication: "to the American String Trio"
Commission: [American String Trio]
Publisher: MMC Publications

Movement(s):
[One untitled movement.]

Instrumentation:
Vln, Vla, Vcl soli.

Sketches:
1 nearly complete draft. 2 folios and 1 bifolio of notes on nomenclature. 1 folio and 1 bifolio of unidentified sketches.

MS Description:
Holograph with printed name, ink on vellum. *Location:* Boston Public Library.

Editorial Notes:
MS is most likely a first draft and contains many corrections and additions. Commission and premiere performance information from the composer.

Performance History:
[† Fall 1968: State University of New York, Albany, NY
American String Trio.]

See also: Trio for Two Violins and Viola (VIII.F.2)

Group V: Trios for Two Instruments and Keyboard

Group V.A: Trios for Flute, Oboe, and Harpsichord

V.A.1 Spring Sonata for Flute, Oboe, and Harpsichord

Date: 7 May 1988 *Duration:* 15'00"
Dedication: "to the Trio Bell'Arte"
Commission: [Trio Bell'Arte]
Publisher: MMC Publications

Movement(s):
I. Twilight: Mormorante (♩.=72)
II. Aubade: Calmo (♩=44)
III. Noonday: Presto (𝅗𝅥=98)
IV. Afternoon: Moderato (♩=63)
V. Evening: Lento (♩=40)
VI. Dusk: Allegretto (♩.=69)
VII. Nocturne: Andante (♩=80)

Instrumentation:
Fl, Ob, Hpschd soli.

MS Description:
Holograph with signature, pencil on vellum. *Location:* Boston Public Library.

Editorial Notes:
Commission information from the composer. 9 Sep 1988 performance information from BMI records.

Performance History:
† 3 Jun 1988: Weill Recital Hall, New York, NY
Trio Bell'Arte (Robert Stallman, Fl; Humbert Lucharelli, Ob; Elaine Comparone, Hpschd).
[9 Sep 1988: Location unknown
Trio Bell'Arte.]
† (Boston) 11 Nov 1988: First and Second Church, Boston, MA
Trio Bell'Arte.

Bibliography:
Crutchfield, Will. "The New and the Rococo, by Trio Bell'Arte." *The New York Times* 5 Jun 1988: II–59.
Buell, Richard. "Orchestral Normalcy, Cleaned-Up Mozart." *The Boston Globe* 15 Nov 1988.

Program Notes:
"This work was written for the talents of the Trio Bell'Arte and their chosen concert theme, 'C.P.E. Bach Meets the Moderns.' I was inspired by this theme to create a work with Baroque-Classical characteristics. Since the Baroque 'Doctrine of Affections' has always interested me, I decided to create a setting which seemed appropriate to this aspect of Baroque thought, framed within a musical structure of economy and unity. Thus, the idea of a sonata cast in

multi-movement form, containing dramatic ideas of contrast and 'affect,' came into being.

"Seven movements depict the cyclic diversity of a complete spring day, ranging from earliest dawn ("Aubade") to midnight ("Nocturne"). It was extremely pleasurable to complete the *Spring Sonata* late one night in early May when, for the first time since the winter solstice, I was able to experience the character of this cycle in its fullest bloom and natural stages of metamorphosis."

—William Thomas McKinley (© 1988), from 3 Jun 1988 and 11 Nov 1988 programs and his notes.

Group V.B: Trios for Clarinet, Percussion, and Piano

V.B.1 Glass Canyons

Date: 1990 *Duration:* 21'39"
Dedication: [The Bella Lewitzky Dancers]
Commission: [The Bella Lewitzky Dance Foundation, funded by the University of California at Los Angeles and Berkeley, Northeastern University, and Chamber Music, Chicago.]
Publisher: MMC Publications

Movement(s):
I. Blue Glass: Majestically
II. Glass Rockets: Jazzy, with fire (𝅗𝅥=ca. 144)
III. Glass Ballerina: Delicately and sweetly
IV. Glass Beads: Capriciously and furiously, prestissimo
V. Glass Canyons: Majestically and dramatically
VI. Shattered Glass: Jazzy 4/4 boogie woogie feeling (♩=ca. 176)
VII. Stained Glass: Grandly, expressively, with some melancholy

Instrumentation:
Cl/Rec, Perc, Pno soli.

Sketches:
Formal plan for the work, including some themes and key designations. 1 complete motivic draft of the clarinet part.

MS Description:
Holograph with printed name, pencil on vellum. *Location:* Boston Public Library.

Editorial Notes:
Commission information from commission contract and 8–9 Mar 1991 program. The draft of the clarinet part as the formal plan were used as motivic models upon which McKinley, Richard Stoltzman (Cl), and Grisha Alexiev (Perc) improvised and recorded in a private session. The recording was then transcribed by the composer. This tape is stored with the MS.

Performance History:
† 9 Feb 1991: University of California at Berkeley, Berkeley, CA
Richard Stoltzman, Cl; Lewitzky Dance Company.
† (Los Angeles) 15–16 Feb 1991: UCLA Center for the Performing Arts, Los Angeles, CA
Richard Stoltzman, Cl; Lewitzky Dance Company.
† (Boston) 8–9 Mar 1991: Blackman Auditorium, Northeastern University, Boston, MA
Richard Stoltzman, Cl; Lewitzky Dance Company.

Bibliography:

Masters, Kim. "Obscenity Ban Altered for Some Arts Grants." *The Washington Post* 20 Jul 1990: D1.

Gere, David. "Lewitzky's Principled Pieces of Principal Art." *The Tribune (Oakland, CA)* 11 Feb 1991.

Green, Judith. "Wide and Airy: Dancing Through Bella Lewitzky's 'Glass Canyons.'" *San José Mercury News* 11 Feb 1991.

Tucker, Marilyn. "Lewitzky Gives World Premiere." *San Francisco Chronicle* 11 Feb 1991: F2.

Ulrich, Allan. "Lewitzky's Grand 'Canyons.'" *San Francisco Examiner* 11 Feb 1991: B1, B4.

Perlmutter, Donna. "Lewitzky and Stoltzman's 'Love Affair' Proves Fruitful." *Los Angeles Times* 15 Feb 1991: F12, F14.

Segal, Lewis. "The Limits of Lewitzky, Stoltzman." *The Los Angeles Times* 18 Feb 1991: F1, F9.

Fanger, Iris. "Dancing Triumphant: Director's Arts-Obscenity Ruling a Victory vs. Censorship." *The Boston Herald* 4 Mar 1991: 33–34.

Rosenberg, Donald. "New Kensington Composer in Demand." *The Pittsburgh Press* 28 Apr 1991: F1, F4.

Group V.C: Trios for Clarinet, Violin, and Piano

V.C.1 Two Romances for Violin, Clarinet, and Piano

Date: [1984] *Duration:* 10'00"
Dedication: "to Richard Stoltzman, Lucy Stoltzman and Richard Goode"
Commission: [Richard and Lucy Stoltzman]
Publisher: MMC Publications

Movement(s):
I. Moderato (♩=80)
II. Allegro fantastico (♩.=72)

Instrumentation:
Cl, Vln, Pno soli.

Sketches:
2 drafts of the opening of II.

MS Description:
Holograph with signature, pencil on vellum. *Location:* Boston Public Library.

Editorial Notes:
Date taken from review of 14 Sep 1987 performance and McKinley's notes. Commission taken from McKinley's notes. Premiere performance information from the composer and Richard Stoltzman.

Performance History:

[† 1986: Jordan Hall, New England Conservatory of Music, Boston, MA
Richard Stoltzman, Cl; Lucy Stoltzman, Vln; Pianist unknown.]

[† (St. Louis)] 14 Sep 1987: [Hall unknown,] St. Louis, MI
Synchronia.

† (New York) 9 Dec 1987: Merkin Concert Hall, New York, NY
Jean Kopperud, Cl; Sarah Kwak, Vln; Cameron Grant, Pno.

Bibliography:
Wierzbicki, James. "Synchronia's Quiet Rock Scores with the Real Thing." *St. Louis Post-Dispatch* 16 Sep 1987.

V.C.a ~~[Untitled for Violin, Piano and Bass Clarinet]~~

Date: [ca. 1968]
Publisher: Unpublished

Movement(s):
I. ♩=48–52

Instrumentation:
BCl, Pno, Vln soli.

Sketches:
4 folios of unidentified sketches.

MS Description:
Holograph, pencil on paper. *Location:* Boston Public Library.

Editorial Notes:
MS ends after 15 measures (3 pages). Date determined through paleographic analysis. Possibly an earlier version of *Attitudes for Flute, Clarinet and Cello* (VIII.F.1).

Group V.D: Trios for Clarinet, Viola, and Piano

V.D.1 Little Sonata for Viola, Clarinet, and Piano

Date: Nov 1973 in Reading, MA ("Linnea Lane") *Duration:* 3'52"
Publisher: MMC Publications

Movement(s):
♩=46

Instrumentation:
Cl, Pno, Vla soli.

Sketches:
6 drafts of the opening.

MS Description:
Holograph with printed name, ink on vellum. *Location:* Boston Public Library.

V.D.2 Trio Appassionato for B♭ Clarinet, Viola, and Piano

Date: [1982] in [Reading, MA ("Lells")] *Duration:* 11'00"
Dedication: "to Richard Stoltzman[, Walter Trampler, and Thomas Stumpf]"
Commission: [Richard Stoltzman]
Publisher: MMC Publications

Movement(s):
Appassionato (𝅗𝅥=180)

Instrumentation:
Cl, Vla, Pno soli.

Sketches:
5 folios of notes, including a formal plan and many themes.

MS Description:
Engraving by McKinley, ink stencil on vellum. *Location:* Boston Public Library.

Editorial Notes:
Date taken from 3 Oct 1983 program and McKinley's notes. Location of composition, and commission also taken from McKinley's notes. Additional dedication information taken from McKinley's program notes.

Performance History:
† 3 Oct 1983: Jordan Hall, New England Conservatory of Music, Boston, MA
Richard Stoltzman, Cl; Walter Trampler, Vla; Thomas Stumpf, Pno.

Bibliography:
Driver, Paul. "Composer McKinley 'Hears the Muses.'" *The Boston Globe* 9 Dec 1983: 48, 52.

Program Notes:
"This is a work in which the classical-symmetrical formal elements of Brahms' Second Symphony (first movement) are synthesized into a dark, brooding, melodic textural fabric. The combination of viola and clarinet emphasizes the dark lines, and each instrument consistently blends into a chamber-like relationship—giving and taking, ebbing and flowing, with equivalent power given to each. The work was composed for tonight's performers."
—William Thomas McKinley (© 1983), from 3 Oct 1983 program.

Group V.E: Trios for Soprano Saxophone, Violoncello, and Piano

V.E.1 Six Pieces for Soprano Sax, Piano and Cello

Date: Jan 1973 in Chicago, IL (Univ. of Chicago) *Duration:* 4'06"
Dedication: "To my wife"
Publisher: MMC Publications

Movement(s):
I. Quasi rubato, espr[essivo] (♩=45)
II. ♩=47
III. With drama
IV. ♩=34
V. Scherzo, but with force and abandon (♪=74)
VI. 𝅘𝅥𝅯=47

Instrumentation:
Sop Sax, Pno, Vcl soli.

Sketches:
1 draft of the opening. 1 draft of the opening of V. 1 draft of the opening of VI. 1 unidentified draft.

MS Description:
Holograph with printed name, pencil on vellum. *Location:* Boston Public Library.

Group V.F: Trios for Violin, Violoncello, and Piano

V.F.1 Trio [No. 1] in One Movement [for] Violin, Cello, [and] Piano

Date: [Spring 1963] in Pittsburgh, PA *Duration:* 8'42"
Dedication: "to Nikolai Lopatnikoff"
Publisher: MMC Publications

Movement(s):
Allegro (♩=120–130)

Instrumentation:
Vln, Vcl, Pno soli.

MS Description:
Holograph, ink on vellum. *Location:* Boston Public Library.

Editorial Notes:
Year of composition taken from binding of MS. McKinley's notes indicate that this piece "won a Fromm Fellowship of study at Tanglewood for the summer of 1963." Also won 1963 BMI Prize. Premiere performance information also taken from McKinley's notes.

Performance History:
[† Aug 1963: Tanglewood Theater Concert Hall, Lenox, MA
Fromm Foundation Players.]

Bibliography:
Grimes, Ev. "Yale University American Music Oral History Series: William Thomas McKinley." Oct 1986, Yale University School of Music: 35–36.

V.F.2 [Trio No. 2 for Violin, Cello and Piano]

Date: [1991]
Duration: 15'35"
Dedication: ["to the Gollab–Kaplan–Carr Trio"]*
Publisher: MMC Publications

Movement(s):
I. Moderato e tenebroso (♩=116)
II. Presto (♩=200)
III. Tango e finale (♩=58)

Instrumentation:
Vln, Vcl, Pno soli.

Sketches:
1 draft of II/10.

MS Description:
Holograph with signature, pencil on paper. *Location:* Boston Public Library.

Editorial Notes:
*McKinley's program notes seem to dedicate the work to the Solati Trio. Title, dedication, and date taken from fair copy.

Performance History:
[†] 26 Mar 1993: Jordan Hall, New England Conservatory of Music, Boston, MA
Solati Trio (Sophia Herman, Vln; Hrant Tatian, Vcl; Ludmilla Lifson, Pno).
† (New York) 14 Mar 1994: Weill Recital Hall, New York, NY
Solati Trio.
3 May 1994: Jordan Hall, New England Conservatory of Music, Boston, MA
Solati Trio.

Recording(s):
MMC Recordings Ltd.: to be recorded in 1995.
Solati Trio.

Program Notes:
"[I]t is a work in the great romantic tradition and was inspired by the conception and style of the Solati Trio."
—William Thomas McKinley (© 1994), from 14 Mar 1994 program.

Group VI: Duos for Solo Instrument and Keyboard

Group VI.A: Duos for Flute and Piano

VI.A.1 Duo Concerto for Flute and Piano

Date: 1983* in Reading, MA ("Lells") *Duration:* 16'00"
Dedication: [Helen Campo]
Commission: Concert Artists Guild
Publisher: MMC Publications

Movement(s):
Vivo (♩.=72)

Instrumentation:
Fl, Pno soli.

Sketches:
4 folios of notes and sketches.

MS Description:
Engraving by McKinley, ink stencil on vellum. *Location:* Boston Public Library.

Editorial Notes:
*McKinley's program notes indicate that the work was completed in January of 1984. The earlier date on the cover of the manuscript may therefore reflect the date the work was begun rather than completed. Dedication taken from McKinley's program notes.

Performance History:
† 22 May 1984: Weill Recital Hall, New York, NY
Helen Campo, Fl; Thomas Stumpf, Pno.
5 Jun 1986: Merkin Concert Hall, New York, NY
Jayn Rosenfeld, Fl; Cameron Grant, Pno.

Bibliography:
Holland, Bernard. "Music: Works by McKinley." *The New York Times* 7 Jun 1986: 12.
Lifchitz, Max. "Composer of Note: William Thomas McKinley." *Living Music* 4(Fall 1986), no. 1: 2.

Program Notes:
"*Duo Concerto* was commissioned by Concert Artists Guild, and is dedicated to Helen Campo. Completed in January, 1984, the *Duo* is unlike most of my recent works, which are traditional in form and predominantly tonal in language. It thus concerns itself with less traditional problems and sets out to explore a more intricate musical terrain and complex compositional ideal. Paradoxically, the melodic basis in the *Duo* is 'folkloristic', borrowing and generating melodic incipits (fragments) which derive from American popular standards. It is the aural transformation of this basis which is given greatest compositional emphasis in the overall understanding of the chosen materials. The melodic incipits—'Stella by Starlight,' 'Stars Fell on Alabama,' 'Hi Fly,' 'Somewhere Over the Rainbow,' and 'How High the Moon'—are woven into a fantasy texture and rhapsodic form. They overlap, change register, undergo

rhythmic permutation, and interact in various dramatic ways suggesting 'free' jazz improvisation and dance movement. These carefully woven fragments are given brilliant and virtuosic treatment in both the flute and piano, resulting in an instrumental dual that is explosive and which creates a vivid aural tapestry that is rich and polyphonically active. Acting as a stabilizing force within the complex musical dialogue, many of these incipits are treated in unison and help provide a clear articulation and perspective between foreground and background elements. Thus the interplay between the musical dialogue which emotes tension in portraying independence and opposition, and the musical dialogue which emotes resolution in portraying dependence and support, is enhanced *quid pro quo*, and becomes the central dramatic force of the entire work. *Duo Concerto* is in one movement and, although through-composed is extremely controlled (every event is fully and traditionally notated), particularly due to the amount of variation and development given to the melodic incipits. There are no events which do not at least in some aspect relate to or derive from the compositional raw materials, and, for the first time, I used to the full extent the variational possibilities of a set of chosen elements in a manner which improvisation itself has never been able to provide—free from 'academic' and 'trendy' influences and at the same time modern and fresh in their dramatic character and aspirations. The exotic and lavishing quality of flute together with piano was indeed an inspiring aural platform for presenting this kind of 'folklore fantasy.' And during its composition, I was often compelled towards a journey which was marked by exciting musical exploration and challenging discovery while at the time striving to sustain a powerful emotional basis, musical necessity, and a common goal of communication and understanding."
—William Thomas McKinley (© 1984), from 22 May 1984 program and his notes.

VI.A.2 Three Romances [Romances No. 1 for Flute and Piano]

Date: [Jul–Aug 1984] in [Reading, MA ("Lells")] *Duration:* 10'30"
Dedication: "to Robert Stallman and Richard Goode"
Commission: [Robert Stallman]
Publisher: Margun Music Inc.

Movement(s):
I. Tempo di valse (𝅗𝅥.=72)
II. Larghetto (♩=56)
III. Molto tempestoso (♩=92)

Instrumentation:
Fl, Pno soli.

MS Description:
Holograph, pencil on vellum. *Location:* Boston Public Library.

Editorial Notes:
Date, commission, and location of composition taken from McKinley's notes. 19 Mar 1991 performance information from BMI records.

Performance History:
† 21 Sep 1984: Alice Tully Hall, New York, NY
Robert Stallman, Fl; Richard Goode, Pno.
† (Boston) 26 Feb 1985: Jordan Hall, New England Conservatory of Music, Boston, MA
Julie Scolnik, Fl; Yukiko Takagi, Pno.
1 Apr 1986: Jordan Hall, New England Conservatory of Music, Boston, MA
Robert Stallman, Fl; Thomas Stumpf, Pno.

8 Feb 1987: Merkin Concert Hall, New York, NY
Stephanie Jutt, Fl; Araceli Chacon, Pno.
[†? (Los Angeles) 19 Mar 1991: Los Angeles County Museum, Los Angeles, CA
Performers unknown.]
† (Washington, DC) 20 May 1992: The John F. Kennedy Center for the Performing Arts, Washington, DC
Sara Stern, Fl; Lisa Emenheiser Logan, Pno.

Recording(s):
GM Recordings: GM2026CD, ©1990 (CD)
Stephanie Jutt, Fl; Randall Hodgkinson, Pno.

Bibliography:
Holland, Bernard. "Music: Robert Stallman, Flutist." *The New York Times* 23 Sep 1984: 2.64.
Carter, Michael. "Flute and Piano." *American Record Guide* 53(Nov–Dec 1990), no. 6: 148.
Vernier, Tom. "William Thomas McKinley: Three Romances. . . ." *CD Review* Oct 1991.
Smith, Arthur R. "Sara Stern." *The Washington Post* 22 May 1992: D4.

Program Notes:
"Inspired by the French Romantic and Impressionist traditions, my *Three Romances for Flute and Piano*, composed during late July and early August 1984, was carefully conceived for the marvelous lyrical and technical gifts of Robert Stallman and Richard Goode, to whom the work is warmly dedicated. All three Romances, although brief in duration, unfold with a sense of large gesture and design and are characterized by through-composed ostinato figurations, richly orchestrated harmonics, and shifting harmonic rhythm. The first Romance is in 3/4 time and flows generally in the manner of a lyrical waltz with occasional turbulent interruptions. The second Romance is in 4/4 time, unfolding in a stately Baroque-like manner, and the third Romance is in 2/4 time, melodically expansive and often tempestuous. All three Romances strive to honor the goals of traditional performance practice while, at the same time, they create an energy and drama of modernity and contemporary richness. And for these goals I am indebted to so many of the most outstanding performers and conductors of our time with whom I have worked and from whom I have learned much—those who have demonstrated the importance of preserving in addition to further developing those significant natural attributes of musical expression and traditional performance practice which are so often ignored in contemporary compositional values."
—William Thomas McKinley (© 1984), from 21 Sep 1984 program and his notes.

"The *Three Romances* were composed in 1984 for an Alice Tully Hall recital by flutist Robert Stallman. The rest of the program was already in place, and Stallman's request was for a piece of suitable length and character to go along with such works as Debussy's *Syrinx* and the Dutilleux *Sonatine*. McKinley's response was three short character pieces, with the third related to the first, particularly through the piano part, which was conceived with Richard Goode in mind. 'I was pursuing what Richard likes to play,' McKinley says, 'and the writing owes a good deal to Chopin, in its passage work in thirds and sixths, and in the twists and turns it takes.'

"The first piece is marked 'Tempo di valse.' Over a murmurous accompaniment in the piano, the flute plays a lilting, off-center waltz that alternates with scherzando passages, almost as if the accumulating excitement of the waltz cannot contain itself. 'This is a technique I learned from my work with Lopatnikoff—it shows up in a lot of the classical Russian pieces, when one rhythmic mood suddenly vanishes and out of nowhere a new rhythm starts darting around.' The piece has a contrasting center section based on a slowed-down version of the scherzando idea, and then it returns to the music of the beginning. The performers are asked to alternate graciousness and fire, and the music dies away to nothing.

"The middle Romance is a Larghetto built over a repeated, 'walking' bass that never interrupts its gait, though the tread becomes increasingly heavy as the line is weighted with octaves. Over this there moves a rather severe and majestic melody of baroque cast that one is surprised to find marked *amoroso* in the score. McKinley attributes this paradox to another one of his teachers, the musicologist Frederick Dorian, who stimulated his interest in baroque music; the *amoroso* refers to the 'doctrine of affectations' or *Affekt.* 'This piece pays homage to my feelings about Bach in that world, a romantic look back, anchored by a steady, baroque bass.'

The third Romance is marked 'Molto tempestoso.' Over a flowing piano part that echoes the one in the first romance, the flute traces increasingly elaborate coloratura figurations that the composer says should 'take flight.'"
—Richard Dyer (©1990), from GM Recordings GM2026CD liner notes.

VI.A.3 Valse for Flute and Piano (An Encore Piece)

Date: [1984] *Duration:* 1'30"
Publisher: MMC Publications

Movement(s):
Tempo di valse (♩.=60)

Instrumentation:
Fl, Pno soli.

MS Description:
Holograph with signature, pencil on paper. *Location:* Boston Public Library.

Editorial Notes:
Date taken from cover of fair copy.

VI.A.4 Poem for Flute and Piano*

Date: [1986] *Duration:* 11'00"
Dedication: [Robert Stallman]
Commission: [Robert Stallman]
Publisher: MMC Publications

Movement(s):
Poco adagio (♩=76)

Instrumentation:
Fl, Pno soli.

MS Description:
Copyist's hand, pencil on vellum. *Location:* Boston Public Library.

Editorial Notes:
*An arrangement by Peter Farmer of the first movement of the Concerto for Flute and String Orchestra (II.D.1). Date and dedication from the printed cover sheet of the MS. Commission information from the composer.

Bibliography:
See Concerto for Flute and String Orchestra (II.D.1).

Program Notes:
See Concerto for Flute and String Orchestra (II.D.1).

VI.A.5 Fantasy on a Theme of J.S. Bach for Flute and Piano

Date: 22 Oct 1987 in Reading, MA ("Lells") *Duration:* 11'30"
Dedication: "to Bob Stallman, a premier flutist"
Commission: [Robert Stallman]
Publisher: MMC Publications

Movement(s):
Prestissimo (♩.=152)

Instrumentation:
Fl, Pno soli.

MS Description:
Holograph with signature, pencil on vellum. *Location:* Boston Public Library.
Markings: Cover page: "(from book II, #12, f minor prelude)."

Editorial Notes:
Commission information from the composer.

Performance History:
† 17 Nov 1987: Weill Recital Hall, New York, NY
Robert Stallman, Fl; Erika Nickrenz, Pno.

Program Notes:
"I am grateful to my friend William Thomas McKinley who has written his *Fantasy on a Theme by Bach* especially for tonight's concert. The *Fantasy* is a one movement *moto perpetuo* that explores a single Bach melody in an improvisatory style. The theme's three-note motive is treated as an *idée fixe*, as McKinley takes us through all the major and minor keys, echoing Bach in the *Well Tempered Clavier*. The theme that has inspired this Fantasy comes from the *Well Tempered Clavier*, but the exact identity of the theme I will leave as an enigma for you to solve."
—Robert Stallman (© 1987), from 17 Nov 1987 program.

VI.A.6 Secrets of the Heart (Romances No. 2) for Flute and Piano

Date: [1990] *Duration:* 18'00"
Dedication: "to Robert Stallman and Erika Nickrenz"
Commission: [Robert Stallman]
Publisher: MMC Publications

Movement(s):
I. Innocence: Innocente (♩.=72)
II. Flirtatiousness: Scherzando (𝅗𝅥.=54)
III. Loneliness: Doloroso (♩=58)
IV. Wildness: Presto (♩=112)
V. Wistfulness: Andante con moto (𝅗𝅥=48)
VI. Prankishness: Vivace (♩.=80)
VII. Triumphantness: Tempo di marcia (♩=120)
VIII. Pensiveness: Andantino (♩=58)
IX. Tormentedness: Tormentoso (♩=80)
X. Glamorousness: Presto (♩=160)*
XI. Trancendentalness: Adagio (𝅗𝅥=69)*
XII. Joyousness: Allegro giubilante (𝅗𝅥=69)

Instrumentation:
Fl, Pno soli.

Sketches:
1 folio of notes on the formal plan of the work. 2 drafts of the opening of I. 1 draft of the opening of II.

MS Description:
Holograph with signature, pencil on paper. *Location:* Boston Public Library.

Editorial Notes:
*In copyist's fair copy, movement X is entitled "Earthiness" and movement XI is entitled "Transcendence." Date taken from 10 Dec 1990 program. Commission information from the composer. 10 May 1992 performance information taken from a newspaper advertisement.

Performance History:
† 10 Dec 1990: Weill Recital Hall, New York, NY
Robert Stallman, Fl; Erika Nickrenz, Pno.
[† (Boston)] 28 Jan 1991: Jordan Hall, New England Conservatory of Music, Boston, MA
Robert Stallman, Fl; Erika Nickrenz, Pno.
[10 May 1992: Lafayette Ave. Presbyterian Church, Brooklyn, NY
Robert Stallman, Fl; Erika Nickrenz, Pno.]
6/7 Jun 1992: Weill Recital Hall, New York, NY
Robert Stallman, Fl; David Buechner, Pno.
24 Jun 1993: Library Gallery, North Essex Community College, Haverhill, MA
Michael Finegold, Fl; David Pihl, Pno.
[† (Europe)] 24 Oct 1993: Záhorská galéria, Bratislava, Slovakia
Marián Turner, Fl; Elena Michalicová, Pno.

Recording(s):
Academy Sound and Vision, Ltd.: CD DCA 869, ©1993 (CD)
Robert Stallman, Fl; David Buechner, Pno.

Bibliography:
Dyer, Richard. "Heiss and McKinley: A Study in Contrasts." *The Boston Globe* 29 Jan 1991.
Kozinn, Allan. "Flute Fest: Weill Recital Hall." *The New York Times* 9 Jun 1992: C12.

Program Notes:
"In my first set of *Romances for Flute and Piano* (premiered at Alice Tully Hall by Robert Stallman and Richard Goode, and subsequently recorded for CD on GM with Stephanie Jutt and Randall Hodgkinson), I created a rather expansive and large-framed developmental structure in a clearly musical Romantic style.

"In this new set of Romances (*Secrets of the Heart*) I decided for contrast, to compose a substantial number (twelve in this set) of smaller—almost bagatelle-like romances each lasting between 1–3 minutes and each expressing a concrete emotional image or affection—hence the sub-title 'Secrets of the Heart.' For in each of our hearts (and minds too!) exist a wide and divergent canvas of emotional mood-images—dramatic—drawn and stored like acorns from our varied and at times quite secret (but ultimately shared) inner experiences at times real and at times vicarious in their origin. In my experience, it seems truly remarkable to observe how universal the agreement among sensitive listeners, performers and conductors is regarding the objective character and cognition of their perceptions *vis-à-vis* their 'received' mood images and dramatic feelings generated by melodic, harmonic, rhythmic and coloristic musical vibrations. We all have experienced gentleness, innocence, triumphantness, prankishness, joyousness, wildness—in fact encompassing the entire gamut of human feelings and emotion. The heart feels and the mind interprets—a fascinating and perfect symbiosis

and one which is at the basis of ART and on which our future styles and musical streams will be nourished and developed. The Romance is a symbol of this state of universal mind and how fortunate we mortals to be able to experience if only for an aesthetic instant these precious gradations of the human heart—a mirror through which the composer may enter in order to continually perfect the deepest and most elegant ideas of universal experience and human understanding."
—William Thomas McKinley (© 1990), from 10 Dec 1990, 28 Jan 1991, 6/7 Jun 1992, and 24 Jun 1993 programs and his notes.

VI.A.a ~~Sonata for Piano and Flute~~

Date: [ca. 1965]
Publisher: Unpublished

Movement(s):
[One untitled movement]

Instrumentation:
Fl, Pno soli.

Sketches:
1 folio of unidentified sketches.

MS Description:
Holograph, pencil on paper. *Location:* Boston Public Library.

Editorial Notes:
MS ends after 17 measures. Date determined through paleographic analysis.

VI.A.b ~~[Untitled for Flute and Piano]~~

Date: [ca. 1972]
Publisher: Unpublished

Movement(s):
Violent attacks with total abandon (♪=120)

Instrumentation:
Fl, Pno soli.

Sketches:
14 drafts of the opening. 3 unidentified drafts.

MS Description:
Holograph, ink on vellum. *Location:* Boston Public Library.

Editorial Notes:
MS ends after one page. Date determined through paleographic analysis.

Group VI.B: Duos for Oboe and Piano

VI.B.1 Four Pieces for Oboe and Piano

Date: 14–15 Nov 1971 in Chicago, IL (Univ. of Chicago) *Duration:* 8'18"
Dedication: "To the spirit of..."
Publisher: MMC Publications

Movement(s):
I. [1/4 inch=1"]
II. [1/4 inch=1"]
III. [1/4 inch=1"]
IV. ♪=87

Instrumentation:
Ob, Pno soli

MS Description:
Holograph with printed name, ink on vellum. *Location:* Boston Public Library.
Markings: Cover page: "1st version."* Pieces I and II dated 14 Nov 1971. Pieces III and IV dated 15 Nov 1971.

Editorial Notes:
*Although the MS is marked "1st version," no later versions were ever written. Premiere performance information from the composer.

Performance History:
[† 1971–1972: Location unknown
Wilma Zonn, Ob.]

VI.B.2 Ten Interludes for Oboe and Piano

Date: 15–24 Nov 1971
Commission: [Wilma Zonn]
Publisher: MMC Publications
Duration: 16'19"

Movement(s):
Interlude I.
Interlude II.
Interlude III.
Interlude IV. Forceful (♩=45)
Interlude V. Legato, dramatic
Interlude VI.
Interlude VII.
Interlude VIII.
Interlude IX.
Interlude X. ♪=75

Instrumentation:
Ob, Pno soli.

Sketches:
1 complete draft of I with draft of the opening of II. 1 draft from X. 3 unidentified drafts.

MS Description:
Holograph with printed name, ink on vellum. *Location:* Boston Public Library.
Markings: Interlude I dated 15 Nov 1971. Interlude II and III dated 19 Nov 1971. Interludes IV, V, and VI dated 20 Nov 1971. Interlude VII dated 21 Nov 1971. Interludes VIII and IX dated 22 Nov 1971. Interlude X dated 24 Nov 1971.

Editorial Notes:
Commission and premiere performance information taken from McKinley's notes.

Performance History:
[† Mar 1972: University of Illinois, Urbana, IL
Wilma Zonn, Ob; Paul Zonn, Pno.]
[† (Chicago)] 26 May 1972: Mandel Hall, University of Chicago, Chicago, IL
Wilma Zonn, Ob; Arthur Maddox, Pno.

Program Notes:
"The compositional features display lyricism, the long line, and the arabesque. They are essentially Baroque in conception as they each deal with a particular 'affection' and its exposition. My prime challenge was to integrate these features with improvisational gestures—to create a synergy between clarity and flexibility, and to balance between them the singing-*cantabile* line."
—William Thomas McKinley (© 1972), from 26 May 1972 program.

Group VI.C: Duos for Clarinet and Piano

VI.C.1 Duo Concertante for B♭ Clarinet and Piano

Date: [Dec 1982] in [Reading, MA ("Lells")] *Duration:* 15'00"
Dedication: [Richard Stoltzman]
Commission: [Richard Stoltzman]
Publisher: MMC Publications

Movement(s):
Lamento (♩=48)

Instrumentation:
Cl, Pno.

Sketches:
3 folios of notes and sketches.

MS Description:
Engraving by McKinley, ink stencil on vellum. *Location:* Boston Public Library.

Editorial Notes:
Date, location of composition, and commission taken from McKinley's notes. Dedication taken from McKinley's program notes.

Performance History:
† 3 Oct 1983: Jordan Hall, New England Conservatory of Music, Boston, MA
Richard Stoltzman, Cl; Thomas Stumpf, Pno.

Bibliography:
Driver, Paul. "Composer McKinley 'Hears the Muses.'" *The Boston Globe* 9 Dec 1983: 48, 52.

Program Notes:
"*Duo Concertante* was specifically designed for Richard Stoltzman's dazzling instrumental virtuosity—it explores particularly the arabesque line, the totality of clarinet registers and wide range of timbre. The piano part is also a *tour de force* bringing out pianistic qualities in the manner of a 20th century Liszt—dazzling, brilliant, and in a continual kaleidoscopic interplay and equivalency with its clarinet partner."
—William Thomas McKinley (© 1983), from 3 Oct 1983 program.

VI.C.2 Intermezzo [No. 1] for B♭ Clarinet and Piano

Date: [1983] in Reading, MA ("Lells") *Duration:* 5'00"
Dedication: [Richard Stoltzman]
Commission: [National Endowment for the Arts]
Publisher: MMC Publications

Movement(s):	*Instrumentation:*
Lamento, brooding (♩=80)	Cl, Pno soli.

MS Description:
Holograph with signature, pencil on paper. *Location:* Owned by Richard Stoltzman.*

Editorial Notes:
*A photocopy of the manuscript has been placed in the Boston Public Library collection. Date, dedication and commission taken from McKinley's program notes. Premiere performance information from advertisement and McKinley's program notes.

Performance History:
[† 3 May 1983: Jordan Hall, New England Conservatory of Music, Boston, MA
Richard Stoltzman, Cl; Thomas Stumpf, Pno.]
3 Oct 1983: Jordan Hall, New England Conservatory of Music, Boston, MA
Richard Stoltzman, Cl; Thomas Stumpf, Pno.
2 Dec 1986: Jordan Hall, New England Conservatory of Music, Boston, MA
Maria Moan, Cl; Linnea Bardarson, Pno.

Bibliography:
Driver, Paul. "Composer McKinley 'Hears the Muses.'" *The Boston Globe* 9 Dec 1983: 48, 52.
Buell, Richard. "Enchanted Circle Series Celebrates 10 Years at NEC." *The Boston Globe* 4 Dec 1986: 98.

Program Notes:
"Completed in 1983, these Intermezzi were written for Richard Stoltzman, and premiered by Stoltzman and pianist Thomas Stumpf on May 3, 1983 in Jordan Hall. The Intermezzi were originally commissioned through the National Endowment for the Arts."
—William Thomas McKinley (© 1986), from 2 Dec 1986 program.

"An Intermezzo is unimaginatively defined as a short movement connecting the main part of a composition. But because William Thomas McKinley's life is a composition—imagine barely opening a door, gently, and hearing a song—almost a dream of a song already begun, slowly spinning, beautiful in long breathed simplicity. Imagine listening, almost motionless, the door slightly open, transfixed. Then, slowly, closing the door, hearing the music no more yet feeling it flowing on and on inside you, inside the door. You have heard a moment of McKinley; a brief breeze from the mountain of McKinley's compositional life—an Intermezzo."
—Richard Stoltzman (© 1983), from the printed score.

VI.C.3 Intermezzo [No. 2] for B♭ Clarinet and Piano

Date: [1983] *Duration:* 3'30"
Dedication: [Richard Stoltzman]
Commission: [National Endowment for the Arts]
Publisher: MMC Publications

Movement(s):	*Instrumentation:*
Presto (♩=120)	Cl, Pno soli.

MS Description:
Holograph with signature, pencil on vellum. *Location:* Boston Public Library.

Editorial Notes:
See Intermezzo No. 1 (VI.C.2).

Performance History:
See *Intermezzo No. 1* (VI.C.2).

Bibliography:
See Intermezzo No. 1 (VI.C.2).

Program Notes:
See Intermezzo No. 1 (VI.C.2).

VI.C.4 Sonata for Clarinet and Piano

Date: [1986] *Duration:* 23'30"
Dedication: "to Richard Stoltzman"
Commission: [Richard Stoltzman]
Publisher: MMC Publications

Movement(s):
I. Andantino (𝅗𝅥=100)
II. Scherzando (♩=160)
III. Largo (♩=48)
IV. Maestoso (𝅗𝅥.=66)

Instrumentation:
Cl, Pno soli.

Sketches:
1 draft of the opening of I.

MS Description:
Holograph with printed name, pencil on vellum. *Location:* Boston Public Library.

Editorial Notes:
Date taken from 25 Apr 1987 program, Oct 1986 article, and McKinley's notes. Commission also taken from McKinley's notes. Premiere confirmation from McKinley's program notes.

Performance History:
[†] 8 Feb 1987: Merkin Concert Hall, New York, NY
Richard Stoltzman, Cl; Irma Vallecillo, Pno.
[† (Boston)] 25 Apr 1987: Jordan Hall, New England Conservatory of Music, Boston, MA
Richard Stoltzman, Cl; Irma Vallecillo, Pno.
3 Jun 1990: Great Hall, State House, Boston, MA
Richard Stoltzman, Cl; Irma Vallecillo, Pno.
8 Dec 1990: [Hall unknown], New England Conservatory of Music, Boston, MA
Stephanie Key, Cl; [Pianist unknown].

Recording(s):
RCA Victor Red Seal: to be released in 1995.
Richard Stoltzman, Cl; Irma Vallecillo, Pno.

Bibliography:
Bouchard, Fred. "Richard Stoltzman: Clarinet Crossover." *Downbeat* 53(Oct 1986), no. 10: 20–22, 61.
Miller, Nancy. "Alea III and All That Jazz." *The Boston Globe* 27 Apr 1987: 12.
Dyer, Richard. "A Season Marked by Many Fond Farewells." *The Boston Globe* 2 Jun 1990: 11.

Program Notes:
"The McKinley *Sonata for Clarinet and Piano* was composed for Richard Stoltzman and was premiered by Richard Stoltzman and Irma Vallecillo at Merkin Hall, New York, on February 8, 1988 [*sic*]. In four movements, this work represents one of McKinley's most ambitious sonatas and embraces a wide gamut of emotional contrasts, juxtapositions of color, and musical sentiment—all ambitiously developed and amply canvassed throughout the large-framed movements. The work does not attempt to disguise its romantic impulses and essentially lyric development. Its inspirational basis is in great part intuitive and its rhythmic momentum is generated by strong contrasts, propelling drive, and development. Since its New York premiere, Mr. Stoltzman has frequently performed the Sonata throughout the United States."
—William Thomas McKinley (© 1994), from his notes.

VI.C.5 Blue Jeans (An Assortment of Blues and "Things" for B♭ Clarinet and Piano)

Date: 7 Jan 1991 *Duration:* 10'40"
Dedication: "to Jean Kopperud and Cameron Grant"
Commission: [Jean Kopperud]
Publisher: MMC Publications

Movement(s):
I. Drone: Blues drone (♩=69)
II. Vamp: Largo tenebre (♩=50)
III. Tango: Andante (♩=88)
IV. To "Bird": Presto (𝅗𝅥=112)

Instrumentation:
Cl, Pno soli.

Sketches:
2 drafts of the opening (earlier titles: *Jazz Suite; Suite; Cooker*).

MS Description:
Holograph with signature, pencil on paper. *Location:* Boston Public Library.
Markings: Final Page: Fine and timing followed by: 'Blue Jeans' | (set no 1.) | William Thomas McKinley | reading ma. Jan 7, 91. 'new year'

Editorial Notes:
Commission information from the composer.

Performance History:
† 4 Mar 1991: Merkin Concert Hall, New York, NY
Jean Kopperud, Cl; Cameron Grant, Pno.
† (Australia) 4 Jul 1991: Basil Jones Theater, Brisbane, Australia
Floyd Williams, Cl; Mitchell Leigh, Pno.
[† (Boston)] 16 Nov 1991: Brown Hall, New England Conservatory of Music, Boston, MA
Jean Kopperud, Cl; Cameron Grant, Pno.
17 Feb 1992: Branscomb Memorial Auditorium, Florida Southern College, Lakeland, FL
Richard Stoltzman, Cl; Cameron Grant, Pno.
27 Feb 1994: Jordan Hall, New England Conservatory, Boston, MA
Chester Brezniak, Cl; David Hagan, Pno.
3 May 1994: Jordan Hall, New England Conservatory, Boston, MA
Chester Brezniak, Cl; David Hagan, Pno.

VI.C.a ~~Waltz~~

Date: [ca. 1983–1985]
Publisher: Unpublished

Movement(s):
♩.=48

Instrumentation:
Cl, Pno soli.

Sketches:
1 incomplete draft.*

MS Description:
Holograph, pencil on vellum. *Location:* Boston Public Library.

Editorial Notes:
MS ends after 22 measures (4 pages). *It is difficult to know which came first, that which I call the "draft" or that which I call the "manuscript." The final decision was made by choosing the cleaner version which bears the title as the manuscript, and the other version, which has no title, as the draft.

See also: Blues Lament for Dick (II.E.3)
Goodbye for B♭ Clarinet and Piano (X.B.1)
Night and Day (X.B.2)
Time on My Hands [Medley] (X.B.4)
~~**My Way**~~ (X.B.a)
~~**Isn't She Lovely**~~ (X.B.b)

Group VI.D: Duos for Horn and Piano

VI.D.1 Two Romances for French Horn and Piano

Date: Nov 1985
Dedication: "to Dale Clevenger"
Commission: [Dale Clevenger]
Publisher: MMC Publications

Duration: 6'00"

Movement(s):
I. Larghetto (♩=63)
II. Allegro molto tempestoso (♩.=116)

Instrumentation:
Hn, Pno soli.

MS Description:
Holograph with signature, pencil on vellum. *Location:* Boston Public Library.

Editorial Notes:
Commission information from the composer. Conversation with Dale Clevenger confirms that he did not perform this work. Therefore, 21 Oct 1986 performance is most likely the premiere.

Performance History:
[†] 21 Oct 1986: Jordan Hall, New England Conservatory of Music
Jay Wadenpfuhl, Hn; Judith Gordon, Pno.

Program Notes:
"*Two Romances for Horn and Piano* were composed for Dale Clevenger, who is the principal Horn with the Chicago Symphony, when Dale asked me to write a Horn Concerto and some solo recital pieces. I immediately set out to create the *Romances*, of which there are two, each with a different character and mood. Both emphasize the rich and wide tessitura of the Romantic Horn, and lush, harmonic capabilities of the piano. Both Romances are brief but rich and passionate."
—William Thomas McKinley (© 1986), from 21 Oct 1986 program.

Group VI.E: Duos for Trumpet and Organ

VI.E.1 Die Mauern (A Symphonic Portrait for Trumpet and Organ)*

Date: [Early 1992] *Duration:* 18'00"
Dedication: "to David Tasa"
Commission: [David Tasa]
Publisher: MMC Publications

Movement(s):
Largo (♩=40)

Instrumentation:
Tpt, Org soli.

MS Description:
Holograph with signature, pencil on paper. *Location:* Boston Public Library.

Editorial Notes:
**Die Mauern* later became the Part One of *Jenseits der Mauer*. Dating based on date of premiere performance. Commission information from the composer.

Performance History:
See *Jenseits der Mauer* (IX.B.9).

Bibliography:
See *Jenseits der Mauer* (IX.B.9).

Program Notes:
See *Jenseits der Mauer* (IX.B.9).

Group VI.F: Duos for Violin and Piano

VI.F.1 Adagio for Violin [and] Piano

Date: [1960] in [Pittsburgh, PA (Carnegie-Mellon Univ.)] *Duration:* Varies
Publisher: MMC Publications

Movement(s):
Quasi improvisare

Instrumentation:
Vln, Pno soli.

Sketches:
MS contains several paste-overs, behind which are earlier drafts.

MS Description:
Holograph, pencil on paper. *Location:* Boston Public Library.

Markings: Cover: Miscellaneous titles of works by other composers and addresses, along with some music. Seems to have been used as scratch paper.

Editorial Notes:
Date taken from cover page of fair copy. Location of composition and premiere performance information taken from McKinley's notes.

Performance History:
[† May 1960: Carnegie-Mellon University, Pittsburgh, PA
Joe Bishkoff, Vln; William Thomas McKinley, Pno.]

VI.F.2 [Sonata for Violin and Piano]

Date: [ca. 1967]
Publisher: Unpublished

Movement(s):
♪=52

Instrumentation:
Vln, Pno soli.

Sketches:
1 incomplete draft of exposition and development ("A")
4 drafts of the opening of A. 2 drafts of mm. 11–16 of A. 1 draft of mm. 11–31 of A. 1 sketch of m. 17 of A. 1 draft of mm. 43–44 of A.
1 incomplete draft of development ("B") 1 draft of the opening of B.

MS Description:
Holograph, pencil on paper. *Location:* McKinley Residence.

Editorial Notes:
MS would seem to be complete, but is extremely light and difficult to read. Title of work taken from sketches. Date determined through paleographic analysis. Judging by the style of handwriting and music, this work and the Untitled work for Trumpet and Bassoon (VIII.G.1) were probably written one right after the other.

VI.F.a ~~Duo Concertante for Violin and Piano~~

Date: 1969 in Chicago, IL (Univ. of Chicago)
Dedication: "to Paul Zukofsky"
Publisher: MMC Publications

Movement(s):
Quasi cadenza (♪=52)

Instrumentation:
Vln, Pno soli.

MS Description:
Holograph with printed name, pencil on vellum. *Location:* Boston Public Library.

Editorial Notes:
MS ends after 5 pages.

Group VI.G: Duos for Viola and Piano

VI.G.1 [Viola Sonata No. 1]

Date: [Jun 1984] *Duration:* 24'30"
Dedication: [Walter Trampler]
Commission: [The Chamber Music Society of Lincoln Center]
Publisher: MMC Publications

Movement(s):
I. Poco allegro appassionato (♩=90)
II. Allegretto (♩=144)
III. Allegro tempestuoso (♩.=110)

Instrumentation:
Vla, Pno soli.

Sketches:
1 draft of the opening of I. 3 drafts of the opening of II. 1 draft of II/227–30. 3 drafts and 1 sketch of the opening of a movement (either very early versions of one of the existing movements or the first drafts of the unwritten fourth movement). 5 unidentified drafts.

MS Description:
Holograph, pencil on paper. *Location:* Boston Public Library.
Markings: Movements apparently re-ordered: IV became I (new IV never written), and III became II.

Editorial Notes:
Date taken from McKinley's notes. Title and commission taken from cover page of fair copy. Dedication taken from McKinley's program notes. A photocopy of a modified fair copy with handwritten edits by McKinley is stored with the manuscript. The original modified fair copy is lost. 10 Apr 1986 performance information from advertisement, however, flyer for 9 Feb 1987 performance indicates Boston premiere.

Performance History:
† 13 Feb 1986: St. Ann's Church, Brooklyn, NY
Walter Trampler, Vla; Charles Wadsworth, Pno.
14, 16 Feb 1986: Alice Tully Hall, New York, NY
Walter Trampler, Vla; Charles Wadsworth, Pno.
[† (Boston) 10 Apr 1986: Jordan Hall, New England Conservatory, Boston, MA
Walter Trampler, Vla; Charles Wadsworth, Pno.]
8 Feb 1987: Merkin Concert Hall, New York, NY
Walter Trampler, Vla; Irma Vallecillo, Pno.
† (Boston)[?] 9 Feb 1987: Jordan Hall, New England Conservatory of Music, Boston, MA
Walter Trampler, Vla; Irma Vallecillo, Pno.
17 Oct 1987: [Location unknown]
P. Jordan, Vla; L. Bardarson, Pno.

Bibliography:
Kandell, Leslie. "Classical Composer With a Passion For Jazz." *The New York Times* 17 Feb 1985: 23, 26.
Zakariasen, Bill. "Sibelius Holds No Terror for Brooklyn." *The New York Daily News* 17 Feb 1986: 36.
Page, Tim. "Music: Lincoln Center Group." *The New York Times* 18 Feb 1986: C 18.

Rooney, Dennis D. "Concert Notes: New York." *The Strad* 96(May 1986), no. 1153: 8.
Tommasini, Anthony. "A White-hot Program on a Cold Winter's Night." *The Boston Globe* 11 Feb 1987.

Program Notes:

"The viola is certainly one of the most difficult instruments for the composer to display convincingly and effectively. Fortunately for me, however, at the time of beginning the Viola Sonata, I had already completed two viola concertos, numerous viola solo pieces, and a trio for viola, clarinet, and piano, which gave me greater confidence in my undertaking. Therefore, this new Sonata, commissioned by The Chamber Music Society of Lincoln Center and dedicated to Walter Trampler, embodies several notable developments of my creative thought.

"First, I envisioned musical ideas drawn from the richest and most resonant tessitura of the viola coupled and integrated with supportive resonances from the piano.

"Second, this Sonata culminates, to some degree, one period in my search for expressive possibilities in the still-present universe of tonality. It incorporates pulse-dance rhythms, vivid harmonic color, and, most important, singing in the manner of opera—specifically 'bel canto.'

"And finally, composing for artists of the magnitude of Walter Trampler and Charles Wadsworth was a continual inspiration. I was always able to hear and see their performance vividly in my musical imagination. Such collaboration needs to be perpetually fostered at the highest level. Herein lies one of the genuine tests for the development, sustenance, and ultimate impact of the composer's contribution to the mainstream repertoire. And to such collaboration and inspiration the Sonata owes its themes, emotional states, developmental stages, movement structure, and harmonic forms. Imagining several movements with a viola cadenza in the first movement, I tried to create a hybrid of Beethovian and Schubertian dialogue, romantically filtered through a contemporary dramatic realism. Indeed, all of these 'wanderings' were psychically powerful, continually reinforced by the thought of Walter and Charles performing the Sonata in Alice Tully Hall."

—William Thomas McKinley (© 1986), from 14, 16 Feb 1986 program.

VI.G.2 Samba for Viola and Piano

Date: 1984 in Reading, MA ("Lells") *Duration:* 12'00"
Dedication: [Walter Trampler and Richard Goode]
Commission: [Lincoln Center Chamber Music Society]
Publisher: MMC Publications

Movement(s):
Lamentoso (♩=60+)

Instrumentation:
Vla, Pno soli.

MS Description:
Copyist's hand, pencil on vellum. *Location:* Lost.*

Editorial Notes:
*The copyist's fair copy has survived and a photocopy has been placed in the Boston Public Library collection. Dedication and commission taken from McKinley's program notes.

Performance History:
† 21 Oct 1985: Jordan Hall, New England Conservatory of Music, Boston, MA
Marcus Thompson, Vla; Randall Hodgkinson, Pno.

Bibliography:

Buell, Richard. "Heiss/McKinley Concert A Study in Warring Contrasts." *The Boston Globe* 23 Oct 1985: 63.

Program Notes:

"The genesis of the *Samba* is unusual. Having been commissioned by the Lincoln Center Chamber Music Society to compose a 25 minute viola sonata for Walter Trampler and Richard Goode, I found, upon the completion of a four movement sonata, that the slow movement (entitled *Samba*) of the piece might be forming an identity of its own. Thus I decided to omit it from the rest of the score and make it an independent [work]. Therefore the movement you will hear is an Adagio in the Romantic sense, incorporating many folkloristica and South American elements into its fabric. This samba is of the slow 2/4 variety and is lyrical, brooding, and in the viola part works up quite a frenzy which derives from authentic Latin-samba rhythms. There is also an element of jazz-samba feeling throughout, set against a droning bass line in the piano part. The richness of the low viola register is particularly suited to this kind of piece."

—William Thomas McKinley (© 1985), from 21 Oct 1985 program.

VI.G.3 Viola Concerto No. 2 [Piano Reduction]

Date: 1985 in Unknown *Duration:* 30'30"
Dedication: "to Sol Greitzer"
Commission: [Sol Greitzer]
Publisher: MMC Publications

Movement(s):
I. Andante ma non troppo (♩=52)
II. Vivo (♩=120+)
III. Molto maestoso (𝅝=48)

Instrumentation:
Vla, Pno.

Sketches:
See Concerto for Viola No. 2 (II.M.2).

MS Description:
Copyist's hand, ink on vellum (mvt. 1), pencil on vellum (mvts. 2 and 3). *Location:* Boston Public Library.

Editorial Notes:
Reduction by copyist. See concerto entry (II.M.2) for more information. Commission information from the composer.

Program Notes:
See Concerto for Viola No. 2 (II.M.2).

Group VI.H: Duos for Violoncello and Piano

VI.H.a ~~{Untitled for Violoncello and Piano}~~

Date: [ca. 1972]
Publisher: Unpublished

Movement(s):
Molto adagio, with plasticity and brilliance (♩=47)

Instrumentation:
Vcl, Pno soli.

MS Description:
Holograph, ink on vellum. *Location:* Boston Public Library.

Editorial Notes:
MS ends after one measure.

Group VII: Works for Solo Instrument

Group VII.A: Works for Solo Flute

VII.A.1 Extemporara for Solo Flute

Date: 1968 in Albany, NY (SUNY Albany) *Duration:* 5'57"
Dedication: "for Irvin Gilman"
Publisher: MMC Publications

Movement(s):
♪=60

Instrumentation:
Fl solo.

MS Description:
Holograph with printed name, ink on vellum. *Location:* Boston Public Library.

Editorial Notes:
Location and date of premiere performance from McKinley's notes.

Performance History:
[† 1968: State University of New York, Albany, NY
Irvin Gilman?, Fl.]
Spring 1976: North Essex Community College, Haverhill, MA
Michael Finegold, Fl.

VII.A.2 Study for Computer Tape and Solo Flute

Date: 1969 in New Haven, CT (Yale Univ.) *Duration:* 2'45"
Commission: [Michael Finegold]
Publisher: Unpublished

Movement(s):
[One untitled movement.]

Instrumentation:
Fl solo; Tape.

MS Description:
Holograph, ink on vellum. *Location:* McKinley Residence.

Editorial Notes:
Commission and premiere performance information from the composer.

Performance History:
[† ca. 1969: Yale University, New Haven, CT
Michael Finegold, Fl.]

VII.A.3 Songs Without Words for Solo Flute (op. 72)

Date: 4 Aug 1976 in Manchester, MA ("Carriage House") *Duration:* 24'00"
Commission: [Massachusetts Council for the Arts]
Publisher: Margun Music Inc.

Movement(s):
I. With introspection (♩=52+)
II. Rapid, with fire (♪=90)
III. ♩=87
IV. With joy (♩=100+)
V. Presto molto (♪=140)
VI. ♩=180+
VII. Majestic, noble power (♩=30)
VIII. ♩=75
IX. Crying (♩=40)
X. ♩=60
XI. Pulsating (♩=120+)
XII. Dance-like (♩=52)
XIII. Largo (♩=30)
XIV. With gypsy abandon, lusty (♩.=92)
XV. Scherzo (𝅘𝅥𝅯=170)
XVI. 𝅘𝅥𝅯=as fast as possible
XVII. With crystalline clarity (♩=60)
XVIII. ♩=48
XIX. 𝅘𝅥𝅯=82
XX. Presto (♩=200)
XXI. ♩=42
XXII. As legato as possible (♪=72)
XXIII. As legato as possible, dazzling, suspended animation (♩=100+)
XXIV. ♩=66
XXV. ♪=82
XXVI. ♪=140
XXVII. Frozen, time suspended (♩=20)
XXVIII. Cantabile (♩=48)

Instrumentation:
Fl solo.

MS Description:
Holograph with printed name, ink on paper. *Location:* Lost.*
Markings: Cover page: "although each page is a self-contained entity, the work is also meant to be a total dramatic statement.... The flutist may wish to isolate a few of the 'songs' (pages) to form a 'smaller' work...in this sense the work is a portfolio, series of technical and aesthetic studies.... Ideally it is the composer's wish to have the entire work performed with only very short (,) pauses between each song or page. The visual layout is like an album of leaves—each varied and yet related by a common organic biology and spirit...."

Editorial Notes:
*A photocopy of the manuscript has survived and been placed in the Boston Public Library collection. Commission taken from McKinley's notes. Premiere performance information taken from McKinley's program notes.

Performance History:
[† Late 1976: Longy School of Music, Cambridge, MA
Stephanie Jutt, Fl.]
17 Oct 1977: Jordan Hall, New England Conservatory of Music, Boston, MA (songs 1–3, 7, 9, 20, 25, 27, and 28 only)
John Heiss, Fl.
13 May 1981: North Essex Community College, Haverhill, MA
Michael Finegold, Fl.
2 Apr 1982: North Essex Community College, Haverhill, MA
Michael Finegold, Fl.
24 Apr 1984: Brown Hall, New England Conservatory of Music, Boston, MA
Helen Campo, Fl.

Bibliography:
Driver, Paul. "Cornucopia Sampled at New England Conservatory." *The Boston Globe* 26 Apr 1984: 71.

Program Notes:
"These epigrammatic studies were initially concerned with the 'spirit' of the traditional virtuoso etude. Therefore they emphasize the realms of technical difficulty which derive from a broadly based musical-stylistic spectrum. Their primary aesthetic inspiration was stimulated by the early Romantics, primarily Chopin, Schumann and Schubert. In addition, I have endowed them with a pragmatic value which embraces the same pedagogical attitudes clearly represented in many of Bach's solo keyboard compositions. It is the amalgam of these tendencies and influences towards which these instrumental songs ideally aspire. *Songs Without Words* was given its world premiere by Stephanie Jutt at the Longy School of Music, Cambridge, Massachusetts in 1976."
—William Thomas McKinley (© 1977), from Margun Music, inc.MM042 published score.

"Of *Songs Without Words*, there are twenty-eight in all. Each movement is a kind of small, dramatic episode, independent in itself, yet also part of an overall progression. Mr. McKinley, who teaches at this conservatory [New England Conservatory], writes that "The visual layout is like an album of leaves—each varied and yet related by a common organic biology and spirit..." He advises that the performer may wish to isolate a few of the songs (pages) to form a 'smaller' work; nine of these have been selected for presentation in this concert."
—John Heiss (© 1977), from 17 Oct 1977 program.

VII.A.4 Elegy for Solo Alto Flute

Date: [Mar 1994] in [Reading, MA ("Lells")] *Duration:* 6'00"
Dedication: "To Robert Stallman in the memory of Robert Black"
Commission: [Robert Stallman]
Publisher: MMC Publications

Movement(s):
Largo elegiaco e libero (♩=46)

Instrumentation:
Alt Fl solo.

MS Description:
Holograph with signature, pencil on paper. *Location:* Boston Public Library.

Editorial Notes:
Author was witness to date and location of composition. Commission information from the composer.

Performance History:
[† See *Recording(s).*]

Recording(s):
Recording firm as yet undetermined: to be released in 1995
Robert Stallman, Fl.

See also: Ancient Memories... (II.M.3)

Group VII.B: Works for Solo Clarinet

VII.B.1 Solo Duet for Clarinet ("Duet for One")

Date: 11 Oct 1968 *Duration:* 4'35"
Dedication: "for Bill Hudson"
Commission: [Bill Hudson]
Publisher: MMC Publications

Movement(s):
[One untitled movement.]

Instrumentation:
Cl solo.

MS Description:
Holograph, pencil on paper. *Location:* Boston Public Library.
Markings: Final page: "begun 8:30 pm | fine 11: pm"; "Solo | Duet for Clarinet"

Editorial Notes:
Commission information from the composer. Premiere performance information taken from McKinley's notes.

Performance History:
[† 1973: University of Wisconsin, Madison, WI
Les Thimmig, Cl.]

VII.B.2 Song for Solo B♭ Clarinet

Date: Oct 1968 in Albany, NY (SUNY Albany) *Duration:* 8'23"
Dedication: "to Bill Hudson"
Commission: [Bill Hudson]
Publisher: MMC Publications

Movement(s):
♩=52–60

Instrumentation:
Cl solo.

MS Description:
Holograph with printed name, ink on vellum. *Location:* Boston Public Library.

Editorial Notes:
Fair copy is a McKinley holograph (ink on vellum, dated, with location "Yale" marked on the first page). Commission and premiere performance information from the composer.

Performance History:
[† Date unknown: Yale University, New Haven, CT
Bill Hudson, Cl.]

VII.B.3 For One

Date: 18 Nov 1971 in Urbana, IL *Duration:* 5'00"
Commission: [Paul Zonn]
Publisher: MMC Publications

Movement(s):
♩=76

Instrumentation:
Cl solo.

MS Description:
Holograph with printed name, ink on vellum. *Location:* Lost.*

Editorial Notes:
*A photocopy of the manuscript has survived and been placed in the Boston Public Library collection. ‡An American Academy and Institute of Arts and Letters grant of $5,000 was awarded for the making of the CRI recording. Commission taken from McKinley's notes.

Performance History:
[†?] 22 Oct 1976: Virgil M. Hancher Auditorium, University of Iowa, Iowa City, IA
Richard Stoltzman, Cl.
[† (New York)] 7 Nov 1976: St. Patrick's Cathedral, New York, NY
Richard Stoltzman, Cl.
[† (San Francisco)] 17 Apr 1977: Alfred Hertz Memorial Auditorium, University of California, Berkeley, CA
Richard Stoltzman, Cl.
12 May 1977: Auditorium of the New York Public Library at Lincoln Center, New York, NY
Richard Stoltzman, Cl.
[† (Boston)] 15 Jan 1980: Sala de Puerto Rico, Massachusetts Institute of Technology, Cambridge, MA
Richard Stoltzman, Cl.
10 May 1981: Brown Hall, New England Conservatory of Music, Boston, MA
Edward Ferris, Cl.
12 Oct 1986: Jordan Hall, New England Conservatory of Music, Boston, MA
Richard Stoltzman, Cl.
15 Mar 1987: Carnegie Hall, New York, NY
Richard Stoltzman, Cl.

Recording(s):
Composers Recordings, Inc.: CRI SD 507, ©1984 (LP)‡
Richard Stoltzman, Cl.

Bibliography:
Hughes, Allen. "Concert: Tashi's Webern Elates." *The New York Times* 14 May 1977: 14.

Rothstein, Edward. "Music Notes: Changes for Mostly Mozart." *The New York Times* 8 May 1983: 2.23.
Spousta, Holly. "A Man of 'Eminently Worthwhile Music': Profiling Reading's William T. McKinley." *Reading Daily Times Chronicle* 21 Aug 1986: 1, 14A.
Grimes, Ev. "Yale University American Music Oral History Series: William Thomas McKinley." Oct 1986, Yale University School of Music: 75.
Miller, Nancy. "A Perfect Doubles Match at Jordan Hall." *The Boston Globe* 14 Oct 1986.
Page, Tim. "Music: Richard Stoltzman." *The New York Times* 21 Mar 1987: 14.
Tassel, Janet. "From Fat Tuesday's to Carnegie Hall." *Musical America* 107(Jan 1988), no. 6: 21–22.

Program Notes:
For Composers Recordings CRI SD 507 liner notes and 15 Mar 1987 program notes, see *Paintings VII* (VIII.B.3).

"*For one* was composed in 1972 [*sic*] while I was in residence for a performance at the University of Illinois at Urbana. The prime content of the work is emotional in origin. I wanted to capture the attitude of a single extemporaneous outburst, as if improvised and yet with a sense of inevitable organic growth from idea to idea. In a phrase, the work is 'through composed,' much in the same manner as the 19th-century abstraction known as *Durchkompaniert*. The ethos of the work then is Romantic, inspired by a Dionysian impulse, with Crocian expressionism. Paul Klee spoke of his desire to capture the totality of a painting in one gesture, without the influence of self criticism or the negative censorship of the conscious mind. I too wanted to 'capture' the same sensation, to create a virtuosic, melismatic, unending melody, which never looks back, is never self critical, and always energized by an intuitive self propelled emotional-psychic fine. The work is dedicated 'for one' Richard Stoltzman and I had his personality and concept of performance always in the foreground of my musical thinking."
—William Thomas McKinley (© 1994), from his notes.

VII.B.4 Composition I for Bass Clarinet

Date: Dec 1972 *Duration:* 4'36"
Dedication: "to Les [Thimmig]"
Publisher: MMC Publications

Movement(s):
[I.*] ♪=74
[II.*] ♪=47
[III.*] ♩=47

Instrumentation:
BCl solo.

Sketches:
1 draft of the opening of I. 7 drafts and 1 sketch of the opening of II. 2 unidentified sketches.

MS Description:
Holograph with printed name, pencil on vellum. *Location:* Boston Public Library.

Editorial Notes:
*The compositional process demonstrated in the sketches indicates a three movement structure, despite the lack of a double bar at the end of each of the first two movements. Premiere performance information from the composer.

Performance History:
[† Date unknown: location unknown
Les Thimmig, BCl.]

Program Notes:
"Growth and Form of Lecture will follow the growth and form of a recent work—a trilogy for solo woodwinds and saxophones entitled *Composition I, Steps Part I* and *II*. The architecture expands from monophony to polyphony. The polyphony is of two kinds—Medieval denotes heterophony and classical denotes traditional common practice polyphonic procedure. The passages of heterophony are not, however, purely random and can not simply be dismissed as aleatoric fragments vertically in musical space. The 'affect' of heterophony is principally achieved and heightened by the various layerings or superpositions of live and pre-taped performance. Since all the parts are performed by one soloist the *Human* Factor plays an especially significant role in attempting to coordinate the many vertical-linear difficulties canonic variants, incipient mensuration canons and the like which are present in the score. *Steps Part II* presents a significant challenge in this arena.

"*Comp[osition] I* is a solo work [that is] monophonic. More difficult to comprehend is my use of the term *Classical*. Classical denotes a process somewhat more vague. Since my work is not tonal the listener will not perceive vertical blocks of harmonic movement and thus be unable on first hearing (or perhaps many hearings) to understand the musical analogs I have substituted for classical common-practice polyphonic procedures. Many passages are related in terms of specific intervallic designs—the imitations, stretti, and episodes which follow are at times composed of similar designs and are meant to create a 'tonal,' i.e. abstract harmonic affect on the listener. These areas shift quickly, kaleidoscopically, thereby continually interrupting any sense of vertical stability. Finally, both polyphonic processes are clearly manifest in the structure of the work consistently in movement creating a synergy between heterophonic polyphonic thought—energy and static—a kineticism exploiting the simultaneities and dualities of both."
—William Thomas McKinley (© 1994), from his notes.

VII.B.5 Steps (Part I) for Solo and Two Pre-Taped Bass Clarinets

Date: 5 Jan 1973 *Duration:* 7'19"
Dedication: "For Les [Thimmig], once again!"
Commission: [Les Thimmig]
Publisher: MMC Publications

Movement(s):
With clarity, pristine (♩=80–87)

Instrumentation:
Cl solo, 2 pre-recorded BCl.

MS Description:
Holograph with signature, pencil on paper. *Location:* Boston Public Library.
Markings: Final Page: "to the new year! for Les, with the deepest admiration—"

Editorial Notes:
Commission information from the composer.

Performance History:
† 20 Feb 1973: Mills Concert Hall, University of Wisconsin, Madison, WI
University of Wisconsin Contemporary Chamber Ensemble, Les Thimmig, Cond.
1 Oct 1973: Morphy Recital Hall, University of Wisconsin, Madison, WI
Les Thimmig, Cl; Dan Harris, Taped BCl.
[† (Boston)] 26 Mar 1974: Jordan Hall, New England Conservatory of Music, Boston, MA
Les Thimmig, Cl; [Dan Harris, Taped BCl.]
[1973–80]: Madison Art Center, Madison, WI
Les Thimmig, Cl; Dan Harris, Taped BCl.
[†? (Europe)] 26 Apr 1987: Opéra de Nice, Nice, France
Dan Harris, Cl; [Dan Harris, Taped BCl.]

Bibliography:
Elsner, Carmen. "New Sound Explored on Campus." *Wisconsin State Journal* 23 Feb 1973: IV 17.

Program Notes:
For 20 Feb 1973 notes see *Cello Music* (VIII.E.5).
For McKinley's handwritten notes see *Composition I* (VII.B.4).

"*Steps* was composed for [New Music Symposium II at the University of Wisconsin]. One of the things I admire most about his music is the blending and synthesis of traditional Western instrumental virtuosity with the unique virtuosity that has emerged from Black American music, as embodied in the art of John Coltrane and Cecil Taylor. Part I is ostensibly a solo piece for bass clarinet which is interrupted near the end by two taped bass clarinets. Part II employs a constantly shifting texture of 'live' player plus three pre-recorded tracks, all of which utilize varying combinations of the four instruments. Future plans call for more parts, and it is not unthinkable that it will eventually become an entire program in itself, utilizing sixteen pre-recorded tracks."
—Les Thimmig (© 1973), from 1 Oct 1973 program.

VII.B.6 Concerto for Solo B♭ Clarinet

Date: 15 Mar 1976 in Manchester, MA ("Carriage House") *Duration:* 50'24"
Dedication: "To Richard Stoltzman" and "To the spirit of...and once again...time transitory...an illusion intensified and meaning restored to all who are truly...and justly alive..."
Commission: [Richard Stoltzman]
Publisher: MMC Publications

Movement(s):
Semplice, a distant past recalled, with hushed vibrations (♩=42)

Instrumentation:
Cl solo.

MS Description:
Holograph with printed name, ink on paper. *Location:* Boston Public Library.
Markings: Page 4: "For Dick Stoltzman with respect and love."

Editorial Notes:
Commission taken from McKinley's notes.

VII.B.7 Entrata [No. 1] for Solo B♭ Clarinet

Date: [Jul 1983] in [Reading, MA ("Lells")] *Duration:* 1'30"
Dedication: [Richard Stoltzman]
Commission: [Richard Stoltzman]
Publisher: Margun Music Inc.

Movement(s):
Scherzo (𝅗𝅥=120)

Instrumentation:
Cl solo.

MS Description:
Holograph with signature, pencil on paper. *Location:* Owned by Richard Stoltzman. *Markings:* Cover page: "Walking tempo=♩=60 per step (or even slower). Soloist walking from near auditorium entrance down main aisle to stage, slowly, playing to the right and left (and to the balcony)—then to stage center, or where the soloist prefers to finish the piece."

Editorial Notes:
Date and location of composition taken from McKinley's notes. Dedication taken from McKinley's program notes. Commission information from *AMC Newsletter* 27(Winter 1985), no. 1: 14 and McKinley's notes.

Performance History:
† 26 Feb 1984: Carnegie Hall, New York, NY
Richard Stoltzman, Cl.
[† (Boston)] 14 Sep 1985: Hatch Shell, Boston, MA
Richard Stoltzman, Cl.

Bibliography:
See *Entrata No. 2* (VII.B.8).

Program Notes:
See *Entrata No. 2* (VII.B.8).

VII.B.8 Entrata No. 2 for Solo B♭ (or E♭) Clarinet

Date: [Jul 1983] in [Reading, MA ("Lells")] *Duration:* 2'30"
Dedication: [Richard Stoltzman]
Commission: [Richard Stoltzman]
Publisher: Margun Music Inc.

Movement(s):
With pronouncement (𝅗𝅥=60+)

Instrumentation:
Pic Cl or Cl solo.

MS Description:
Holograph with signature, pencil on paper. *Location:* Owned by Richard Stoltzman. *Markings:* Cover page: "Same walk-on instructions as *Entrata No. 1*" See also *Entrata No. 1* (VII.B.7).

Editorial Notes:
Date and location of composition taken from McKinley's notes. Dedication taken from McKinley's program notes. Commission information from *AMC Newsletter* 27(Winter 1985), no. 1: 14 and McKinley's notes.

Performance History:
[†] 3 Feb 1984: Jordan Hall, New England Conservatory of Music, Boston, MA
Richard Stoltzman, Cl.
† [NY] 26 Feb 1984: Carnegie Hall, New York, NY
Richard Stoltzman, Cl.
14 Sep 1985: Hatch Shell, Boston, MA
Richard Stoltzman, Cl.
[†? (Europe)] 17 Feb 1986: Musée d'art et d'historie, Ville de Genève, France
Richard Stoltzman, Cl.

Bibliography:
Rich, Alan. "Pied Piper of the Clarinet." Newsweek 19 Mar 1984: 105.
Buell, Richard. "Noise One Doesn't Mind Along Storrow Drive." *The Boston Globe* 16 Sep 1985: 24.

Program Notes:
"These two short companion works [*Entratas Nos. 1 and 2*] may be performed separately or together. Apropos of their title the *Entratas* are fanfares, calls-to-attention intended to open a concert (or half a concert), and were written specifically for Mr. Stoltzman's virtuoso talents. According to the composer, these two pieces unlike most of his works, are intended for 'lay audiences' (a perhaps inadvertent reminder of the polarities inflicted upon classical music today). Though not written in a deliberately jazz-oriented style, both *Entratas* 'flirt with jazz... and with the audience.'"
—Peter Kristian Mose (© 1983), from 3 Feb 1984 program.

VII.B.a ~~Impressions of Marlene~~

Date: [ca. 1972]
Publisher: Unpublished

Movement(s):
I. ♪=60
II. ♪=76

Instrumentation:
Cl solo.

MS Description:
Holograph, ink on paper. *Location:* Boston Public Library.

Editorial Notes:
MS ends shortly after the beginning of the second movement. Date determined through paleographic analysis.

See also: Poem of Light... (II.K.2).

Group VII.C: Works for Solo Saxophone

VII.C.1 For Les (Three Pieces for Soprano Sax)

Date: 13 Sep 1972 *Duration:* 2'53"
Dedication: [Les Thimmig]
Commission: [Les Thimmig]
Publisher: MMC Publications

Movement(s):
I. ♪=52
II. ♪=120
III. Bold (♪=76)

Instrumentation:
Sop Sax solo.

MS Description:
Holograph with printed name, ink on vellum. *Location:* Boston Public Library.

Editorial Notes:
Dedication inferred from the title of the work. Commission information from the composer. Verification of 11 Oct 1974 as premiere performance from McKinley's notes.

Performance History:
[†] 11 Oct 1974: Murphy Hall, University of Wisconsin, Madison, WI
Les Thimmig, Sop. Sax.
26 Jan 1980: Mills Concert Hall, University of Wisconsin, Madison, WI
Les Thimmig, Sop Sax.

Program Notes:
"My programs never seem to be without the services of some McKinley music. He's my man, and I play his music. It's just that simple. *Three Pieces for Les* was written between 4 and 8 a.m. on September 13, 1972. We had played a jazz concert that evening (in Chicago) and wound up back at his apartment wolfing down vast amounts of scrambled eggs, bacon, and black coffee. (Thanks, Marlene. Sure tasted good.) One by one, we repaired to assorted chairs and sofas and passed out: except for Tom, that is. He claims that something he heard me play on soprano saxophone that night stuck and intrigued him. Neither one of us knows what it was, but he grabbed a pen and these three small pieces are the result. (Must have been the bacon.)"
—Les Thimmig (© 1980), from 26 Jan 1980 program.

VII.C.2 Solo Tenor Saxophone Piece No. 1

Date: 22 Feb 1975 in Reading, MA ("Linnea Lane") *Duration:* 10'22"
Dedication: "For Les Thimmig"
Commission: [Les Thimmig]
Publisher: MMC Publications

Movement(s):
To Coltrane: Brilliant, soaring (♪=137–142)

Instrumentation:
Ten Sax solo.

MS Description:
Holograph with printed name, ink on vellum. *Location:* Boston Public Library.

Editorial Notes:
Commission information from the composer. Premiere performance information taken from McKinley's notes.

Performance History:
[† 1975: University of Wisconsin, Madison, WI
Les Thimmig, Ten Sax.]
18 May 1976: Lovejoy Library Auditorium, Southern Illinois University, Edwardville, IL
Les Thimmig, Ten Sax.

Program Notes:
"[*Solo Tenor Saxophone Piece*] was composed February 22, 1975 in a single sitting from approximately 10:00 p.m. to 8:00 a.m. I was arriving in Boston that morning for a week of playing and teaching at the New England Conservatory, where [Tom] teaches. He simply decided to compose me a little gift. However, sitting up all night working caused him to pass out immediately upon completion of the piece, and he missed my plane, leaving me sitting at Logan airport for hours with five horns, stands, music, tapes, luggage, and mad as hell. It was a most poignant experience when he finally did show up and let me know that the delay was caused by the birth of a new piece. I would have gladly waited all day. As for the music itself, little needs to be said. The contrasts of tempo, register, loudness, etc. are clear and direct. Of most interest, possibly, is the way it moves, non-stop, from beginning to end. Just as an improvisation is played in one take, this piece was written in one take."
—Les Thimmig (© 1976), from 18 May 1976 program.

VII.C.3 Ballade for Soprano Saxophone

Date: [Jun 1983] in [Reading, MA ("Lells")] *Duration:* 8'31"
Dedication: [Les Thimmig]
Commission: [Les Thimmig]
Publisher: Unpublished

Movement(s):
[One untitled movement]

Instrumentation:
Sop Sax solo.

Sketches:
1 sketch of the opening.

MS Description: Uncertain–probably ink on vellum. *Location:* Lost.

Editorial Notes:
Date, Location of composition, dedication and commission from McKinley's notes. Notes also indicate premiere performance by Les Thimmig during his 1984 Midwest tour.

Performance History:
5 Jun 1986: Merkin Concert Hall, New York, NY
Les Thimmig, Sop Sax.
6 Jan 1988: Weill Recital Hall, New York, NY
Les Thimmig, Sop Sax.

Bibliography:
Holland, Bernard. "Music: Works by McKinley." *The New York Times* 7 Jun 1986.
Lifchitz, Max. "Composer of Note: William Thomas McKinley." *Living Music* 4(Fall 1986), no. 1: 2.

Group VII.D: Works for Solo Bassoon

VII.D.1 Charts and Shapes for Bassoon Solo

Date: 1968 in New Haven, CT (Yale Univ.) *Duration:* 4'30"
Dedication: "to Bill [Douglas]"
Publisher: MMC Publications

Movement(s):
]Four untitled movements.]

Instrumentation:
Bsn solo.*

MS Description:
Holograph with printed name, pencil on vellum. *Location:* Boston Public Library.

Editorial Notes:
*Program of 27 Apr 1968 indicates the accompaniment of the bassoon by an improvisation ensemble. There is no notation in the score for such instrumentation, however. Confirmation of 27 Apr 1968 as premiere performance from McKinley's notes.

Performance History:
[†] 27 Apr 1968: The Master's House, Erza Stiles College, Yale University, New Haven, CT William Douglas, Bsn; [Untitled ensemble].

VII.D.2 Twelve Stages for Solo Bassoon

Date: 16 Nov 1971 *Duration:* 25'41"
Commission: [Bill Douglas]
Publisher: MMC Publications

Movement(s):
I. Ana
II. Lai
III. Talea
IV. Time: ♩=70
V. Chanson: ♩=46
VI. Organum
VII. Plainsong: ♩=56
VIII. Chart: Agitated (♪=66)
IX. Pretty
X. Maze
XI. Epilogue: ♪=57
XII. Cadenza

Instrumentation:
Bsn solo; Tape (some sections must be pre-recorded).

Sketches:
7 folios of notes, primarily on the design of the tenth "Stage."

MS Description:
Holograph with printed name, ink on vellum. *Location:* Boston Public Library.
Markings: Stages I and II dated 11 Nov 1971. Stages III though VIII dated 13 Nov 1971, with VIII also marked "evening." Stage XI dated 14 Nov 1971. Stage XII dated 16 Nov 1971.

Editorial Notes:
Commission and premiere performance information from McKinley's notes.

Performance History:
[† 4 Nov 1978: Jordan Hall, New England Conservatory of Music, Boston, MA
Janet Grice, Bsn.]

Group VII.E: Works for Solo French Horn

VII.E.1 Three Pieces for Solo French Horn

Date: 29 Jul 1979 in Reading, MA ("Barn") *Duration:* 9'28"
Dedication: "for Phillip Myers"
Commission: [Phillip Myers]
Publisher: MMC Publications

Movement(s):
I. Amabile (♩=76)
II. ♩=90
III. Appassionato (𝅗𝅥=30)

Instrumentation:
Hn solo.

MS Description:
Engraving by McKinley, ink stencil on vellum. *Location:* Boston Public Library.

Editorial Notes:
Commission information from the composer.

VII.E.2 Portraits for Solo French Horn

Date: Sep 1985 *Duration:* 19'30"
Dedication: "to Dale Clevenger"
Commission: [Dale Clevenger]
Publisher: MMC Publications

Movement(s):
I. Grandioso (♩=72)
II. Allegro burlesco (♩=126)
III. Andante ma non troppo (♩.=84)
IV. Larghetto (♩=66)

Instrumentation:
Hn solo.

MS Description:
Holograph with signature, pencil on vellum. *Location:* Boston Public Library.

Editorial Notes:
Commission information taken from McKinley's notes.

VII.E.3 Three Bagatelles for Solo French Horn

Date: Oct 1985 *Duration:* 4'30"
Dedication: "to Dale Clevenger"
Commission: [Dale Clevenger]
Publisher: MMC Publications

Movement(s):
I. Andante Amabile (♩=76)
II. Larghetto (♩=48)
III. Allegro tempestoso (♩=144)

Instrumentation:
Hn solo.

MS Description:
Holograph with signature, pencil on vellum. *Location:* Boston Public Library.

Editorial Notes:
Commission and premiere performance information from the composer. Additional premiere information from Dale Clevenger.

Performance History:
[† ca. 1985: Santa Fe Chamber Music Festival, Santa Fe, NM.
Dale Clevenger, Hn.]

Group VII.F: Works for Solo Guitar

VII.F.1 Ballade for Solo Guitar

Date: 1972
Duration: 1'55"
Commission: [Ronald Anthony]
Publisher: MMC Publications

Movement(s):
♩=50

Instrumentation:
Gtr solo.

MS Description:
Holograph with printed name, ink on vellum. *Location:* Boston Public Library.

Editorial Notes:
Commission and premiere performance information from the composer.

Performance History:
[† Date unknown: Location unknown
Ronald Anthony, Gtr.]

Group VII.G: Works for Solo Harp

VII.G.1 [Etude No. 1 for Solo Harp]

Date: 17 Oct 1973 in Reading, MA ("Linnea Lane")
Duration: 7'00"
Dedication: ["To Marlene"]
Commission: [Susan Allen]
Publisher: MMC Publications

Movement(s):
Expansive, with great freedom of gesture (♩=42)

Instrumentation:
Hp solo.

MS Description:
Holograph, pencil on paper. *Location:* Boston Public Library.

Markings: Dedication page of fair copy: "Extend the limits... | with internal | contact... | energy fused..."

Editorial Notes:
MS contains a great deal of shorthand. Fair copy is a McKinley holograph (ink on vellum with printed name, dated Nov 1973). Title and dedication taken from fair copy. Commission and European premiere performance information taken from McKinley's notes.

Performance History:
† 28 Feb 1974: Museum of Fine Arts, Boston, MA
Susan Allen, Hp.
[†? (Europe) Aug 1976: Dutch National Radio, Netherlands
Susan Allen, Hp.]
6 Oct 1979: Weill Recital Hall, New York, NY
Susan Allen, Hp.

Recording(s):
1750 Arch Records: S-1787, ©1982 (LP)
Susan Allen, Harp

Bibliography:
Horowitz, Joseph. "New Music: Susan Allen on the Harp." *The New York Times* 8 Oct 1979.
Dyer, Richard. "Susan Allen: *New Music for Harp, Vol. 1* (1750 Arch)." *The Boston Globe* 13 Oct 1983: Calendar 7.

Program Notes:
"[Etude no. 1] is superior music-making in the *lingua franca* of advanced musical thought, ranging in an improvisatory flow over vast terrains of expressivity. Poignant, dark, contemplative, always fervent, the composition expands the boundary conditions of harp literature in confident knowledge of the instrument's resources. This single-movement work contains a world of invention displaying contrasts so stark as to bring to mind Gertude Stein's comment about how well Americans handle at one and the same time extremes of violence and tenderness. The listener is bound to sense at once that McKinley traffics in a spacious art sustaining a personal, unbroken vision: expressionism free and wild yet controlled and confined. In this and other unions of opposites the composer asserts a persuasive, beautiful grandeur."
—Mel Powell (©1982), from 1750 Arch Records S-1787 liner notes

VII.G.2 Etude No. 2 for Solo Harp

Date: Feb 1974 in Reading, MA ("Linnea Lane") *Duration:* 7'25"
Commission: [Susan Allen]
Publisher: MMC Publications

Movement(s):
With bravura and flight (♩=50)

Instrumentation:
Hp solo.

Sketches:
20 drafts of the opening. 29 drafts of page 2. 4 unidentified drafts.

MS Description:
Holograph with printed name, ink on paper. *Location:* Boston Public Library.

Editorial Notes:
Commission and premiere performance information taken from McKinley's notes.

Performance History:
[† Aug 1976: Dutch National Radio, Netherlands
Susan Allen, Hp.]

Group VII.H: Works for Solo Keyboard

VII.H.1 Four Piano Pieces [Piano Pieces Nos. 1–4]

Date: 9–11 Nov 1971 in Chicago, IL (Univ. of Chicago) *Duration:* 8'01"
Dedication: "to my wife"
Commission: [Arthur Maddox]
Publisher: MMC Publications

Movement(s):
I. [1/4 inch=1"]
II. Quasi improvisare (♩=40)
III. ♩=40
IV. [1/4 inch=1"]

Instrumentation:
Pno solo.

Sketches:
1 nearly complete draft.

MS Description:
Holograph with printed name, ink on vellum. *Location:* Boston Public Library.
Markings: Pieces I and II dated 9 Nov 1971. Piece III dated 10 Nov 1971. Piece IV dated 11 Nov 1971.

Editorial Notes:
Commission taken from McKinley's notes. Premiere performance information from the composer.

Performance History:
[† Date unknown: Location unknown
Arthur Maddox, Pno.]

VII.H.2 Eleven Interludes for Solo Piano [Piano Pieces Nos. 5–15]

Date: 12–13 Nov 1971 in Chicago, IL (Univ. of Chicago) *Duration:* 10'20"
Dedication: "to my wife"
Commission: [Arthur Maddox]
Publisher: MMC Publications

Movement(s):
Interlude I. [1/4 inch=1"]
Interlude II. [1/4 inch=1"]
Interlude III. ♪=40
Interlude IV. [1/4 inch=1"]
Interlude V. 𝅘𝅥𝅯=100
Interlude VI. [1/4 inch=1"]

Instrumentation:
Pno solo.

Interlude VII. ♩=76
Interlude VIII. [1/4 inch=1"]
Interlude IX. ♪=50
Interlude X. ♪=40
Interlude XI. ♩=76

Sketches:
1 incomplete draft. 6 folios and 1 bifolio of unidentified sketches.

MS Description:
Holograph with signature, ink on vellum. *Location:* Boston Public Library.
Markings: Interludes V–VIII dated 12 Nov 1971. Interludes IX–XI dated 13 Nov 1971.

Editorial Notes:
Commission taken from McKinley's notes.

Performance History:
† 4 Apr 1985: University of Lowell, Lowell, MA
Thomas Stumpf, Pno.
[† (Boston)] 9 Feb 1986: Brown Hall, New England Conservatory of Music, Boston, MA
Thomas Stumpf, Pno.
19 Feb 1987: Jordan Hall, New England Conservatory of Music, Boston, MA
Thomas Stumpf, Pno.

VII.H.3 Piano Piece [No.] 16

Date: 13 Nov 1971 in Chicago, IL (Univ. of Chicago) *Duration:* 2'59"
Dedication: "To the spirit of..."
Commission: [Arthur Maddox]
Publisher: MMC Publications

Movement(s):
♩=40

Instrumentation:
Pno solo.

Sketches:
3 drafts of the opening.

MS Description:
Holograph with printed name, ink on vellum. *Location:* Boston Public Library.

Editorial Notes:
Commission taken from McKinley's notes.

VII.H.4 Fantasies and Inventions for Solo Harpsichord*

Date: 27 Apr–12 May 1972 in Chicago, IL (Univ. of Chicago) *Duration:* 34'02"
Commission: [Arthur Maddox]
Publisher: MMC Publications

Movement(s):
[Invention I]. Presto (♪=160)
[Invention II]. Very fast, but maintain gestural clarity (♪=130–150)

Instrumentation:
Hpschd solo.

[Invention III]. Arioso, maintain tempo, strict (♪=30)
[Invention IV]. Detached, scherzo (♪=70)
Fantasia. ♪=75
[Invention V].
[Invention VI]. Quasi improvisare
[Invention VII]. Quiet, legato (♪=40)
[Invention VIII]. Caprice (𝅘𝅥𝅯=60)
[Invention IX]. Legato possible, short pause between each 4 note group

Sketches:
1 draft of the opening of I. 1 draft of the opening of II. 11 drafts of the opening of III. 1 draft of page 2 of III. 1 draft of the opening of IV. 1 draft of the opening of the Fantasia. 1 draft of page 2 of the Fantasia. 1 draft of the opening of V. 1 draft of page 2 of VII. 1 draft of the opening of VIII. 1 draft of page 2 of VIII. 2 drafts of the opening of IX. 15 unidentified drafts.

MS Description:
Holograph with printed name, ink on paper. *Location:* Boston Public Library.
Markings: Invention II dated 27 Apr 1972. Invention III dated 1 May 1972. Invention IV dated 2 May 1972. Fantasia dated 4 May 1972. Inventions V and VI dated 5 May 1972. Invention VII dated 6 May 1972. Invention VIII dated 10 May 1972. Invention IX dated 12 May 1972.

Editorial Notes:
*Title originally appears with "Fantasies" spelled as "Fantasys." Commission taken from McKinley's notes. Premiere performance information from the composer. There is nothing to suggest that these works should be performed in any particular order. The manuscript has no page or movement numbers and, upon first examination, was completely unordered. The above movement listing represents my best attempt at establishing some form of order, based upon the dates found on some of the pieces. As it is common for McKinley to begin dating work collections such as this after the second or third work, I have listed the undated invention first. It was not possible, however, to establish an order within each date. Therefore the order for the inventions written on 5 May 1970 is random. An analysis of the sketches indicates that the work began with Invention III and was originally conceived as a piano piece.

Performance History:
[† Date unknown: Location unknown
Arthur Maddox, Pno.]

Bibliography:
Grimes, Ev. "Yale University American Music Oral History Series: William Thomas McKinley." Oct 1986, Yale University School of Music: 64–65.

VII.H.5 Piano Piece No. 18 ("Journeys")

Date: Nov 1973 in Reading, MA ("Linnea Lane") *Duration:* 3'04"
Publisher: MMC Publications

Movement(s):
Wild (𝅘𝅥𝅰=75)

Instrumentation:
Pno solo.

Sketches:
1 incomplete draft.

MS Description:
Holograph with printed name, ink on vellum. *Location:* Boston Public Library.

VII.H.6 Piano Piece No. 19

Date: Nov 1973 in Reading, MA ("Linnea Lane") *Duration:* 3'05"
Publisher: MMC Publications

Movement(s):
♪=57

Instrumentation:
Pno solo.

MS Description:
Holograph with printed name, ink on vellum. *Location:* Boston Public Library.

VII.H.7 Fantasy for Piano Solo

Date: Sep 1974 in Reading, MA ("Linnea Lane") *Duration:* 17'28"
Publisher: MMC Publications

Movement(s):
Presto molto (♪=120)

Instrumentation:
Pno solo.

MS Description:
Holograph with printed name, ink on paper. *Location:* Boston Public Library.

Editorial Notes:
Article in 3 Apr 1985 *Lowell Sun* indicates premiere performance by Thomas Stumpf. Additional premiere information taken from McKinley's notes.

Performance History:
[† 3 Mar 1979: Longy School of Music, Cambridge, MA
Thomas Stumpf, Pno.]
11 Jun 1982: [Location unknown]
Thomas Stumpf, Pno.

Bibliography:
Berg, Frances. "Thomas Stumpf to Perform Tomorrow Night at ULowell." *Lowell Sun* 3 Apr 1985.

VII.H.8 Piano Piece [No.] 20 ("From a Private Monologue")

Date: 23 Apr 1975 in Reading, MA ("Linnea Lane") *Duration:* 11'48"
Publisher: MMC Publications

Movement(s):
Maintain dotted feel of anxiety (𝅘𝅥𝅯=47)

Instrumentation:
Pno solo.

Sketches:
41 drafts of the opening (earlier titles: Etude No. 1 for Solo Piano; Etude; Etudes for Two Pianos). 3 unidentified drafts.

MS Description:
Holograph with printed name, ink on paper. *Location:* Boston Public Library.

VII.H.9 Piano Piece [No.] 21 ("From a Private Monologue")

Date: 6 May 1975 in Reading, MA ("Linnea Lane") *Duration:* 3'17"
Publisher: MMC Publications

Movement(s):
♪=85+

Instrumentation:
Pno solo.

MS Description:
Holograph with printed name, ink on vellum. *Location:* Boston Public Library.

VII.H.10 Piano Piece No. 22 ("Blues")

Date: 9 Dec 1975 in Manchester, MA ("Carriage House") *Duration:* 23'09"
Publisher: MMC Publications

Movement(s):
Blues (♪=48)

Instrumentation:
Pno solo.

MS Description:
Holograph with printed name, ink on vellum. *Location:* Boston Public Library.

Editorial Notes:
Confirmation of 24 Mar 1978 as premiere performance from McKinley's notes.

Performance History:
[†] 24 Mar 1978: Jordan Hall, New England Conservatory of Music, Boston, MA
Thomas Stumpf, Pno.

Bibliography:
Berg, Frances. "Thomas Stumpf to Perform Tomorrow Night at ULowell." *Lowell Sun* 3 Apr 1985.

VII.H.11 Piano Study

Date: [1975] *Duration:* 1'41"
Publisher: MMC Publications

Movement(s):
𝅗𝅥=60

Instrumentation:
Pno solo.

Sketches:
1 draft of the opening.

MS Description:
Holograph, pencil on vellum. *Location:* Boston Public Library.

Editorial Notes:
Dating determined through paleographic analysis and discovery of sketch among other sketches from 1975.

VII.H.12 [Preludes]

Date: [ca. 1988] *Duration:* 2'30"
Publisher: MMC Publications

Movement(s):
Prelude No. I. Allegro (𝅗𝅥.=60)
Prelude No. II. Largo lamentoso (♩=30)
Prelude No. III. Più animato e flessible (𝅗𝅥.=56)*

Instrumentation:
Pno solo.

Sketches:
1 draft of the opening.

MS Description:
Holograph, pencil on vellum. *Location:* Boston Public Library.

Editorial Notes:
*Prelude No. 3 is unfinished (MS ends after 18 measures). Title taken from draft. Date determined through paleographic analysis.

VII.H.13 Waltzes for Piano

Date: [Mar 1993] in [Reading, MA ("Lells")] *Duration:* 7'40"
Dedication: "to Nick Underhill (and Chopin)"
Commission: [Nicholas Underhill]
Publisher: MMC Publications

Movement(s):
I. Dolce e con ritmo (♩=112)
II. Con moto e agitato (𝅗𝅥.=63)
III. Andante amoroso (♩=84)
IV. Prestissimo, á la minute waltz (𝅗𝅥.=72)

Instrumentation:
Pno solo.

Sketches:
1 draft of the opening.

MS Description:
Holograph with signature, pencil on paper. *Location:* Boston Public Library.

Editorial Notes:
Author was witness to date and location of composition. Commission information from the composer.

Performance History:
† 14 Jun 1993: Weill Recital Hall, New York, NY
  Nicholas Underhill, Pno.
13 Feb 1994: Unitarian-Universalist Church, Portsmouth, NH
  Nicholas Underhill, Pno.
[† (Boston)] 14 Feb 1994: First and Second Church, Boston, MA
  Nicholas Underhill, Pno.

Program Notes:
"These short waltzes are written in the spirit of Chopin yet expressed with a modern sensibility."
—William Thomas McKinley (© 1993), from 14 Jun 1993, 13 and 14 Feb 1994 programs.

VII.H.a ~~Etude~~

Date: [ca. 1963]
Publisher: Unpublished

Movement(s):
♩=40

Instrumentation:
Pno solo.

MS Description:
Holograph, ink on paper. *Location:* Boston Public Library.

Editorial Notes:
MS ends after 3 pages. Date determined through paleographic analysis—writing is similar to that in *Orchestral Study* (I.C.1).

VII.H.b ~~Exercises in Composition~~

Date: [ca. 1968]
Publisher: Unpublished

Movement(s):
Freely, tender (♩=52)

Instrumentation:
Pno solo.

MS Description:
Holograph, ink on paper and vellum. *Location:* Boston Public Library.

Editorial Notes:
11 pages of the manuscript survive, but they are not consecutive. It is therefore not possible to determine the work's original length. Date determined through paleographic analysis.

VII.H.c ~~Water Color for Marlene's Beauty~~

Date: [ca. 1972]
Publisher: Unpublished

Movement(s):
[One untitled movement.]

Instrumentation:
Pno solo.

MS Description:
Holograph, pencil on paper. *Location:* Boston Public Library.

Editorial Notes:
MS ends in the middle of page 2. Date determined through paleographic analysis.

VII.H.d ~~Studies~~*

Date: [ca. 1972]
Publisher: Unpublished

Movement(s):
[♩=50]

Instrumentation:
Pno solo.

Sketches:
1 drafts of the opening. 1 chart of chord permutations.

MS Description:
Holograph, ink on paper. *Location:* Boston Public Library.

Editorial Notes:
*Title originally appears with "Studies" spelled as "Studys." MS ends after three measures. Tempo taken from draft of opening of the work.

VII.H.e ~~Good Morning~~

Date: [ca. 1973]
Publisher: Unpublished

Movement(s):
♪=76

Instrumentation:
Pno solo.

MS Description:
Holograph, pencil on paper. *Location:* Boston Public Library.

Editorial Notes:
MS contains four non-contiguous measures. Date determined through paleographic analysis.

VII.H.f ~~[Piano Piece No. 17]~~

Date: [ca. 1973]*

Movement(s):
[None]

Instrumentation:
Pno solo.

MS Description:
Unwritten.

Editorial Notes:
*No evidence exists to support the existence of this work. Most likely, McKinley incorrectly remembered the last Piano Piece number when he continued the cycle in 1973 with *Piano Piece No. 18* (VII.H.5).

VII.H.g ~~[Untitled Two-Part Invention in B♭ for Piano]~~

Date: [Early 1975]
Publisher: Unpublished

Movement(s):
[One untitled movement.]

Instrumentation:
Pno solo.

MS Description:
Holograph, pencil on paper. *Location:* Boston Public Library.
Markings: First Page: "2 Part."

Editorial Notes:
MS ends after 8 measures. MS was found with and on the same paper as early sketches for Piano Piece No. 20, thus allowing it to be dated as above.

VII.H.h ~~[Untitled for Piano No. 1]~~

Date: [ca. 1976]
Publisher: Unpublished

Movement(s):
Dolce, introspective (♩=60+)

Instrumentation:
Pno solo.

MS Description:
Holograph, ink on paper. *Location:* Boston Public Library.

Editorial Notes:
MS ends in the middle of page 2. Date determined though paleographic analysis.

VII.H.i ~~[Untitled for Piano No. 2]~~

Date: [ca. 1982]
Publisher: Unpublished

Movement(s):
Rich, weighted texture (♩=72)

Instrumentation:
Pno solo.

MS Description:
Holograph, pencil on paper. *Location:* Boston Public Library.

Editorial Notes:
MS ends after 49 measures. Date determined through paleographic analysis.

Group VII.I: Works for Solo Violin

VII.I.1 Arabesques for Solo Violin*

Date: 24–29 Dec 1971
Duration: 20'36"
Dedication: "to Paul [Zukofsky]"
Commission: [Paul Zukofsky]
Publisher: MMC Publications

Movement(s):
Arabesque I: ♪=44
Arabesque II: ♩=42
Arabesque III: ♪=35
Arabesque IV: ♩=52
Arabesque V: ♩=47
Arabesque VI: ♪=137
Arabesque VII: ♪=137
Arabesque VIII: Allegro molto (♪=120)
Arabesque IX: With boldness (𝅘𝅥𝅯=84)
Arabesque X: ♩=44

Instrumentation:
Vln solo.

Sketches:
9 drafts of the opening of I. 10 drafts of the opening of IX (Earlier title: "Pulses"). 8 unidentified sketches.

MS Description:
Holograph with printed name, ink on vellum. *Location:* Boston Public Library.
Markings: Arabesques I, II, III, and IV dated 24 Dec 1971. Arabesques V, VI, VII, and VIII dated 27 Dec 1971. Arabesque IX dated 28 Dec 1971. Arabesque X dated 29 Dec 1971.

Editorial Notes:
*Title originally appears with "Arabesque" spelled as "Arabasque." The movement titles have been likewise corrected. One of the drafts of Arabesque IX contains the title "Pulses," suggesting that it was begun first, then set aside until later for completion in its final form. Commission taken from McKinley's notes. Premiere performance information from the composer.

Performance History:
[† Date unknown: Sanders Theater, Cambridge, MA
Lucy Stoltzman, Vln.]

VII.I.2 Bagatelles and Finale for Solo Violin

Date: 1985 *Duration:* 16'45"
Dedication: "to Joel [Smirnoff], Lucy [Stoltzman], Syoko [Aki Erle] and my fiddler friends"
Commission: [Lucy Stoltzman]
Publisher: MMC Publications

Movement(s):
I. Presto (𝅗𝅥=100)
II. Andantino (♩=72)
III. Allegro ma non troppo (♩=84)
IV. Allegro molto burlesco (♩=132)
V. Andante tranquillo (♩=80)
VI. Prestissimo rustico (♪=176)
VII. Allegro moderato, ma non troppo (𝅗𝅥=120)
Finale: Larghetto dramatico (♪=108)

Instrumentation:
Vln solo.

MS Description:
Holograph with signature, pencil on vellum. *Location:* Boston Public Library.
Markings: Cover: "Bagatelle no. 1 is written in honor of Gunther Schuller's 60th Birthday— to a man of greatness and love—"

Editorial Notes:
Commission information from the composer.

Performance History:
† 19 Nov 1985: Jordan Hall, New England Conservatory of Music, Boston, MA (fourth movement only)
Lucy Stoltzman, Vln.
† 24 Jul 1986: Sanders Theater, Cambridge, MA (complete)
Lucy Stoltzman, Vln.
12 Oct 1986: Jordan Hall, New England Conservatory of Music, Boston, MA
Lucy Stoltzman, Vln.
[† (New York)] 8 Feb 1987: Merkin Concert Hall, New York, NY
Lucy Stoltzman, Vln.

Bibliography:

Tommasini, Anthony. "Red Sneakers' Mixed Bag Has Fun and Foolishness." *The Boston Globe* 26 Jul 1986.

Program Notes:

"*Seven Bagatelles and Finale* is dedicated to a distinguished group of violinists who have performed my music, including Joel Smirnoff, Nancy Cirillo, Eric Rosenblith, Joseph Silverstein, Ida Kavafian, and tonight's soloist Lucy Stoltzman.

"Although the overall character and style of the Seven Bagatelles conform to traditional expectation, the additional Finale movement, equal to one-third of the work's entire duration, considerably increases the temporal magnitude, formal architecture, and ultimate impact of the whole work's character. Although the soloist is given license to abridge this work, to mix and match the various Bagatelles, and to include or omit the Finale, tonight's performance premieres all seven Bagatelles and the Finale.

"Each Bagatelle is one to two minutes in length, with a unique emotive and formal character. The succession gradually gathers impetus, ultimately adopting the guise of symphonic movement-structures, culminating in the more elaborate and extensively developed Finale.

"The ambitious Finale then acts as a summation of the principal characteristics explored in the preceding movements and is consequently the most demanding. All of the pieces contain virtuosic, but idiomatic elements, and their cumulative development coupled with the extensive Finale should prove to be large."

—William Thomas McKinley (© 1986), from 24 Jul 1986 and 12 Oct 1986 programs.

Group VII.J: Works for Solo Viola

VII.J.1 Portraits for Solo Viola

Date: Nov 1973 in Reading, MA ("Linnea Lane") *Duration:* 21'08"
Commission: [James Dunham]
Publisher: MMC Publications

Movement(s):
I. Autumn: With intense mystery (♩=60)
II. Weapons: With noble gesture and tenderness (♪=57)
III. Prayer: Dance (♩=75)
IV. Granite: Brilliant (♩=48)
V. Clay: With vitriolic wildness and anger (♩=60)
VI. Silver: Majestic and with great calm (♪=47)
VII. Flowers: ♩=57
VIII. Ivory: With absolute precision and directness (♪=87)
IX. Crystals: With grace and clarity (♪=50)

Instrumentation:
Vla solo.

Sketches:
5 drafts of the opening of I. 1 draft of the opening of II. 2 drafts of the opening of III. 1 draft of the opening of IV. 1 draft of the opening of V. 1 draft of the opening of VII. 2 drafts of the opening of IX.

MS Description:
Holograph with printed name, ink on vellum. *Location:* Boston Public Library.
Markings: Each movement is individually marked with "fine," composer's printed name, date, and location. Movements I, II, IV, and VII–IX dated Nov 1973. Movement III dated "Thanksgiving 1973"

Editorial Notes:
Commission and premiere performance information from the composer.

Performance History:
[† Date unknown: Location unknown
James Dunham, Vla.]

VII.J.2 Waves (A Study for Solo Viola)

Date: Nov 1973 in Reading, MA ("Linnea Lane") *Duration:* 5'23"
Commission: [James Dunham]
Publisher: MMC Publications

Movement(s):
With dignity and strength (♪=57)

Instrumentation:
Vla solo.

MS Description:
Holograph with printed name, ink on vellum. *Location:* Boston Public Library.

Editorial Notes:
Commission and premiere performance information from the composer.

Performance History:
[† ca. 1973: Location unknown
James Dunham, Vla.]

Group VII.K: Works for Solo Violoncello

VII.K.1 Suite for Violoncello Solo

Date: Apr 1984 *Duration:* 25'07"
Dedication: "to Lawrence Lesser"
Commission: [Lawrence Lesser]
Publisher: MMC Publications

Movement(s):
I. Andante ma non troppo (♩=60)
II. Allegro vivace (♩=140)
III. Andantino (♩.=52, flexible)
IV. Largo (♩=42)
V. Allegretto (♪.=90)
VI. Maestoso (♩=84)

Instrumentation:
Vcl solo.

Sketches:
2 drafts of the opening of I (earlier title: Sonata).

MS Description:
Holograph with signature, pencil on vellum. *Location:* Boston Public Library.

Editorial Notes:
Commission information from the composer. Nov 1987 performance information from McKinley's notes.

Performance History:
† 6 Jan 1988: Weill Recital Hall, New York, NY
Ronald Thomas, Vcl.
[† (Boston) Late Nov 1987: WGBH Radio, Boston, MA
Bruce Coppock, Vcl.]
4 Nov 1989: Theresa L. Kaufmann Concert Hall, The 92nd St. YM-YWCA, New York, NY
Colin Carr, Vcl.
28 Feb 1990: Jordan Hall, New England Conservatory of Music, Boston, MA
Colin Carr, Vcl.

Bibliography:
Oestreich, James R. "Colin Carr, a British Cellist." *The New York Times* 6 Nov 1989: C16.
Goldsmith, Harris. "Concert Notes: New York." *The Strad* 101(Apr 1990), no. 1200: 258.

Program Notes:
"The work is a homage to the Bach cello suites and inspired by Casals' performances. It is modeled after them in length, scope, style, and form."
—William Thomas McKinley (© 1989), from 4 Nov 1989 and 28 Feb 1990 programs.

Group VII.L: Works for Solo Contrabass

VII.L.1 Variations for Contrabass

Date: 1968 in New Haven, CT (Yale Univ.) *Duration:* 5'56"
Dedication: "for Roger Cooke"
Commission: [Bert Turetsky]
Publisher: MMC Publications

Movement(s):
[One untitled movement.]

Instrumentation:
Cb solo.

MS Description:
Holograph with signature, ink on vellum. *Location:* Boston Public Library.

Editorial Notes:
Commission taken from McKinley's notes. Dedication suggests, however, that this work may have been used to fill an earlier commission by Roger Cooke for the Concerto for Solo Double Bass (II.O.a), which was never finished.

VII.L.2 Two Pieces for Solo Contrabass

Date: [Jul] 1985 in [Reading, MA ("Lells")] *Duration:* 7'00"
Dedication: "to Miroslav Vitous"
Commission: [Miroslav Vitous]
Publisher: MMC Publications

Movement(s):
I. Memory: Largo (♩=42, a piacére)
II. Awakening: Allegro (♩=120, giusto)

Instrumentation:
Cb solo.

MS Description:
Holograph with signature, pencil on vellum. *Location:* Boston Public Library.

Editorial Notes:
Month and location of composition and commission taken from McKinley's notes. According to those notes, the piece was written for an ECM recording to be made by Vitous in October of 1985 which never took place.

Performance History:
See Editorial Notes.

Group VIII: Works for Assorted Instruments

Group VIII.A: Works for Large Chamber Ensemble

VIII.A.1 Premises and Expositions for Flute, Oboe, Clarinet, Bassoon, Two Violins, Viola, [and] Cello

Date: 1968 in New Haven, CT (Yale Univ.) *Duration:* 20'18"
Dedication: "to the Fromm Foundation"
Commission: [Fromm Music Foundation (10 Oct 1967)]
Publisher: MMC Publications

Movement(s):
I.
II.
III. ♩=60
IV.
V.

Instrumentation:
Fl, Ob, Cl, Bsn, 2 Vln, Vla, Vcl soli.

Sketches:
2 formal plans. 1 complete draft. 9 folios of unidentified sketches. 16 unidentified drafts.

MS Description:
Holograph with printed name, ink on paper. *Location:* Boston Public Library.

Editorial Notes:
Fair copy is a McKinley holograph (ink on vellum, engraved name, no date). Commission information from commission letter.

Performance History:
† 6 Aug 1968: Tanglewood Theater-Concert Hall, Lenox, MA
[Untitled ensemble], Ronald Stoffel, Cond.

Bibliography:
Grimes, Ev. "Yale University American Music Oral History Series: William Thomas McKinley." Oct 1986, Yale University School of Music: 49, 56–57.

Program Notes:
"*Premises and Expositions* is comprised of five pieces each of which is governed by a specific premise or rationale which is then set forth in an expository manner. It is scored for woodwind and string quartets.

"The first piece deals with a set level of density, duration, dynamic, and velocity.

"The second piece is a monolithic, ostinato, recurring idea and is essentially a 'one thing' piece.

"The third piece deals with the abstraction of the dance. Unlike many neoclassic dance forms, the composer sought to eliminate any semblance of melodic contour thereby focusing entirely on the essence of the dance: namely, physical gesture.

"The fourth piece shows retrospective tribute to the *Klangfarben* melody of Schoenberg as well as one attempt to eliminate any aspect of mobility which occurs within the other pieces. This piece is to be thought of as one elongated, legato gesture with isolated woodwind attacks occurring within the structure. Intrinsically this piece exemplifies a kind of 'tone painting.'

"The fifth piece is a collage and variation of the first piece, emphasizing, unlike the first piece, more radical shifts of velocity, tempo, and attack. In this piece, the performer is required to make choices from a pitch gamut and within this gamut he must also perform specific ideas composed in a leitmotif fashion. This piece may be considered by some to be aleatoric but at no time does the composer relinquish any of the parameters."
—William Thomas McKinley (© 1968), from 6 Aug 1968 program.

VIII.A.2 Three Movements for Wind Ensemble

Date: 1980 in [Reading, MA ("Barn")] *Duration:* 11'15"
Commission: [Massachusetts Council for the Arts]
Publisher: MMC Publications

Movement(s):
I. Moderato (♩=84)
II. Marcia (♩=150)
III. Largo (𝅗𝅥=20)

Instrumentation:
Pic, 2 Fl, 2 Ob, EHn, 2 Bsn, CBsn, Pic Cl, 6 Cl, Alt Cl, BCl, CbCl, 2 Alt Sax, Ten Sax, Bar Sax, 4 Hn, Bar Hn, 4 Tpt, 4 Tbn, 2 Tba, Timp, 2 Perc, 4 Cb.

MS Description:
Engraving by McKinley, ink stencil on vellum. *Location:* Boston Public Library.

Editorial Notes:
Location of composition and commission taken from McKinley's notes.

Performance History:
† 11 Dec 1980: Jordan Hall, New England Conservatory of Music, Boston, MA
Conservatory Wind Ensemble, Frank Battisti, Cond.

Bibliography:
Buell, Richard. "Wind Ensemble Gives Lots of a Nice Thing." *The Boston Globe* 15 Dec 1980: 32.

VIII.A.3 Symphony for Thirteen Players [Chamber Symphony No. 1]

Date: 1 Mar 1983 in [Reading, MA ("Lells")] *Duration:* 27'30"
Dedication: "to Vic Firth and the B[oston] S[ymphony] O[rchestra] Chamber Players"
Commission: [National Endowment for the Arts and Music Today]
Publisher: MMC Publications

Movement(s):
I. Poco adagio (♩=72)
II. Scherzo (♩=120+)
III. Presto (𝅗𝅥=160+)

Instrumentation:
Fl, Ob, Cl, Bsn, Hn, Tpt, Tbn, Timp/Perc, Pno, Vln, Vla, Vcl, Cb soli.

Sketches:
Pages 2–3 (6 measures) of an earlier lost draft.

MS Description:
Holograph with signature, pencil on paper. *Location:* Boston Public Library.

Editorial Notes:
Location of composition and commission taken from McKinley's notes.

Performance History:
† 19 Oct 1983: Merkin Concert Hall, New York, NY
Jonathan Haas, Perc; Music Today, Gerard Schwarz, Cond.
† (Boston) 15 Oct 1984: Jordan Hall, New England Conservatory of Music, Boston, MA
Dean Anderson, Perc; [Untitled ensemble], Robert Black, Cond.

Bibliography:
Page, Tim. "Concert: Music Today." *The New York Times* 21 Oct 1983: C31.
Driver, Paul. "Composer McKinley 'Hears the Muses.'" *The Boston Globe* 9 Dec 1983: 48, 52.

Program Notes:

"The *Symphony for Thirteen Players,* featuring one each of the principal orchestral instruments, was composed for Vic Firth and the Boston Symphony Chamber Players. Its world premiere was given last November [*sic*] at the Music Today Series, conducted by Gerard Schwarz. The percussion writing, a *tour de force* for a single player, is dramatically prominent in each of the work's three movements and highlighted by a long snare drum cadenza as the Trio of the second movement. The first movement is a sonata; the second, a scherzo-trio; and the third, a rondo."
—William Thomas McKinley (© 1984), from 15 Oct 1984 program.

"Victor Firth, principal percussionist with the Boston Symphony Orchestra, likes to hear jazz drummers and so he makes the rounds of the Boston clubs. Often, he had heard composer/pianist William Thomas McKinley with drummers like Roy Haynes and Billy Hart. Knowing McKinley slightly on a collegial basis—they both teach at the New England Conservatory—Firth struck up a friendship with Tom, as he is known in jazz circles, who proposed a work for the Boston Symphony Orchestra Chamber Players with whom Firth also performs. Firth told him to go ahead—a friendly commission—and McKinley, over a three-year period, finally responded with a work actually not begun until the winter of 1981–82 and finished until late winter, 1982–83.

"McKinley, who writes in numerous dialects from jazz to Expressionism, initially conceived of the *Symphony for Thirteen Instruments* as a three-movement chamber work scored for single winds, strings, and six percussion instruments. The idea of a jazz-related language crept in as Firth talked about improvisation. But Firth, a fine soloist, is not a jazz drummer.

"The percussion, featured prominently in the work, often initiate ideas or carry the rhythmic thread. From time to time, other instruments perform fairly substantial parts, too, but as the work progressed, it began to resemble a concerto more and more. The percussion is not treated flamboyantly by any measure: the work calls for only two instruments per movement so that the percussionist need not dive from one part of the orchestra floor to another. So the Symphony is not really a concerto in the usual sense of the word. The drums have a part somewhat analogous to the viola in Berlioz's symphony, and McKinley, rather whimsically, has begun to refer to his work as 'Victor in Boston.'

"McKinley has not written a collage; he does not copy progressions from Schubert or Mahler; he does not serialize atonal sonorities; he does not reiterate the same chord in different ways *ad infinitum*; nor does he use jazz clichés. But jazz plays an important part in the development of the work's harmonic language. McKinley notes that he uses Beethovenian structural elements, themes, and developments of harmonic features that originate in Impressionism, jazz, and early Stravinsky. The rich harmonic vocabulary derives from expansions and extensions of triadically-based sonorities found in Ravel and Debussy and then in the jazz of musicians like Gil and Bill Evans, pushed to the nth degree and treated somewhat in the manner of the progressive tonality of the late-Romantic symphony.

"The Adagio of the first movement serves as Introduction to an Allegro that unfolds as a sonata form with clear primary and secondary groups (the latter beginning with a trumpet theme). After a Development and Recapitulation, the Adagio returns as Coda.

"A Scherzo follows. Its Trio, centerpiece of the symphony, features a virtuosic snare-drum cadenza. A fast, straightforward Rondo, ABACABA, brings the symphony to a close."
—Peter Eliot Stone (© 1983), from 19 Oct 1983 program.

VIII.A.4 A Small Rhapsody for Alto Sax, Two Tenor Saxes, Trombone, Guitar, Piano, Bass, [and] Drums

Date: [ca. 1984] *Duration:* 1'56"
Publisher: MMC Publications

Movement(s):
Moderate

Instrumentation:
Alt Sax, 2 Ten Sax, Tbn, Gtr, Pno, Cb, Dr soli.

MS Description:
Holograph, pencil on paper. *Location:* Boston Public Library.

Editorial Notes:
Date determined through paleographic analysis.

VIII.A.5 Grand Finale [No. 1] for Chamber Ensemble

Date: 1986 *Duration:* 10'00"
Dedication: "to David Stock and the Pittsburgh New Music Ensemble"
Commission: [Pittsburgh New Music Ensemble with a grant from the Pennsylvania Council on the Arts]
Publisher: MMC Publications

Movement(s):
Celestial (𝅝 ♩=60)

Instrumentation:
Pic/Fl, Ob, Cl, Bsn, Hn, Tpt, Tbn, Perc, Pno, Hp, Vln, Vla, Vcl, Cb soli.

MS Description:
Holograph with signature, pencil on vellum. *Location:* Boston Public Library.

Editorial Notes:
Commission taken from 5 May 1986 program.

Performance History:
† 5 May 1986: Campell Memorial Chapel, Chatham College, Pittsburgh, PA
The Pittsburgh New Music Ensemble, David Stock, Cond.
† (New York) 5 Jun 1986: Merkin Concert Hall, New York, NY
The New York New Music Ensemble, Robert Black, Cond.
[† (Boston)] 25 Apr 1987: Jordan Hall, New England Conservatory of Music, Boston, MA
ALEA III, Theodore Antoniou, Cond.

6 Jun [1988]: Fulton Theater, Pittsburgh, PA
The Pittsburgh New Music Ensemble, David Stock, Cond.
11 Jun 1989: Merkin Concert Hall, New York, NY
The Pittsburgh New Music Ensemble, David Stock, Cond.
[† (Columbus)] 21 Apr 1990: Weigel Hall, Columbus, OH
ProMusica Chamber Orchestra of Columbus, David Stock, Cond.
17 Aug 1990: School of Music, Dusquesne University, Pittsburgh, PA
The Pittsburgh New Music Ensemble, David Stock, Cond.

Bibliography:

Vranish, Jane. "New Music: Rousing Season Finale." *Pittsburgh Post-Gazette* 6 May 1986.
Holland, Bernard. "Music: Works by McKinley." *The New York Times* 7 Jun 1986.
Lifchitz, Max. "Composer of Note: William Thomas McKinley." *Living Music* 4(Fall 1986), no. 1: 2.
Miller, Nancy. "Alea III and All That Jazz." *The Boston Globe* 27 Apr 1987: 12.
Apone, Carl. "New Music Ensemble Delights Small Crowd." *The Pittsburgh Press* 7 Jun 1988.
Schulz, Richard. "Pittsburgh New Music Ensemble." *WQED-FM Sunday Arts Magazine* 12 Jun 1988.
Kozinn, Allan. "New Work From Pittsburgh Ensemble." *The New York Times* 13 Jun 1989: C19.

Program Notes:

"*Grand Finale* is intended as a jubilant, celebratory work creating an orchestral palette in one grandly gestured movement. Scored for one each of flute, oboe, clarinet, bassoon, trumpet, horn and trombone, piano, harp, percussion and strings, the work was first designed to feature the wonderfully virtuosic talents of the Pittsburgh New Music Ensemble and is cast sonically in the traditional manner of a grand finale."
—William Thomas McKinley (© 1990), from 21 Apr 1990 program.

VIII.A.6 Symphony of Winds

Date: 18 Jul 1988 in Reading, MA ("Lells") *Duration:* 13'00"
Commission: "to the Detroit Chamber Winds"
Publisher: MMC Publications

Movement(s):
Adagio maestoso (♩=50)

Instrumentation:
2 Pic/2 Fl, 2 Ob/EHn, Pic Cl/2 Cl/BCl, 2 Bsn/CBsn, 3 Hn, 2 Tpt, Tbn, 2 Perc.

MS Description:
Holograph with printed name, pencil on vellum. *Location:* Boston Public Library.

Performance History:

† 11 Sep 1988: Wallace F. Smith Performing Arts Theater, Detroit, MI
Detroit Chamber Winds, H. Robert Reynolds, Cond.
† (Boston) 16 Feb 1989: Jordan Hall, New England Conservatory of Music, Boston, MA
Conservatory Wind Ensemble, Frank Battisti, Cond.

Bibliography:

Guinn, John. "A Few Words With William Thomas McKinley: Jazz and Classics Merge in Composer's Mind." *Detroit Free Press* 19 Sep 1988.

VIII.A.7 Chamber Symphony No. 2 in One Movement

Date: 27 Aug 1989 in Reading, MA ("Lells") *Duration:* 16'00"
Dedication: "to Alexander Ivashkin"
Commission: [Bolshoi Theater Orchestra]
Publisher: MMC Publications

Movement(s):
Lento molto e largamente (♩=40)

Instrumentation:
Pic/Fl, Ob/EHn, Cl, Bsn, Hn, Tpt, Tbn, Timp, 2 Perc, Pno, Hp, 2 Vln, Vla, Vcl, Cb soli.

Sketches:
3 drafts of the opening.

MS Description:
Holograph with signature, pencil on paper. *Location:* Boston Public Library.

Editorial Notes:
Premiere information taken from 14 Apr 1990 article. Commission information from the composer.

Performance History:
[† May 1991: Bolshoi Theater, Moscow, Russia
Bolshoi Theater Orchestra.]
† (United States) 31 Mar 1992: Foellinger Great Hall, University of Illinois, Urbana, IL
UI Contemporary Players/UI New Music Ensemble, Paul Martin Zonn, Cond.

Bibliography:
Dyer, Richard. "NEC, BU, Harvard Cook Up Hot Week of Student Opera." *The Boston Globe* 14 Apr 1990: 12.

VIII.A.8 Chamber Concerto No. 3*

Date: 1991 *Duration:* 22'45"
Dedication: "to David Stock and P[itt]s[burg]h New Music Ensemble"
Commission: [Pittsburgh New Music Ensemble "to mark the ensemble's anniversary"]
Publisher: MMC Publications

Movement(s):
I. Rapsodico e lirico, ma tenebre e tumultuoso (♩=92)
II. Tranquillo e misterioso (♩=120)
III. Prestissimo (𝅗𝅥=192)

Instrumentation:
Pic/Fl/Alt Fl, Ob/EHn, Cl/BCl, 2 Perc, Pno, 2 Vln, Vcl soli.

Sketches:
1 draft of the opening of II. 1 draft of II/183. 1 draft of II/177–78.

MS Description:
Holograph with signature, pencil on paper. *Location:* Boston Public Library.

Editorial Notes:
*Chamber Concerti 1 and 2 are actually Chamber Symphonies 1 and 2 (VIII.A.3 and 7). Commission taken from 30 Apr 1991 review.

Performance History:
† 29 Apr 1991: J. Leonard Levy Hall, Rodef Shalom Temple, Pittsburgh, PA
The Pittsburgh New Music Ensemble, David Stock, Cond.
† (Boston) 5 Nov 1991: Jordan Hall, New England Conservatory of Music, Boston, MA
[Untitled ensemble].
10 Feb 1992: Jordan Hall, New England Conservatory of Music, Boston, MA
[Untitled ensemble], David Stock, Cond.

Bibliography:
Rosenberg, Donald. "New Kensington Composer in Demand." *The Pittsburgh Press* 28 Apr 1991: F1, F4.
Croan, Robert. "Composers Come Home For Joint Concert." *Pittsburgh Post-Gazette* 30 Apr 1991.
Rosenberg, Donald. "Premieres Keep it Fresh for New Music Ensemble." *The Pittsburgh Press* 30 Apr 1991.
Dyer, Richard. "Teachers' Works Put Musicians to the Test." *The Boston Globe* 11 Feb 1992.

VIII.A.a ~~Introduction, Statement and Epilogue for Wind Orchestra, Percussion, Piano, Contrabass, Improvisation Ensemble and Harp~~

Date: 1963–1964
Commission: [Robert Reynolds]
Publisher: Unpublished

Movement(s):
[One untitled movement.]

Instrumentation:
Wind Orchestra (Pic, Pic/2 Fl, Alt Fl, 2 Ob, EHn, 2 Cl, A Cl, BCl, 3 Bsn, 2 CBsn, 4 Hn, 5 Tpt, 3 Tbn, BTbn, Tba); Perc, Hp, Pno, Cb, Improv Ens. (unspecified).

Sketches:
4 folios of detailed notes.

MS Description:
Holograph, pencil on paper. *Location:* Boston Public Library.

Editorial Notes:
There is no MS for this work. Commission information from the composer.

VIII.A.b ~~[Untitled for Four Trios and Piano]~~

Date: [ca. 1967–1969]
Publisher: Unpublished

Movement(s):
[One untitled movement]

Instrumentation:
Pic, Fl, Vln soli; Cl, Tpt, Vla soli; Ob, Bsn, Vcl soli; Hn, Tbn, Tba soli; Pno solo.

Sketches:
19 drafts of the opening. 5 folios and 2 bifolios of unidentified sketches and drafts.

MS Description:
Holograph, pencil on paper. *Location:* Boston Public Library.

Editorial Notes:
There is no MS for this work. Date determined through paleographic analysis.

See also: Again the Distant Bells (II.H.1)
Arabesques for Assorted Instruments (VIII.E.3)
The Mountain for Large Chamber or Full Symphony Orchestra (I.C.4)
Nostradamus... (II.C.4)
~~**Shapes**~~ (VIII.G.d)
To My Friend Dick (II.E.5)

Group VIII.B: Septets for Assorted Instruments

VIII.B.1 Paintings [No. 1] for Seven Players

Date: Nov 1972
Duration: 11'10"
Dedication: [Les Thimmig]
Commission: [University of Wisconsin]
Publisher: MMC Publications

Movement(s):
I. Fancy: ♩=52
II. Wheels: ♪=75
III. Cubes: With abandon (♪=57)
IV. Purple: Dark (♩=47)
V. Question: Quasi cadenza (♪=57)

Instrumentation:
2 Cl/BCl, Bsn, 2 Perc, Vln, Vcl soli.

Sketches:
3 drafts of the opening of I. 9 drafts of page 2 of I. 14 drafts of the opening of II. 5 drafts of page 2 of III. 2 drafts of the opening of IV. 1 draft of page 2 of IV. 26 drafts of the opening of V (earlier title: "Sleep"). 10 drafts of page 2 of V. 4 drafts of page 3 of V. 7 unidentified drafts. 4 folios of notes, containing mostly numbers and instrumentation layouts.

MS Description:
Holograph with printed name, ink on vellum. *Location:* Boston Public Library.
Markings: Movement I dated 7 Nov 1972. Movement II dated 9 Nov 1972. Movements III–V dated Nov 1972.

Editorial Notes:
Dedication inferred from citation on 20 Feb 1973 program: "PAINTINGS and STEPS were composed specifically for [this] occasion." and dedications to Les Thimmig on *Steps (Part I)* and *(Part II)* MSS. Commission taken from McKinley's notes. 4 Nov and 8 Nov 1985 performance information from advertisements.

Performance History:
† 20 Feb 1973: Mills Concert Hall, University of Wisconsin, Madison, WI
University of Wisconsin Contemporary Chamber Ensemble, Les Thimmig, Cond.
23 May 1973: Wheaton College, Wheaton, IL
[Specific performers unknown], Howard Whitaker, Cond.
[† (San Francisco) 4 Nov 1985: Herbst Hall, San Francisco, CA
San Francisco Contemporary Music Players, Gunther Schuller, Cond.]

[†(Sacramento) 8 Nov 1985: Music Recital Hall, California State University, Sacramento, CA
San Francisco Contemporary Music Players, Gunther Schuller, Cond.]

Bibliography:

Elsner, Carmen. "New Sound Explored on Campus." *Wisconsin State Journal* 23 Feb 1973: IV 17.

Program Notes:

For 20 Feb 1973 notes see *Cello Music* (VIII.E.5).

VIII.B.2 Paintings [No.] 5 for Flute, B♭ Clarinet, [Bass Clarinet,] Trumpet in C, Violin, Viola, and Cello

Date: 1979 in Reading, MA ("Barn") *Duration:* 18'00"
Dedication: "To David Stock and the Pittsburgh New Music Ensemble"
Commission: [Pittsburgh New Music Ensemble]
Publisher: MMC Publications

Movement(s):
Delicate motion (♪=72+)

Instrumentation:
Pic/Fl, Cl, BCl, C Tpt, Vln, Vla, Vcl soli.

Sketches:

10 drafts of the opening. 7 drafts of mm. 246–50.

MS Description:

Holograph with printed name, ink on vellum. *Location:* Boston Public Library.

Editorial Notes:

Commission taken from McKinley's notes. Premiere performance information from *AMC Newsletter* 21(Summer 1979), no. 3: 12.

Performance History:

[† 22 Apr 1979: Campbell Memorial Chapel, Chatham College, Pittsburgh, PA
Pittsburgh New Music Ensemble, David Stock, Cond.]
[ca. 1979]: WQED Radio Studios, Pittsburgh, PA
Pittsburgh New Music Ensemble, David Stock, Cond.

VIII.B.3 Paintings No. 6 ("To Hear the Light Dancing")—A Chamber Concerto for Flute, B♭ Clarinet, Percussion, Violin, Viola, Cello, and Pianoforte

Date: 1981 in Reading, MA ("Barn") *Duration:* 17'00"
Dedication: "to Richard Pittman and the Boston Musica Viva"
Commission: National Endowment for the Arts
Publisher: Margun Music Inc.

Movement(s):
Tranquillo (♩.=120)

Instrumentation:
Fl, Cl, Perc, Vln, Vla, Vcl, Pno soli.

MS Description:

Engraving by McKinley, ink stencil on vellum. *Location:* Boston Public Library.
Markings: Score contains numerous programmatic impressions written above the music.

Editorial Notes:

Liner notes of Northeastern Records NR 203 indicate choreographed premiere in October 1981. 17 May 1989 performance information from BMI records.

Performance History:

† 1 May 1981: Sanders Theater, Cambridge MA
The Boston Musica Viva, Richard Pittman, Cond.
[† (Hartford)] 3 May 1981: Millard Auditorium, Hartford University, Hartford, CT
The Boston Musica Viva, Richard Pittman, Cond.
[† (ballet performance, Boston)] 2 Oct 1981: Sanders Theater, Cambridge MA
The Boston Musica Viva, Richard Pittman, Cond.
[† (New Haven)] 4 Oct 1981: Sprague Hall, Yale University, New Haven, CT
The Boston Musica Viva, Richard Pittman, Cond.
27 Jun 1982: DeCordova Museum, Lincoln, MA
The Boston Musica Viva, Richard Pittman, Cond.
[† (Lenox)] 2 Aug 1982: Tanglewood Theater-Concert Hall, Lenox, MA
[Specific performers unknown], Theodore Antoniou, Cond.
4 Mar 1988: First and Second Church, Boston, MA
The Boston Musica Viva, Richard Pittman, Cond.
[† (Toledo) 17 May 1989: Hall unknown, Toledo, OH
Toledo Symphony Orchestra.]
See also *Program Notes.*

Recording(s):

Northeastern Records: NR 203, ©1982 (LP)
Boston Musica Viva, Richard Pittman, Cond.

Bibliography:

Charles, Eleanor. "Preview of Chamber Tour." *The New York Times* 3 May 1981: XICT-14.
Buell, Richard. "Musica Viva Airs Works for European Tour." *The Boston Globe* 5 May 1981: 29.
Buell, Richard. "Hijinks from Musica Viva." *The Boston Globe* 7 Oct 1981: 53.
Driver, Paul. "Composer McKinley 'Hears the Muses.'" *The Boston Globe* 9 Dec 1983: 48, 52.
Rockwell, John. "Tanglewood: Fromm Week Returns to Normal." *The New York Times* 4 Aug 1982: C17.
Tommasini, Anthony. "McKinley's Recent Works Lack Discernment and Taste." *The Boston Globe* 5 Mar 1988: 14.

Program Notes:

"*Paintings VI* was commissioned by the National Endowment for the Arts and the Boston Musica Viva. It is scored for flute, B♭ clarinet, piano, percussion (one player), violin, viola, and cello. The work was composed with a dual purpose in mind and is thus a ballet and a chamber concerto. A fully staged and choreographed world premiere was to have been given on May 1, 1981. However, the staging and choreographing was postponed until October, 1981, and the instrumental version was given its world premiere by the Boston Musica Viva at Sanders Theater, Richard Pittman conducting, on May 1, 1981. Subsequently, the Boston Musica Viva has taken the Chamber Concerto version on its European Tour, and since May 15, 1981, *Paintings VI* has been premiered in Bulgaria, Spain, Portugal, Berlin, Germany, Belgium, and London, England. In addition, it was recorded for television in Belgium and for a broadcast on the BBC in London. The Boston Musica Viva will also participate in the October performance with full complement.

"In the printed score verbal indications and suggestions or cues are given which serve as interpretive guides for the light director and choreographer. The choreographer is given a separate scenario which is more linear and more detailed. This scenario dramatizes the process witnessed in human affairs from pre-life to post-life and the major forces, ideas, and attitudes therein. The symbolic development of this process is represented in the concrete forms of an individual existence seen as a metaphor for all existence. Perhaps, in a certain sense, *Paintings VI* is autobiographical. As the various metaphors, depicted in the scenario, unfold, they are given correspondent relationships in the musical structure. For example, at the stage of life symbolized by midnight, wherein the darkest nocturnal forces play upon the psyche, a musical texture and motivic interplay quote elements of the immortal jazz classic 'Round about Midnight,' and at a climactic point culminate in a literal quotation of the melody, 'Round about Midnight,' evoking the very powerful and suggestive metaphor of the nocturnal fantasy and its relationship to the dark phantasmagoric overtones of jazz, dark-night-towns, sensory fantasy, illusions of transformation and escaping into realms of non-reality. Another example which is adumbrated in the early going and which climaxes in the final moments, is the overpowering and insistently repeated gong crash (and choke). Metaphorically, these fervored repetitions represent the element of 'white light' which ultimately converts physical-material substance into ethereal substance—all with blinding dominance and brilliant projection. The dominant symbolic presence of 'white light' in the final moments of *Paintings VI* is an exact metaphor dramatizing the cosmic transporting of the human spirit into realms unknown and unexplored. Another example which may be more easily perceived is embodied in the solo violin cadenza. This cadenza functions in several ways: it acts as a dramatic relief—the complex textures and polyphony which lead up to the cadenza create a very strong musical necessity for contrast and relief. The ballet scenario also demands physical and visual relief and the metaphorical character of the violin cadenza which represents the individual soul's traversal and transition through the latter stages of life culminates when the full ensemble returns and begins its development toward a final apotheosis.

"In purely abstract musical terms, there are many structural elements which exist independently in much the same manner as the musical structural elements contained in Alban Berg's *Wozzeck.* There are powerful rhythmic motives which are ubiquitous and unify the total musical structure, creating long-range contrapuntal goals and resolutions. These elements are supported by a harmonic language which, although atonal or pantonal throughout, derives from a very cohesive unfolding of the total chromatic, creating the aural impression of harmonic balance and homogeneity throughout the entirety of the work's discourse. The use of registral invariance and the polyphonic network of clearly audible linear patterns which develop temporally over long periods, create a sense of ongoing (teleological) continuity and convincing physical motion highlighted by several major climactic points. These climactic points guide the listener through various stages of structural evolution (related, of course, to the earlier descriptions of the dramatic-metaphorical scenario) and transformation of the musical motives and harmonic materials—acting ultimately as architectonic pillars or formal guide posts within a very large single movement framework."

—William Thomas McKinley (© 1982), from Northeastern Records NR 203 liner notes and his notes.

VIII.B.4 Paintings No. 7 for Bass Clarinet, Percussion, Piano, Harp, Violin, Viola, and Cello

Date: 1982 in Reading, MA ("Lells") *Duration:* 14'00"
Dedication: "to Frank Epstein, Gunther Schuller, and Collage"
Commission: [Collage]
Publisher: Margun Music Inc.

Movement(s):
I. Grandioso (♩=52)
II. Grandioso (♩=36)

Instrumentation:
BCl, Perc, Pno, Hp, Vln, Vla, Vcl soli.

Sketches:
1 draft of the opening.

MS Description:
Engraving by McKinley, ink stencil on vellum. *Location:* Boston Public Library.

Editorial Notes:
*An American Academy and Institute of Arts and Letters grant of $5,000 was awarded for the making of the CRI recording. Commission taken from McKinley's notes. Premiere performance confirmed in *AMC Newsletter* 28(Mar–Apr 1986), no. 1: 16 and McKinley's notes.

Performance History:
[†] 22 Feb 1982: Sander's Theater, Cambridge, MA
Collage, Gunther Schuller, Cond.

Recording(s):
Composers Recordings, Inc.: CRI SD 507, ©1984 (LP)*
Collage, Gunther Schuller, Cond.

Bibliography:
Grimes, Ev. "Yale University American Music Oral History Series: William Thomas McKinley." Oct 1986, Yale University School of Music: 78–79.

Program Notes:
"*Paintings VII* and *For One* share many musical and dramatic characteristics though a number of years separates their times of composition. Each work derives its essential energy and compositional spirit from a predominantly expressionistic musical palette which results in a widely contrasting array of emotional states. These states are juxtaposed in short rapid-fire order—often suddenly—creating at times the impression of 'psychic' motion or force throughout their development.

"The gestures of *Paintings VII* derive from 'physical' patterns, suggesting dance and improvisational movement. I would like to think of its form as 'organic'—that is, evolving and yet strongly goal-oriented.

"*Paintings VII* creates a scenario which displays the explosive percussion talents of Frank Epstein, while at the same time articulating an overall dramatic portrait of instrumental levels. Thus, I set up the following hierarchy in terms of dramatic importance: (1) percussion, (2) bass clarinet, (3) piano, (4) violin, (5) harp, (6) cello, (7) viola. Most of the instruments are given soloistic passages to varying length which dominate the entire group for short periods of time, thus taking over the momentary compositional direction. Nonetheless, the essential musical drive and development is distributed principally among the first three instruments (in the above order) while the others generally take on subordinate roles. The percussion dramatizes volcanic gestures—dominating and wild; the bass clarinet provides a perpetual obbligato-like blanket or undertow—rhapsodizing in a sometimes nonchalant manner and occasionally engaging in difficult cadenza-like passages; and the piano reacts in sometimes explosive fashion, also rhapsodizing, but in a manner different from the others, with unique cadenzas occurring intermittently. Richard Stoltzman has remarked concerning my music: 'McKinley's music is traditional in the sense that all fine music is. It assimilates respected sounds and forms of history, reflects the qualities of its own ear, and forges fresh bonds with the future. I find it challenging, spontaneous, exciting, sincere, and eminently worthwhile.' *For One* is an extroverted, Fauvistic, and virtuosic work—a fitting companion to *Paintings VII*—which seems to be fulfilling my hope that it will become a significant contribution to the clarinet repertoire. Because of the unavoidable fact that the single line creates its own unique effect, one asked to hear lines which occur in different registers as multiple lines that contain many melodic levels within them. The listening experience in *For One* creates the same aural challenges that are encountered in listening to a solo work of Bach, wherein the perception to linear polyphony [is] paramount in obtaining enjoyment and the fullest understanding.

"The mastery of Stoltzman's performance brings the polyphonic levels to the foreground, helping the listener to follow the work's continuity, melodic connections, and overall dramatic progress."

—William Thomas McKinley (© 1984), from Composers Recordings CRI SD 507 liner notes.

"*Paintings VII* embraces a wide array of aesthetical and compositional characteristics. Many of these characteristics synthesize and refine musical ideas that are explored and developed in *Paintings II, IV,* and *VI.* The most important among them include the partitioning of in-time/out-of-time (metric/non-metric) structures; the expansion and transformation of canonic ideas such as stretto, fugal polyphony, and the monadic individuation and independence of musical line; the juxtaposition and interweaving of detailed polyphonic structures with improvisatory-like structures (or heterophonic structures); the spinning and weaving of intricate rhythmic constellations against an unending and configurative melodic thread or *cantus firmus*; a striving towards a 'new' refraction of ideas through the development of a musical syntax which fosters a pan-tonal linear and harmonic universe that manifests as a language 'heard' rather than as language 'derived' solely from artificial construct; creating a sustained sense of psychic expectation and musical discovery through the evocation of perpetual variation and continual invention of musical ideas; and finally revealing a condition of musical-dramatic resolve in juxtaposition against musical-dramatic resolution (i.e., measuring the unknown against the known). It is not difficult to observe the intricate paradoxes spawned by these characteristics. And to those listeners who are acquainted with other works in the *Paintings* series, perhaps some of these characteristics, in combination and synthesis, will be musically observable, although it is extremely important for the listener to discover as the work evolves, characteristics which immediately relate to his/her own 'personal' vision sense of expectation and perception of dramatic conflict and resolution.

"The dominant character of *Paintings VII* is abstract and is undoubtedly the most intense and complex composition in the *Paintings* series. Its complexity is sustained and reinforced by a metric-temporal undercurrent which rapidly develops and continually transforms. At times this rapidity evokes a veritable 'explosion' of musical energy and intensity. Architecturally, the work is divided into three sub-movements and a set of polyphonic cadenzas which are compressed together, forming a single movement. A virtuoso concerto-like (or concertante) treatment of the bass clarinet, percussion, and piano pervades the work's entirety but is given its greatest elaboration during extended polyphonic triple-cadenza. Many of the most intricate compositional details include the presentation of timbre melody, metric proportions, metronomic proportions, the partitioning of in-time/out-of-time elements (notable in the third section) and the exploration of very complex polyphony derived from numerical relationships which help to control linear details on both the macro and micro (moment to moment) levels. For example, the ratios of 3/7, 11/7, 10/7, and 10/3 are of particular rhythmic significance, and they help to generate and extend the moment to moment musical continuity into larger periods which eventually shapes the overall structure and polyphonic surface. This manner of complexity paradoxically yields a gestural quality of improvisational freedom coupled with and intensified by extreme dynamic contrasts, textural expansiveness, intricate solo dialogue, antiphonal interplay, all underscored by a long-term cumulative sense of musical expectation and surprise. Perhaps the most challenging task was to blend and integrate formidable a priori relationships into an intuitive flow of musical thought—to create a web of musical-dramatic conflict, heightened by an intensely personal and musically dynamic palette. Therefore the bass clarinet, percussion, and piano (concertante group) are often given the most powerful musical status, traversing the widest gamut of emotional conflict, and responding as principal antagonists within the entire ensemble scenario. At times, however, the percussion dominates all and is given moments of action which seek dramatic supremacy and eminent musical status within both the concertante group and the entire ensemble. The percussion seeks its own personal dominion and its musical discourse erupts in highly ornate musical gestures and polyrhythmic patterns. Nevertheless, it should not be inferred that the remaining instruments are treated with less significance. To the contrary, they have their say in quite important and brilliant fashion. The violin, viola, cello, and harp group is given considerably virtuosic passage work and intricate ensemble activity which is, at times, on equal footing with the activity in the concertante group and contributes importantly to the total musical energy and fabric. Occasionally, they act as a 'string quilting,' lending a transparent blanketing and support to the concertante group. And although they are not involved in the polyphonic triple-cadenzas, they assume greater and greater importance towards the end of *Paintings VII*. The sound of sleigh bells adumbrates the final section whereupon a resolution and tendency towards unity becomes increasingly evident, and the multi-leveled conflicts set forth from the beginning are gradually abated. The effect of the 'string quilting,' which creates a harmonic calm and balance, brings to end the last stages of dramatic conflict, generating a powerful musical quieting and sense of transcendence."

—William Thomas McKinley (© 1982), from his notes (excerpts appear in Margun Music, inc. MP5030 published score).

VIII.B.5 Curtain Up for Flute, Oboe, Clarinet, Percussion, Piano, Violin, [and] Cello

Date: 14 Aug 1988 in Reading, MA ("Lells") *Duration:* 11'30"
Dedication: "to the Pittsburgh New Music Ensemble"
Commission: Pittsburgh New Music Ensemble
Publisher: MMC Publications

Movement(s):
Allegro vivace (𝅝=60+)

Instrumentation:
Pic/Fl/Alt Fl, Ob/EHn, Cl/BCl, Perc, Pno, Vln, Vcl soli.

MS Description:
Holograph with signature, pencil on vellum. *Location:* Boston Public Library.
Markings: Page 1: MS contains an erroneous tempo marking for the strings. Tempo for all parts should read 𝅝=60+.

Editorial Notes:
27 Jul 1989 performance date from BMI records.

Performance History:
† 19 Sep 1988: J. Leonard Levy Hall, Rodef Shalom Temple, Pittsburgh, PA
Richard Stoltzman, Cl; The Pittsburgh New Music Ensemble, David Stock, Cond.
28 Jan 1989: The Mauch Chunk Opera House, Jim Thorpe, PA
The Pittsburgh New Music Ensemble, David Stock, Cond.
[† (Allentown)] 29 Jan 1989: Paul C. Emple Theater, Muhlenberg College, Allentown, PA
The Pittsburgh New Music Ensemble, David Stock, Cond.
20 Feb 1989: West Virginia College of Creative Arts, Morgantown, WV
The Pittsburgh New Music Ensemble, David Stock, Cond.
5 May 1989: Erie Art Museum, Erie, PA
The Pittsburgh New Music Ensemble.
† (New York) 11 Jun 1989: Merkin Concert Hall, New York, NY
The Pittsburgh New Music Ensemble, David Stock, Cond.
[27 Jul 1989]: Touchstone Center for Crafts, New York, NY
The Pittsburgh New Music Ensemble, David Stock, Cond.
28 Jul 1989: School of Music, Dusquesne University, Pittsburgh, PA
The Pittsburgh New Music Ensemble, David Stock, Cond.
[† (Chautauqua)] 27 Jun 1994: Elizabeth S. Lenna Hall, Chautauqua, NY
The Pittsburgh New Music Ensemble, David Stock, Cond.

Bibliography:
Croan, Robert. "Clarinetist Shines in Jazz." *Pittsburgh Post-Gazette* 20 Sep 1988.
Kozinn, Allan. "New Work From Pittsburgh Ensemble." *The New York Times* 13 Jun 1989: C19.

VIII.B.a ~~[Red]~~

Date: [ca. 1979]
Publisher: Unpublished

Movement(s):
I. Red (♪=90)

Instrumentation:
Pic/Fl, Cl, 3 Perc, Pno, Vcl soli.

Sketches:
25 drafts of the opening of I (earlier title: "Red Goblets").

MS Description:
Engraving by McKinley, ink stencil on vellum. *Location:* Boston Public Library.

Editorial Notes:
MS ends after 19 measures. Work title taken from the title of the surviving first movement.

See also: Arabesques for Assorted Instruments (VIII.E.3)
Nostradamus... (II.C.4)
~~**Shapes**~~ (VIII.G.d)

Group VIII.C: Sextets for Assorted Instruments

VIII.C.1 Paintings No. 2 for Double Trio

Date: 16 Jun 1975 in Reading, MA ("Linnea Lane") *Duration:* 12'00"
Dedication: "to Yale School of Music, Norfolk, Conn."
Commission: [Yale University]
Publisher: Margun Music Inc.

Movement(s):
I. Winter: ♩=47+
II. Spring: With elegance (♩=70)
III. Summer: 𝅗𝅥=48-
IV. Autumn: With a feeling of intense murmuring, whispered (♩=94+)
V. Epilogue: ♪=Fast as possible, 100+

Instrumentation:
Pic/Fl, Ob, Cl, Vln, Vla, Vcl soli.

Sketches:
55 drafts of the opening of I (earlier titles: "Points"; "Swarming Bees"). 1 draft of III/24. 1 draft of IV/24–25. 1 draft of V/4–5.

MS Description:
Holograph with printed name, ink on paper. *Location:* Boston Public Library.

Editorial Notes:
Commission taken from McKinley's program notes.

Performance History:
† 28 Feb 1976: Jordan Hall, New England Conservatory of Music, Boston, MA
The New England Conservatory Contemporary Music Ensemble, Gunther Schuller, Cond.
[† (Lenox)] 14 Aug 1976: Tanglewood Theater-Concert Hall, Lenox, MA
Fellows of the Berkshire Music Center, Michael Pratt, Cond.
[† (New York)] 3 Feb 1978: The Great Hall, Cooper Union, NY
[Untitled ensemble], Gunther Schuller, Cond.

Recording(s):
Golden Crest Records Inc.: NEC-119, ©1979 (LP)
New England Conservatory Contemporary Music Ensemble, Gunther Schuller, Cond.

Bibliography:
Porter, Andrew. "Musical Events: Playing in Earnest." *The New Yorker* 20 Feb 1978: 116–17.
Grimes, Ev. "Yale University American Music Oral History Series: William Thomas McKinley." Oct 1986, Yale University School of Music: 76.

Program Notes:
"*Paintings No. 1* was premiered at the University of Wisconsin at Madison with their contemporary Chamber ensemble conducted by Les Thimmig in 1972. As in *Paintings No. 1*, I was concerned with the Baroque concept of *Affektenlehre* or the Doctrine of Affections.

The link between this doctrine and the nineteenth-century tone poem ideal is convincing. Therefore, each piece is designed to express a particular 'affect' or mood. In *Paintings No. 2,* the pieces are titled as follows: Winter, Spring, Summer, Autumn, and Epilogue. The connection with Vivaldi's *Seasons* is obvious, but I, as so many of my predecessors, am deeply affected by the drama inherent in these natural changes and was thus moved to attempt painting these transformations in sound. It is not expected that each listener perceive these changes. Each painting is a self-contained musical structure which has much in common with the language found in certain freer present-day styles of improvisation. Though strictly composed and notated, the overall attitude of the work is one of plasticity and flexibility of musical gesture within a carefully woven network of motivic and rhythmic detail."
—William Thomas McKinley (© 1976), from 28 Feb 1976 program.

"*Paintings No. 2* was composed on a commission from Yale University in 1974, but its first performance did not take place until Gunther Schuller premiered the work in February 1976 with the New England Conservatory Contemporary Music Ensemble during the annual ASUC Festival.

"Its setting is quite simple. The seasons have always inspired me as they have inspired many other composers from Vivaldi to Prokofiev. Living in New England, one witnesses a dramatic seasonal metamorphosis. It is precisely the nature of these changes which caused me to 'paint' their characters in a sound portrait. However, the work is not to be interpreted in a strict programmatic sense. The illusions are subjective, although vivid to the imagination of the composer.

"Each seasonal portrait in *Paintings No. 2*, as well as the fifth movement *Epilogue*, is a self-contained musical organism in which motivic and structural details can be aurally perceived and followed throughout their individual stylistic development. Although I feel the language of the work to be a synthesis of both Afro-American musical gestures and influences of the Viennese school (Webern, Schoenberg and Berg), I hope that the total sound fabric demonstrates a personal musical style and statement."
—William Thomas McKinley (© 1976), from Margun Music, inc. MM015 published score, 14 Aug 1976 and 3 Feb 1978 programs, and his notes.

VIII.C.2 Summer Light

Date: 18 May 1991 in Reading, MA ("Lells") *Duration:* 12'00"
Dedication: "to Robert Stallman and the Marblehead Chamber Players"*
Commission: [Marblehead Chamber Players]
Publisher: MMC Publications

Movement(s):
Felice (♩=112)

Instrumentation:
Fl, Cl, Vln, Vla, Vcl, Pno soli.

MS Description:
Holograph with signature, pencil on paper. *Location:* Boston Public Library.

Editorial Notes:
*McKinley's program notes dedicate the work to Robert Stallman and the *Cambridge* Chamber Players. Commission information from the composer.

Performance History:
† 4 Aug 1991: Old North Church, Marblehead, MA
The Cambridge Chamber Players, Robert Stallman, Cond.

Program Notes:
"*Summer Light* represents a continuation in a series of my single movement chamber music works, devoted to the compositional expression and development of color and texture and the many various musical facets in which these techniques of color and texture are expressed within a narrative musical structure or framework. Tonal harmony and melody also play important roles and are continually woven into the fabric of the color and texture, providing enrichment and dramatic support throughout the work's discourse.

"While I was composing *Summer Light*, a very compelling musical form gradually emerged which greatly influenced the overall design and temporal direction, and hence the work's primary impulses were expanded into an accumulating dramatic intensity. Having found myself withholding the voice of the viola, I then decided to assign the viola a metaphorical character to create a sense of excitement and anticipation centering around its eventual appearance into the musical dialogue. The viola came to represent the richness and paradoxical weight and darkness of summer light, the embodied intense warmth and heat of summer—summer itself—and the viola's presence remains in the dialogue until a pattern of gradual disappearance (*á la* Haydn's *Farewell* Symphony) occurs *poco a poco* throughout the remaining instrumental parts, symbolizing a farewell to summer, until only the solo flute remains as a solitary remembrance carrying the musical-dramatic thread towards the penultimate *tutti* in the closing pages, while gathering the work's energies into a final conclusion. One will indeed notice at times the allusion to the ubiquitous Gershwin tune *Summertime*, and this is no accident. My own background in jazz improvisation, dance, and theater encourages this process of musical interpolation; and for me, at least, the work's metaphorical basis is thereby strengthening this association with the 'mundane,' thus helping to create (and reinforce) an anchor for the listener while at the same time making the many abstract and original details of color and texture within the primary musical palette more accessible and evocative.

"*Summer Light* is dedicated to Robert Stallman and the Cambridge Chamber Players, and to their continued musical prosperity and luminous creative development and longevity."
—William Thomas McKinley (© 1991), from 4 Aug 1991 program.

VIII.C.3 [Sextet]

Date: 20 May 1992 in Reading, MA ("Lells") *Duration:* 6'20"
Dedication: ["Dedicated to Robert Stallman, Helen Campo and my other great flutist friends"]
Publisher: MMC Publications

Movement(s):	*Instrumentation:*
Tempestoso (♩=144+)	6 Fl soli.

MS Description:
Holograph with signature, pencil on paper. *Location:* Boston Public Library.

Editorial Notes:
Title taken from cover page of fair copy. Dedication taken from McKinley's program notes. 7 Jun 1992 advertised performance at Weill Recital Hall in New York did not include this work.

Program Notes:
"Dedicated to Robert Stallman, Helen Campo and my other great flutist friends. This work engages the instrumentalists in a fierce virtuoso workout while maintaining a hair-

raising tempo (♩=144) from beginning to end (as in a *perpetuo moto*) dramatically conveying an intense celebratory spirit, festiveness and equanimity throughout."
—William Thomas McKinley (© 1994), from his notes.

VIII.C.a ~~[Untitled for Chamber Ensemble]~~

Date: [ca. Late 1968]
Publisher: Unpublished

Movement(s):
[One untitled movement.]

Instrumentation:
Fl, Ob, Cl, Vln, Vla, Vcl soli.

Sketches:
1 draft of the opening.

MS Description:
Holograph, pencil on paper. *Location:* Boston Public Library.

Editorial Notes:
MS ends after 11 pages. Written on same paper as and found with *Solo Duet for Clarinet ("Duet for One")* (VII.B.1).

See also: Arabesques for Assorted Instruments (VIII.E.3)
Jean's Dream... (II.E.4)
~~**Shapes**~~ (VIII.G.d)

Group VIII.D: Quintets for Assorted Instruments

VIII.D.1 Trio and Poem for Flute, Piano, Contrabass, Soprano, and Snare Drum

Date: [1967] in [New Haven, CT (Yale Univ.)] *Duration:* 8'18"
Publisher: MMC Publications

Movement(s):
Largo (♩=48)

Instrumentation:
Sop, Fl, Pno, Cb, Snare Dr soli.

Sketches:
1 complete draft.

MS Description:
Holograph with printed name, pencil on vellum. *Location:* Boston Public Library.

Editorial Notes:
Poem "I am" by Marlene Marie McKinley. Date taken from 8 Dec 1967 program. Location of composition taken from McKinley's notes.

Performance History:
† 8 Dec 1967: Sprague Recital Hall, Yale University School of Music, New Haven, CT
Audrey Naarden, Sop; Michael Finegold, Fl; Roger Cooke, Cb; Frank W. Bennett, Snare Dr; William Thomas McKinley, Pno; Thomas C. Fay, Cond.

VIII.D.2 Steps (Part II) for Bass Clarinet, Basset Horn, Soprano Sax, Tenor Sax, and Contrabass Clarinet

Date: Dec 1972—Jan 1973 *Duration:* 4'16"
Dedication: "For Les [Thimmig], once more"
Commission: [Les Thimmig]
Publisher: MMC Publications

Movement(s):
[One untitled movement.]

Instrumentation:
BCl, Basset Hn, Sop Sax, Ten Sax, CbCl soli;
Tape (some sections must be pre-recorded).

Sketches:
10 drafts of the opening. 1 draft of page 2. 2 unidentified drafts.

MS Description:
Holograph with printed name, pencil on vellum. *Location:* Boston Public Library.

Editorial Notes:
Commission information from the composer.

Performance History:
† 20 Feb 1973: Mills Concert Hall, University of Wisconsin, Madison, WI
University of Wisconsin Contemporary Chamber Ensemble, Les Thimmig, Cond.
1 Oct 1973: Morphy Recital Hall, University of Wisconsin, Madison, WI
Les Thimmig, Cl; Dan Harris, Taped BCl; [Other specific performers unknown].
[† (Boston)] 26 Mar 1974: Jordan Hall, New England Conservatory of Music, Boston, MA
Les Thimmig, Cl; [Other specific performers unknown].

Bibliography:
Elsner, Carmen. "New Sound Explored on Campus." *Wisconsin State Journal* 23 Feb 1973: IV 17.

Program Notes:
For 20 Feb 1973 notes see *Cello Music* (VIII.E.5).
For 1 Oct 1973 notes see *Steps (Part I)* (VII.B.5).
For McKinley's handwritten notes see *Composition I* (VII.B.4).

VIII.D.3 Six Impromptus for Flute, B♭ Clarinet, Violin, Viola, [and] Cello

Date: 27 Jul 1978 in Boston, MA *Duration:* 11'00"
Dedication: "To Richard Pittman [and Boston Musica Viva]"
Commission: [National Endowment for the Arts]
Publisher: MMC Publications

Movement(s):
I. ♩=60
II. ♩.=90
III. ♩=60
IV. ♪ =72
V. ♩=50
VI. ♪ =180

Instrumentation:
Pic/Fl, Cl, Vln, Vla, Vcl soli.

MS Description:
Holograph with printed name, ink on vellum. *Location:* Boston Public Library.

Editorial Notes:
Commission and additional dedication taken from McKinley's program notes. Premiere performance information from McKinley's notes.

Performance History:
[† 21 Nov 1978: Sanders Theater, Cambridge, MA
The Boston Musica Viva, Richard Pittman, Cond.]
23 Mar 1979: [Location unknown]
The Boston Musica Viva, Richard Pittman, Cond.
4 Mar 1988: First and Second Church, Boston, MA
The Boston Musica Viva, Richard Pittman, Cond.
See also *Program Notes.*

Recording(s):
Northeastern Records: NR 203, ©1982 (LP)
Boston Musica Viva, Richard Pittman, Cond.

Bibliography:
Grimes, Ev. "Yale University American Music Oral History Series: William Thomas McKinley." Oct 1986, Yale University School of Music: 73–74.
Tommasini, Anthony. "McKinley's Recent Works Lack Discernment and Taste." *The Boston Globe* 5 Mar 1988: 14.

Program Notes:
"William Thomas McKinley's *Six Impromptus* was commissioned by the National Endowment for the Arts and completed in 1978. It is dedicated to Richard Pittman and members of the Boston Musica Viva and is scored for flute (doubling piccolo), B♭ clarinet, violin, viola, and cello. It was given its world premiere during the 1978–1979 season of the Boston Musica Viva with Mr. Pittman conducting. Subsequently, it has been performed at the Eastman School of Music, the New England Conservatory of Music, and recently (1981) recorded for the BBC in London, England. In May, 1981, the Boston Musica Viva recorded the work on Northeastern Records, along with Mr. McKinley's *Paintings No. 6.* This recording is scheduled for release in the fall of 1981.

"Essentially, the *Six Impromptus* is simple in form (ABA or ABA' varied) and improvisatory in character. Unlike the other works of McKinley which often espouse literary or programmatic ideals, the *Impromptus* is abstract in nature and does not consciously attempt portrayal of extra-musical poetic ideas or metaphors. It is therefore a classical work, and its intrinsic elements exist as 'pure' musical thought, containing compositional complexities that unfold within short time periods, and that display considerable virtuosity and linear-polyphonic density. Thus, great demands are placed on both performer and listener, and comprehension requires intense concentration and aural effort. The work demands flawless execution and intonation, being at times very fragile and at times very rugged, sounding nearly orchestral. At first, its manner might suggest to the listener the character of studies or etudes. But the listener must strive to hear the virtuosic interplay among all of the parts. This will eventually lead him to the perception of the whole musical fabric, at which point the character of etude or study will diminish, the musical dramatic action dominate, and the listener will then perceive with less difficulty the classically constructed and developed foreground of articulated phrases, motives, and cadences. Ideally, the *Six Impromptus* seeks a synthesis or balance between ordered structure (phrases, motives, cadences, etc.) and

ornamentation (those particular events which decorate the shifting temporal patterns and which display a linear velocity suggesting improvisational time as set apart from metric time). Given repeated listenings, new events, new details, and new inter-relationships will surface. And, this will serve to strengthen the dramatic effect and continuity in each of the impromptus as well as the dramatic effect and continuity of the entire work. But, ultimately, the *Six Impromptus* must be heard as an entity and understood as a cumulative, organic, and classically unified musical statement and musical form."
—William Thomas McKinley (© 1982), from Northeastern Records NR 203 liner notes and his notes.

VIII.D.4 Paintings No. 4 ("Magical Visions")

Date: 2 Sep 1978 in Reading, MA ("Barn") *Duration:* 13'00"
Dedication: "To Frank Epstein and the members of Collage"
Commission: [National Endowment for the Arts]
Publisher: Margun Music Inc.

Movement(s):
With great contemplation
and inner strength (♩=52)

Instrumentation:
Pic/Fl, Cl, Perc, Vcl, Pno soli.

MS Description:
Holograph with signature, Blue wax pencil on vellum. *Location:* Boston Public Library.

Editorial Notes:
Commission taken from McKinley's notes. 13 Jan 1988 performance information from advertisement.

Performance History:
† 4 Dec 1978: Longy School of Music, Cambridge, MA
Collage, Gunther Schuller, Cond.
[† (Lenox)] 7 Aug 1979: Tanglewood Theater Concert Hall, Lenox, MA
Collage, Gunther Schuller, Cond.
29 Feb 1980: Jordan Hall, New England Conservatory of Music, Boston, MA
The Conservatory Contemporary Ensemble, Larry Livingston, Cond.
8 Jul 1980: Chautauqua Park, Boulder, CO
Colorado Music Festival Chamber Orchestra, Giora Bernstein, Cond.
[† (New York) 13 Jan 1988: Merkin Concert Hall, New York, NY
Music Today, Gerard Schwarz, Cond.]

Bibliography:
Grimes, Ev. "Yale University American Music Oral History Series: William Thomas McKinley." Oct 1986, Yale University School of Music: 76.

Program Notes:
"*Paintings No. 4* was originally conceived as a collection of musical tone portraits. However, during the earliest stages of the creative process, it soon became vivid in my imagination that a single, dramatically uninterrupted movement structure was forming. Hence a single painting 'magical visions' resulted; an imaginary landscape, chimerical, whirling, and perpetually evolving and transforming back and forth from concrete into amorphous musical texture.

"Throughout the work's entirety, the role of percussion is of principal importance (*Paintings No. 4* is dedicated to Frank Epstein, eminent percussionist with the Boston Symphony Orchestra). In its dramatic construction, the percussion acts both as an antagonist and a protagonist and is given very elaborate polyphonic and contrapuntal detail, complex textural and melodic transformations, and, when musically necessary, simple, direct and singular dramatic interjections. Fundamentally, therefore, the percussion acts as a *cantus firmus*, a rhythmic and melodic thread of continuity surrounded by an embroidered network of arabesques and kaleidoscopic play generated by the other instruments. However, the percussion activity, regardless of its sonic importance, should never relegate the surrounding instrumental activity to a position of secondary importance. It is the combined dramatic 'affect' which seeks to release in the listener's imagination a realm of magic, that uncertain and equivocally mystical spiritual ingredient shelved within the human psyche.

"No one will deny that vibrant chimerical visions exist within each one of us. We need only to recollect childhood dreams and fantasies. *Paintings No. 4* attempts to evoke and unlock each listener's personal vision, magic, those subconscious paintings, images, and perceptions which are often very distant and nebulous, but at times so very near and distinct. It is the 'concretion' of both worlds, the magical and the real, and their ultimate meeting point in time which initiates vision. And given the insight and genius of a great painter or the technological development of some future camera with which to precisely photograph mental images, each of us would then be able to permanently capture our most brilliant and private magical visions, crystallizing a myriad of fantasies and a plethora of the deepest projections and essence of mind.

"Thus, from the realm of 'pure' sound I have tried to dramatically capture and musically expand a few crystallized moments from the mental diary of my most personal and private dream visions, hoping to unleash within the listener the infinite sounds of the mind's magical and visionary eye."

—William Thomas McKinley (© 1979), from 7 Aug 1979 and 29 Feb 1980 programs and Margun Music, inc. MP5009 published score.

VIII.D.5 Quintet in One Movement for Flute, Clarinet, Oboe, French Horn, [and] Bassoon

Date: Feb 1980 in [Reading, MA ("Barn")] *Duration:* 20'00"
Dedication: [John Heiss, Robert Annis, Frederic Cohen, David Hoose, and Peter Schoenbach]
Commission: [National Endowment for the Arts]
Publisher: Margun Music Inc.

Movement(s):
Brillante (♩=90)

Instrumentation:
Pic/Fl/Alt Fl, Cl/BCl/CbCl, Ob/EHn, Hn, Bsn soli.

MS Description:
Engraving by McKinley, ink stencil on vellum. *Location:* Boston Public Library.

Editorial Notes:
Dedication taken from McKinley's program notes. Location of composition and commission taken from McKinley's notes.

Performance History:
† 10 Nov 1980: Jordan Hall, New England Conservatory of Music, Boston, MA
John Heiss, Fl; Robert Annis, Cl; Frederic Cohen, Ob; David Hoose, Hn; Peter Schoenbach, Bsn.

Bibliography:
Buell, Richard. "A Triumph of Tightrope Walking." *The Boston Globe* 14 Nov 1980: 26.

Program Notes:
"The McKinley Quintet, composed for the exact five players appearing here, is in part a response by the composer to their performance of the quintet by John Harbison last season. In one extended movement with several sections, the work grows out of ideas which are improvisatory in nature and moves toward others which, more homophonically defined, create an increasing sense of broad, oncoming resolution. What is quiet and pastoral expands to become intense and brilliant. McKinley uses a rich pallet of evocative sounds, colored especially by the use of bass and contrabass clarinet, English horn, piccolo and alto flute. In this context, the long-delayed and subtle entrances of the flute and French horn are particularly effective."
—John Heiss (© 1980), from 10 Nov 1980 program.

VIII.D.6 March Symphony

Date: 1984 in [Reading, MA ("Lells")] *Duration:* 26'00"
Dedication: "to Andre Emelianoff and Da Capo"
Commission: [National Endowment for the Arts]
Publisher: MMC Publications

Movement(s):
I. Allegro appassionato (♩=120)
II. Andante grazioso (𝅗𝅥=60)
III. Scherzo, presto (♩=140)
IV. Presto, joyous (𝅗𝅥=90)

Instrumentation:
Fl, Cl, Vln, Vcl, Pno soli.

Sketches:
1 draft of I/16. 1 draft of I/101. 1 draft of III/83–86.

MS Description:
Holograph with signature, pencil on vellum. *Location:* Boston Public Library.

Editorial Notes:
Commission and location of composition from McKinley's notes.

Performance History:
† 21 Jan 1985: Jordan Hall, New England Conservatory of Music, Boston, MA
The Da Capo Chamber Players (Patricia Spencer, Fl; Laura Flax, Cl; Joel Lester, Vln; Andre Emelianoff, Vcl; Sarah Rothenberg, Pno).
† (New York) 5 Jun 1986: Merkin Concert Hall, New York, NY
The New York New Music Ensemble, Robert Black, Cond.

Bibliography:
Dyer, Richard. "Da Capo Chamber Players Premiere McKinley Work." *The Boston Globe* 23 Jan 1985.
Holland, Bernard. "Music: Works by McKinley." *The New York Times* 7 Jun 1986.

Lifchitz, Max. "Composer of Note: William Thomas McKinley." *Living Music* 4(Fall 1986), no. 1: 2.

VIII.D.7 Cadenzas (An Instrumental Opera in Two Movements)

Date: Oct 1985 *Duration:* 23'00"
Dedication: "to Eddie Gomez and Omega [Ensemble]"
Commission: [Omega Ensemble]
Publisher: MMC Publications

Movement(s):
I. Prologue: Larghetto tranquillo (♩=63)
II. Narrative; epilogue: Prestissimo (♩=192)

Instrumentation:
Cl, Pno, Vln, Vcl, Cb soli.

MS Description:
Holograph with signature, pencil on vellum. *Location:* Boston Public Library.

Editorial Notes:
Premiere performance confirmed in *AMC Newsletter* 28(Mar–Apr 1986), no. 1: 16 and in McKinley's notes. Commission also taken from McKinley's notes.

Performance History:
[†] 25 Feb 1986: Carnegie Hall, New York, NY
Eddie Gomez, Cb; Omega Ensemble (Jean Kopperud, Cl; Doris Konig, Pno; Richard Rood, Vln; Andre Emelianoff, Vcl).

VIII.D.8 A Different Drummer ["An Instrumental Omnibus"]

Date: 22 Jul 1989 in Reading, MA ("Lells") *Duration:* 18'00"
Dedication: "to Danny Druckman and the New York New Music Ensemble"
Commission: [The New York New Music Ensemble]
Publisher: MMC Publications

Movement(s):
Prestissimo (♩=208)

Instrumentation:
Pic/Fl/Alt Fl, Cl/BCl, Perc, Pno, Vcl soli.

Sketches:
Formal plan for the work.

MS Description:
Holograph with signature, pencil on paper. *Location:* Boston Public Library.

Editorial Notes:
Subtitle, "An Instrumental Omnibus," from fair copy cover page and McKinley's program notes. Commission information from McKinley's program notes.

Performance History:
† 30 Oct 1989: Jordan Hall, New England Conservatory of Music, Boston, MA
The New York New Music Ensemble, Robert Black, Cond.
† (New York) 3 Nov 1989: Symphony Space, New York, NY
The New York New Music Ensemble, Robert Black, Cond.
† (Houston) 5 Nov 1989: Hammen Hall, Rice University School of Music, Houston, TX
The New York New Music Ensemble, Robert Black, Cond.

[† (New Orleans)] 6 Nov 1989: Contemporary Arts Center, New Orleans, LA
The New York New Music Ensemble, Robert Black, Cond.
[† (Chautauqua)] 30 Jul 1990: The Hall of Christ, Chautauqua Institution, Chautauqua, NY
[Untitled ensemble], David Stock, Cond.

Bibliography:

Tommasini, Anthony. "The Celebrated New York New Music Ensemble." *The Boston Globe* 1 Nov 1989.
Holland, Bernard. "A Concert of New Music 'In Celebration of the Soloist.'" *The New York Times* 5 Nov 1989: 94.
Cunningham, Carl. "Rice's Festival of American Music Less Than Riveting." *The Houston Post* 7 Nov 1989: A15.
Ward, Charles. "Fest Demonstrates Vitality of New Music." *Houston Chronicle* 7 Nov 1989: 4D.
Gagnard, Frank. "Fest Features the Offbeat." *New Orleans Times-Picayne* 12 Nov 1989.

Program Notes:
"This work was commissioned by the New York New Music Ensemble and features the outstanding individual virtuosic talents of its members, highlighting the drumming and mallet technique of Daniel Druckman. Subtitled 'An Instrumental Omnibus,' *A Different Drummer* presents a large and varied gestural-sonic canvas of duets, trios, quartets, and *tutti* combinations. In fact, there are over thirty varied and kaleidoscopically changing instrumental combinations (i.e., piccolo and clarinet, clarinet and drums, piano, cello, and flute; piano, clarinet, cello, and percussion; percussion alone, and so forth) which unfold throughout a large single-movement rondo structure gradually defining a chain of ever-expanding, developing, overlapping, and recapitulating musical elements. The percussion music connects these manifold combinations and acts as a *cantus firmus* and catalyst through the entire movement. Each new percussion set-up helps to amplify the essential dramatic tone and compositional pacing—suggesting to me the idea of an instrumental omnibus—with Dan at the helm and the others individually taking over the lead from time to time, allowing this 'different drummer' intervals of rest and preparation for the various musical entrances which lie ahead. Hence, a journey of discovery, rapprochement and renewal is continually filtered and carried along by the intensity and precision of Dan's persona—for Dan is indeed a 'different drummer,' different in many ways, not the least of which is his incredible versatility and brilliance which sets him quite apart from the ordinary drummer."
—William Thomas McKinley (© 1989), from 30 Oct 1989 and 3 Nov 1989 programs and his notes.

VIII.D.9 [Grand] Finale [No. 2]

Date: [Mar 1992] in [Reading, MA ("Lells")] *Duration:* 6'00"
Dedication: "To the Maryland Bach Aria Group"
Commission: [Maryland Bach Aria Group]
Publisher: MMC Publications

Movement(s):
Molto tempestoso e giubilante (♩=100)

Instrumentation:
Bsn, C Tpt, Pno, Vln, Vcl soli.

MS Description:
Holograph with signature, pencil on paper. *Location:* Boston Public Library.

Editorial Notes:
Date and location of composition from Elliott Miles McKinley. Commission information from the composer.

Performance History:
† 6 Apr 1992: Weill Recital Hall, New York, NY
Maryland Bach Aria Group (Deborah Greitzer, Bsn; Jeff Silberschlag, Tpt; Shirley Greitzer or Joel Wizansky, Pno; José Cuerto, Claudia Chudakoff, or Susan Aquila, Vln; Pamela Greitzer, Vcl).

VIII.D.10 Fleeting Moments

Date: 24 Aug 1992 in [Reading, MA ("Lells")] *Duration:* 11'00"
Dedication: "to the Maryland Bach Aria Group"
Commission: [Maryland Bach Aria Group]
Publisher: MMC Publications

Movement(s):
I. Con moto e grazioso (𝅗𝅥=104)
II. Prestissimo (♩=152)
III. Andantino e sensuale (𝅗𝅥.=40)
IV. Tempesto e presto (♩=184)
V. Largo e amabile (♩=40)
VI. Tango rag (𝅝‿♩=48)
VII. Larghetto e cantabile (♩.=50)
VIII. Più mosso e languido (♩=144)
IX. Allegro brillante (♩=132)
X. Lullaby: Andante e simplice (♩=92)
XI. Allegro energico (♩=138)

Instrumentation:
Cl, Bsn, Vln, Vcl, Pno soli.

MS Description:
Holograph with signature, pencil on paper. *Location:* Boston Public Library.

Editorial Notes:
Author was witness to location of composition. Commission information from the composer.

Performance History:
† 28 Oct 1992: Teatro Filarmonico, Verona, Italy
Maryland Bach Aria Group.

Bibliography:
Dalla Chiara, Albertina. "Il veronese Torelli fra Bach e Bernstein." *Il Nuovo Veronese* 28 Oct 1992: 29.
Gasdia, Elena. "Tutta colpa del barocco: Dal Maryland a Verona il Bach Aria Group." *La Cronaca di Verona* 28 Oct 1992: 23.
Villani, Gianni. "Musicisti dagli USA: Tra America e Europa col Maryland Bach Aria." *L'Arena di Verona* 28 Oct 1992: 29.

See also: Arabesques for Assorted Instruments (VIII.E.3)
Shapes (VIII.G.d)

Group VIII.E: Quartets for Assorted Instruments

VIII.E.1 Directions '65 for E♭ Alto Saxophone, Guitar, Contrabass, and Percussion

Date: Apr 1965 *Duration:* 5'02"
Dedication: "to my wife, Marlene"
Publisher: MMC Publications

Movement(s):
♩=60

Instrumentation:
Alt Sax, Perc, Gtr, Cb.

Sketches:
Formal plan for the work, including some themes and key designations. 2 complete drafts. 1 incomplete draft. 4 folios and 1 bifolio of sketches and 1 draft of the opening. 4 folios of unidentified sketches.

MS Description:
Holograph with printed name, pencil on vellum. *Location:* Boston Public Library.

Editorial Notes:
Performance information taken from McKinley's notes.

Performance History:
[†? Aug 1965: National Educational Television
Performers unknown.]

VIII.E.2 From Opera [No. 1]

Date: 1968 in Albany, NY (SUNY Albany) *Duration:* 19'38"
Dedication: "for Paul and Wilma Zonn"
Commission: [Paul Zonn]
Publisher: MMC Publications

Movement(s):
I.
II. Tactus=66

Instrumentation:
Pic/Fl/Alt Fl, Ob/EHn, Cl/BCl/Sop Sax, Pno soli.

Sketches:
1 complete draft.

MS Description:
Holograph with printed name, ink on vellum. *Location:* Boston Public Library.
Markings: Page b: Performance instructions followed by "Again, Violence and Instruments of Introspection are put into poetic conflict, our time our hate, black war but... just cause... if violence."

Editorial Notes:
In addition to the holograph MS, there exists a revised holograph piano part of the second movement (ink on vellum, undated). The first draft indicates the work was originally divided into five sections (an introduction and four "arias"), which were later combined in the final manuscript. The former introduction became the first movement and the four arias became the second movement. Commission and premiere performance information from McKinley's

notes. A recording of what is presumably this performance exists in McKinley's private collection.

Performance History:
[† Spring 1969: Yale University, New Haven, CT
Yale Players.]

VIII.E.3 Arabesques for Assorted Instruments*

Date: 1969–1970 in Chicago, IL (Univ. of Chicago) *Duration:* 10'37"
Dedication: "to Marlene"
Publisher: MMC Publications

Movement(s):
[Eight untitled movements.]

Instrumentation:
"Any number of assorted instruments." Originally written for Pno, Tpt, Vcl, and Rec soli.

MS Description:
Holograph with printed name, ink on vellum. *Location:* Boston Public Library.

Editorial Notes:
*Title originally appears with "Arabesque" spelled as "Arabasque." Supplementary premiere performance information from McKinley's notes.

Performance History:
[†] 6 Feb 1980: Teatro Nacional, Caracas, Venezuela (for Flute and Harp)
[Helen Campo, Fl; Susan Allen, Hp.]

VIII.E.4 Progeny for Flute, Piccolo, Oboe, Clarinet, Soprano Sax, Bass Clarinet, Percussion, and Tape

Date: 1971 in [Chicago, IL (Univ. of Chicago)] *Duration:* 21'29"
Dedication: "to Paul Zonn"
Commission: [University of Illinois, Urbana Chamber Ensemble]
Publisher: MMC Publications

Movement(s):
[One untitled movement.]

Instrumentation:
Pic/Fl, Ob, Cl/BCl/Sop Sax, Perc, Tape.

MS Description:
Holograph with printed name, pencil on vellum. *Location:* Boston Public Library.

Editorial Notes:
Commission and location of composition from McKinley's notes. Premiere performance information from the composer.

Performance History:
[† Date unknown: University of Wisconsin, Madison, WI
Performers unknown.]

VIII.E.5 Cello Music (A Portfolio for Solo, Two, Three, and Four Cellos)

Date: 12–27 Apr 1972 in Chicago, IL (Univ. of Chicago) *Duration:* 49'23"
Commission: [Roger Malitz]
Publisher: MMC Publications

Movement(s):
Episode A: With intense pulsation (♪=170)
Episode B: ♩=52
Episode C: With passion (♪=57)
Dances for Four Cellos:
I. Pristine Drops: ♩=47
II. Blue Expansion: ♪.=50
III. Kinetic Haze: As legato as possible
IV. Solo Excursion [1]: Molto espr[essivo] (♪=42)
V. Time Steps: Flautando (♪=54/60)
VI. Solo Excursion 2: Long lined (♩=30)
Solo Excursion 3: With great lyricism (♩=40)
VII. Solo Excursion 4: ♪.=52
Solo Excursion 5: Quasi recitativo (♪=56)
VIII. Dialogue 1: Col legno (♩=76)
Dialogue 2: Flowing (♩.=90)
IX. Static Flight: Sul pont, molto legato, whispered (♪=40)
X. Triple: Legato (♩=50)
XI. Solo Excursion 6: With intense statement (♩=40)
XII. Solo Excursion 7: Adagio (♩=52)
XII[I]. Winter Muse: ♩=30

Instrumentation:
4 Vcl soli.

Sketches:
8 sketches from "Solo Excursion [1]." 2 drafts of the opening of "Time Steps." 1 draft of the opening of "Solo Excursion 4." 2 drafts of the opening of "Dialogue 1."

MS Description:
Holograph with printed name, ink on vellum. *Location:* Boston Public Library.
Markings: "Episode A" dated 24 Apr 1972. "Episode B" dated 21 Apr 1972. "Episode C" dated 22 Apr 1972. "Pristine Drops" dated 12 Apr 1972. "Blue Expansion" and "Time Steps" dated 13 Apr 1972. "Kinetic Haze" and "Solo Excursions" [1]—3 dated 14 Apr 1972. "Solo Excursion" 4 and 5, "Dialogue" 1 and 2, and "Static flight" dated 16 Apr 1972. "Triple" dated 20 Apr 1972. "Solo Excursion 6" dated Apr 21 1972. "Solo Excursion 7" dated Apr 23 1972. "Winter Muse" dated Apr 27 1972.

Editorial Notes:
Commission taken from McKinley's notes.

Performance History:
† 20 Feb 1973: Mills Concert Hall, University of Wisconsin, Madison, WI (Solo Excursions III–IV only)
Lowell Creitz, Vcl.
[† (Chicago)] 6 Mar 1973: Mandel Hall, University of Chicago, Chicago, IL (3 solo excursions only)
Roger Malitz, Vcl.

Bibliography:

Elsner, Carmen. "New Sound Explored on Campus." *Wisconsin State Journal* 23 Feb 1973: IV 17.

Program Notes:

"In many of my recent scores, I have become increasingly intrigued with notions of virtuosity and complexity considered as dramatic and audible musical elements of considerable magnitude within a given compositional fabric. However, I have never sought to exceed boundaries of traditional performance practice. Yet those boundaries remain at present in considerable dispute (as perhaps they have always remained) due to the ageless, irrational, but incidentally imperative, symbiosis between composer and performer. I have never wanted to merely indulge in the commonplace juxtaposition of 'novelties,' which, due to its seeming unorthodoxy, nearly always creates havoc and hazardous going for even the most dedicated musicians.

"Instead, I have continually hoped to expand the boundaries of traditional performance technics—to create a new virtuosity which attempts to constantly challenge and stimulate the creativity of the individual performer. As a result, my music creates considerable networks of complexities which at first seem unfathomable to both listener and performer. I have observed that in time performers admirably come to grips with these demands and find excitement, and, yes, even reward in the challenges presented. At this stage, listeners begin to sense the vibrations of communication, and the dramatic content of my work gradually becomes less foreboding. (I hope that will be the case this evening.)

"All of the works to be heard, and in particular the Trio [for Two Violins and Viola] and *Steps*, dramatize in full blossom the notions of virtuosity and complexity I have been discussing. The solo *Cello Music* to be played is but a small portion of an entire portfolio of pieces for 1, 2, 3, and 4 celli. The cellist is free to choose those pieces which are felt suitable for a given occasion. Some of these pieces are considerable in size and can function as separate solo works. Others are in the nature of interludes which can be played in companion cycles. Mr. Creitz has chosen four of the Solo Excursions, which are representative of the latter classification.

"*Paintings* [*No. 1*] attempts to express a greater distinction between these antipodal states of lyricism and vehemence. And yet, in servitude to my basic credo, I have not diluted or simplified the complexities and virtuosic demands which *Paintings* requires of the performers. I simply gave myself a greater latitude in this particular work—a latitude which, for want of a more sophisticated term, encompasses clearly audible 'Impressionist' technics which have their conscious roots clearly in some of the more significant Debussy works: *Jeux*, Trio for flute, viola and harp, and a few other late pieces.

"The chamber work, *Paintings*, is a special case. Unlike *Steps* and the Trio, I have attempted to bring to the listener's attention strong lyrical elements which serve as a contrast and relief to the more vividly complex and varied musical events within the score. I speak here only in terms of degree. In all of my work I consciously attempt to stress what I believe to be lyrical qualities. But because these qualities are often manifest in non-melodic and non-linear fashion, the percipient at times cannot hear these areas in which I attempt to provide structurally clear portions of lyrical release. The undeniable surface loudness and gestural environments in my work seem to cloud the issue. Listeners often cannot remember anything else.

"I have never been certain which I admire most—the violence of Debussy or that of Schoenberg! In any case, metaphors and analogs of both appear in my work. But I would hope that my life's experience in improvisation will dominate any influences which may be felt. Perhaps improvisation is the philosophical source of these notions concerning virtuosity, complexity and the like.

"Finally, I wish my music to sound as if it were continuously being invented, challenging the unyielding strength and mysterious enigma of the creative mind—of the performer's will to break away, if only momentarily, from the normal practice of clichés—to be constantly on the periphery of the impossible, and yet to survive having experienced the challenge, as did the late John Coltrane.

"It is wise to remember: Who Listens If You Care!"

—William Thomas McKinley (© 1973), from 20 Feb 1973 program.

VIII.E.6 Quartet for Piano, Soprano Sax, Bass [and] Drums

Date: 1975 *Duration:* 19'00"
Publisher: MMC Publications

Movement(s):
Wildly (♪=120)

Instrumentation:
Sop Sax, Dr, Pno, Cb soli.

MS Description:
Holograph with printed name, ink on paper. *Location:* Boston Public Library.

VIII.E.7 Quartet No. 1 for B♭ Clarinet, Violin, Cello and Piano (op. 99) ["Tashi"]

Date: 25 Jul 1977 in Manchester, MA ("Carriage House") *Duration:* 4'48"
Dedication: "to Tashi"
Commission: National Endowment for the Arts
Publisher: MMC Publications

Movement(s):
With great movement, molto legato, whispered, the awakening (♪=40+)

Instrumentation:
Cl, Vln, Vcl, Pno soli.

Sketches:
1 earlier, unfinished version of the work (MS ends after 26 measures). 7 drafts of the opening of the early version. 4 drafts of m. 25 of the early version. 57 drafts of the opening of the final version.

MS Description:
Holograph with printed name, ink on vellum. *Location:* Boston Public Library.

Editorial Notes:
The work is often referred to as the *Tashi Quartet* in McKinley's notes.

Performance History:
[†?] 10 May 1979: The Straus Building, Milton Academy
Tashi (Richard Stoltzman, Cl; Peter Serkin, Pno; Ida Kavafian, Vln; Fred Sherry, Vcl).

Bibliography:
Grimes, Ev. "Yale University American Music Oral History Series: William Thomas McKinley." Oct 1986, Yale University School of Music: 75.

Program Notes:

"My primary purpose was to create a rich and varied textural, temporal, and gestural fabric. The challenges were fascinating and formidable. My musical imagination was continually 'haunted' by the individualistic, rugged, intensely romantic and yet beautifully controlled B♭ clarinet sound which Richard Stoltzman achieves. And combining the B♭ clarinet with the 'traditional' trio of violin, cello, and piano increased the possibilities of obtaining an active, kaleidoscopic, and heterogeneous sound portrait. (The 'traditional' piano trio ensemble is, for the most, homogeneous in its overall sound constitution and personality, and the certainty which it would have offered was not, for obvious reasons, available.) And during this gestation period, these possibilities, specifically those details which concerned time and timbre, became increasingly lucid; the heterogeneous sound portrait of the quartet was thus gradually revealed and illuminated.

"Equally important, I was soon to discover the wonderful *Quartet for the End of Time* by Olivier Messiaen (recorded by Tashi). This proved to be a most 'dramatic' musical encounter, providing me with a compositional 'model' and a spiritual 'catalyst.' I never consciously imitated Messiaen's quartet. It was not difficult to 'apprehend' the heterogeneous nature of its sound personality. Driven by a lyrical intensity, its total 'affect' was at once both chimerical and introspective. Comparing both quartets, it would be aurally apparent that their 'sensuous' surfaces are, in fact, quite similar and to some ears perhaps identical. (I realize that these quartets differ considerably in terms of syntax or linguistic-musical content. An appropriate study of these differences would carry beyond the purview of these notes.)

"Alas, my challenge was magnified! And an important question occurred to me. How might it be possible to musically 'photograph' the collective sound personality in this combination of instruments? How could I enlarge the sound, creating an orchestral expanse? And how might it be possible to objectify this personality, enabling listeners to easily identify it, to 'apprehend' its fundamental 'aura'?

"First, it was decided that the piano was to be given an important role, acting as a dramatic protagonist. And the violin, cello, and clarinet 'embellish' this role which in itself is most often lyrical, harmonic, and texturally transparent. But in all of the parts, arabesques, coloristic and textural embellishment, and other aspects of motivic dialogue find their basic stimuli, origins, and essential meaning and activity *vis-à-vis* powerful associations with the kinesthetic world of dance movement. Consequently, as the musical shapes unfold, subtle transformations of temporal movement (analogous to kinesthetic change) measured against 'real' time elements (not necessarily metric changes) take place within large spatial-time areas. And these changes determine to my ears at least the primary levels of architectural design and ultimately the entire musical structure of the quartet. The work is in one movement. Many states of temporal flux are concentrated within it. Considerable complexity results on every musical level. But despite the complexity, I wanted the total sound personality to portray a very clear and direct statement, magical and lyrical in nature.

"Fundamentally, this quartet is very traditional, controlled, and 'classically' detailed composition. One need only to examine and study the musical score. Its shapes, motifs, and motivic development are considerably dominant and of foreground importance. And the performers must 'display' the very same patterns of discipline, understanding, and musical intelligence which they must command in order to put forth a convincing interpretation of, say, a Mozart or Brahms composition.

"But to what extent can the listener be held accountable in fathoming these difficulties? In my judgment, if the listener is made aware of the mental attitudes necessary to begin initial stages of active and constructive participation in the listening process, many of these

difficulties vanish and understanding would follow close behind. Ideally, it would be desirable if each listener could link his/her own creative imaginations with the 'emotive' powers which emanate from the music itself, experiencing these powers as if in a state of child-like innocence, putting aside all of his/her preconceptions, prejudices, and value judgments. In the final analysis, my Quartet strives through its directness to enable the listener greater understanding of the tonal movement, the syntactical logic, and the "naturalness" of the temporal flow—all kaleidoscopically threaded together by a clearly articulated harmonic rhythm. The latter exhibits tonal gravity, tonal weight, tonal tension, and tonal resolution no differently, in terms of the classical control inherent in the melodic-contrapuntal movement, than any given traditional tonal example one might cite for comparison. However, these familiar harmonic movements are never literal. They are illusory, nebulous, and transcendental. And it is my most sincere hope that all whose 'good' ears occasion to grace this Quartet will remain open-minded to the possibility that all music, perhaps all creation, is in the final judgment, an activity of labor, love, and magic!"
—William Thomas McKinley (© 1979), probably from 10 May 1979 program.

VIII.E.8 August Symphony for Piano, Clarinet in B♭, Violin, and Cello

Date: [Aug] 1983 *Duration:* 21'30"
Dedication: "to Omega [Ensemble]"
Commission: [Omega Ensemble]
Publisher: MMC Publications

Movement(s):
I. Tragic, dark and deeply singing (𝅗𝅥.=60)
II. Adagio (♩=48)
III. Scherzando (♩.=72)
IV. Tragic, dark and deeply singing (𝅗𝅥.=60)

Instrumentation:
Cl, Pno, Vln, Vcl soli.

Sketches:
1 draft of the opening of II. 1 draft of III/27. 1 draft of III/77–78.

MS Description:
Holograph with signature, pencil on vellum. *Location:* Boston Public Library.

Editorial Notes:
Month of composition and commission taken from McKinley's notes.

Performance History:
† 11 Apr 1984: Weill Recital Hall, New York, NY
Omega Ensemble (Jean Kopperud, Cl; Doris Konig, Pno; Richard Rood, Vln; Andre Emelianoff, Vcl).
[† (Boston)] 21 Oct 1985: Jordan Hall, New England Conservatory of Music, Boston, MA
Thomas Hill, Cl; Nancy Cirillo, Vln; Bruce Coppock, Vcl; Randall Hodgkinson, Pno.

Bibliography:
Hughes, Allen. "Concert: Omega Group in a Premiere." *The New York Times* 15 Apr 1984: 50.
Buell, Richard. "Heiss/McKinley Concert A Study in Warring Contrasts." *The Boston Globe* 23 Oct 1985: 63.

Program Notes:
"*August Symphony* was commissioned by Omega and premiered in Carnegie Recital Hall. It is a lyrical work made up of simple outlines and broad structures. Composed in four

movements, the work's architecture and development evolve slowly and spaciously throughout its entirety. The *August Symphony* is conceived along very classical lines and accordingly with restraint. Perhaps the dramatic high-points occur in the Dirge (second movement), where the greatest dissonantal tension is placed. The third movement is a relatively brief Scherzo-Trio, and the fourth in fact continues as well as recapitulates the material of the first movement. The title refers to the month in which the work was composed, as well as the use of the first three melody notes of 'Stormy Weather' as a metaphor for the month of August. Finally, the work is a chamber symphony in the most traditional meaning." —William Thomas McKinley (© 1985), from 21 Oct 1985 program.

VIII.E.9 Paintings No. 8

Date: [1986] *Duration:* 20'30"
Dedication: [Dinosaur Annex]
Commission: [Dinosaur Annex]
Publisher: MMC Publications

Movement(s):
I. Landscape: Voluttuosamente (𝅗𝅥=80)
II. Elegy: Elegante (♩=66)
III. Cathedrals: Presto (𝅗𝅥=126)
IV. Clowns: Burlesco (𝅗𝅥.=76)

Instrumentation:
3 Cl/2 BCl/2 Pic Cl/A Cl, Perc.

Sketches:
1 extended draft of the opening (earlier title: *Climbing Waves*).

MS Description:
Holograph, pencil on vellum. *Location:* Boston Public Library.

Editorial Notes:
Dating based on premiere performance date and paleographic analysis. Dedication taken from draft. Commission taken from McKinley's notes.

Performance History:
† 25 Jan 1987: First and Second Church, Boston, MA (first three movements only)
Dinosaur Annex Music Ensemble (Diane Heffner, Ian Greitzer, Katherine Matasy, Cl; Michael Parola, Perc).
[†] 26 Feb 1987: Chapel, Massachusetts Institute of Technology, Cambridge, MA (complete)
Dinosaur Annex Music Ensemble.

Bibliography:
Miller, Nancy. "Piston's Craft Sparkles." *The Boston Globe* 28 Jan 1987: 53.

Program Notes:
"I had not planned to title the new work *Paintings VIII*, but all of the other *Paintings* are composed for eclectic combinations, and a work for three clarinets and percussion suited the *Paintings* series perfectly. For me, the challenge was to structure an ambitious set of movements and create maximum variety out of minimal instrumental means. The dramatic idea of a gradual ascension occurred to me and with the possibility of doubling as well as the availability of various clarinets I came up with the plan that involved one percussion instrument in each of the four movements and a family of clarinets beginning with two bass

clarinets in B♭ plus vibraphone in the first movement; one bass clarinet, plus two B♭'s and marimba in the second movement; three B♭ clarinets and tubular chimes in the third; and two E♭ clarinets, clarinet in A and xylophone in the fourth movement. Thus, there is a general spectral shift from movement to movement and an overall or gradually induced sense of ascension through the works' entirety. Seen as a whole, the general dramatic personality of *Paintings VIII* is neither heavy nor complex in nature. I prefer to view its moods in the same way as one might interpret the different moods of a clown—ranging from the tragic and serious to the jovial and jestful—but ultimately playful, bright and fun-filled in its eventual outcome and purpose. From this vantage point, *Paintings VIII* may well be my most entertaining work and indeed the nature of its instrumentation as well as its overall design inspired me to envision this particular outcome in musical environment."
—William Thomas McKinley (© 1987), from 25 Jan 1987 program.

VIII.E.10 Can You Sing Me a Song? (Rhythm Section Reduction)*

Date: 1988 *Duration:* 33'00"
Dedication: "to Stan Getz"
Commission: [Stan Getz]
Publisher: MMC Publications

Movement(s):
Ballad tempo, very slowly (♩=52)

Instrumentation:
Ten Sax, Pno, Cb, Dr.

MS Description:
Copyist's hand, pencil on vellum. *Location:* Boston Public Library.

Editorial Notes:
*An arrangement by Michael Shea of *Can You Sing Me A Song? (A Lyric Concerto in One Movement)* (II.B.5). Commission information from the composer.

Program Notes:
See *Can You Sing Me A Song? (A Lyric Concerto in One Movement)* (II.B.5).

VIII.E.11 Serenata for Flute, Clarinet, Cello, and Piano

Date: 20 Oct 1989 in Reading, MA ("Lells") *Duration:* 17'00"
Dedication: "to the The Boston Chamber Music Society"
Commission: [The Boston Chamber Music Society]
Publisher: MMC Publications

Movement(s):
I. Ragtime: Ragtime tempo and feeling (𝅗𝅥=76–84)
II. Waltz: Tempo di valse (𝅗𝅥.=52)
III. March: Tempo di marcia (♪=264)
IV. Lullaby: Largo e tenero (♪=80)
V. Jig: Presto vivace (♩.=76)
VI. Polka: Giacosamente (♩=126)
Finale. Ad libitum (♩=66)

Instrumentation:
Pic/Fl, Pic Cl/Cl, Vcl, Pno soli.

MS Description:
Holograph with signature, pencil on paper. *Location:* Boston Public Library.

Editorial Notes:
Commission information from the composer.

Performance History:
† 12 Jan 1990: Jordan Hall, New England Conservatory of Music, Boston, MA
The Boston Chamber Music Society, Ronald Thomas, Cond.
† (New York) 13 Jan 1990: Alice Tully Hall, New York, NY
The Boston Chamber Music Society, Ronald Thomas, Cond.
14 Jan 1990: Sanders Theater, Cambridge, MA
The Boston Chamber Music Society, Ronald Thomas, Cond.

Bibliography:
Oestreich, James R. "Mozart to Neo-Baroque, By Boston Chamber Players." *The New York Times* 15 Jan 1990: C15.

Program Notes:
"*Serenata* was completed in 1989 and is dedicated to a marvelous group of artists—The Boston Chamber Music Society—who as individuals have performed and recorded many of my works over the past fifteen years. It is my pleasure to compose this work for them collectively; I salute each of them and look forward to a never-ending creative relationship.

"Essentially, *Serenata* is a set of instrumental dances (drawn from among my favorite) except for the 'Lullaby' (which is in some sense a 'rocking chair' dance) and the 'Finale.' Each of the movements is treated with idiomatic care while at the same time striving to 'abstract' and view certain characteristics through a contemporary lens. For instance, the 'Ragtime' movement, while preserving certain general mannerisms and idiomatic traits heard in Ragtime style, at the same time presents musical elements which are often more syncopated and rhythmically complex than those heard in Ragtime. These presentations are sometimes 'mirrored' or transformed through juxtaposition as well as antiphony. But never are those elements 'abstracted' to a point wherein their traditional musical character is lost or their idiomatic and stylistic basis blurred or destroyed. Similarly, each of the remaining movements seeks a balance between the stated character and the abstraction of that character from a contemporary vantage point and looking glass.

"Instrumentally, *Serenata* gives each of the performers (flute, clarinet, piano, and cello) a considerable virtuosic workout and I have 'lovingly' spotlighted each instrument from time to time throughout the work (e.g. the flute cadences in the 'Finale' and other surprises for my friends en route.)"

—William Thomas McKinley (© 1990), from 12, 13, and 14 Jan 1990 programs and his notes.

VIII.E.12 Four Saxophone Blues

Date: 5 Oct 1992 in Reading, MA ("Lells") *Duration:* 12'15"
Dedication: "to the Berlin Saxophone Quartet"
Commission: [Berlin Saxophone Quartet]
Publisher: MMC Publications

Movement(s):	*Instrumentation:*
I. Moderato (♩=54)	Sop Sax, Alt Sax, Ten Sax, Bar Sax.
II. Prestissimo (♩=208)	
III. Allegretto e dolce (♩.=54)	
IV. Presto e molto feroce con loco moto (𝅗𝅥=176)	

MS Description:
Holograph with signature, pencil on paper. *Location:* Boston Public Library.

Editorial Notes:
Commission information from the composer.

Performance History:
† 25 Apr 1993: Jordan Hall, New England Conservatory of Music, Boston, MA
Berliner Saxophon Quartett (Detlef Bensmann, Sop Sax; Klaus Kreczmarsky, Alt Sax; Christof Griese, Ten Sax; Friedemann Graef, Bar Sax).
† (New York) 28 Apr 1993: Weill Recital Hall, New York, NY
Berliner Saxophon Quartett.

See also: ~~**Composition for Flute, Guitar and Piano**~~ (VIII.F.a)
~~**Shapes**~~ (VIII.G.d)

Group VIII.F: Trios for Assorted Instruments

VIII.F.1 Attitudes for Flute, Clarinet and Cello

Date: 1967 *Duration:* 8'11"
Dedication: "to Mel Powell"
Publisher: MMC Publications

Movement(s):	*Instrumentation:*
I. Chorale: ♩=60	Fl, Cl, Vcl soli.
II. Variation: ♩=72–80	
III. Transformation: ♩=60	
IV. Epilogue: ♩=72	

Sketches:
1 nearly complete draft (includes multiple drafts of some pages). 8 folios of thematic sketches, pitch functionality charts, and tone rows. 4 folios of theme and variation layouts. 1 draft and 2 extended drafts of the opening (earlier titles: *Variations for Flute, Clarinet and Cello; Variations, Psychological for Flute, Clarinet and Cello*). 4 folios of "additions" to I. 1 draft of the end of I and opening of I. 8 folios and 1 bifolio of unidentified sketches.

MS Description:
Holograph with printed name, pencil on paper. *Location:* Boston Public Library.

Editorial Notes:
Fair copy is a McKinley holograph (pencil on paper, no signature or date, owned by Richard Stoltzman). Confirmation of 4 May 1967 as premiere performance from McKinley's notes.

Performance History:
[†] 4 May 1967: Sprague Memorial Hall, Yale University School of Music, New Haven, CT
Michael Finegold, Fl; Richard Stoltzman, Cl; Eric Jensen, Vcl.
14 May 1967: Pierson College, Yale University, New Haven, CT
Michael Finegold, Fl; Richard Stoltzman, Cl; Eric Jensen, Vcl.

Bibliography:
Bouchard, Fred. "Richard Stoltzman: Clarinet Crossover." *Downbeat* 53(Oct 1986), no. 10: 20–22, 61.
Grimes, Ev. "Yale University American Music Oral History Series: William Thomas McKinley." Oct 1986, Yale University School of Music: 53–54.
Tassel, Janet. "From Fat Tuesday's to Carnegie Hall." *Musical America* 107(Jan 1988), no. 6: 21–22.

VIII.F.2 Trio for Two Violins and Viola

Date: [Dec 1971] in [Chicago, IL (Univ. of Chicago)] *Duration:* 18'57"
Dedication: "to Paul Zukofsky"
Commission: [Paul Zukofsky]
Publisher: MMC Publications

Movement(s):
[One untitled movement.]

Instrumentation:
2 Vln, Vla soli.

Sketches:
33 drafts of the opening (earlier title: *Fragments*). 1 draft of page 15. 1 draft of page 16. 4 folios of notes, including motives and a formal plan. 37 unidentified drafts.

MS Description:
Holograph, pencil on vellum. *Location:* Boston Public Library.

Editorial Notes:
Dating based draft dated 26 Nov 1971 and 20 Feb 1973 program and McKinley's notes which indicate 1971 as the year of composition. Location of composition and commission from McKinley's notes.

Performance History:
† 20 Feb 1973: Mills Concert Hall, University of Wisconsin, Madison, WI
Norman Paulu and Martha Blum, Vln; Marna Street, Vla.

Program Notes:
For 20 Feb 1973 notes see *Cello Music* (VIII.E.5).

VIII.F.3 Dance Piece (A Format for Improvisation)

Date: 1972 *Duration:* Varies
Commission: [University of Chicago Dance Ensemble]
Publisher: MMC Publications

Movement(s):
As fast as possible

Instrumentation:
Perc, Pno, Cb soli; 5 dancers.

Sketches:
1 complete draft—much of it in prose.

MS Description:
Holograph with signature, pencil on paper. *Location:* Boston Public Library.

Editorial Notes:
Commission information from the composer. Premiere performance information from McKinley's notes.

Performance History:
[† 1973: University of Chicago, Chicago, IL
William Thomas McKinley, Pno; University of Chicago Dance Ensemble; Other performers unknown.]

VIII.F.4 Downtown Walk No. 2 for Violin, Marimba, and Contrabass

Date: 5 Mar 1989 in Reading, MA ("Lells") *Duration:* 14'00"
Dedication: "to Rufus Reid and Marimolin"
Commission: [Marimolin]
Publisher: MMC Publications

Movement(s):
♩=48

Instrumentation:
Mar, Vln, Cb soli.

Sketches:
1 folio of notes on tempo markings.

MS Description:
Holograph with signature, pencil on vellum. *Location:* Boston Public Library.

Editorial Notes:
Commission information from the composer.

Performance History:
† 29 Apr 1989: Cambridge Multicultural Arts Center, E. Cambridge, MA
Rufus Reid, Cb; Marimolin (Sharan Leventhal, Vln; Nancy Zeltsman, Mar).
[† (New York)] 14 May 1989: Weill Recital Hall, New York, NY
Rufus Reid, Cb; Marimolin.

Program Notes:
"*Downtown Walk No. 2* is part of a cycle of pieces composed for my bass playing friends. *No. 1* was composed for Marc Johnson and his wife, flutist Stephanie Jutt, and *No. 2* is dedicated to Rufus Reid and Marimolin. The series is intended to feature primarily the pizzicato walking bass line indigenous to jazz time playing. This is unequivocally the natural habitat of the jazz bassist and the most immediately effective and gratifying to hear. This intrinsic characteristic also allowed me to explore different tempi or time feelings particularly in *Downtown Walk No. 2*, which is divided into fifteen different through composed tempi each with a different manner and 'groove.' The violin and marimba are integrated into the tempo changes and the overall effect is of a dialogue among all three instruments with about equal virtuosic interplay spread among them. There are a few segments of arco playing within the total framework, but this serves only as a coloristic relief to the ubiquitous pizzicato."

"All the parts are fully notated and the improvisational interplay is a result of control rather than freedom. This is a very important aspect. I want to create a notated or permanent

statement drawn from our rich jazz heritage helping to crystallize the important qualities for other bassists to be able to play in the future—to create a common ground for the two realities of classical and jazz, without compromising either genre. As a final note *Downtown Walk* does mean literally what it says. The jazz pizzicato bass epitomizes the earthiness implied and the richness desired."
—William Thomas McKinley (© 1989), from 29 Apr/14 May 1989 program.

VIII.F.5 Singletree for Flute, Marimba, and Tuba

Date: Mar 1992 *Duration:* 9'00"
Dedication: "to Singletree"
Commission: [Singletree]
Publisher: MMC Publications

Movement(s):
I. Branches: Con moto e grazioso (♩=144)
II. Leaves: Vivace (𝅗𝅥=63)
III. Roots: Lamento (♩=63)
IV. Buds: Vivo (♩=120)
V. Twigs: Prestissimo (♩.=168)

Instrumentation:
Fl, Tba, Mar soli.

MS Description:
Holograph with signature, pencil on paper. *Location:* Boston Public Library.

Editorial Notes:
Commission information from the composer.

Performance History:
† 29 Mar 1992: Knitting Factory, New York, NY
Singletree (Helen Campo, Fl; Marcus Rojas, Tba; William Moersch, Mar).

VIII.F.a ~~Composition for Flute, Guitar and Piano~~

Date: 1965 *Duration:* 2'15"
Dedication: "to my wife"
Publisher: Unpublished

Movement(s):
♩=60

Instrumentation:
[Voice,] Fl, Gtr, Pno soli.

Sketches:
2 folios of descriptive notes and tone rows. 8 folios and 3 bifolios of sketches and drafts of the opening. 3 folios and 1 bifolio of unidentified sketches and drafts.

MS Description:
Holograph, pencil on paper. *Location:* Boston Public Library.

Editorial Notes:
Notes indicate that the composer intended to add voice in the last 30 seconds and that the work would not exceed two and a half minutes in length.

VIII.F.b ~~Smoke~~

Date: [ca. 1972]
Publisher: Unpublished

Movement(s):
Static immobile quality
with quiet intensity (♩=60)

Instrumentation:
Fl, Hp, Vla soli.

Sketches:
1 draft of the opening.

MS Description:
Holograph, ink on paper. *Location:* Boston Public Library.

Editorial Notes:
MS ends after 4 measures.

See also: Arabesques for Assorted Instruments (VIII.E.3)
~~Shapes~~ (VIII.G.d)

Group VIII.G: Duos for Assorted Instruments

VIII.G.1 [Untitled for Trumpet and Bassoon]

Date: [ca. 1967]
Publisher: Unpublished

Movement(s):
[One untitled movement.]

Instrumentation:
Tpt, Bsn soli; Tape (some sections must be pre-recorded).

MS Description:
Holograph, pencil on paper. *Location:* McKinley Residence.

Editorial Notes:
MS seems to be complete, but is extremely light and difficult to read. Date determined through paleographic analysis. Judging by the style of handwriting and music, this work and the Sonata for Violin and Piano (VI.F.2) were probably written one right after the other.

VIII.G.2 Interim Pieces [No. 1] for Violin and Bass Clarinet

Date: 1968 in New Haven, CT (Yale Univ.) *Duration:* 17'28"
Dedication: "For Les [Thimmig] and Syoko [Aki Erle]"
Commission: [Les Thimmig and Syoko Aki Erle]
Publisher: MMC Publications

Movement(s):
I. ♪=30
Interlude.
II. ♪=30

Instrumentation:
BCl, Vln soli

III. ♪=42
IV.
Interlude.
V.
VI.
Interlude.
VII.

Sketches:
1 nearly complete draft. 1 draft of the opening (earlier instrumentation: Ob, BCl, Tpt, Pno, Vln soli). 1 harmonic layout using the earlier instrumentation. 10 folios of unidentified sketches.

MS Description:
Holograph with printed name, ink on vellum. *Location:* Lost*.

Editorial Notes:
*A photocopy of the MS survives and is stored at Boston Public Library. Commission information from the composer.

Performance History:
† 9 Feb 1968: Sprague Memorial Hall, Yale University, New Haven, CT
Les Thimmig, BCl; Syoko Aki Erle, Vln.
14 Apr 1968: Morse College, Yale University, New Haven, CT
Les Thimmig, BCl; Syoko Aki Erle, Vln.

Program Notes:
"These seven pieces and three interludes encompass several objectives. In them I attempted for the first time to explore a freer use of *mensural principles*. The bar line as well as metric constancy have been abolished in favor of a more *spatially* and *gesturally* oriented notation. In this, I wished to obliterate *periodicity* as well as reduce the foolish and excessive notational complexities which pervade so much of new music. Also, for the first time, contained in the 2nd interlude, I introduced *graphic shapes* of various sizes and definitions (not unlike, conceptually, those many and varied ornaments in Baroque music) which would hopefully stimulate, psychologically, a state of *improvisation* in the performers. The prime objectives of these pieces transcend, however, such notational procedures. These *objectives* can be regarded in two ways—*initially* they should remain as distinct personalities—singular and differentiated in their aural characteristics and developmental goals. *Secondly*, and most important perhaps this work strives for a *total dramatic* effect—a scenario in which the individual parts or pieces become only the trees within the density of the forest—this commitment to total organic unity is certainly the prime philosophic, aesthetic and compositional *raison d'etre* for the *Interim Pieces*—and it is in this way that the work should ultimately be perceived and aurally admitted into the domain of musical reality...."
—William Thomas McKinley (© 1968), from 9 Feb 1968 program.

VIII.G.3 Sonatas for Two Pianos

Date: Oct–Nov 1972 *Duration:* 17'31"
Commission: [James Winn and Cameron Grant]
Publisher: MMC Publications

Movement(s):
I.
II.
III. On the Eve: ♩=52
Sunshine
Holidays

Instrumentation:
2 Pno soli.

Sketches:
5 drafts of the opening of I. 2 drafts of page 2 of I. 1 draft of page 4 of I. 1 draft of page 6 of I. 1 draft of page 10 of I. 4 drafts of page 11 of I. 1 draft of page 12 of I. 2 drafts of the opening of II. 2 drafts of page 4 of II. 2 drafts of page 5 of II. 7 drafts of page 6 of II. 2 drafts of page 8 of II. 6 drafts of page 7 of II. 1 draft of the opening of the first movement of III. 4 drafts of the opening of the third movement of III. 39 unidentified drafts.

MS Description:
Holograph with printed name, ink on vellum. *Location:* Boston Public Library.
Markings: Each sonata is individually dated and has its own title page. Sonatas I and II dated Oct 1972. Sonata III dated Nov 1972.

Editorial Notes:
Commission information from the composer.

Performance History:
† 18 Apr 1975: Lecture Center 105, State University of New York, Stony Brook, NY
George Fisher and Rebecca La Brecque, Pno.
† (Boston) 8 May 1975: Jordan Hall, New England Conservatory of Music, Boston, MA
Cameron Grant and James Winn, Pno.

Program Notes:

"To Sound. . . Sonic Forms . . Sonata Allegro Metamorphosed . .
Circle of 5ths . . B♭ Major . . Sublimated
and Fused . . Equal Temperament
. . All Temperaments . . Asceticism to Wildness
and with Prayer . . Reverence
To Beethoven and Coltrane . . No Rollos . .
No Oleos . . . Sonata Allegro Once
Again Metamorphosed . . .
Unity, Transmuted, the Apocalypse . . ."

—William Thomas McKinley (© 1975), from 8 May 1975 program.

VIII.G.4 Interim Piece No. 2

Date: 28–29 Sep 1974 in Reading, MA ("Linnea Lane") *Duration:* 6'48"
Dedication: "For Les Thimmig and Lowell Creitz with fondness and respect"
Commission: [University of Wisconsin]
Publisher: MMC Publications

Movement(s):
♪=182

Instrumentation:
Sop Sax/CbCl, Vcl soli.

Sketches:
10 drafts of the opening. 3 drafts of page 2. 1 unidentified draft.

MS Description:
Holograph with printed name, ink on vellum. *Location:* Boston Public Library.
Markings: Cover page: "an excursion | a journey | a prayer | all worlds | spin | about | cosmic | powder | turned | loose! | or | laughing | ...rags of mundane Mondays...."

Editorial Notes:
Confirmation of 11 Oct 1974 as premiere performance and additional premiere information from McKinley's notes. Commission also taken from McKinley's notes.

Performance History:
[†] 11 Oct 1974: Murphy Hall, University of Wisconsin, Madison, WI
Les Thimmig, Sop. Sax; [Lowell Creitz, Vcl.]

VIII.G.5 Concerto for Oboe and Percussion

Date: Mar 1978 *Duration:* 20'00"
Dedication: "To Fred Cohen"
Commission: [Fred Cohen]
Publisher: MMC Publications

Movement(s):
Largo, crying out (𝅗𝅥=20)

Instrumentation:
Ob/EHn/ObD'am, Perc soli.

MS Description:
Holograph with printed name, ink on paper. *Location:* Boston Public Library.

Editorial Notes:
Commission information from the composer.

Performance History:
† 11 Apr 1978: Jordan Hall, New England Conservatory of Music, Boston, MA
Fredric T. Cohen, Ob (EHn, ObD'am); Sara Tenney, Perc.
27 Mar 1979: Studio One at WGBH Radio, Boston, MA
Fredric T. Cohen, Ob (E Hn, ObD'am); Sara Tenney, Perc.
22 Nov 1982: Jordan Hall, New England Conservatory of Music, Boston, MA
Sandra Gerster, Ob (E Hn, ObD'am); Nancy Zeltsman, Perc.

VIII.G.6 Nocturnes for Cello and Clarinet in B♭

Date: [Jan 1984] in [Reading, MA ("Lells")] *Duration:* 11'00"
Dedication: [Fred Sherry and Richard Stoltzman]
Commission: [Richard Stoltzman]
Publisher: MMC Publications

Movement(s):
I. Lento (♩=48)
II. Prestissimo (♩=120)

Instrumentation:
Cl, Vcl soli.

Sketches:
5 drafts of the opening.

MS Description:
Holograph, pencil on vellum. *Location:* Boston Public Library.

Editorial Notes:
Date and location of composition taken from McKinley's notes. Dedication from cover of fair copy. Commission information from *AMC Newsletter* 27(Winter 1985), no. 1: 14 and McKinley's notes.

Performance History:
† 16 May 1984: Heinz Hall for the Performing Arts, Pittsburgh, PA
Richard Stoltzman, Cl; Hampton Mallory, Vcl.
[† (Boston)] 21 Jan 1985: Jordan Hall, New England Conservatory of Music, Boston, MA
Laura Flax, Cl; Andre Emelianoff, Vcl.
[† (Indianapolis)] 27 Feb 1985: Ruth Allison Lilly, Children's Museum, Indianapolis, IN
Richard Stoltzman, Cl; Fred Sherry, Vcl.
[† (San Francisco)] 4 Mar 1985: Herbst Theater, San Francisco, CA
Richard Stoltzman, Cl; Fred Sherry, Vcl.
8 Mar 1985: Sherwood Auditorium, La Jolla Museum of Contemporary Art, La Jolla, CA.
Richard Stoltzman, Cl; Fred Sherry, Vcl.
10 Mar 1985: Johnson Theater, University of New Hampshire, Durham, NH
Richard Stoltzman, Cl; Fred Sherry, Vcl.
19 Feb 1987: Alumni Auditorium, Northeastern University, Boston, MA
Richard Stoltzman, Cl; Fred Sherry, Vcl.
6 Nov. 1987: Lynman Hall, Pomona College, Claremont, CA
Kalman Bloch, Cl; Michael Mathews, Vcl.
[† (New York)] 6 Jan 1988: Weill Recital Hall, New York, NY
Richard Stoltzman, Cl; Fred Sherry, Vcl.

Bibliography:
Dyer, Richard. "Da Capo Chamber Players Premiere McKinley Work." *The Boston Globe* 23 Jan 1985.
Staff, Charles. "Good Fortune Befalls Enthralled Audience." *The Indianapolis News* 28 Feb 1985: 28.
Pontzious, Richard. "Good Fortune Strikes Ears of Concert-goers." *San Francisco Examiner* 5 Mar 1985.
Commanday, Robert. "Good Programming but Players Don't Mesh." *San Francisco Chronicle* 6 Mar 1985.
Shere, Charles. "Good Fortune Comes to Chamber Music." *The Tribune (Oakland, CA)* 6 Mar 1985.
Gregson, David. "Tashi Displays High Spirits, Polished Musicianship." *San Diego Union* 9 Mar 1985: D 9.
Scher, Valerie. "Tashi Has Changed with Times, but Remains Terrific." *San Diego Tribune* 9 Mar 1985.
Koontz, Barbara. "Tashi Finishes National Tour at UNH." *The New Hampshire* 12 Mar 1985: 14.
Tommasini, Anthony. "A Dazzling Performance by Tashi." *The Boston Globe* 23 Feb 1987.
Bernheimer, Martin. "'Tashi'—Elegant Foss Premiere." *Los Angeles Times* 3 Mar 1987: VI-1.
Cariaga, Daniel. "McKinley Premiere." *Los Angeles Times* 16 Mar 1987.
Rubinstein, Leslie. "Creative Spirit: Richard Stoltzman." *Carnegie Hall Stagebill* 10(Feb 1988), no. 6: 22, 27–28.

Program Notes:
"In these Two Nocturnes for B-flat Clarinet and Cello I set out to create a musical fabric that was simple, direct, traditional in form, and imbued with a dramatic character that would

evoke in the listener a sense of some of the mysteries and complex sensations which are so very often aroused and sustained during the night. And since the genre of the nocturne does not necessarily bring to mind the instrumental combination I had already chosen, my creative task was thus the more challenging: to try to communicate, *through the music itself*, those musical ideas which would vividly call up nocturnal emotions.

"I had already composed a large number of 'heavy' works for Richard Stoltzman, and now decided to compose a work in a 'lighter' and more accessible musical language, though I might occasionally use 'heavier' musical shadings to preserve the subtle essence and ambiance of the nocturne. Both of my Nocturnes are tonal and make extended use of a diatonic and modally chromatic language. The first Nocturne moves slowly and is built predominantly around a drone-like ostinato figure (in the cello's lowest register). This figure supports shimmering gestures and gossamer-like arabesques throughout all of the clarinet's registers, particularly the chalumeau.... By contrast, the second Nocturne is predominantly fast-moving and considerably more forceful than the first. To me, the second Nocturne seems more closely related to the manner of Chopin (a composer of nocturnes who *does* come readily to mind when contemplating that form) and presents an atmosphere which dramatically portrays that time of night when daybreak intrudes and begins to spread the energy and movement of light over us.

"It is rewarding for a composer to delve into musical character portraits, to try to capture a single essence and a single mood or expressive idea. These Two Nocturnes for Clarinet and Cello offered me the possibility of wedding together two very contrasting movements that at the same time reflect a common dramatic purpose, character, unified emotive goal, and ultimate musical outcome."

—William Thomas McKinley (© 1984), from 16 May 1984 program.

VIII.G.7 rim (Rhythm In Motion)—An Instrumental Ballet for Violin and Marimba in Ten Movements

Date: 6 Sep 1987 in Reading, MA ("Lells") *Duration:* 21'00"
Dedication: "to Marimolin (Nancy and Sharan)"
Commission: [Marimolin]
Publisher: MMC Publications

Movement(s):
I. Little wooden soldiers:
Allegro ma non troppo (♩=126)
II. Waltz of the toy machines: Presto (♩=200)
III. The mournful ballerina: Adagietto (𝅗𝅥=72)
IV. In the hands of time: Andantino (♩=96)
V. Burning tigers: Allegro (♩.=132)
VI. Little blue boy: Moderato (♪=132)
VII. Hot city nights: Larghetto (♩=56)
VIII. Jumpin' jacks: Prestissimo (𝅝‿𝅗𝅥.=54)
IX. Dancing song: Andante con moto (♩=104)
X. Puppets: Andantino (♩=96)

Instrumentation:
Mar, Vln soli.

MS Description:
Holograph with printed name, pencil on vellum. *Location:* Boston Public Library.

Editorial Notes:
Commission taken from McKinley's program notes. 17 Mar and 1 Sep 1988 performance information from BMI records.

Performance History:
† 8 Oct 1987: Cambridge Multicultural Arts Center, E. Cambridge, MA
Marimolin (Sharan Leventhal, Vln; Nancy Zeltsman, Mar).
10 Oct 1987: Sanders Theater, Cambridge, MA
Marimolin.
† (New York) 25 Oct 1987: Weill Recital Hall, New York, NY
Marimolin.
[17 Mar 1988: Location unknown
Marimolin.]
5 Apr 1988: Jordan Hall, New England Conservatory of Music, Boston, MA
Marimolin.
[1 Sep 1988: Location unknown
Marimolin.]
29 Apr 1989: Cambridge Multicultural Arts Center, E. Cambridge, MA (mvts. I and X only)
Marimolin.
14 May 1989: Weill Recital Hall, New York, NY (mvts. I and X only)
Marimolin.

Bibliography:
Holland, Bernard. "Music: Marimolin, Duo at Weill Hall." *The New York Times* 29 Oct 1987: C21.
Lawrence, R.D. "Concert Notes: New York" *The Strad* 99(Mar 1988), no. 1175: 187.

Program Notes:
"*Rim* (*Rhythm In Motion*) Composed specifically for the dazzling, virtuosic talents of Nancy Zeltsman and Sharan Leventhal, *Rim* (taken from Ma*rim*olin) is an instrumental ballet cast in ten moderately brief movements. Each movement has a specific programmatic character with very definite choreographic forms and images in mind. It is the first work of mine which is directed toward the medium of dance while at the same time serving the purpose of a virtuoso workout for the violin and extended concert grand marimba. The unique technical and timbral possibilities of these two instruments in tandem were a continued source of surprise and inspiration which made it easy for the composer to envision the dual roles. It is to Eva Rubenstein that the composer owes the first suggestion to create a work which would be of interest to Mr. Peter Martins and the New York City Ballet, and composing for this splendid blend of percussion and string sound helped to bring her friendly suggestion to fruition in this new work (completed September 1987) commissioned by Marimolin."
—William Thomas McKinley (© 1987), from 25 Oct 1987 and 29 Apr/14 May 1989 programs and his notes.

VIII.G.8 Rags 'n Riches for Two Pianos (A Slow and Bluesy Foxtrot Omnibus)

Date: 20 Sep 1987 *Duration:* 12'30"
Dedication: "to Roland Nadeau, Bob Winter and WGBH radio"
Commission: [Roland Nadeau]
Publisher: MMC Publications

Movement(s):
Lazy, bluesy (♩=66)

Instrumentation:
2 Pno soli.

MS Description:
Holograph with signature, pencil on vellum. *Location:* Boston Public Library.

Editorial Notes:
Commission taken from McKinley's notes.

Performance History:
† 8 Nov 1987, 10pm: "A Note to You," WGBH Radio, Boston, MA
Roland Nadeau and Bob Winter, Pno.

VIII.G.9 New York Rhapsody for B♭ Clarinet and Harp

Date: 30 Sep 1987 *Duration:* 12'00"
Dedication: "to Dick Stoltzman with love and friendship"
Commission: [Richard Stoltzman]
Publisher: MMC Publications

Movement(s):
Flowing (♩.=42)

Instrumentation:
Cl, Hp soli.

MS Description:
Holograph with signature, pencil on vellum. *Location:* Boston Public Library.

Editorial Notes:
Commission taken from McKinley's program notes. 5 Oct 1990 performance information from BMI records.

Performance History:
† 16 Oct 1987: Metropolitan Museum of Art, New York, NY
Richard Stoltzman, Cl; Nancy Allen, Hp.
[5 Oct 1990: Pennsylvania State University, University Park, PA
Richard Stoltzman, Cl; Nancy Allen, Hp.]
30 Jan 1993: Theresa L. Kaufmann Concert Hall, The 92nd St. YM-YWCA, New York, NY
Richard Stoltzman, Cl; Nancy Allen, Hp.
See also *Program Notes.*

Program Notes:

"*New York Rhapsody* is a large concertante structure in a single movement which holds strong programmatic attachment to the images of New York City. One will readily hear popular motifs (particularly 'I Hear a Rhapsody') and improvisatory gestures unfolding in an expansive rhapsodic atmosphere. The concertante element presents a virtuoso workout particularly as the work progresses as well as coloristic impressionist textures, emphasized by the timbre of the harp set against the oftentimes brilliance in the higher registers of the clarinet. The overall gesture of the rhapsody is embroidered in a giant arabesque-like web of swirling sound, set against introspective and distant evocations—memories of New York.

"*New York Rhapsody* was commissioned by Richard Stoltzman and premiered by Richard Stoltzman and Nancy Allen at the Metropolitan Museum of Art in 1987. Subsequent performances have been given by Stoltzman and Allen throughout the United States."
—William Thomas McKinley (© 1993), from 30 Jan 1993 program and his notes.

VIII.G.10 Marcatissimo for Flute and Contrabass [Downtown Walk No. 1]

Date: 7 Nov 1987 in Reading, MA ("Lells") *Duration:* 11'00"
Dedication: "to Marc Johnson and Stephanie [Jutt]" and "to the spirit of..."
Commission: [Marc Johnson and Stephanie Jutt]
Publisher: MMC Publications

Movement(s):
Con brio e vivamente (𝅗.=48)

Instrumentation:
Fl, Cb soli.

MS Description:
Holograph with signature, pencil on vellum. *Location:* Boston Public Library.

Editorial Notes:
Commission information from the composer.

Performance History:
† 6 Jan 1988: Weill Recital Hall, New York, NY
Marc Johnson, Cb; Stephanie Jutt, Fl.

VIII.G.11 Upstairs, Downstairs for E♭ Soprano Clarinet and B♭ Bass Clarinet

Date: Jan 1988 *Duration:* 11'00"
Dedication: "To Les Thimmig"
Commission: [Les Thimmig]
Publisher: MMC Publications

Movement(s):
I. Upstairs: Allegro molto e brilliante (♩=184+)
II. Downstairs: Con moto (♩=138)

Instrumentation:
Pic Cl, BCl soli.

Sketches:
MS contains many earlier drafts which have been crossed out. 2 drafts of the opening of I. 1 draft of I/126–164. 3 drafts of the opening of II.

MS Description:
Holograph with signature, ink on paper. *Location:* Boston Public Library.

Editorial Notes:
Commission information from the composer.

Performance History:
† 20 Feb 1988: Elizabeth Killian Hall, Massachusetts Institute of Technology, Cambridge, MA
Les Thimmig, Cl.
4 Mar 1988: First and Second Church, Boston, MA
Les Thimmig, Cl; The Boston Musica Viva, Richard Pittman, Cond.

Bibliography:
Tommasini, Anthony. "McKinley's Recent Works Lack Discernment and Taste." *The Boston Globe* 5 Mar 1988: 14.

VIII.G.12 Miniature Portraits for Trumpet and Bassoon

Date: 12 May 1988 *Duration:* 16'00"
Dedication: "to Debbie Greitzer and Jeff Silberschlag"
Commission: [Deborah Greitzer]
Publisher: MMC Publications

Movement(s):
I. Burlesco: ♩=144
II. Humoresque: Presto (♩.=152)
III. Satirico: Satirico (♩=54)
IV. Sarcasmo: Presto (♩=180)
V. Ironico: Moderato (♩=120)
VI. Fantastico: Allegro molto (♩=144)
VII. Triste: Jazzy, andante (♩=76)
VIII. Enigmatico: Prestissimo (♩=184)

Instrumentation:
B♭ Pic Tpt/Tpt/Optional: F Tpt/D Tpt/C Tpt, Bsn soli.

Sketches:
Draft of the opening appears just before the beginning of I. At the end of I is a draft of the opening measures of II. At the end of V is a draft of the opening measures of VI.

MS Description:
Holograph with signature, pencil on paper. *Location:* Boston Public Library.
Markings: Cover page: "hello Mr. Pelican," surrounded by a few musical notes.

Editorial Notes:
Commission taken from McKinley's notes. 13 Jul 1988 is first performance present in BMI records. 1 Apr 1989 performance information from BMI records.

Performance History:
[†] 13 Jul 1988: Montgomery Fine Arts Recital Hall, St. Mary's College, MD
Jeffrey Silberschlag, Tpt; Deborah Greitzer Silberschlag, Bsn.
† (Boston) 23 Oct 1988: Jordan Hall, New England Conservatory of Music, Boston, MA
Jeffrey Silberschlag, Tpt; Deborah Greitzer Silberschlag, Bsn.
[1 Apr 1989: International Brass Festival
Jeffrey Silberschlag, Tpt; Deborah Greitzer Silberschlag, Bsn.]

Program Notes:
"This work was composed for my friend Debbie Greitzer and her husband Jeff Silberschlag. Indeed, it was a formidable challenge in combining the characteristics of a trumpet and bassoon. I realized early on that a lengthy single movement or set of large movements was out of the question. Endurance in the trumpet part was the first consideration. And the kind of dramatic expression the duo could evoke was yet another important consideration.

"It became clear that a group of miniatures (*not* in the Weberian sense) would best suit this combination—a set of portraits, each with a unique dramatic persona, and each lasting around two minutes. My thoughts turned to ideas of satire, humor, irony, jazz inflections, and the like—ideas which the character of the trumpet and bassoon could best evoke and which could carry the strongest aural impression and musical interest. And as the work progressed I found that the metaphoric nature of these ideas strengthened and to my mind began to take on a far more serious character than I originally envisioned. Thus I became more and more engrossed in various possibilities such as the wide tessitura from the lowest regions of the bassoon to the potential unlimited high region of the trumpet, the use of trumpet mutes, and the change of trumpets from movement to movement (although the trumpet player can choose to play the entire work on his main instrument with the exception of the B♭ piccolo trumpet).

"And finally it is intended that the pieces will serve as recital concert material for my many trumpet and bassoon playing friends who will now have a new opportunity to perform together and which may help to extend the repertoire beyond the standard fare."
—William Thomas McKinley (© 1994), from his notes.

VIII.G.13 A Family Portrait

Date: 16 Jul 1989 in Reading, MA ("Lells") *Duration:* 10'25"
Dedication: "to Meggie, Peter John, Dick and Lucy Stoltzman"
Commission: [Richard Stoltzman]
Publisher: MMC Publications

Movement(s): *Instrumentation:*
I. Peter John: Allegro ma non troppo (♩=120) Cl, Vln soli.
II. Lucy: Largo (𝅗𝅥=42)
III. Meggie: Prestissimo (𝅗𝅥=160)
IV. Dick: Veloce e perpetuo moto (𝅗𝅥.=76+)
V. The Family: Allegro ma non troppo (♩=108±)

MS Description:
Holograph with signature, pencil on paper. *Location:* Boston Public Library.

Editorial Notes:
Commission taken from McKinley's notes.

Performance History:
† 18 Nov 1989: The John F. Kennedy Center for the Performing Arts, Washington, DC
Richard Stoltzman, Cl; Lucy Stoltzman, Vln.
[†(Boston)] 19 Nov 1989: Jordan Hall, New England Conservatory of Music, Boston, MA
Richard Stoltzman, Cl; Lucy Stoltzman, Vln.

Bibliography:
Gewertz, Daniel. "Pianist Writes Classically, Plays Jazzily." *The Boston Herald* 17 Nov 1989: S15.
Tommasini, Anthony. "Old Friends With Very Different Styles." *The Boston Globe* 22 Nov 1989.

Program Notes:
"The great affection and respect which I hold towards the Stoltzman family was the inspirational basis of *A Family Portrait*. Each of the five movements contains a 'motto' theme based on the names of family members 1. Peter John (duet), 2. Lucy (Dick's solo), 3. Meggie (duet), 4. Dick (Lucy's solo), 5. The Family (duet). The movements depict certain personality traits and human characteristics which, over many years, I have fondly observed. Viewed abstractly, this *Family Portrait* is a virtuosic showcase for both performers, and each of its movements, although modest in proportion, allows time for considerable development and working out of musical texture and detail."
—William Thomas McKinley (© 1989), from 19 Nov 1989 program and his notes.

VIII.G.a ~~[Untitled for Two Violins]~~

Date: [ca. 1965]
Publisher: Unpublished

Movement(s):
♪=120

Instrumentation:
2 Vln soli.

Sketches:
2 drafts of the opening. 2 unidentified drafts.

MS Description:
Holograph, ink on paper. *Location:* Boston Public Library.

Editorial Notes:
MS ends after two pages (1 bifolio). Date determined through paleographic analysis.

VIII.G.b ~~[Untitled for Flute and Bass]~~

Date: [ca. 1968]
Dedication: "For Bert Turetsky"
Publisher: Unpublished

Movement(s):
Quasi ad libitum (♩=58)

Instrumentation:
Fl, Cb soli.

MS Description:
Holograph, pencil on paper. *Location:* Boston Public Library.

Editorial Notes:
Date determined through paleographic analysis and location of discovery. MS ends after 5 pages. Page 2 of MS is lost.

VIII.G.c ~~Duo Fantasy for Trumpet and Bassoon and Tape~~

Date: 1969 in Chicago, IL (Univ. of Chicago)
Dedication: "to Wes[ley Ward] and Jim"
Commission: [Wesley Ward]
Publisher: Unpublished

Movement(s):
[One untitled movement.]

Instrumentation:
Bsn, Tpt soli; Tape (some sections must be pre-recorded).

MS Description:
Holograph with printed name, pencil on vellum. *Location:* Boston Public Library.

Editorial Notes:
MS ends after 6 pages. Commission information from the composer.

VIII.G.d ~~Shapes~~

Date: [ca. 1972]
Dedication: "to Ralph Shapey with respect and affection"
Publisher: Unpublished

Movement(s):
I. Haze

Instrumentation:
2 Pno soli. Sketches sometimes include one or more of the following: Fl, Cl, BCl, Vln, Vla, Vcl.

Sketches:
210 drafts of the opening.

MS Description:
Holograph, ink on paper and vellum. *Location:* Boston Public Library.

Editorial Notes:
None of the drafts was significantly more complete than the others and thus deserving of the title "manuscript."

See also: Arabesques for Assorted Instruments (VIII.E.3)

Group IX: Works for Voice

Group IX.A: Choral Works

IX.A.1 Eliot for Mixed Chorus

Date: 1972 in Chicago, IL (Univ. of Chicago) *Duration:* 6'26"
Dedication: "to James Mack and the University of Chicago Chorus"
Commission: [University of Chicago]
Publisher: MMC Publications

Movement(s):	*Instrumentation:*
Burnt Norton	SATB (64 Voices)/64 Perc.

Sketches:
3 drafts of the opening of the work. 1 draft of page 2. 4 drafts of page 3. 17 drafts of page 4. 13 drafts of page 5. 2 drafts of page 7. 1 draft of page 8. 8 unidentified drafts.

MS Description:
Holograph with printed name, ink on vellum. *Location:* Boston Public Library.
Markings: Cover page: "Based on 'Burnt Norton' from the 4 Quartets of T.S. Eliot." Cover page draft is dated 1971–72.

Editorial Notes:
Commission taken from McKinley's notes.

IX.A.2 Carol for Mixed Chorus

Date: 12 Feb 1976 in Manchester, MA ("Carriage House") *Duration:* 7'17"
Publisher: MMC Publications

Movement(s):	*Instrumentation:*
♩=72+	SATB.

Sketches:
3 drafts of the opening.

MS Description:
Holograph with signature, ink on vellum. *Location:* Boston Public Library.

Editorial Notes:
The letters "KY," which appear as the text for two of the drafts, may indicate that the original conception for the work was a Kyrie. Location of composition taken from McKinley's notes.

IX.A.3 Four Text Settings for A Cappella Mixed Chorus (op. 109)

Date: 1 Oct 1979 in Reading, MA ("Barn") *Duration:* 17'00"
Dedication: "to John Oliver"
Commission: [The John Oliver Chorale]
Publisher: Margun Music Inc.

Movement(s):
Introduction. ♩=52
Text 2. Con fuoco (♩=100+)
Text 3. Con spirito (♩=180)
Text 4. ♩=76

Instrumentation:
SATB (8 Sop, 8 Alt, 6 Ten, 6 Bs).

MS Description:
Engraving by McKinley, ink stencil on vellum. *Location:* Boston Public Library.

Editorial Notes:
Texts by Marlene Marie McKinley. Commission taken from McKinley's notes. Premiere performance date confirmed in *AMC Newsletter* 23(Summer 1981), no. 3: 20 and McKinley's notes.

Performance History:
[†] 4 Apr 1981: First Congregational Church, Cambridge, MA
The John Oliver Chorale, John Oliver, Cond.

Recording(s):
Koch International Classics: 3–7178–2, ©1994 (CD)
John Oliver Chorale, John Oliver, Cond.

Bibliography:
"*Four Text Settings*." *Anonymous IV* 0(8 Apr 1981), no 1: 2.
Grimes, Ev. "Yale University American Music Oral History Series: William Thomas McKinley." Oct 1986, Yale University School of Music: 76.
"JOC Awarded Grant from NEA to Produce New Compact Disc." *High Notes: Newsletter of the John Oliver Chorale* Fall 1991: 1.

Program Notes:
"My *Four Text Settings for A Cappella Mixed Chorus* was composed for John Oliver. During the Fromm Festival, August 1979, John heard the Tanglewood premiere of my *Paintings IV* conducted by Gunther Schuller.... After the performance John asked me if I had ever written music for chorus. I told him that I had two choral works to my credit but that I would be most honored and delighted to compose a new score for his chorale. He accepted, and I began the score almost immediately."
—William Thomas McKinley, from 4 Apr 1981 program.

IX.A.4 Deliverance, Amen (An Oratorio)

Date: [May] 1983 in [Reading, MA ("Lells")] *Duration:* 38'00"
Dedication: "To John Oliver and Frank Epstein"
Commission: [National Endowment for the Arts]
Publisher: MMC Publications

Movement(s):
Scene I. Misterioso (♩=60)
Scene II. Allegro molto (♩.=100+)
Scene III. Presto, military (♩=160)
Scene IV. Anthem: With quiet movement
and inner passion, singing and yet austere (♩=60)
Scene V. Lively, robust (♩.=76)
Scene VI. Moving (♩=90)
Scene VII. ♩=48
Scene VIII. 𝅗𝅥.=80
Scene IX. Dramatic, isolated, calling forth (♩=90)
Scene X. Poco non vibrato, almost hushed and distant (♩=72)

Instrumentation:
Pic/Fl, Pic Cl/Cl/BCl, 2 Perc, Pno, Org, Vln, Vcl, MSop, Ten, Bar soli; SATB.

Sketches:
2 drafts of the opening of I.

MS Description:
Holograph with signature, pencil on paper. *Location:* Boston Public Library.

Editorial Notes:
Text by Marlene Marie McKinley. Month and location of composition from McKinley's notes. Commission information from *AMC Newsletter* 27(Winter 1985), no. 1: 14 and McKinley's notes.

Performance History:
† 12 Dec 1983: First Congregational Church, Cambridge, MA
John Oliver Chorale, Collage New Music, John Oliver, Cond.
12 Mar 1989: Jordan Hall, New England Conservatory of Music, Boston, MA
Collage New Music and Chorus, Robert Black, Cond.

Bibliography:
Driver, Paul. "Composer McKinley 'Hears the Muses.'" *The Boston Globe* 9 Dec 1983: 48, 52.
Driver, Paul. "McKinley Oratorio Has a Rewarding Premiere." *The Boston Globe* 15 Dec 1983: 99.
Grimes, Ev. "Yale University American Music Oral History Series: William Thomas McKinley." Oct 1986, Yale University School of Music: 95
Creasey, Beverly. "Brighton Flutist Celebrates Modern Works." *The Allston-Brighton Journal* 9 Mar 1989: 9.
Tommasini, Anthony. "McKinley's Popularity a Mystery." *The Boston Globe* 14 Mar 1989: 29.

Program Notes:
"The text of this work was formed around Tom's ideas: the inclusion of comic book and radio 'superheroes' with meditative and contemplative elements. Therefore, in order to combine such seemingly disparate features, I based the text on perhaps the overused theme of the Fall and its effects.

"Needless to say, the scope of such ideas ranges well beyond the limits of this work. Therefore, I did not penetrate even one of them in any depth; but rather, I only suggested and recalled within a dream-like flow, using allusions and direct quotations from literature to help convey ideas and experiences which I intentionally kept general so that they might have some meaning to everyone, regardless of religious persuasions. I should also add that this text includes humor in its overall seriousness and that it does not conform and adhere to any traditional literary structures because doing so would have confined Tom's musical ideas. Therefore my selection of words was based on those sounds and rhythms which I felt were most harmonious to Tom's music.

"Finally, though I ruthlessly had to cut words, lines, sections, and whole scenes due to time constraints after which I could only hope the text still 'lived' in some fashion, I needn't have worried at all. For Tom, as always, rose above such obstacles and wrote a most beautiful, unified, coherent, dramatic work, well beyond my limited sight. He has indeed created a magnificent VISION, *Deliverance, Amen*."

Scene i	Exposition—The Fall and Our Present State
Scene ii	Reflective Interlude or Transition—Three Views of Man's Relation to 'Nature' (Nature incorporating the trinity of Human Nature, Nature and Super Nature or Spirit)
Scene iii	Man's Call to Ancient and Modern Heroes or Superheroes
Scene iv	Realizing the Extent of the Fallen Condition and of the Impotent Calls for Help and Impotent Solutions
Scene v	One Determines to Seek Another Path—A Path Forsaking 'Saviors'. Forsaking the Things of this World
Scenes vi & vii	The Inner Seeking—Meeting Aspects of One's Self: Fears, Truth, False Hopes
Scene vii	The Inner Seeking Progresses to Horror, Dread, and Despair. The Utter Wanhope Causes a Psychic Break, Abandonment and Loss of the Self, the Ego. At This Point, then,
Scene ix	One Can Penetrate and break through to the Real Self— Deliverance. This Mystic Union, at-One-Ment, Transfiguration Is Conveyed (and perhaps can only be conveyed) by and in the Music.
Scene x	(The following comes from one who has experienced UNION and is now once again 'in the body', 'in this world'.) A subsequent reflection on Man— Hope Deliverance, Amen.

—Marlene Marie McKinley (© 1983), from 12 Dec 1983 and 12 Mar 1989 programs.

"*Deliverance, Amen* embodies the traditional oratorio form. It unfolds into an extended religious (non sectarian) setting composed for mixed chorus, solo singers, organ, and instrumental ensemble. There are ten scenes, several of which are interlocked into larger units, connected together without musical pause and, therefore, developed and extended over longer time periods. Although the traditional setting calls for the use of full orchestra, practical necessity limited the adaptation of larger instrumental forces. However, the basic aural conception is nearly always orchestral. For this reason the organ plays a vital harmonically supportive function, evoking the power and mass of a full orchestra, particularly in the major tutti sections.

"The baritone, tenor, and mezzo soprano soloists were not in any way conceived as 'characters.' Since there is no action (a traditional concept, too), the soloists thereby often assume a more abstract character, providing contrast against the weight of the full chorus, intensifying the textual elements, such as word articulation and word painting. In addition, the soloists mediate between the instrumental ensemble and chorus, occasionally taking on

virtuoso characteristics and more instrumental-like gestures. Essentially, however, the vocal solos and choral writing are lyrical and intensely *bel canto*. The organic development throughout the ten scenes 'spins' from the opening solo clarinet line directly and unequivocally to the very end. In addition, each scene may be viewed and heard as an entity or separate musical structure containing ideas which are unique and expository and which develop along abstract lines into independent movements. The scenes which combine without pause into larger units are similarly marked by the same development. A 'Deliverance' harmony and a 'Deliverance, Amen' harmonic phrase permeate the entire oratorio and help to establish the identity of an important pillar in the musical structure, thereby helping the listener to perceive and remember some aspects in the larger architectural design."
—William Thomas McKinley (© 1983), from 12 Dec 1983 program.

IX.A.5 Mauern

Date: [Late 1992] in [Reading, MA ("Lells")] *Duration:* 18'00"
Commission: [Cambridge Madrigal Singers]
Publisher: MMC Publications

Movement(s):
[I. Bild: der Tanz beginnt:]
Largo (𝅗𝅥=52)
Aria [and chorus]: Allegro furioso (♩=126)
[II. Bild: der Auszug ("der verlorne Sohn")]
Recit.: Libero (♩=56)
[Chorus:] Largamente (♩=48)
[III. Bild: der Turm von Babel]
[Aria:] Allegro molto (♩.=126)
[Chorale:] Lento e molto appass[ionato] (𝅗𝅥=46)

Instrumentation:
Cl, Sop, Alt, Ten, Bs soli; SATB.

MS Description:
Holograph with signature, pencil on paper. *Location:* Boston Public Library.

Editorial Notes:
Texts by Hans-Jörg Modlmayr. Bracketed text in *Movements* appears only in the premiere performance program. Date and location of composition from Elliott Miles McKinley. Commission information from the composer.

Performance History:
† 19 Dec 1992: Jordan Hall, New England Conservatory of Music, Boston, MA
Richard Stoltzman, Cl; Margaret Richardson, Sop; Ann Busby, Alt; Jonathan Solomon, Ten; Robert Ruplenas, Bar; Cambridge Madrigal Singers, Raymond D. Fahrner, Cond.

Bibliography:
Buell, Richard. "Madrigal Singers Span the Centuries with Style." *The Boston Globe* 21 Dec 1992: 40.

Program Notes:
"This work represents a collaboration in the most real of senses. Both the poet, Hans-Jörg Modlmayr, and the clarinetist Richard Stoltzman are friends of the composer who share a common vision....
"The text is a fusion of passages from the Bible and original poetry. While it is about the Berlin Wall and the struggles of Germany and Europe, it transcends politics to deal with the

concept of walls themselves, offering both security and limits. The images verge on Expressionistic, and McKinley has chosen music of extreme contrast to portray the essential *Angst* of these *Mauern*. The role of the clarinet is individualistic, by turns counterpointing the chorus, making its own statements, and providing a backdrop over which the vocal statements are made."
—Raymond D. Fahrner (©1992), from 19 Dec 1992 program.

See also: Can You Sing Me a Song? (II.B.5)

Group IX.B: Works for Voice and Instrumental Ensemble

IX.B.1 Song for Piccolo, Bassoon and Soprano

Date: 1968 in New Haven, CT (Yale Univ.) *Duration:* 1'45"
Dedication: "To my wife"
Publisher: MMC Publications

Movement(s):
[One untitled movement]

Instrumentation:
Sop, Pic, Bsn soli.

Sketches:
2 bifolios of unidentified sketches.

MS Description:
Holograph with printed name, ink on vellum. *Location:* Boston Public Library.

Editorial Notes:
Poem, "Tribute to the Opium Eaters," by Marlene Marie McKinley. Premiere performance information from the composer.

Performance History:
[† Date unknown: Yale University, New Haven, CT
Performers unknown.]

IX.B.2 Five Songs for Soprano, Bass Clarinet, Cello, [and] Piano

Date: [Late] 1973 in Reading, MA ("Linnea Lane") *Duration:* 6'19"
Dedication: "to my wife Marlene"
Commission: [University of Wisconsin]
Publisher: MMC Publications

Movement(s):
Song I. ♪=42
Song II. ♩=42
Song III. ♪=42
Song IV. ♪=47
Song V. ♪=47

Instrumentation:
Sop, BCl, Vcl, Pno soli.

Sketches:
74 drafts of the opening.

MS Description:
Holograph with signature, ink on paper. *Location:* Boston Public Library.
Markings: Cover page: "begun in Chicago, Illinois, Summer '73."

Editorial Notes:
Sketches suggest the poems were written spontaneously at the time of the music's composition. National Endowment grant application for a proposed three act opera verifies text composition by the composer. Commission information from the composer. Premiere performance information from McKinley's notes.

Performance History:
[† Sep 1975: University of Wisconsin, Madison, WI
Les Thimmig, BCl; Other performers unknown.]

IX.B.3 When the Moon is Full

Date: 29 Jun 1989 *Duration:* 15'30"
Dedication: [St. Mary's College in honor of its 150th anniversary]
Commission: "Commissioned by St. Mary's College on the occasion of their 150th birthday"
Publisher: MMC Publications

Movement(s):
I. ♩=84
II. Presto (𝅗𝅥=152)
III. Lento (♩=46)
IV. Tempo di valse (𝅗𝅥.=52)

Instrumentation:
MSop, Bar, Fl, Cl, Bsn, Tpt, 2 Perc, Pno soli.

Sketches:
Formal plan for the work. Complete text (11 pages) from which lyrics were chosen (includes McKinley's notes).

MS Description:
Holograph with printed name, pencil on vellum. *Location:* Boston Public Library.

Editorial Notes:
Texts by Marlene Marie McKinley. Dedication inferred from commission citation on MS.

Performance History:
† 7–9 July 1989: Montgomery Fine Arts Center, St. Mary's College, MD
Tidewater Chamber Players, Deborah Greitzer, Cond.
[† (New York)] 1 Mar 1990: Weill Recital Hall, New York, NY
Tidewater Chamber Players, Robert Black, Cond.
[† (Washington, DC)] 5 Mar 1990: Hammer Auditorium, Corcoran Gallery of Art, Washington, DC
Tidewater Chamber Players, Robert Black, Cond.
23 Mar 1990: Montgomery Fine Arts Center, St. Mary's College, MD
Tidewater Chamber Players, Robert Black, Cond.
[† (Boston)] 10 Feb 1992: Jordan Hall, New England Conservatory of Music, Boston, MA
Members of the Tidewater Chamber Players, David Stock, Cond.

Bibliography:
Scarupa, Henry. "St. Mary's College Plans to Premiere Song Cycle." *The Baltimore Sun* 2 Jul 1989.

Duncan, Scott. "A Vivid Premiere for St. Mary's." *Baltimore Evening Sun* 10 Jul 1989.
Holland, Bernard. "Tidewater Ensemble." *The New York Times* 4 Mar 1990: 52.
Krehbiel, Ken. "Tidewater Chamber Players." *The Washington Post* 6 Mar 1990: C3.
Dyer, Richard. "Teachers' Works Put Musicians to the Test." *The Boston Globe* 11 Feb 1992: 54.

IX.B.4 Ceremonies of the Guild

Date: 25 Dec 1990 in Reading, MA ("Lells") *Duration:* 7'20"
Dedication: ["to the Concert Artists Guild in celebration of their 40th anniversary"]
Commission: [Concert Artists Guild]
Publisher: MMC Publications

Movement(s):
Quietamente e mormorio (♩=144)

Instrumentation:
MSop, Hn, Pno, Vln, Vcl soli.

MS Description:
Holograph with signature, pencil on paper. *Location:* Boston Public Library.
Markings: Over mm. 238–40: "to L.B. ('Lenny') + his passion."

Editorial Notes:
Text by Marlene Marie McKinley. Dedication taken from cover of fair copy. Commission taken from 15 Jan 1991 program.

Performance History:
† 15 Jan 1991: Merkin Concert Hall, New York, NY
Concert Artists Guild (Mary Ann Hart, MSop; Maria Bachmann, Vln; Semyon Fridman, Vcl; David Jolly, Hn; Michael Rodgers, Pno.)

Program Notes:
"A meditative and rejoicing text (inscription) for the Guild and in the hope for peace during the days and nights throughout this year.

Ceremonies of the Guild
Celebration song of joy
Welcome and rejoice
Inspire
Grace
Renew
All is well

First Refrain: Welcome and rejoice
Welcome and rejoice
Ceremonies of the Guild

Second Refrain: Ceremonies of the Guild
Rejoice, the Guild...
Rejoice..."

—Marlene Marie McKinley, from text insert to 15 Jan 1991 program.

IX.B.5 Emsdettener Totentanz

Date: 27 Sep 1991 *Duration:* 43'00"
Dedication: ["dedicated to Hildegard Modlmayr-Heimath, who designed the project, to Fritz Möser who created the graphic cycle 'TOTENTANZ' in 1962, to Hans-Jörg Modlmayr whose texts cycle 'TOTENTANZ' was inspired by Fritz Möser's work, to Bernhard Volkenhoff who commissioned the writing of 'TOTENTANZ,' the cantata, to Albert Göken, the musical director of the project to whom we owe the musical cast of performers, and to my lifelong Muse Marlene. [W]ritten for the Berliner Saxophon Quartett and the Silesian String Quartet from Katowice, Poland."]

Commission: [Bernhard Volkenhoff]
Publisher: MMC Publications

Movement(s):
Overture. Tod: Allegro (♩=144)
Prelude I. Es ist ein Schnitter...
I. Das Rendezvous
II. Der Tod und der Playboy: Più mosso (♩=84)
III. Der Tod und das Mädchen
IV. Das Mahl: Presto (𝅗𝅥=162)
Prelude II. Dies irae
I. Das Urteil
II. Der Kommandant: Più mosso e tempo di marcia (𝅗𝅥=138)
III. Die Eingeschlossenen
Prelude III. Media vita
I. Der Schrei: ♩=88
II. Der Reigen: ♩=176
III. Die Überfahrt
Finale. Vision

Instrumentation:
Sop, Alt, Bar, 4 Sop Sax/3 Alt Sax/2 Ten Sax/ Bar Sax, 2 Perc, 2 Vln, Vla, Vcl soli.

Sketches:
Preliminary programs, with McKinley's markings (includes his plan for the work's structure and the translation of the German text from which he worked). Copies of the chants and hymns which served as the foundation for the movements.
"Dies Irae" in *Liber Usualis* (Tournai and New York: Desclee Co., 1959), 1810–1813.
"Veni Creator Spiritus" in *Liber Usualis*, 885.
"Es ist ein Schnitter" (1638) in Wilhelm Bäumker, *Das katholische deutsche Kirchenlied in seinen Singweisen* (Hildesheim: Georg Olms Verlagsbuchhandlung, 1962), IV:694–95.
"Mitten wir in Leben sind" (1524) in Bäumker, IV:585–95.
(Above sources are not original, but contain the same melodies used by McKinley)

MS Description:
Holograph with signature, pencil on paper. *Location:* Boston Public Library.

Editorial Notes:
Dedication and commission from printed cover page of the MS. Text: 10 poems by Hans-Jörg Modlmayr on 10 graphics by Fritz Möser.

Performance History:
† 15 Mar 1992: St. Joseph Kirche, Emsdetten, FRG
Regine Gebhardt, Sop; Ursula Krämer, Alt; Volker Schwarz, Bass/Bar; Stefan Feurich, Thomas Hoffmann Perc; Berliner Saxophon Quartett (Detlef Bensmann, Sop Sax; Klaus Kreczmarsky, Alt Sax; Christof Griese, Ten Sax; Friedemann Graef, Bar Sax), Silesian String Quartet (Marek Mos, Poitr Janosik, Vln; Arkadiusz Kubica, Vla; Lukasz Syrnicki, Vcl), Albert Göken, Cond.
[† (Berlin)] 30 Dec 1992: Kammermusiksaal der Philharmonie, Berlin, FRG
Vera Gantner, Wolfgang Forester, Nar; Regine Gebhardt, Sop; Ursula Krämer, Alt; Volker Schwarz, Bass/Bar; Stefan Feurich, Thomas Hoffmann, Perc; Berliner Saxophon Quartett, Silesian String Quartet, Albert Göken, Cond.

† (United States) 24 Apr 1993: C. Walsh Theater, Suffolk University, Boston
Bernhard Volkenhoff, Nar; Regine Gebhardt, Sop; Ursula Krämer, Alt; Volker Schwarz, Bass/Bar; Robert Schulz, Gardner Cook, Perc; Berliner Saxophon Quartett, Silesian String Quartet, Albert Göken, Cond.

Bibliography:

Lüttmann, Hans. "'Totentanz' soll in St. Joseph uraufgeführt werden." *Emsdettener Tageblatt* 21 Sep 1991.
"'Ja' zum 'Totentanz.'" *Emsdettener Tageblatt* 26 Sep 1991.
"Der Totentanz wird bezuschußt." *Emsdettener Volkszeitung* 27 Sep 1991.
Lüttmann, Hans. "Totentanz zwischen Angst und Erlösung." *Westfälische Nachrichten* 1 Oct 1991.
"Komponist aus den USA mag Dorstener Herbst." *WAZ Dorsten* 1 Nov 1991.
"Konzertanter Höhepunkt in St. Joseph bringt menschliche Begegnung mit sich." *Emsdettener Volkszeitung* 2 Nov 1991.
"'Totentanz' soll Emsdetten im Namen tragen." *Emsdettener Tageblatt* 4 Nov 1991.
"Lebhafter Dialog zwischen Dirigent und Musikern." *Ruhrnachrichten Dorsten* 5 Nov 1991.
Volkenhoff, Bernhard. *Dokumentation Emsdettener Totentanz.* Fürstenfeldbruck: Europäische Totentanz Vereinigung, 1992.
"Mösers Totentanz ist ein Jahrhundertwerk." *Emsdettener Tageblatt* 11 Feb 1992.
"Tod mit anderen Augen sehen." *Emsdettener Volkszeitung* 12 Feb 1992.
"Der Emsdettener Totentanz soll ein Jahrhundertereignis werden." *Emsdettener Tageblatt* 13 Feb 1992.
"Der Emsdettener Totentanz: Mit Bildern von Fritz Möser." *Memminger Zeitung* 15 Feb 1992.
Kneisel, Volker. "Die Totentänze sollten Abtrünnige schrecken." *Emsdettener Tageblatt* 17 Feb 1992.
"Musik spricht eine ganz eigene Sprache." *Emsdettener Volkszeitung* 17 Feb 1992.
Kopmann, Beate. "Bußernst und Sinnenlust: 'Totentanz' wird in Emsdetten uraufgeführt." *Westfälische Nachrichten* 27 Feb 1992.
"Ein neues Leben für Totentanz." *WAZ Dorsten* 27 Feb 1992.
Eibel, Brigitte. "Beschäftigung mit dem Thema Tod hat Vorbehalte und Ängste abgebaut." *Emsdettener Volkszeitung* 11 Mar 1992.
"Selbst in Estland ist der 'Totentanz' im Gespräch." *Emsdettener Tageblatt* 11 Mar 1992.
"Der Mensch wird zum Täter und Opfer degradiert." *Emsdettener Tageblatt* 12 Mar 1992.
"Motive im Mittelteil: 'Emsdettener Totentanz.'" *Emsdettener Volkszeitung* 12 Mar 1992.
"Nicht hinnehmen, daß der Tod ausgebürgert worden ist." *Emsdettener Tageblatt* 13 Mar 1992.
"Reprise des ersten Blattes." *Emsdettener Volkszeitung* 13 Mar 1992.
"Ab heute besteht Gelegenheit, eigene Eindrücke zu sammeln." *Emsdettener Volkszeitung* 13 Mar 1992.
"Bald seid ihr im Garten." *Emsdettener Tageblatt* 14 Mar 1992.
"Totentanz in Emsdetten: Welturaufführung eines alten Themas ganz modern." *Kirche und Leben* 15 Mar 1992: 5.
Eibel, Brigitte. "Zuhörer arbeiten engagiert am eigenen Zugang zur Symbiose von Texten, Tönen und Bildern: 'Emsdettener Totentanz': angeregte Diskussion nach der Generalprobe." *Emsdettener Volkszeitung* 16 Mar 1992: EV2.
Lüttmann, Hans. "Meine Seele wurde vom ersten Takt an regelrecht mitgerissen." *Emsdettener Tageblatt* 16 Mar 1992.

Elling, E. "Der Schnitter ist leise: W.T. McKinleys 'Emsdettener Totentanz' uraufgeführt." *Westfälischer Anzeiger* 17 Mar 1992.
Schulte im Walde, Christoph W. "Kratzspuren an der 'heilen Welt': Emsdettener 'Totentanz' heftig umstritten." *Emsdettener Tageblatt* 17 Mar 1992: RKL 1.
Tettke, Chris. "Emsdettener Totentanz: ... das Lamm, der Wolf, hurz." *Emsdettener Volkszeitung* 17 Mar 1992.
Weitkamp,Andreas. "Der Prophet spielt Saxophon." *Emsdettener Volkszeitung* 17 Mar 1992: M8.
"Totentanz löst Diskussion aus." *WAZ Dorsten* 18 Mar 1992.
"Reiches Lob für 'Totentanz'-Premiere." *Ruhrnachrichten Dorsten* 18 Mar 1992.
Cisek, Georg. "Gehandelt mit viel Weitblick." *Emsdettener Volkszeitung* 19 Mar 1992.
Cisek, Georg. "Über Vorwürfe entsetzt." *Emsdettener Tageblatt* 19 Mar 1992.
Tettke, Chris. "Lamm und Wolf und hurz." *Emsdettener Tageblatt* 19 Mar 1992.
Mock, Edwin. "Kyrie eleison nur noch ein Hurz?" *Emsdettener Volkszeitung* 20 Mar 1992.
Mock, Edwin. "Aalglatte Häme und gemeine Art der Kritik." *Emsdettener Tageblatt* 20 Mar 1992.
Kortmann, Reinhold. "Intolerant und dogmatisch." *Emsdettener Tageblatt* 21 Mar 1992.
Tettke, Chris. "Zustimmung und Bewunderung." *Emsdettener Tageblatt* 21 Mar 1992.
Steinle, Werner. "Der Emsdettener Totentanz-Zyklus machte Fritz Mösers Namen zu einem Begriff." *Memminger Zeitung* 28 Mar 1992.
"Der Tod weckt aus falschem Schlaf." *Kirche und Leben* 29 Mar 1992: 16–17.
Hochgartz, Michael. "Keine Angst vor dem Tod." *Münstersche Zeitung* 31 Mar 1992.
Schulte im Walde, Christoph W. "Todeserfahrung aus der Distanz: Künstlerische Auseinandersetzung mit einem Tabuthema in Rheine." *Westfälische Nachrichten* 31 Mar 1992.
Jeismann, Marlies. "Örtliche Kleingeisterei." *Emsdettener Volkszeitung* 1 Apr 1992.
"Modlmayr-Verse zu Möser-Totentanz." *Allgäuer Zeitung* 2 Apr 1992.
"Es war ein Erlebnis: Späte, aber begeisterte Resonanz auf die Premiere des 'Totentanzes.'" *Emsdettener Tageblatt* 4 Apr 1992.
Köster, Konrad. "Totentanz schenkte mir neue Zuversicht." *Emsdettener Volkszeitung* 6 Apr 1992.
"Gäste sind nachhaltig beeindruckt: Spätes Echo auf 'Totentanz.'" *Emsdettener Volkszeitung* 7 Apr 1992.
"Emsdetten vorher kein Begriff." *Emsdettener Volkszeitung* 7 Apr 1992.
"Gegen Jugendideal." *Emsdettener Volkszeitung* 7 Apr 1992.
Köster, Konrad. "Glaubensvolle Ermutigung." *Emsdettener Tageblatt* 8 Apr 1992.
Pasterkamp, Bettina. "Thema Tod kein Tabu mehr." *Emsdettener Volkszeitung* 14 Apr 1992.
Scholten, Ursula. "Emsdettener Totentanz: Geborgenheit." *Kirche und Leben* 19 Apr 1992: 9.
"Totentanz: Vom Hören zum Tun." *Emsdettener Volkszeitung* 15 May 1992: ED 3.
"Der 'Totentanz' im Unterricht: Ein möglicher Weg der Annäherung?" *Emsdettener Tageblatt* 21 May 1992.
Modlmayr, Hans-Jörg. "Getanzt muss sein, sag ja, sag nein: Die europäische Totentanz-Vereinigung tagte-international." *Basler Zeitung* 7 Oct 1992.
"Lehrer reden über Tod und Sterben." *Emsdettener Volkszeitung* 8 Oct 1992.
"Fiebern Berlin entgegen: Dorstener haben mit 'Totentanz' einen großen Auftritt." *WAZ Dorsten* 15 Oct 1992.
"Mauern fallen erneut: Uraufführung in USA." *WAZ Dorsten* 19 Dec 1992.
"'Emsdettener Totentanz' hat jetzt in Berlin Premiere." *Emsdettener Tageblatt* 22 Dec 1992.
"Berliner Premiere vom 'Totentanz.'" *Emsdettener Volkszeitung* 22 Dec 1992.
"Totentanz im Berliner Saal: Dorstener schreib Liedzyklus." *WAZ Dorsten* 28 Dec 1992.

Huwe, Gisela. "Poetische Endzeit-Visionen rütteln auf." *Berliner Morgenpost* 29 Dec 1992: 20.
Asel, Harald. "Mitten im Leben: Neue Seuchen, Hunger, Kriege, kaputte Umwelt—die Zeit ist reif für Totentänze." *Berlin Magazin* Jan 1993.
Helmig, Martina. "Annäherung an das Thema 'Tod' durch sensible Musik." *Berliner Morgenpost* 2 Jan 1993: 9
Richter, Andreas. "*Totentanz*: Neue Stücke von Friedemann Graef und McKinley." *Der Tagesspiegel (Berlin)* 2 Jan 1993: 16.
"Premiere in Berlin war ein Riesenerflog." *Emsdettener Tageblatt* 5 Jan 1993.
"Emsdettener Totentanz: Amerikanische Premiere in Boston ermöglicht." *Borkener Zeitung* 24 Apr 1993.
"Tod und Sterben auf der Bühne." *Oldenburgische Volkseitung* 22 Apr 1993: 29.
Buell, Richard. "Modern Meets Medieval in 'Dance of Death."*The Boston Globe* 27 Apr 1993: 59.
"Lebensbaum folgt dem Totentanz." *WAZ Dorsten* 28 Sep 1994.
"Der 'Baum des Lebens' wächst in St. Joseph." *Emsdettener Tageblatt* 11 Oct 1994.
Lüttmann, Hans. "Emsdettener Projekt ist beeindrukend und rundherum geglückt." *Emsdettener Tageblatt* 19 Oct 1994.

Program Notes:

"Erst wenn man sich dem Tod stellt und ihn annimmt als unausweichlichen Teil unseres Lebens, d.h. erst wenn man 'mit dem Tod tanzt,' kann man wirklich bewußt spirituell leben im dann noch übrigbleibenden physischen Leben ('man muß sterben, um zu leben'). Deshalb hat der Tod keinen Stachel.

"Für mich ist der Totentanz ein LEBENSTANZ, eine Bestärkung des Lebens durch den ewigen Kreislauf, eine Feier und keine Erwartung des Weltgerichts, der entgültigen Verdammnis. Das Leben selbst beinhaltet all diese gegensätzlichen Gefühle, und für mich ist der Tod eine Spiegelung oder ein Tor in die andere Wirklichkeit."

—William Thomas McKinley (© 1992), from 30 Dec 1992 program. Translator unknown, original lost.

IX.B.6 Westfälischer Pan [First Version]

Date: [1991] *Duration:* 5'45"
Dedication: "To Solo Esprit"
Commission: [D'anna Fortunato]
Publisher: MMC Publications

Movement(s):
I. Westfälischer Pan: Poco larghetto (♩=63)
II. Die Landschaft: Poco scherzando (♩=152)

Instrumentation:
MSop, Cl, Pno soli.

MS Description:
Holograph with signature, pencil on paper. *Location:* Boston Public Library.

Editorial Notes:
Texts by Hans-Jörg Modlmayr. Date taken from the cover sheet of the fair copy. Commission and premiere performance information from the composer. Additional premiere information from BMI records.

Performance History:
[† 25 Jan 1992: New School of Music, Cambridge, MA
D'anna Fortunato, MSop.]

IX.B.7 [Three Poems of] Pablo Neruda

Date: 14 Jan 1992 in Reading, MA ("Lells") *Duration:* 12'00"
Dedication: "to Isabelle Ganz"
Commission: [Isabelle Ganz]
Publisher: MMC Publications

Movement(s):
I. Black Vulture: Tenebre e tragico (♩.=54)
II. Chilean Tinamou: Prestissimo e barbaroso (𝅗𝅥=112)
III. Octobrine: Largo e triste (♩=48)

Instrumentation:
Sop solo; Orchestra (3 Pic/2 Fl, 2 Ob, EHn, 2 Pic Cl/2 Cl, BCl, 2 Bsn, CBsn, 4 Hn, 2 Tpt, 3 Tbn, Tba, Timp, 3 Perc, Hp, Strings).

Sketches:
2 errata sheets of the original MS (all corrected in the fair copy).

MS Description:
Holograph with signature, pencil on paper. *Location:* Boston Public Library.

Editorial Notes:
The title as written above appears only on the cover page of the fair copy. Texts by Pablo Neruda, from *Arte de Pajoras*. Commission information from the composer.

Performance History:
[† See *Recording(s)*.]

Recording(s):
MMC Recordings Ltd.: to be released in 1995
Isabelle Ganz, Sop; Slovak Radio Symphony, Robert Black, Cond.

IX.B.8 Westfälischer Pan [Second Version]

Date: [Aug 1992] in [Reading, MA ("Barn")] *Duration:* 17'00"
Dedication: "To Neva Pilgrim and the Society for New Music, Syracuse"
Commission: [Neva Pilgrim and the Society for New Music, Syracuse]
Publisher: MMC Publications

Movement(s):
I. Die Landschaft: Con moto e misterioso (𝅗𝅥.=46)
Interlude: Poco scherzando (♩=152)
II. Gemen: Largo (♩=40)
III. Raesfeld: Feroce (𝅗𝅥=160)
Interlude II: Molto rapsodico e florido (♩=46)
IV. Westfälischer Pan: Poco larghetto (♩=63)
Postlude: Più mosso (♩=63)

Instrumentation:
MSop, Pic/Fl, Cl, Perc, Pno, Vln, Vcl soli.

MS Description:
Holograph with signature, pencil on paper. *Location:* Boston Public Library.

Editorial Notes:
Texts by Hans-Jörg Modlmayr. Author was witness to date and location of composition. Commission information from the composer.

Performance History:
† 13 Oct 1992: Crouse College Auditorium, Syracuse, NY
Neva Pilgrim, Sop; Linda Greene, Fl; John Friedrichs, Cl; Ernest Muzquiz, Perc; Steven Heyman, Pno; Dmitri Gerikh, Vln; Walden Bass, Vcl.

IX.B.9 Jenseits der Mauer

Date: Oct 1992 in [Reading, MA ("Lells")] *Duration:* 28'20"
Dedication: [David Tasa]
Commission: [David Tasa]
Publisher: MMC Publications

Movement(s):
Part I: Largo (♩=40)*
Part II: Misterioso e religioso (♩=69)
Part III: Largo e dramatico (♩.=44)

Instrumentation:
Bar, Tpt, Org soli.

MS Description:
Holograph with signature, pencil on paper. *Location:* Boston Public Library.

Editorial Notes:
Text by Hans-Jörg Modlmayr. *Part one of *Jenseits der Mauer* was originally written as *Die Mauern* and is not filed with the *Jenseits der Mauer* MS. For MS description of Part one, see *Die Mauern* (VI.E.1). Author was witness to location of composition. Dedication carried over from *Die Mauern*. Commission information from the composer.

Performance History:
† 24 May 1992: St. Martin Kirche, Ober-Erlenbach, FRG (Part I only)
David Tasa, Tpt; Albert Göken, Org.
† 26 Feb 1993: St. Joseph Kirche, Emsdetten, FRG
Volker Schwarz, Bar; David Tasa, Tpt; Albert Göken, Org.
27 Feb 1993: St. Barbara Kirche, Dorsten-Wulfen-Barkenberg, FRG
Volker Schwarz, Bar; David Tasa, Tpt; Albert Göken, Org.
[† (Costa Rica)] 8 Aug 1993: Teatro Nacional, San José, Costa Rica (Part I only)
David Tasa, Tpt; Albert Göken, Org.
† (UK) 14 Oct 1993: College Chapel, University of London, Egham, UK
Volker Schwarz, Bar; David Tasa, Tpt; Albert Göken, Org.
[† (Cambridge)] 16 Oct 1993: Trinity College Chapel, Cambridge, UK.
Volker Schwarz, Bar; David Tasa, Tpt; Albert Göken, Org.

Bibliography:
Kneisel, Volker. "Die 'neue Welt' lebt nur als Traum: 'Jenseits der Mauern': Generalprobe in St. Joseph verlangte viel von Musikern und Zuhörern." *Emsdettener Tageblatt* 1 Mar 1992.
"Organist probt Konzert auf amerikanische Art: Kirchenmusiker spielt bei McKinley-Welturaufführung." *WAZ Dorsten* 19 May 1992.
Dellith, Michael. "Trompete schreit nach Fall der Mauer." *Taunus-Zeitung: Bad Homburg* 27 May 1992.
"Wulfener pressen ihre eigene Kirchen-Platte: CD-Aufnahme in St. Barbara mit Trompeter David Tasa." *WAZ Dorsten* 18 Sep 1992.
"Gesprächsabend am Freitag zur Musik 'Jenseits der Mauern.'" *Emsdettener Volkszeitung* 27 Jan 1993.

"'Jenseits der Mauer' beeindrukte: Generalprobe des Triptychons von McKinley am Freitag 20 Uhr in der Josephkirche." *Emsdettener Volkszeitung* 1 Feb 1993.
"Modlmayr-Sonette mit Musik von McKinley." *Emsdettener Tageblatt* 1 Feb 1993.
"Noch vor dem Fall der Mauer: Welt-Uraufführung." *WAZ Dorsten* 17 Feb 1993
"Keine einfache Story über die Berliner Mauer: Dorstener Lehrer shrieb für einen Amerikaner." *WAZ Dorsten* 18 Feb 1993.
"'Jenseits der Mauer': Generalprobe am Freitag in St. Joseph." *Emsdettener Volkszeitung* 24 Feb 1993.
"Jenseits der Mauern: In St. Joseph Generalprobe zur Welturaufführung." *Emsdettener Tageblatt* 24 Feb 1993.
"'Jenseits der Mauer' wird in Barkenberg uraufgeführt: Hochkarätige Musiker sind in Dorsten am Werk." *Stadtspiegel Dorsten* 24 Feb 1993: 1.
"Begeisterter Beifall für exzellente Leistung: Kirche St. Barbara—Uraufführung der Komposition 'Jenseits der Mauer.'" *Ruhrnachrichten Dorsten* 1 Mar 1993.

Program Notes:

"Early in 1988 the Boston composer William Thomas McKinley, sensing very strongly that the fall of the Berlin Wall was imminent, asked the German poet Hans-Jörg Modlmayr (educated at Cambridge University) to write a cycle of poems on the Wall. This cycle explores the ambivalences of walls and memories associated with, for example, Jericho and the Berlin Wall The cycle of poems also recalls the dark years which Berlin witnessed under Hitler—terrible years without which the Berlin Wall would never have been erected....

"McKinley, who has recorded with the London Sinfonietta and whose music is played all the world over, wrote the cantata *Jenseits der Mauer / Beyond the Wall* for David Tasa, the solo trumpeter of Frankfurt Opera. The cantata has three movements: trumpet and organ—organ solo—bass baritone, trumpet and organ....

"William Thomas McKinley and Hans-Jörg Modlmayr have collaborated on other projects: *Emsdettener Totentanz / Dance of Death* with Albert Göken conducting the Berlin Philharmonic; *Mauern / Walls* with clarinetist Richard Stoltzman and the Cambridge Madrigal Singers; *Westfälischer Pan / Westphalian Pan* with soprano Neva Pilgrim (Syracuse University, N.Y.)."

—Author unknown, from 16 Oct 1993 program.

IX.B.10 Der Lebensbaum [The Life-Tree]

Date: July 1994 in [Reading, MA ("Lells")] *Duration:* 37'40"
Dedication: [Hildegard Modlmayr]
Commission: [Hildegard Modlmayr]
Publisher: MMC Publications

Movement(s):
Prelude: Dolce con moto (♩=52)
Rilke–Sonnette an Orpheus: Grandioso (♩=80)*
Bobrowski–Der Muschelbläser: Tempo di valse (♩.=72)*
Celan–Du liegst hinaus: Scherzando e sardonico (♩=152)*
Modlmayr–Europa: Lamento e triste (♩=44)*
Interlude: Adagio
Das 1,000 jahrige Reich: Largo e tragico (♩=48)
Postlude: Più mosso (♩=126)

Instrumentation:
Sop, MSop, Bar, 2 Vln, Vla, Vcl soli.

Sketches:
See *Baum des Lebens* (IV.C.12).

MS Description:
Holograph with signature, pencil on paper. *Location:* Boston Public Library.

Editorial Notes:
*Movements I–IV ("Rilke"—"Modlmayr") are from *Baum des Lebens* (IV.C.12). Please see that entry for MS and sketch information. Based on the book of Revelation, poems by Rainer Maria Rilke (1922), Johannes Bobrowski (1958), Paul Celan (1976), and Hans-Jörg Modlmayr (1989), and graphics by Fritz Möser. Dedication and commission taken from *Baum des Lebens* and confirmed by McKinley. Author was witness to location of composition.

Performance History:
† 30 Oct 1994: St. Joseph Kirche, Emsdetten, FRG
Regine Gebhardt, Sop; Ursula Krämer, MSop; Volker Schwarz, Bar; Silesian String Quartet (Marek Mos, Poitr Janosik, Vln; Arkadiusz Kubica, Vla; Lukasz Syrnicki, Vcl), Albert Göken, Cond.

Bibliography:
"Lebensbaum folgt dem Totentanz." *WAZ Dorsten* 28 Sep 1994.
"Der 'Baum des Lebens' wächst in St. Joseph." *Emsdettener Tageblatt* 11 Oct 1994.
"Uraltes, überlefertes Symbol der Menschen." *Emsdettener Volkszeitung* 15 Oct 1994.
Lüttmann, Hans. "Emsdettener Projekt ist beeindrukend und rundherum geglückt." *Emsdettener Tageblatt* 19 Oct 1994.

See also: Can You Sing Me a Song? (II.B.5)
Quadruplum (II.B.1)

Group IX.C: Works for Voice and Piano

IX.C.1 Six Pieces for Soprano Voice and Piano

Date: Summer 1972 in Chicago, IL (Univ. of Chicago) *Duration:* 10'05"
Dedication: "To my wife"
Commission: [Elsa Charlston]
Publisher: MMC Publications

Movement(s):
I. Remain: With quiet energy (♩=72)
II. Rosebud: Gossamer, like glass (♪.=90)
III. Melting: Legato espr[essivo] (♩=48)
IV. Drum: Boldly (♩=52)
V. Pearls: ♩=52
VI. Sigh: ♪=210

Instrumentation:
Sop, Pno soli.

Sketches:
1 nearly complete draft (pages 4–5 of the MS are missing). 3 drafts of the opening of I. 1 draft of the opening of IV. 2 drafts of the opening of VI. 1 unidentified sketch.

MS Description:
Holograph with printed name, ink on vellum. *Location:* Boston Public Library.

Editorial Notes:
Text by William Thomas McKinley. Commission information from the composer. Premiere performance information from McKinley's notes.

Performance History:
[† 15 Apr 1973: University of Chicago, Chicago, IL
Elsa Charlston, Sop; John Cobb, Pno.]

IX.C.2 New York Memories for Soprano Voice and Piano

Date: 20 Dec 1987 *Duration:* 17'00"
Commission: "to Leslie Kandell"
Publisher: MMC Publications

Movement(s): *Instrumentation:*
I. Songs to Remember: Largo sensuale (♩=54) Sop, Pno soli.
II. Shiva in New York: Presto (♩=160)
III. Workday Mornings: Andantino (♩.=72)
IV. Stone Settings: Lento, poco libero e rubato (♩=42)
V. A City Nightscape: Poco allegro (♩=112)
Epilogue. Larghetto (♩=56)

MS Description:
Holograph with printed name, pencil on vellum. *Location:* Boston Public Library.

Editorial Notes:
Texts by Marlene McKinley (II), Robert K. Johnson (III, IV, V), and William Thomas McKinley (I, Epilogue).

Performance History:
† 6 Jan 1988: Weill Recital Hall, New York, NY
Lisa Safer, Sop; Judith Gordon, Pno.
† (Boston) 23 Oct 1988: Jordan Hall, New England Conservatory of Music, Boston, MA
Joan-Marie Zimmerman, Sop; Judith Gordon, Pno.
28 Feb 1990: Jordan Hall, New England Conservatory of Music, Boston, MA
Joan-Marie Zimmerman, Sop; Judith Gordon, Pno.

Program Notes:
"The text of the opening and concluding sections of *New York Memories* is based on fragments of popular songs about New York and on dream reveries about New York. This work was commissioned by Leslie Kandell and premiered by Lisa Safer and Judith Gordon in Carnegie Recital Hall, New York."
—William Thomas McKinley (© 1990), from 28 Feb 1990 program.

IX.C.a **~~Chaconne (Plain-song)~~**

Date: [ca. 1970] *Duration:* 2'00"
Publisher: Unpublished

Movement(s):
♩=72

Instrumentation:
[Voice?]

MS Description:
Holograph with signature, pencil on paper. *Location:* Boston Public Library.

Editorial Notes:
MS ends after 49 measures. Date determined through paleographic analysis and location of discovery (with other 1970 sketches).

Group X: Arrangements

Group X.A: Classical Arrangements

X.A.1 Mozart Cadenza

Date: [ca. 1967]
Duration: I. 3'39"; II. 0'39"; III. 1'11"
Publisher: Unpublished

Movement(s):
[One untitled movement]

Instrumentation:
Pno solo.

MS Description:
Holograph, pencil on paper. *Location:* Boston Public Library.

Editorial Notes:
Cadenzas for Mozart's Piano Concerto in C minor (No. 24, K. 491). Date determined through paleographic analysis.

X.A.2 The Fisherman and His Wife

Date: 23 Mar 1975
Duration: 60'
Commission: [Boston Opera Company]
Publisher: Margun Music Inc.

Movement(s):
Scene I: ♩=60
Scene II: ♩=80
Scene III: ♩=116
Scene IV: ♩=88
Scenes V–VII: Maestoso (♩=60)
Scene VIII: ♩=96–100
Scene IX: Maestoso (♩=60)
Scene X: ♩=100–104
Scene XI: Molto maestoso (♩=40–46)
Scene XII: ♩=60
Scene XIII: ♩=60

Instrumentation:
Sop (The Cat), Alt (The Wife), Ten (The Fisherman), Bar (The Fish); Orchestra (Pic/Fl, Cl/Alt Sax, Bsn/CBsn, Hn, Tpt, Tbn, Perc, Org, Strings); Tape. Optional: Elec Bass.

MS Description:
Holograph with signature. *Location:* Unknown.*

Editorial Notes:
McKinley's re-orchestration of Gunther Schuller's 1970 opera. *A blueprint of the MS has survived and been placed in the Boston Public Library collection. Commission taken from National Endowment grant application made in the mid-1970s. Premiere performance information from the composer.

Performance History:
[† ca. 1975: Hall unknown, Boston, MA
Boston Opera Company.]

Group X.B: Jazz and Pop Arrangements

X.B.1 Goodbye for B♭ Clarinet and Piano

Date: [1981] in [Reading, MA ("Lells")] *Duration:* 9'30"
Dedication: "To Dick [Stoltzman] with great love and admiration—this is no. 1 of your wonderful commission. I give you thanks and may we continue on this beautiful path.—Tom"
Commission: Richard Stoltzman
Publisher: MMC Publications

Movement(s):
Slow ballad (♩=48)

Instrumentation:
Cl, Pno soli.

MS Description:
Holograph with signature. *Location:* Lost.*

Editorial Notes:
Original melody Gordon Jenkins. *A photocopy of manuscript has survived and been placed in the Boston Public Library collection. Since this work is "no. 1" of Richard Stoltzman's arrangement commission, a commission made in 1981 (see *Program Notes*), and since *Night and Day*, the second work in this commission series, was written in 1981, this work must also have been written in 1981. Location of composition taken from McKinley's notes. McKinley's notes indicate 28 Apr 1982 as premiere performance.

Performance History:
[†] 28 Apr 1982: Carnegie Hall, New York, NY
Richard Stoltzman, Cl; Irma Vallecillo, Pno.
17 Nov 1991: Jordan Hall, New England Conservatory of Music, Boston, MA
Richard Stoltzman, Cl; Irma Vallecillo, Pno.

Bibliography:
Henahan, Donal. "Clarinetist: Richard Stoltzman Gives Recital." *The New York Times* 29 Apr 1982: C16.
Henahan, Donal. "The Philharmonic: Bolet and Rex." *The New York Times* 30 Apr 1982: C32.
Grimes, Ev. "Yale University American Music Oral History Series: William Thomas McKinley." Oct 1986, Yale University School of Music: 88–89, 92, 95.
Dyer, Richard. "The Savvy Sound of Richard Stoltzman." *The Boston Globe* 18 Nov 1991: 29.

Program Notes:
"The idea to compose and adapt extended jazz improvisations based on standard popular tunes was first stimulated and encouraged by Richard Stoltzman. Richard's first 'urgings' began when we were classmates at Yale University fifteen years ago. One late night after a jazz improvisation session, he asked me why I did not write down my improvisations. And he continued to ask me the same question for many years after that. Although I did compose many classical chamber and orchestral works for Richard, as well as several quasi 'third stream' works for other occasions, one of which I performed as piano soloist with the Chicago

Symphony in 1972, my reluctance to write down jazz improvisations *literally* note for note did not wane. Finally, however, during the early summer of 1981, Richard's perennial 'urgings' were amplified in a direct commission for me to compose some thirty or more such pieces, over the next few years, for clarinet and piano, clarinet and string quartet, and clarinet and orchestra. The time was right, and thus I set anxiously forth on the project. (I should add that this project was intensified by the fact that at that time I had been, and still am, performing extensively with my own jazz trio, featuring Miroslav Vitous and Billy Hart—together with whom I recently recorded a Jazz Alive national broadcast in addition to a commercial recording which will be released this month on GunMar Records.)

"To date, I have completed seven extended jazz improvisations among which are the two performed tonight, *Goodbye* and *Night and Day*. In them I have combined the richness of contemporary jazz harmony with the kinds of textures and lines which suggest the school of post be-bop and contemporary mainstream jazz. They are completely realized in a manner which I might improvise in a given jazz performance situation and are standard fare in the jazz repertory, being among my personal favorites. But it must be emphasized that these works are *more* than jazz arrangements. They contain classical procedures of development, extension, and manipulation of phrases and periods, elaborate harmonic weaving and layering, cadenza interpolations, counterpoint, and thematic variation. But, paradoxically, they never lose sight of their jazz roots; and to listeners already familiar with the original melodies, they are quite easy to follow throughout their multiple developments and transformations. In addition, they present to both listener and performer an immediate and emotionally communicative experience, revealing a synthesis of musical styles drawn from my own deeply intense and personal involvement in the contemporary jazz experience, evoking in the listener's psyche the great musical riches which the eloquent language of jazz forcefully and uninhibitedly generates to each of us."

—William Thomas McKinley (© 1994), from his notes.

X.B.2 Night and Day

Date: [1981] *Duration:* 2'59"
Commission: [Richard Stoltzman]
Publisher: MMC Publications

Movement(s):
With great movement and sense of "up" tempo character (♩=180+)

Instrumentation:
Cl, Pno soli.

Sketches:
1 draft of mm. 41–54.* 1 draft of mm. 57–68.*

MS Description:
Holograph, pencil on paper. *Location:* Boston Public Library.
Markings: Over m. 105: "Free Tags for Dick [Stoltzman]"

Editorial Notes:
Original melody by Cole Porter. *Sketches are written on the backs of pages of the MS. MS is missing page 2 (mm. 24–40). A complete fair copy does exist. Date taken from cover page of fair copy. Commission information from the composer.

Performance History:
See *Goodbye* (X.B.1).

Bibliography:
See *Goodbye* (X.B.1).

Program Notes:
See *Goodbye* (X.B.1).

X.B.3 All The Things You Are

Date: [ca. 1984] *Duration:* 2'49"
Commission: [Tashi]
Publisher: MMC Publications

Movement(s):
V[ery] slow (♩=52)

Instrumentation:
Cl, 2 Vln, Vla, Vcl soli.

MS Description:
Holograph, pencil on paper. *Location:* Boston Public Library.

Editorial Notes:
Original work by Jerome Kern. Date determined through paleographic analysis. Commission and premiere performance information from the composer.

Performance History:
[† Date unknown: Location unknown
Tashi (Richard Stoltzman, Cl; Ida Kavafian and Theodore Arm, Vln; Il-Hwan Bae, Vla; Fred Sherry, Vcl).]

X.B.4 Time On My Hands [Medley]

Date: [ca. 1984] *Duration:* 2'58"
Commission: [Richard Stoltzman]
Publisher: MMC Publications

Movement(s):
♩=80

Instrumentation:
Cl, Pno soli.

MS Description:
Holograph with printed name, pencil on paper. *Location:* Boston Public Library.

Editorial Notes:
Date determined through paleographic analysis. Commission and premiere performance information from the composer.

Performance History:
[† ca. 1984: Location unknown
Richard Stoltzman, Cl.]

X.B.a ~~My Way~~

Date: [ca. 1981]
Publisher: Unpublished

Movement(s):
See editorial notes.

Instrumentation:
Cl, Pno soli.

MS Description:
Holograph, pencil on paper. *Location:* Boston Public Library/Lost.

Editorial Notes:
Only page 7 of the MS exists. Date determined through paleographic analysis and discovery of MS with the *Night and Day* MS.

X.B.b ~~Isn't She Lovely~~

Date: [ca. 1982]
Publisher: Unpublished

Movement(s):
Moderato, singing (♩=60)

Instrumentation:
Cl, Pno soli.

MS Description:
Holograph with signature, pencil on paper. *Location:* Boston Public Library.

Editorial Notes:
Original melody by Stevie Wonder.

General Bibliography

Writings by William Thomas McKinley

McKinley, William Thomas. "Mel Powell's Pedagogy." *Aperiodical* 2(Spring 1988), no. 1: 47–48.

McKinley, William Thomas. "Composer's Views: Excerpts from Testimonial Letters." In *Boston Musica Viva at Twenty*. Boston: Boston Musica Viva, 1988: 27–28.

Monographs and Articles on William Thomas McKinley

(for writings on specific pieces, see Works, Performances, and Bibliography)

Elsner, Carmen. "New Sound Explored on Campus." *Wisconsin State Journal* 23 Feb 1973: IV 17.

Stein, Robert. "McKinley Auditions for Red Sox." *New Kensington Valley News Dispatch* 19 Apr 1975: 21.

Kozinn, Allan. "How to Win Prominence Playing the Clarinet." *The New York Times* 5 Mar 1978: D 15, D 20.

Dyer, Richard. "William Thomas McKinley." *Showcase: The Magazine of the Minnesota Orchestra* 11(29 Nov 1978–6 Jan 1979), no. 3: 13–14.

Solow, Linda I., ed. *The Boston Composers Project: A Bibliography of Contemporary Music.* Cambridge, MA: The MIT Press, 1983: 338–345.

Moss, Howard. "Parnassus on Upper Broadway: The Cream That Rises to the Top." *Vanity Fair* Aug 1983: 59–60.

"Koussevitzky Music Foundation Awards Nine Commissions." *Library of Congress Information Bulletin* 5 Dec 1983: 413–14.

Driver, Paul. "Composer McKinley 'Hears the Muses.'" *The Boston Globe* 9 Dec 1983: 48, 52.

Kandell, Leslie. "Classical Composer With a Passion For Jazz." *The New York Times* 17 Feb 1985: 23, 26.

Hitchcock, H. Wiley, ed. *The New Grove Dictionary of American Music*. Vol. 3. New York: Grove's Dictionaries of Music, 1986: 151–52.

McLaughlin, Jeff. "Nurturing Home-Grown Artistry." *The Boston Globe* 20 Apr 1986: B33, B43.

Kart, Larry. "Schools Offer the Mechanical While Fostering the Spiritual." *Chicago Tribune* 13 Jul 1986: 13.8–13.10.

Spousta, Holly. "A Man of 'Eminently Worthwhile Music': Profiling Reading's William T. McKinley." *Reading Daily Times Chronicle* 21 Aug 1986: 1, 14A.

Grimes, Ev. "Yale University American Music Oral History Series: William Thomas McKinley." Oct 1986, Yale University School of Music.

Lifchitz, Max. "Composer of Note: William Thomas McKinley." *Living Music* 4(Fall 1986), no. 1: 2.

Coffler, Gail. "Interview: William Thomas McKinley." *Collage Newsletter* 1987/88: 4–5.

Tassel, Janet. "Prodigy." *Boston Magazine* 80(Jan 1987), no. 1: 67–69.

Nissen, Phyllis. "He's Not Just Your Average Guy Next Door." *Reading Daily Times Chronicle: Middlesex East Supplement* 6 May 1987: S1, S4.

Tassel, Janet. "From Fat Tuesday's to Carnegie Hall." *Musical America* 107(Jan 1988), no. 6: 21–22.

Kanny, Mark. "Best of Both Worlds: McKinley Quartet Plays Carnegie Hall, Jazz Club." *Pittsburgh Post-Gazette* 4 Jan 1988: 11–12.

Rubinstein, Leslie. "Creative Spirit: Richard Stoltzman." *Carnegie Hall Stagebill* 10(Feb 1988), no. 6: 22, 27–28.

Coffler, Gail. "Interview: William Thomas McKinley." *Perspectives of New Music* 26(Summer 1988), no. 2: 254–271.

Guinn, John. "A Few Words With William Thomas McKinley: Jazz and Classics Merge in Composer's Mind." *Detroit Free Press* 19 Sep 1988.

Creasey, Beverly. "Brighton Flutist Celebrates Modern Works." *The Allston-Brighton Journal* 9 Mar 1989: 9.

Tommasini, Anthony. "McKinley's Popularity a Mystery." *The Boston Globe* 14 Mar 1989: 29.

Page, Tim. "Tanglewood's Contemporary Bag." *Newsday* 7 Aug 1989: II.7.

Gewertz, Daniel. "Pianist Writes Classically, Plays Jazzily." *The Boston Herald* 17 Nov 1989: S15.

Reitershan, Jürgen. "Herz mit Kopf: McKinley über Uraufführung in Bad Kreuznach." *Rhein-Zeitung* 10/11 Feb 1990.

Hampton, Mitch. "William Thomas McKinley: On Music in Life, Life in Music." *Organica Quarterly* Spring 1990: 21 and Summer 1990: 21.

Mott, Gilbert H. "Change of Tune: Composer William Thomas McKinley Rejects Atonality to Make Contemporary Classical Music That's Accessible." *Fairfield Fairpress* 1 Jun 1990: F3.

Snider, Vada. "Composers and Critics Forum continues in Hall of Christ." *The Chautauquan Daily* 30 Jul 1990: 1, 12.

Turner, Megan. "Popular Composer Puts Jazz, Classics Together." *The Courier Mail (Brisbane, Australia)* 7 Sep 1990: 16.

Rosenberg, Donald. "New Kensington Composer in Demand." *The Pittsburgh Press* 28 Apr 1991: F1, F4.

Cic, Emil. "Glazbeni Virtouzitet." *Glasnik Hrvatski Politicki Tjednik* 14 Jun 1991: 46.

Karlovits, Robert. "Jazz, Classical Music Meet in McKinley's Mind." *The Pittsburgh Press* 16 Jan 1992.

Taylor, Charles. "'Bilingual' Composer Speaks Classical, Jazz." *The Richmond News Leader* 29 Feb 1992: A–40.

McKinley, Marlene M. "The Creative Processes of Composer William Thomas McKinley." *Music Theory Explorations and Applications* 1(Fall 1992): 20–29.

Hampton, Aubrey. "Master Musicians Collective." *Organica Quarterly* Autumn 1993: 10–11, 24–25.

Zagorski, William. "On the Building of Pipelines: William Thomas McKinley and the Master Musicians Collective." *Fanfare* 17(Nov–Dec 1993), no. 2: 116–131.

Wheeler, Denise, J. "An Art Form of Note." *Portsmouth Herald* 30 Jan 1994: C1.

Mootz, William. "Arts: Frederick Speck." *The Courier-Journal* 31 Jul 1994: 11.

William Thomas McKinley as Performer

Metalitz, Steve. "McKinley, Friends Play Jazz Delights." *Grey City Journal* 12 Feb 1971: 9.

Whitehead, Kevin. "Tom McKinley and Ed Schuller, Life Cycle, GunMar GM 3001." *Cadence* Sep 1982: 67–68.

Kandell, Leslie. "Classical Composer With a Passion For Jazz." *The New York Times* 17 Feb 1985: 23, 26.

Schneider, Edward. "Catholic Taste Gives Variety to a New Label." *The New York Times* 24 Feb 1985: H 31–32

Dyer, Richard. "Feeling, Not Technique Is Stoltzman's Secret." *The Boston Globe* 17 Mar 1985.

Gewertz, Daniel. "Artists Jam at Jazz Marathon." *The Boston Herald* 27 Aug 1985: 26.

Sherry, Fred. "Cellist Fred Sherry Talks With William Thomas McKinley." *Lincoln Center Stagebill* 13(Feb 1986), no. 6: 12B–12D, 37.

Bouchard, Fred. "Richard Stoltzman: Clarinet Crossover." *Downbeat* 53(Oct 1986), no. 10: 20–22, 61.

Dyer, Richard. "Burton, Stoltzman Unite Jazz, Classical Music." *The Boston Globe* 7 Feb 1987: 17.

Dubois, Cherrie. "Creative Arts 10th Anniversary a Grand Time." *Reading Daily Times Chronicle* 19 May 1987.

Tassel, Janet. "From Fat Tuesday's to Carnegie Hall." *Musical America* 107(Jan 1988), no. 6: 21–22.

Pareles, Jon. "Jazz: Tom McKinley Group." *The New York Times* 7 Jan 1988: C26.

Rubinstein, Leslie. "Creative Spirit: Richard Stoltzman." *Carnegie Hall Stagebill* 10(Feb 1988), no. 6: 22, 27–28.

Croan, Robert. "Clarinetist Shines in Jazz." *Pittsburgh Post-Gazette* 20 Sep 1988.

Blumenthal, Robert. "Consider Getz and Taylor and Mourn Roy Eldridge." *The Boston Phoenix* 10 Mar 1989: 10, 18.

Tommasini, Anthony. "Concert Honors the Legislature." *The Boston Globe* 5 Jun 1990: 63.

Tommasini, Anthony. "Celebrating the Many Sides of Schuller." *The Boston Globe* 29 Nov 1990.

Gonzalez, Fernando. "Jazz Composer's Alliance Stays Fresh." *The Boston Globe* 14 Dec 1990.

Young, Robert. "Pianist Scores With Fusion." *The Boston Herald* 15 Dec 1990: 23.

Gonzalez, Fernando. "New Jazz Pieces Show Skill But Lack Soul." *The Boston Globe* 17 Dec 1990: 40.

Garelick, Jon. "Local Jazz Hits Stride." *The Boston Phoenix* 21 Dec 1990: III–15.

Discography

The Recorded Works of William Thomas McKinley

(in alphabetical order)

Andante and Scherzo for Piano and Orchestra (II.K.5)
MMC Recordings, Ltd.: MMC2009, ©1994 (CD)
Frances Burnett, Pno; Slovak Radio Symphony Orchestra, Robert Stankovsky, Cond.

Boston Overture (I.B.1)
MMC Recordings, Ltd.: MMC2008, ©1993 (CD)
Silesian Philharmonic, Robert Black, Cond.

Clarinet Concerto No. 3 ("The Alchemical") (II.E.9)
MMC Recordings Ltd.: to be released in 1995
Richard Stoltzman, Cl; Warsaw Philharmonic Orchestra, George Manahan, Cond.

Concert Variations for Violin, Viola and Orchestra [Version I] (II.C.7a)
MMC Recordings Ltd.: to be recorded in 1995.
Glenn Dicterow, Vln; Karen Dreyfus, Vla; The Seattle Symphony, Gerard Schwarz, Cond.

Concerto Domestica for Trumpet, Bassoon, and Orchestra (II.C.6)
MMC Recordings, Ltd.: MMC2002, ©1993 (CD)—movement 3 only
Slovak Radio Symphony Orchestra, Robert Black, Cond.

Concerto for Flute and String Orchestra (II.D.1)
Owl Recording, Inc: Owl-34, ©1989 (CD)
Robert Stallman, Fl; The Prism Orchestra, Robert Black, Cond.

Concerto for Orchestra No. 2 (II.A.3)
MMC Recordings Ltd.: to be recorded in 1995.

Concerto for Piano No. 2 (The "O'Leary") (II.K.3)
MMC Recordings Ltd.: to be released in 1995
Jeffrey Jacobs, Pno; Silesian Philharmonic, J. Swoboda, Cond.

[Concerto for Piano No. 3] (II.K.7)
MMC Recordings Ltd.: to be recorded in 1995.

Concerto for the New World... (II.B.7)
MMC Recordings, Ltd.: MMC2002, ©1993 (CD)—variation 5 only
Slovak Radio Symphony Orchestra, Robert Black, Cond.
MMC Recordings Ltd.: to be released in 1995
Quintet of the Americas; The Manhattan School Chamber Orchestra, Glen Cortese, Cond.

[Concerto No. 2 for B♭ Clarinet and Orchestra] (II.E.7)
RCA Victor Red Seal: to be released in 1995.
Richard Stoltzman, Cl; Berlin Radio Symphony, Lukas Foss, Cond.

Concerto No. 3 for Viola and Orchestra (II.M.4)
MMC Recordings Ltd.: to be released in 1995
Karen Dreyfus, Vla; The Manhattan School Chamber Orchestra, Glen Cortese, Cond.

Elegy for Solo Alto Flute (VII.A.4)
Recording firm as yet undetermined: to be released in 1995
Robert Stallman, Fl.

[Etude No. 1 for Solo Harp] (VII.G.1)
1750 Arch Records: S-1787, ©1982 (LP)
Susan Allen, Harp

Fantasia Concertante for String Quartet [String Quartet No. 4] (IV.C.4)
GM Recordings: GM 2014, ©1985 (LP)
Sequoia String Quartet

Fantasia Variazioni (Fantasy Variations) for Harpsichord and Orchestra (II.K.6)
MMC Recordings, Ltd.: MMC2016, ©1994 (CD)
Elaine Comparone, Hpschd; Slovak Radio Symphony Orchestra, Robert Stankovsky, Cond.

For One (VII.B.3)
Composers Recordings, Inc.: CRI SD 507, ©1984 (LP)
Richard Stoltzman, Cl.

Four Text Settings for A Cappella Mixed Chorus (op. 109) (IX.A.3)
Koch International Classics: 3-7178-2, ©1994 (CD)
John Oliver Chorale, John Oliver, Cond.

Golden Petals... (II.C.2)
MMC Recordings, Ltd.: MMC2005, ©1993 (CD)
Richard Nunemaker, Sop Sax/BCl; Peter Herbert, Cb; Pierrot Plus Ensemble, David Colson, Cond.

Jubilee Concerto for Brass Quintet and Symphony Orchestra (II.B.6)
Staatsorchester Rheinische Philharmonie: SRP-D 92, ©1992. (CD)
Staatsorchester Rheinische Philharmonie, James Lockhart, Cond.

Lightning (An Overture) (I.B.4)
MMC Recordings Ltd.: to be released in 1995
Prague Radio Symphony, Vladimir Valek, Cond.

Miniature Portraits for Trumpet, Bassoon and String Orchestra (II.C.5)
Delos International Inc.: to be recorded in 1995.
Jeffrey Silberschlag, Tpt; Deborah Greitzer Silberschlag, Bsn; The Seattle Symphony, Gerard Schwarz, Cond.

New York Overture (I.B.2)
Vienna Modern Masters: VMM 3005, ©1991 (CD)
Warsaw National Philharmonic Orchestra, Robert Black, Cond.
MMC Recordings Ltd.: to be recorded in 1995.

Paintings No. 2 for Double Trio (VIII.C.1)
Golden Crest Records Inc.: NEC-119, ©1979 (LP)
New England Conservatory Contemporary Music Ensemble, Gunther Schuller, Cond.

Paintings No. 6 ("To Hear the Light Dancing")... (VIII.B.3)
Northeastern Records: NR 203, ©1982 (LP)
Boston Musica Viva, Richard Pittman, Cond.

Paintings No. 7... (VIII.B.4)
Composers Recordings, Inc.: CRI SD 507, ©1984 (LP)
Collage, Gunther Schuller, Cond.

Patriotic Variations ["Reading Festival Overture"] (I.B.3)
MMC Recordings Ltd.: to be released in 1995
Slovak Radio Symphony, Robert Stankovsky, Cond.

Secrets of the Heart (Romances No. 2) for Flute and Piano (VI.A.6)
Academy Sound and Vision, Ltd.: CD DCA 869, ©1993 (CD)
Robert Stallman, Fl; David Buechner, Pno.

Silent Whispers for Solo Piano and Orchestra (II.K.4)
MMC Recordings, Ltd.: MMC2004, ©1994 (CD)
Victoria Griswold, Pno; Warsaw National Philharmonic, Robert Black, Cond.

Sinfonie Concertante... (II.B.4)
MMC Recordings Ltd.: to be recorded in 1995.

SinfoNova (A Sinfonietta for String Orchestra in Two Movements) (I.C.5)
MMC Recordings, Ltd.: MMC2001, ©1993 (CD)
Slovak Radio Symphony Orchestra, Robert Black, Cond.

Six Impromptus for Flute, B♭ Clarinet, Violin, Viola, [and] Cello (VIII.D.3)
Northeastern Records: NR 203, ©1982 (LP)
Boston Musica Viva, Richard Pittman, Cond.

Sonata for Clarinet and Piano (VI.C.4)
RCA Victor Red Seal: to be released in 1995.
Richard Stoltzman, Cl; Irma Vallecillo, Pno.

Symphony No. 3 for Chamber Ensemble [“Romantic”] (I.A.3)
MMC Recordings, Ltd.: MMC2003, ©1993 (CD)
Warsaw National Philharmonic, Robert Black, Cond.

Symphony No. 4 (I.A.4)
MMC Recordings Ltd.: to be released in 1995
Slovak Radio Symphony, Robert Stankovsky, Cond.

Symphony No. 5 (The “Irish”) (I.A.5)
Vienna Modern Masters: VMM 3005, ©1991 (CD)
Warsaw Philharmonic Orchestra, Robert Black, Cond.
MMC Recordings Ltd.: to be recorded in 1995.

[Symphony No. 6] (I.A.6)
MMC Recordings Ltd.: to be recorded in 1995.

The Mountain for Large Chamber or Full Symphony Orchestra (I.C.4)
MMC Recordings Ltd.: to be released in 1995
St. Petersburg Philharmonic, Alexander Titov, Cond.

[Three Poems of] Pablo Neruda (IX.B.7)
MMC Recordings Ltd.: to be released in 1995
Isabelle Ganz, Sop; Slovak Radio Symphony, Robert Black, Cond.

Three Romances [Romances No. 1 for Flute and Piano] (VI.A.2)
GM Recordings: GM2026CD, ©1990 (CD)
Stephanie Jutt, Fl; Randall Hodgkinson, Pno.

[Trio No. 2 for Violin, Cello and Piano] (V.F.2)
MMC Recordings Ltd.: to be recorded in 1995.
Solati Trio.

Two Movements for Flute and String Orchestra (II.D.2)
MMC Recordings Ltd.: to be recorded in 1995.

Viola Concerto [No. 2] (II.M.2)
MMC Recordings Ltd.: to be recorded in 1995.

Recordings of William Thomas McKinley as Performer

(in chronological order)

Ralph Shapey: Rituals, for Symphony Orchestra; String Quartet No. 6
Composers Recordings Inc.: CRI SD 275, ©1972 (LP)
William Thomas McKinley, Pno; Lexington Quartet of the Contemporary Chamber Players of the University of Chicago; London Sinfonietta, Ralph Shapey, Cond.

Life Cycle: Tom McKinley—Ed Schuller
GM Recordings: GM 2014, ©1982 (LP)
Tom McKinley, Pno; Ed Schuller, Cb; Tom Harrell, Tpt; Gary Valente, Tbn; Joe Lovano, Sax; Billy Hart, Dr.

Shlomi Goldenberg: To You (Jazz in Israel, Vol. 18)
Jazzis Records: Jazzis 1018, ©1992 (CD)
Tom McKinley, Pno; Shlomi Goldenberg, Sax; Gary Peacock, Cb; Alex Deutsch, Dr.

Plain Talk: Charles Licata
Charles Publishing: CL1, ©1992 (CD)
Tom McKinley, Pno; George Garzone, Sax; Gary Peacock, Cb; Alex Deutsch, Dr.

Jazz Alive at Pittsburgh: Tom McKinley Trio
MMC Recordings Ltd.: MMC2006, ©1993 (CD)
Tom McKinley, Pno; Rufus Reid, Cb; Billy Hart, Dr.

Tom McKinley—Miroslav Vitous
MMC Recordings Ltd.: MMC2013, ©1994 (CD)
Tom McKinley, Pno; Miroslav Vitous, Cb, Roger Ryan, Dr.

Appendix I: Chronological List of Works

(Pieces within each year are in order from specific to general.)

String Quartet No. 1 (IV.C.1)	[1959]
Adagio for Violin [and] Piano (VI.F.1)	[1960]
Trio [No. 1] in One Movement... (V.F.1)	[Spring 1963]
Orchestral Study (I.C.1)	[Summer] 1963
~~Etude~~ (VII.H.a)	[ca. 1963]
~~Introduction, Statement and Epilogue...~~ (VIII.A.a)	1963–1964
Directions '65... (VIII.E.1)	Apr 1965
~~Canons for Orchestra~~ (I.C.a)	[1965]
~~Composition for Flute, Guitar and Piano~~ (VIII.F.a)	1965
~~Music for Improvisation Ensemble and Orchestra...~~ (II.B.a)	[ca. 1965]
~~Sonata for Piano and Flute~~ (VI.A.a)	[ca. 1965]
~~[Untitled for Two Violins]~~ (VIII.G.a)	[ca. 1965]
Attitudes for Flute, Clarinet and Cello (VIII.F.1)	1967
Trio and Poem... (VIII.D.1)	[1967]
Mozart Cadenza (X.A.1)	[ca. 1967]
[Sonata for Violin and Piano] (VI.F.2)	[ca. 1967]
[Untitled for Trumpet and Bassoon] (VIII.G.1)	[ca. 1967]
~~[Untitled for Four Trios and Piano]~~ (VIII.A.b)	[ca. 1967–1969]
Solo Duet for Clarinet ("Duet for One") (VII.B.1)	11 Oct 1968
Song for Solo B♭ Clarinet (VII.B.2)	Oct 1968
Studies for String Trio (IV.F.1)	Oct 1968
~~[Untitled for Chamber Ensemble]~~ (VIII.C.a)	[ca. Late 1968]
Charts and Shapes for Bassoon Solo (VII.D.1)	1968

Extemporara for Solo Flute (VII.A.1)	1968
From Opera [No. 1] (VIII.E.2)	1968
Interim Pieces [No. 1]… (VIII.G.2)	1968
Premises and Expositions… (VIII.A.1)	1968
Song for Piccolo, Bassoon and Soprano (IX.B.1)	1968
Variations for Contrabass (VII.L.1)	1968
~~Exercises in Composition~~ (VII.H.b)	[ca. 1968]
~~Proportionalisms~~ (I.C.b)	[ca. 1968]
~~[Untitled for Flute and Bass]~~ (VIII.G.b)	[ca. 1968]
~~[Untitled for Violin, Piano and Bass Clarinet]~~ (V.C.a)	[ca. 1968]
~~Duo Concertante for Violin and Piano~~ (VI.F.a)	1969
~~Duo Fantasy for Trumpet and Bassoon and Tape~~ (VIII.G.c)	1969
Study for Computer Tape and Solo Flute (VII.A.2)	1969
Quadruplum… (II.B.1)	30 Jan–25 Feb 1970
Circular Forms for Grand Orchestra (I.C.2)	3–10 Mar 1970
Triple Concerto… (II.B.2)	4–12 May 1970
Arabesques for Assorted Instruments (VIII.E.3)	1969–1970
~~Violin Concerto~~ (II.L.a)	[1970]
~~Chaconne (Plain-song)~~ (IX.C.a)	[ca. 1970]
~~Double Concerto~~ (II.C.a)	[ca. 1970]
Four Piano Pieces (VII.H.1)	9–11 Nov 1971
Eleven Interludes for Solo Piano (VII.H.2)	12–13 Nov 1971
Piano Piece [No.] 16 (VII.H.3)	13 Nov 1971
Four Pieces for Oboe and Piano (VI.B.1)	14–15 Nov 1971
Twelve Stages for Solo Bassoon (VII.D.2)	16 Nov 1971
For One (VII.B.3)	18 Nov 1971
Ten Interludes for Oboe and Piano (VI.B.2)	15–24 Nov 1971
Arabesques for Solo Violin (VII.I.1)	24–29 Dec 1971
Trio for Two Violins and Viola (VIII.F.2)	[Dec 1971]
Progeny… (VIII.E.4)	1971
Ballade for Solo Guitar (VII.F.1)	1972
Cello Music… (VIII.E.5)	12–27 Apr 1972
Fantasies and Inventions for Solo Harpsichord (VII.H.4)	27 Apr–12 May 1972

Six Pieces for Soprano Voice and Piano (IX.C.1)	Summer 1972
For Les (Three Pieces for Soprano Sax) (VII.C.1)	13 Sep 1972
Sonatas for Two Pianos (VIII.G.3)	Oct–Nov 1972
Paintings [No. 1] for Seven Players (VIII.B.1)	Nov 1972
Composition I for Bass Clarinet (VII.B.4)	Dec 1972
Dance Piece (A Format for Improvisation) (VIII.F.3)	1972
Eliot for Mixed Chorus (IX.A.1)	1972
~~Impressions of Marlene~~ (VII.B.a)	[ca. 1972]
~~Shapes~~ (VIII.G.d)	[ca. 1972]
~~Smoke~~ (VIII.F.b)	[ca. 1972]
~~Studies~~ (VII.H.d)	[ca. 1972]
~~[Untitled for Flute and Piano]~~ (VI.A.b)	[ca. 1972]
~~[Untitled for Violoncello and Piano]~~ (VI.H.a)	[ca. 1972]
~~Water Color for Marlene's Beauty~~ (VII.H.c)	[ca. 1972]
Steps (Part I)... (VII.B.5)	5 Jan 1973
Steps (Part II)... (VIII.D.2)	Dec 1972–Jan 1973
Six Pieces for Soprano Sax, Piano and Cello (V.E.1)	Jan 1973
[Etude No. 1 for Solo Harp] (VII.G.1)	17 Oct 1973
Little Sonata for Viola, Clarinet, and Piano (V.D.1)	Nov 1973
Piano Piece No. 18 ("Journeys") (VII.H.5)	Nov 1973
Piano Piece No. 19 (VII.H.6)	Nov 1973
Portraits for Solo Viola (VII.J.1)	Nov 1973
Waves (A Study for Solo Viola) (VII.J.2)	Nov 1973
Galaxy (A Short Sonata for String Quartet) (IV.C.2)	Dec 1973
Five Songs for Soprano, Bass Clarinet, Cello, [and] Piano (IX.B.2)	[Late] 1973
Quiet (IV.C.3)	[1973]
~~Good Morning~~ (VII.H.e)	[ca. 1973]
~~[Piano Piece No. 17]~~ (VII.H.f)	[ca. 1973]
Etude No. 2 for Solo Harp (VII.G.2)	Feb 1974
Concerto for Grand Orchestra [No. 1] (op. 53) (II.A.1)	2–22 Mar 1974
Interim Piece No. 2 (VIII.G.4)	28–29 Sep 1974
Fantasy for Piano Solo (VII.H.7)	Sep 1974
Concerto for Piano No. 1 (op. 60) (II.K.1)	29 Dec 1974

Interruptions... (II.B.3)	29 Jan 1975
Solo Tenor Saxophone Piece No. 1 (VII.C.2)	22 Feb 1975
The Fisherman and His Wife (X.A.2)	23 Mar 1975
Piano Piece [No.] 20 ("From a Private Monologue") (VII.H.8)	23 Apr 1975
Piano Piece [No.] 21 ("From a Private Monologue") (VII.H.9)	6 May 1975
Paintings No. 2 for Double Trio (VIII.C.1)	16 Jun 1975
~~[Untitled Two-Part Invention in B♭ for Piano]~~ (VII.H.g)	[Early 1975]
Piano Piece No. 22 ("Blues") (VII.H.10)	9 Dec 1975
Canzona for Brass Quintet (III.B.1)	19–24 Dec 1975
Brass Quintet (III.B.2)	[ca. 25–31 Dec 1975]
Piano Study (VII.H.11)	[1975]
Quartet for Piano, Soprano Sax, Bass [and] Drums (VIII.E.6)	1975
~~Set No. 1 for Orchestra~~ (I.C.c)	[ca. 1975]
Carol for Mixed Chorus (IX.A.2)	12 Feb 1976
From Opera No. 2 for B♭ Clarinet and String Quartet (IV.B.1)	20 Feb 1976
Concerto for Solo B♭ Clarinet (VII.B.6)	15 Mar 1976
Paintings No. 3... (op. 70) (IV.B.2)	Mar 1976
Concertino for Grand Orchestra (op. 71) (II.A.2)	30 Apr 1976
Songs Without Words for Solo Flute (op. 72) (VII.A.3)	4 Aug 1976
Fantasia Concertante for String Quartet (IV.C.4)	21 Aug 1976
Sinfonia for String Quartet [String Quartet No. 3] (IV.C.5)	8 Sep 1976
October Night for Orchestra (I.C.3)	Oct 1976
Rhapsody for Solo Harp and Concert Band (II.J.1)	27 Dec 1976
~~[Untitled for Piano No. 1]~~ (VII.H.h)	[ca. 1976]
Concerto No. 1 for Cello and Orchestra (op. 80) (II.N.1)	18 Jan 1977
Symphony No. 1 in One Movement (I.A.1)	10 Feb 1977
Six Movements for String Quartet (IV.C.6)	26 May 1977
Quartet No. 1... (op. 99) ["Tashi"] (VIII.E.7)	25 Jul 1977
Concerto No. 1 for Clarinet in B♭ and Orchestra... (II.E.1)	25 Dec 1977
Rhapsody Fantasia for Solo A Clarinet and Orchestra (II.E.2)	Jan 1978
Symphony No. 2 ["Of Time and Future Monuments"] (I.A.2)	9 Mar 1978
Concerto for Oboe and Percussion (VIII.G.5)	Mar 1978
Concerto Fantasy for Viola and Orchestra (II.M.1)	5 Jul 1978

Six Impromptus… (VIII.D.3)	27 Jul 1978
Paintings No. 4 ("Magical Visions") (VIII.D.4)	2 Sep 1978
A Short Symphony for Brass and Percussion (Op. 103) (III.A.1)	20 Jul 1979
Three Pieces for Solo French Horn (VII.E.1)	29 Jul 1979
Four Text Settings for A Cappella Mixed Chorus (op. 109) (IX.A.3)	1 Oct 1979
Paintings [No.] 5… (VIII.B.2)	1979
~~[Red]~~ (VIII.B.a)	[ca. 1979]
Quintet in One Movement… (VIII.D.5)	Feb 1980
Three Movements for Wind Ensemble (VIII.A.2)	1980
Again the Distant Bells (II.H.1)	20 Dec 1981
Blues Lament for Dick (II.E.3)	[1981]
Goodbye for B♭ Clarinet and Piano (X.B.1)	[1981]
Night and Day (X.B.2)	[1981]
Paintings No. 6 ("To Hear the Light Dancing")… (VIII.B.3)	1981
~~My Way~~ (X.B.a)	[ca. 1981]
The Mountain… (I.C.4)	31 Aug 1982
Duo Concertante for B♭ Clarinet and Piano (VI.C.1)	[Dec 1982]
Paintings No. 7… (VIII.B.4)	1982
Trio Appassionato for B♭ Clarinet, Viola, and Piano (V.D.2)	[1982]
~~Concerto for Solo Double Bass~~ (II.O.a)	[ca. 1982]
~~Isn't She Lovely~~ (X.B.b)	[ca. 1982]
~~[Untitled for Piano No. 2]~~ (VII.H.i)	[ca. 1982]
Symphony for Thirteen Players… (VIII.A.3)	1 Mar 1983
Deliverance, Amen (An Oratorio) (IX.A.4)	[May] 1983
Ballade for Soprano Saxophone (VII.C.3)	[Jun 1983]
Poem of Light… (II.K.2)	[Jun 1983]
Entrata [No. 1] for Solo B♭ Clarinet (VII.B.7)	[Jul 1983]
Entrata No. 2 for Solo B♭ (or E♭) Clarinet (VII.B.8)	[Jul 1983]
August Symphony… (VIII.E.8)	[Aug] 1983
Duo Concerto for Flute and Piano (VI.A.1)	1983
Intermezzo [No. 1] for B♭ Clarinet and Piano (VI.C.2)	[1983]
Intermezzo [No. 2] for B♭ Clarinet and Piano (VI.C.3)	[1983]
~~Waltz~~ (VI.C.a)	[ca. 1983–1985]

Nocturnes for Cello and Clarinet in B♭ (VIII.G.6)	[Jan 1984]
Symphony No. 3 for Chamber Ensemble ["Romantic"] (I.A.3)	Feb 1984
Scarlet [Version I] (III.A.2a)	[Mar 1984]
Suite for Violoncello Solo (VII.K.1)	Apr 1984
[Viola Sonata No. 1] (VI.G.1)	[Jun 1984]
Three Romances [Romances No. 1...] (VI.A.2)	[Jul–Aug 1984]
Viola Concerto [No. 2] (II.M.2)	[Aug 1984]
Summer Dances (II.L.1)	[Sep 1984]
Double Concerto ("Lucy" Variations...) (II.C.1)	[1984]
March Symphony (VIII.D.6)	1984
Samba for Viola and Piano (VI.G.2)	1984
Two Romances for Violin, Clarinet, and Piano (V.C.1)	[1984]
Valse for Flute and Piano (An Encore Piece) (VI.A.3)	[1984]
A Small Rhapsody... (VIII.A.4)	[ca. 1984]
All The Things You Are (X.B.3)	[ca. 1984]
Time On My Hands [Medley] (X.B.4)	[ca. 1984]
Golden Petals... (II.C.2)	Jan 1985
Dedication Overture for Brass Quintet (III.B.3)	1 May 1985
Two Pieces for Solo Contrabass (VII.L.2)	[Jul] 1985
Portraits for Solo French Horn (VII.E.2)	Sep 1985
SinfoNova... (I.C.5)	Sep 1985
Cadenzas (An Instrumental Opera in Two Movements) (VIII.D.7)	Oct 1985
[Concert Music for Brass Quintet] (III.B.4)	Oct 1985
Three Bagatelles for Solo French Horn (VII.E.3)	Oct 1985
Two Romances for French Horn and Piano (VI.D.1)	Nov 1985
Bagatelles and Finale for Solo Violin (VII.I.2)	1985
Sinfonie Concertante... (II.B.4)	1985
Symphony No. 4 (I.A.4)	1985
Viola Concerto No. 2 [Piano Reduction] (VI.G.3)	1985
Scarlet [Version II] (III.A.2b)	[ca. 1985]
American Blues (II.C.3)	31 Dec 1986
Boston Overture (I.B.1)	1986
Concerto for Cimbalom and Chamber Ensemble (II.I.1)	1986

Concerto for Flute and String Orchestra (II.D.1)	[1986]
Grand Finale [No. 1] for Chamber Ensemble (VIII.A.5)	1986
Paintings No. 8 (VIII.E.9)	[1986]
Poem for Flute and Piano (VI.A.4)	[1986]
Sonata for Clarinet and Piano (VI.C.4)	[1986]
String Quartet [No. 6] (IV.C.7)	[1986]
Jean's Dream... (II.E.4)	11 Jan 1987
Nostradamus... (II.C.4)	26 Jan 1987
Quintet Romantico (IV.A.1)	13 May 1987
Concerto for Piano No. 2 ("O'Leary") (II.K.3)	13 Aug 1987
rim (Rhythm In Motion)... (VIII.G.7)	6 Sep 1987
Rags 'n Riches for Two Pianos... (VIII.G.8)	20 Sep 1987
New York Rhapsody for B♭ Clarinet and Harp (VIII.G.9)	30 Sep 1987
Fantasy on a Theme of J.S. Bach for Flute and Piano (VI.A.5)	22 Oct 1987
Marcatissimo... [Downtown Walk No. 1] (VIII.G.10)	7 Nov 1987
Overture for Brass Quintet (III.B.5)	20 Nov 1987
New York Memories for Soprano Voice and Piano (IX.C.2)	20 Dec 1987
New Year's Carol (III.B.6)	29 Dec 1987
Adagio for Strings (I.C.6)	[1987]
Upstairs, Downstairs... (VIII.G.11)	Jan 1988
Tenor Rhapsody for Solo Tenor Sax and Orchestra (II.F.1)	22 Apr 1988
Spring Sonata for Flute, Oboe, and Harpsichord (V.A.1)	7 May 1988
Miniature Portraits for Trumpet and Bassoon (VIII.G.12)	12 May 1988
Symphony of Winds (VIII.A.6)	18 Jul 1988
Curtain Up... (VIII.B.5)	14 Aug 1988
Piano Quartet No. 1 (IV.E.1)	26 Sep 1988
String Quartet No. 7 (IV.C.8)	1 Oct 1988
Can You Sing Me a Song[?]... (II.B.5)	20 Nov 1988
Can You Sing Me a Song? (Rhythm Section Reduction) (VIII.E.10)	1988
To My Friend Dick (II.E.5)	[1988]
[Preludes] (VII.H.12)	[ca. 1988]
Downtown Walk No. 2... (VIII.F.4)	5 Mar 1989
When the Moon is Full (IX.B.3)	29 Jun 1989

A Family Portrait (VIII.G.13)	16 Jul 1989
A Different Drummer… (VIII.D.8)	22 Jul 1989
Chamber Symphony No. 2 in One Movement (VIII.A.7)	27 Aug 1989
Serenata for Flute, Clarinet, Cello, and Piano (VIII.E.11)	20 Oct 1989
Ancient Memories… (II.M.3)	1989
From Stadler to Stoltzman… [McKinley Segment] (II.E.6)	1989
Huntington Horn Concerto (II.G.1)	1989
New York Overture (I.B.2)	1989
Symphony No. 5 (The "Irish") (I.A.5)	1989
Jubilee Concerto for Brass Quintet and Symphony Orchestra (II.B.6)	1 Jan 1990
[Concerto No. 2 for B♭ Clarinet and Orchestra] (II.E.7)	16 Mar 1990
[Symphony No. 6] (I.A.6)	25 Jul 1990
Concerto for Clarinet and Jazz Orchestra (II.E.8)	2 Dec 1990
Ceremonies of the Guild (IX.B.4)	25 Dec 1990
Glass Canyons (V.B.1)	1990
Secrets of the Heart (Romances No. 2) for Flute and Piano (VI.A.6)	[1990]
Blue Jeans… (VI.C.5)	7 Jan 1991
Summer Light (VIII.C.2)	18 May 1991
Miniature Portraits for Trumpet, Bassoon and String[s] (II.C.5)	[Early 1991]
Emsdettener Totentanz (IX.B.5)	27 Sep 1991
Concerto for the New World… (II.B.7)	Oct 29 1991
Greene and Blues (IV.C.9)	8 Nov 1991
Chamber Concerto No. 3 (VIII.A.8)	1991
Concerto Domestica for Trumpet, Bassoon, and Orchestra (II.C.6)	[1991]
[Trio No. 2 for Violin, Cello and Piano] (V.F.2)	[1991]
Westfälischer Pan [First Version] (IX.B.6)	[1991]
[Three Poems of] Pablo Neruda (IX.B.7)	14 Jan 1992
[Grand] Finale [No. 2] (VIII.D.9)	[Mar 1992]
Singletree for Flute, Marimba, and Tuba (VIII.F.5)	Mar 1992
[String Quartet No. 8] (IV.C.10)	2 Mar 1992
String Quartet No. 9 (Moments Musicals) (IV.C.11)	2 May 1992
[Sextet] (VIII.C.3)	20 May 1992
Die Mauern… (VI.E.1)	[Early 1992]

Fleeting Moments (VIII.D.10)	24 Aug 1992
Concerto No. 3 for Viola and Orchestra (II.M.4)	[Aug 1992]
Westfälischer Pan [Second Version] (IX.B.8)	[Aug 1992]
Four Saxophone Blues (VIII.E.12)	5 Oct 1992
Jenseits der Mauer (IX.B.9)	Oct 1992
Silent Whispers for Solo Piano and Orchestra (II.K.4)	[Dec 1992]
Mauern (IX.A.5)	[Late 1992]
Andante and Scherzo for Piano and Orchestra (II.K.5)	21 Jan 1993
Waltzes for Piano (VII.H.13)	[Mar 1993]
Fantasia Variazioni (Fantasy Variations)... (II.K.6)	2 Apr 1993
Concerto for Orchestra No. 2 (II.A.3)	Summer 1993
Der Baum des Lebens (The Tree of Life) (IV.C.12)	[26 Aug 1993]
Concert Variations... [Version I] (II.C.7a)	2 Sep 1993
Patriotic Variations ["Reading Festival Overture"] (I.B.3)	Sep 1993
Lightning (An Overture) (I.B.4)	17 Nov 1993
Concert Variations... [Version II] (II.C.7b)	[23 Dec 1993]
Clarinet Concerto No. 3 ("The Alchemical") (II.E.9)	[Jan 1994]
Blues Pieces (IV.D.1)	[Feb 1994]
Elegy for Solo Alto Flute (VII.A.4)	[Mar 1994]
Two Movements for Flute and String Orchestra (II.D.2)	Mar 1994
[Concerto for Piano No. 3] (II.K.7)	[20 May 1994]
Der Lebensbaum [The Life-Tree] (IX.B.10)	July 1994

Appendix II: Alphabetical List of Works

Work	Catalog No.
Adagio for Strings	I.C.6
Adagio for Violin [and] Piano	VI.F.1
Again the Distant Bells	II.H.1
All The Things You Are	X.B.3
American Blues	II.C.3
Ancient Memories...	II.M.3
Andante and Scherzo for Piano and Orchestra	II.K.5
Arabesques for Assorted Instruments	VIII.E.3
Arabesques for Solo Violin	VII.I.1
Attitudes for Flute, Clarinet and Cello	VIII.F.1
August Symphony...	VIII.E.8
Bagatelles and Finale for Solo Violin	VII.I.2
Ballade for Solo Guitar	VII.F.1
Ballade for Soprano Saxophone	VII.C.3
Blue Jeans...	VI.C.5
Blues Lament for Dick	II.E.3
Blues Pieces	IV.D.1
Boston Overture	I.B.1
Brass Quintet	III.B.2
Cadenzas (An Instrumental Opera in Two Movements)	VIII.D.7
Can You Sing Me a Song? (Rhythm Section Reduction)	VIII.E.10
Can You Sing Me a Song[?]...	II.B.5
~~Canons for Orchestra~~	I.C.a

Work	Catalog No.
Canzona for Brass Quintet	III.B.1
Carol for Mixed Chorus	IX.A.2
Cello Music...	VIII.E.5
Ceremonies of the Guild	IX.B.4
~~Chaconne (Plain-song)~~	IX.C.a
Chamber Concerto No. 3	VIII.A.8
Chamber Symphony No. 2 in One Movement	VIII.A.7
Charts and Shapes for Bassoon Solo	VII.D.1
Circular Forms for Grand Orchestra	I.C.2
Clarinet Concerto No. 3 ("The Alchemical")	II.E.9
~~Composition for Flute, Guitar and Piano~~	VIII.F.a
Composition I for Bass Clarinet	VII.B.4
[Concert Music for Brass Quintet]	III.B.4
Concert Variations... [Version II]	II.C.7b
Concert Variations... [Version I]	II.C.7a
Concertino for Grand Orchestra (op. 71)	II.A.2
Concerto Domestica for Trumpet, Bassoon, and Orchestra	II.C.6
Concerto Fantasy for Viola and Orchestra	II.M.1
Concerto for Cimbalom and Chamber Ensemble	II.I.1
Concerto for Clarinet and Jazz Orchestra	II.E.8
Concerto for Flute and String Orchestra	II.D.1
Concerto for Grand Orchestra [No. 1] (op. 53)	II.A.1
Concerto for Oboe and Percussion	VIII.G.5
Concerto for Orchestra No. 2	II.A.3
Concerto for Piano No. 1 (op. 60)	II.K.1
Concerto for Piano No. 2 ("O'Leary")	II.K.3
[Concerto for Piano No. 3]	II.K.7
Concerto for Solo B♭ Clarinet	VII.B.6
~~Concerto for Solo Double Bass~~	II.O.a
Concerto for the New World...	II.B.7
Concerto No. 1 for Cello and Orchestra (op. 80)	II.N.1
Concerto No. 1 for Clarinet in B♭ and Orchestra...	II.E.1
[Concerto No. 2 for B♭ Clarinet and Orchestra]	II.E.7

Concerto No. 3 for Viola and Orchestra	II.M.4
Curtain Up...	VIII.B.5
Dance Piece (A Format for Improvisation)	VIII.F.3
Dedication Overture for Brass Quintet	III.B.3
Deliverance, Amen (An Oratorio)	IX.A.4
Der Baum des Lebens (The Tree of Life)	IV.C.12
Der Lebensbaum [The Life-Tree]	IX.B.10
Die Mauern...	VI.E.1
A Different Drummer...	VIII.D.8
Directions '65...	VIII.E.1
Double Concerto ("Lucy" Variations...)	II.C.1
~~Double Concerto~~	II.C.a
Downtown Walk No. 2...	VIII.F.4
Duo Concertante for B♭ Clarinet and Piano	VI.C.1
~~Duo Concertante for Violin and Piano~~	VI.F.a
Duo Concerto for Flute and Piano	VI.A.1
~~Duo Fantasy for Trumpet and Bassoon and Tape~~	VIII.G.c
Elegy for Solo Alto Flute	VII.A.4
Eleven Interludes for Solo Piano	VII.H.2
Eliot for Mixed Chorus	IX.A.1
Emsdettener Totentanz	IX.B.5
Entrata [No. 1] for Solo B♭ Clarinet	VII.B.7
Entrata No. 2 for Solo B♭ (or E♭) Clarinet	VII.B.8
~~Etude~~	VII.H.a
[Etude No. 1 for Solo Harp]	VII.G.1
Etude No. 2 for Solo Harp	VII.G.2
~~Exercises in Composition~~	VII.H.b
Extemporara for Solo Flute	VII.A.1
A Family Portrait	VIII.G.13
Fantasia Concertante for String Quartet	IV.C.4
Fantasia Variazioni (Fantasy Variations)...	II.K.6
Fantasies and Inventions for Solo Harpsichord	VII.H.4
Fantasy for Piano Solo	VII.H.7

Fantasy on a Theme of J.S. Bach for Flute and Piano	VI.A.5
The Fisherman and His Wife	X.A.2
Five Songs for Soprano, Bass Clarinet, Cello, [and] Piano	IX.B.2
Fleeting Moments	VIII.D.10
For Les (Three Pieces for Soprano Sax)	VII.C.1
For One	VII.B.3
Four Piano Pieces	VII.H.1
Four Pieces for Oboe and Piano	VI.B.1
Four Saxophone Blues	VIII.E.12
Four Text Settings for A Cappella Mixed Chorus (op. 109)	IX.A.3
From Opera No. 2 for B♭ Clarinet and String Quartet	IV.B.1
From Opera [No. 1]	VIII.E.2
From Stadler to Stoltzman… [McKinley Segment]	II.E.6
Galaxy (A Short Sonata for String Quartet)	IV.C.2
Glass Canyons	V.B.1
Golden Petals…	II.C.2
~~Good Morning~~	VII.H.e
Goodbye for B♭ Clarinet and Piano	X.B.1
Grand Finale [No. 1] for Chamber Ensemble	VIII.A.5
[Grand] Finale [No. 2]	VIII.D.9
Greene and Blues	IV.C.9
Huntington Horn Concerto	II.G.1
~~Impressions of Marlene~~	VII.B.a
Interim Piece No. 2	VIII.G.4
Interim Pieces [No. 1]…	VIII.G.2
Intermezzo [No. 1] for B♭ Clarinet and Piano	VI.C.2
Intermezzo [No. 2] for B♭ Clarinet and Piano	VI.C.3
Interruptions…	II.B.3
~~Introduction, Statement and Epilogue…~~	VIII.A.a
~~Isn't She Lovely~~	X.B.b
Jean's Dream…	II.E.4
Jenseits der Mauer	IX.B.9
Jubilee Concerto for Brass Quintet and Symphony Orchestra	II.B.6

Lightning (An Overture)	I.B.4
Little Sonata for Viola, Clarinet, and Piano	V.D.1
Marcatissimo... [Downtown Walk No. 1]	VIII.G.10
March Symphony	VIII.D.6
Mauern	IX.A.5
Miniature Portraits for Trumpet and Bassoon	VIII.G.12
Miniature Portraits for Trumpet, Bassoon and String[s]	II.C.5
The Mountain...	I.C.4
Mozart Cadenza	X.A.1
~~Music for Improvisation Ensemble and Orchestra...~~	II.B.a
~~My Way~~	X.B.a
New Year's Carol	III.B.6
New York Memories for Soprano Voice and Piano	IX.C.2
New York Overture	I.B.2
New York Rhapsody for B♭ Clarinet and Harp	VIII.G.9
Night and Day	X.B.2
Nocturnes for Cello and Clarinet in B♭	VIII.G.6
Nostradamus...	II.C.4
October Night for Orchestra	I.C.3
Orchestral Study	I.C.1
Overture for Brass Quintet	III.B.5
Paintings No. 2 for Double Trio	VIII.C.1
Paintings No. 3... (op. 70)	IV.B.2
Paintings No. 4 ("Magical Visions")	VIII.D.4
Paintings No. 6 ("To Hear the Light Dancing")...	VIII.B.3
Paintings No. 7...	VIII.B.4
Paintings No. 8	VIII.E.9
Paintings [No. 1] for Seven Players	VIII.B.1
Paintings [No.] 5...	VIII.B.2
Patriotic Variations ["Reading Festival Overture"]	I.B.3
~~[Piano Piece No. 17]~~	VII.H.f
Piano Piece No. 18 ("Journeys")	VII.H.5
Piano Piece No. 19	VII.H.6

Piano Piece No. 22 ("Blues")	VII.H.10
Piano Piece [No.] 16	VII.H.3
Piano Piece [No.] 20 ("From a Private Monologue")	VII.H.8
Piano Piece [No.] 21 ("From a Private Monologue")	VII.H.9
Piano Quartet No. 1	IV.E.1
Piano Study	VII.H.11
Poem for Flute and Piano	VI.A.4
Poem of Light...	II.K.2
Portraits for Solo French Horn	VII.E.2
Portraits for Solo Viola	VII.J.1
[Preludes]	VII.H.12
Premises and Expositions...	VIII.A.1
Progeny...	VIII.E.4
~~Proportionalisms~~	I.C.b
Quadruplum...	II.B.1
Quartet for Piano, Soprano Sax, Bass [and] Drums	VIII.E.6
Quartet No. 1... (op. 99) ["Tashi"]	VIII.E.7
Quiet	IV.C.3
Quintet in One Movement...	VIII.D.5
Quintet Romantico	IV.A.1
Rags 'n Riches for Two Pianos...	VIII.G.8
~~[Red]~~	VIII.B.a
Rhapsody Fantasia for Solo A Clarinet and Orchestra	II.E.2
Rhapsody for Solo Harp and Concert Band	II.J.1
rim (Rhythm In Motion)...	VIII.G.7
Samba for Viola and Piano	VI.G.2
Scarlet [Version II]	III.A.2b
Scarlet [Version I]	III.A.2a
Secrets of the Heart (Romances No. 2) for Flute and Piano	VI.A.6
Serenata for Flute, Clarinet, Cello, and Piano	VIII.E.11
~~Set No. 1 for Orchestra~~	I.C.c
[Sextet]	VIII.C.3
~~Shapes~~	VIII.G.d

A Short Symphony for Brass and Percussion (Op. 103)	III.A.1
Silent Whispers for Solo Piano and Orchestra	II.K.4
Sinfonia for String Quartet [String Quartet No. 3]	IV.C.5
Sinfonie Concertante...	II.B.4
SinfoNova...	I.C.5
Singletree for Flute, Marimba, and Tuba	VIII.F.5
Six Impromptus...	VIII.D.3
Six Movements for String Quartet	IV.C.6
Six Pieces for Soprano Sax, Piano and Cello	V.E.1
Six Pieces for Soprano Voice and Piano	IX.C.1
A Small Rhapsody...	VIII.A.4
~~Smoke~~	VIII.F.b
Solo Duet for Clarinet ("Duet for One")	VII.B.1
Solo Tenor Saxophone Piece No. 1	VII.C.2
Sonata for Clarinet and Piano	VI.C.4
~~Sonata for Piano and Flute~~	VI.A.a
[Sonata for Violin and Piano]	VI.F.2
Sonatas for Two Pianos	VIII.G.3
Song for Piccolo, Bassoon and Soprano	IX.B.1
Song for Solo B♭ Clarinet	VII.B.2
Songs Without Words for Solo Flute (op. 72)	VII.A.3
Spring Sonata for Flute, Oboe, and Harpsichord	V.A.1
Steps (Part I)...	VII.B.5
Steps (Part II)...	VIII.D.2
String Quartet No. 1	IV.C.1
String Quartet [No. 6]	IV.C.7
String Quartet No. 7	IV.C.8
[String Quartet No. 8]	IV.C.10
String Quartet No. 9 (Moments Musicals)	IV.C.11
~~Studies~~	VII.H.d
Studies for String Trio	IV.F.1
Study for Computer Tape and Solo Flute	VII.A.2
Suite for Violoncello Solo	VII.K.1

Summer Dances	II.L.1
Summer Light	VIII.C.2
Symphony for Thirteen Players...	VIII.A.3
Symphony No. 1 in One Movement	I.A.1
Symphony No. 2 ["Of Time and Future Monuments"]	I.A.2
Symphony No. 3 for Chamber Ensemble ["Romantic"]	I.A.3
Symphony No. 4	I.A.4
Symphony No. 5 (The "Irish")	I.A.5
[Symphony No. 6]	I.A.6
Symphony of Winds	VIII.A.6
Ten Interludes for Oboe and Piano	VI.B.2
Tenor Rhapsody for Solo Tenor Sax and Orchestra	II.F.1
Three Bagatelles for Solo French Horn	VII.E.3
Three Movements for Wind Ensemble	VIII.A.2
Three Pieces for Solo French Horn	VII.E.1
[Three Poems of] Pablo Neruda	IX.B.7
Three Romances [Romances No. 1...]	VI.A.2
Time On My Hands [Medley]	X.B.4
To My Friend Dick	II.E.5
Trio and Poem...	VIII.D.1
Trio Appassionato for B♭ Clarinet, Viola, and Piano	V.D.2
Trio for Two Violins and Viola	VIII.F.2
Trio [No. 1] in One Movement...	V.F.1
[Trio No. 2 for Violin, Cello and Piano]	V.F.2
Triple Concerto...	II.B.2
Twelve Stages for Solo Bassoon	VII.D.2
Two Movements for Flute and String Orchestra	II.D.2
Two Pieces for Solo Contrabass	VII.L.2
Two Romances for French Horn and Piano	VI.D.1
Two Romances for Violin, Clarinet, and Piano	V.C.1
~~[Untitled for Chamber Ensemble]~~	VIII.C.a
~~[Untitled for Flute and Bass]~~	VIII.G.b
~~[Untitled for Flute and Piano]~~	VI.A.b

~~[Untitled for Four Trios and Piano]~~	VIII.A.b
~~[Untitled for Piano No. 1]~~	VII.H.h
~~[Untitled for Piano No. 2]~~	VII.H.i
[Untitled for Trumpet and Bassoon]	VIII.G.1
~~[Untitled for Two Violins]~~	VIII.G.a
~~[Untitled for Violin, Piano and Bass Clarinet]~~	V.C.a
~~[Untitled for Violoncello and Piano]~~	VI.H.a
~~[Untitled Two-Part Invention in B♭ for Piano]~~	VII.H.g
Upstairs, Downstairs…	VIII.G.11
Valse for Flute and Piano (An Encore Piece)	VI.A.3
Variations for Contrabass	VII.L.1
Viola Concerto No. 2 [Piano Reduction]	VI.G.3
Viola Concerto [No. 2]	II.M.2
[Viola Sonata No. 1]	VI.G.1
~~Violin Concerto~~	II.L.a
~~Waltz~~	VI.C.a
Waltzes for Piano	VII.H.13
~~Water Color for Marlene's Beauty~~	VII.H.c
Waves (A Study for Solo Viola)	VII.J.2
Westfälischer Pan [First Version]	IX.B.6
Westfälischer Pan [Second Version]	IX.B.8
When the Moon is Full	IX.B.3

APPENDIX III: UNIDENTIFIED SKETCHES

Sketch No.	*No. of (bi)folios*	*Instrumentation/Contents*	*Approx. Date*
1	2	Pno, Unspecified (treble clefs)	1982
2	5	Strings, Unspecified (no clefs), notes	1984
3	13	Unspecified (treble/bass pairs), notes	1982
4	15	Orchestra, notes	1970
5	1	Pic, CBsn, Cl	1965
6	1	Notes describing two mvt. orchestral work	1965
7	1	Notes, tone rows	1965
8	1	Pno, 2 unspecified (no clefs)	1965
9	1	Formal plan for a work for Cl, Tpt, Hp, Vln, Vcl	1965
10	2, 1b	Pno (possibly teaching aids)	1965
11	11	Fl, Ob, 1 or 2 Pno, Banjo, Perc, Strings	1968
12	3	Orchestra	1968
13	2	Notes on percussion battery from an unidentified work	1967
14	1	Notes, tone rows	1967
15	5	Orchestra	1967
16	7	Brass Quintet	1978
17	3	Pno, unspecified	1965
18	17	Pno, tone rows and other notes and sketches	1965
19	2	Rhythmic sketches	1965
20	1	Pno	1968
21	1	Pno, unspecified (treble clef)	1968
22	1b	2 unspecified (treble clefs)	1968
23	2, 1b	Pno, Voice, Perc, lead sheet	1968

24	2	Vln, Vla, Vcl	1968
25	1	Pno, marked "Vertical Constructs"	1968
26	1	4 Fl	1968
27	2	Pno. Possibly teaching aids	1968
28	1b	Instrumentation list	1968
29	1	Strings in short score (single staff)	1968
30	1	Unspecified treble instrument (possibly short score)	1985
31	1	Instrumentation list	1985
32	1	Cl, Pno	1972
33	2	Vln, Pno (2 folios taped together)	1970
34	1	Pno	1970
35	1	2 Vln?, Vla	1970
36	2	Fl, Vln, Vcl, Pno	1985
37	1	Fl, Ob, Cl, Bsn, Vln	1965
38	1	Unspecified Perc	1970
39	1	Chord chart	1970
40	1	Notes labeled "canonic patterns"	1970
41	1	Pno	1970
42	4	One or two unspecified treble instruments (Vln?)	1972
43	1	Pno	1972
44	1	Pno, Vln, Vla?, Vcl	1972
45	1	Unspecified bass instrument	1972
46	1	Brass quintet?	1972
47	2	2 unspecified instruments or Pno	1972
48	1	Vln	1972
49	1	Unspecified instrument	1972
50	1b	3 Unspecified instruments	1972
51	1	Sop, Fl, Elec Pno	1972
52	1	Unspecified treble instrument	1972
53	1	Unspecified treble instrument	1972
54	1	Pno	1972
55	3	2 unspecified treble instruments or Pno	1975
56	1	Ten Sax, Pno	1972
57	1	1 to 7 unspecified instruments	1972
58	1	Pno?	1972
59	1	Notes on a piece commissioned[?] by Collegium, to Gustav Meir	1969

Appendix IV: Directory of Publishers and Record Labels

Publishers of McKinley's Works

Margun Music, Inc.
167 Dudley Road
Newton Centre, MA 02159
Phone: (617) 332–6398
Fax: (617) 969–1079

MMC Publications
240 West Street
Reading, MA 01867–2847
Phone: (617) 944–0959
Fax: (617) 944–7341

Record Labels with Works by McKinley

1750 Arch Records
1750 Arch Street
Berkeley, CA 94709
No longer in business

Academy Sound and Vision, Ltd.
179–181 North End Road
London W14 9NL
United Kingdom

BMG Classics
1133 Avenue of the Americas, 2nd Floor
New York, NY 10036–6758
Phone: (212) 930–4000

Charles Publishing
78 Division Ave.
Summit, NJ 07901

Composers Recordings Inc.
73 Spring St., Rm. 506
New York, NY 10012
Phone: (212) 941–9673
Fax: (212) 941–9704

Delos International Inc.
1032 N. Sycamore Ave.
Los Angeles, CA 90038
Phone: (213) 962–2626
Fax: (213) 962–2636

Golden Crest Records Inc.
220 Broadway
Huntington Station, NY 11746
No longer in business

GunMar Recordings, Inc.
167 Dudley Road
Newton Centre, MA 02159
Phone: (617) 332–6398
Fax: (617) 969–1079

Jazzis Records
P.O. Box 1106
IL–26105 Kiriat Haim
Israel

Koch International Corp.
177 Contiague Rock Road
Westbury, NY 11590
Phone: (516) 938–8080
Fax: (516) 938–8055

MMC Recordings
240 West Street
Reading, MA 01867–2847
Phone: (617) 944–0959
Fax: (617) 944–7341

Northeastern Records
P.O. Box 3589
Saxonville, MA 01701-0605
Phone: (508) 820–4440

Owl Recording, Inc.
P.O. Box 4536
Boulder, CO 80306
Phone: (303) 449–6510
Fax: (303) 447-8762

RCA Victor Red Seal
See *BMG Classics.*

Staatsorchesters Rheinische Philharmonie
Intendanz des Staatsorchesters Rheinische Philharmonie
Eltzerhofstraße 6a
DW–5400 Koblenz
Germany
Phone: (0261) 3900592
Fax: (0261) 38829

Vienna Modern Masters
Margetetenstraße 125/15
A–1050 Vienna
Austria
Phone: (0431) 5451778
Fax: (0431) 5440785

Index

About the Author

JEFFREY S. SPOSATO, a musicologist, is currently teaching and finishing his doctoral dissertation at Brandeis University. Mr. Sposato also writes program notes for many performing organizations in the Boston and New York areas and for compact discs produced on the MMC Recordings label. In addition, he holds degrees in Vocal Performance from the New England Conservatory of Music and in German Studies from Tufts University. He continues to perform with various ensembles throughout the Boston area.

Recent Titles in
Bio-Bibliographies in Music

Alec Wilder: A Bio-Bibliography
David Demsey and Ronald Prather

Alun Hoddinott: A Bio-Bibliography
Stewart R. Craggs

Elinor Remick Warren: A Bio-Bibliography
Virginia Bortin

Howard Hanson: A Bio-Bibliography
James E. Perone

Peter Sculthorpe: A Bio-Bibliography
Deborah Hayes

Germaine Tailleferre: A Bio-Bibliography
Robert Shapiro

Charles Wuorinen: A Bio-Bibliography
Richard D. Burbank

Elliott Carter: A Bio-Bibliography
William T. Doering

Leslie Bassett: A Bio-Bibliography
Ellen S. Johnson

Ulysses Kay: A Bio-Bibliography
Constance Tibbs Hobson and Deborra A. Richardson, compilers

John Alden Carpenter: A Bio-Bibliography
Joan O'Connor, compiler

Paul Creston: A Bio-Bibliography
Monica J. Slomski, compiler

ISBN 0-313-28923-9
EAN
9 780313 289231
90000>
HARDCOVER BAR CODE